Billy's
War

by
James C. McKay

Eio Books

Published in the United States by

Eio Books
P.O. Box 1392
Port Orchard, Washington, 98366 U.S.A.

www.eiobooks.com

Library of Congress Cataloging-in-Publication Data

McKay, James C.
 Billy's war / by James C. McKay.
      pages cm
 ISBN 978-1-937819-06-4
1. World War, 1939-1945--Naval operations, Ameri-
can--Fiction I. Title.
 PS3613.C54515B55 2013
 813'.6--dc23

                              2013002044

Cover designed by Shane Roberts
Book designed by Shane Roberts

Billy's War

by
James C. McKay

CHAPTER 1

My pounding heart and heavy breathing seemed to echo the throb of the passenger car generators and the mournful sighs of steam drifting across the platform from underneath the huge black locomotive. A variety of emotions swept over me—sadness, apprehension, even fear, mingled with excitement and anticipation. Shivering in spite of the warm September sun, I glanced uneasily at my well-wishers, standing in a circle by the open door of the Bethlehem, Pennsylvania, depot a few yards away, chatting and laughing just like nothing unusual was happening or going to happen. The carefree group included Mom and Dad and Uncle Dan, and, to my amazement, my friend Dee, who'd taken the bumpy bus ride from Allentown. She probably skipped classes at Muhlenberg just to see me off to college, to Cornell University located in a little town in Western New York called Ithaca.

Dee returned my glance, her dark eyes alight with amusement, a bright smile showing that dimple. "Hey, Billy Creelman," she called over, "don't look so glum. This isn't a funeral. You're going to be one of those important college boys. You probably won't even speak to us after a couple of months."

I could only smile weakly and shrug my shoulders. Dee always had a wisecrack to make, especially to me or about me. I'd never been able to figure her out. I'd seen her only two or three times during the past twelve months. A couple of years ago, we had that scary adventure together, looking for Spike, my Border collie, I gave up for dead until she came along and insisted that we search for him. I'd lost track of her for more than a year. Then she unexpectedly showed up in Bethlehem last Christmas, even though we were almost completely snowed in the day before. And last February, she had surprised the daylights out of me by sneaking out of her dorm so she could attend my birthday party. She gave me a big kiss after I blew out the eighteen candles on the chocolate cake Mom had made. I shivered again, recalling the softness of her lips. I worried about my crooked front teeth, but they hadn't seemed to bother her. Then she spoiled it all by patting my head and making a dumb remark about once being a young kid of eighteen, like she'd suddenly become a grown woman, instead of only going on twenty.

Typical Dee, I thought. First do something nice, then make up for it with a cutting remark. My stomach tightened. Would she kiss me goodbye now? In one way, I hoped not— not in front of Mom and Dad and Uncle Dan, and yet...I took a deep breath. It had felt good.

Two shrill blasts of a whistle snapped me out of my daydream. "All aboard!" After shouting his warning, the uniformed conductor jammed his railroad watch into his vest pocket and strolled toward the baggage car. Mom and Dad and Uncle Dan shuffled forward and lined up in front of me. We stared at each other for a few seconds. Dad coughed a couple of times. "Well, Billy, you take care of yourself. And don't forget to write." He patted my shoulder. "I stowed your suitcases in the rack above seat number 16. Hang on to them. They're holding all your worldly goods. Except what you're wearing." He managed a grin.

"Okay, Dad," I mumbled.

Mom averted her face, a few tears streaming down her cheeks. "Yes, dear," she said, "please be careful. Stay warm and eat plenty of good food."

"Oh, come on," Uncle Dan said, "I agree with Dee. We should be happy that Billy's strong right arm got him a scholarship to such a great school. Not many kids these days have that opportunity." I was lucky enough to get a baseball scholarship that would cover my tuition to the Agriculture College at Cornell and also the cost of books and fees. After starting to live with Uncle Dan, I worked for a year, mowing lawns, washing cars, delivering newspapers, and doing other odd jobs to earn money. Then I attended Bethlehem High School my senior year, where I was the star pitcher for the baseball team. We didn't lose a single game. I pitched four shutouts.

Uncle Dan's going to pay my room rent at a dormitory called Cascadilla Hall. I never could have gone to college without a scholarship and Uncle Dan's help. I couldn't figure out how he managed to do all he did. He's a foreman at the Bethlehem Steel plant. Besides paying his own expenses, he helped support Mom and Dad, who live with him now.

Mom pitched in by doing housecleaning work for the wives of two of the company big shots, and Dad worked part time at the plant. In the late summer of 1937, the country still hadn't recovered from the Depression, although President Roosevelt kept promising that better times were right around the corner.

Uncle Dan's been so generous and kind to all of us. Even to Dee. He had written an old war buddy of his, a professor at Muhlenberg College, and helped her get a four-year scholarship—an academic scholarship she made sure to remind me of in a letter after I wrote her about my baseball scholarship. She was in her third year now, another thing she didn't let me forget. Uncle Dan will send me an allowance of twenty-five dollars a month. The coach told me I probably could get my meals free by waiting on tables at one of the fraternity houses.

I reached over and grabbed my uncle's hand. I really admired my Uncle Dan. He'd been a World War hero, an ace. He flew with Eddy Rickenbacker's squadron in France. Even tangled with the Red Baron's Flying Circus. Uncle Dan had come through the war without a scratch, but bad luck caught up with him when a plant explosion burned off his eyebrows, leaving his forehead and cheeks lined with white scars. A black patch covered where his left eye used to be.

"So long, Uncle Dan," I whispered. I couldn't stop my voice from trembling. "Thanks for keeping Spike. I hope he won't be a bother to you."

"Oh, come on, Billy," Uncle Dan said. "You know I love that old sheepdog. He's great company."

My eyes looked past Uncle Dan to Dee, standing a couple of yards away. She was hanging back, not joining in the goodbyes. The train was about to leave. Is she just going to stand there, I wondered. I'd about given up hope of her saying or doing anything and had started toward the car steps, when she rushed over and threw her arms around me. I smelled the freshness of her dark curls in my face. "I'll be thinking of you, Billy," she whispered. She swung around, hurried toward the depot door, and disappeared into the station without looking back.

CHAPTER 2

A sudden lurch of the train caused me to stumble as I walked down the aisle, looking for my seat. Reaching out to steady myself, I grabbed the first thing I could, which turned out to be the shoulder of a guy across from seat number 16. "Uh, sorry," I mumbled.

"Jesus, watch where you're going!" The snarling voice took me by surprise.

I slipped into my seat and looked across the aisle. A pair of black eyes glared at me. "I said I was sorry, sir." Right away I wanted to kick myself for calling him "sir."

He didn't look any older than me. Much better dressed, though. The beat-up mackinaw Uncle Dan bought for me at the thrift store looked seedy alongside this guy's sleek camel's-hair topcoat. The thick black hair on his square head lay slicked back with some kind of gook. His puffy face resembled a ripe tomato from Mom's garden.

He sniffed and spread out a newspaper he was holding on his lap and started reading. I recognized the *Inquirer* and figured he must have boarded the train in Philadelphia. I slid across the seat and craned my neck, hoping to get a last look at Mom and Dad and Uncle Dan...and Dee. But we passed through the overhang of the station and were slowly threading our way between two lines of freight cars. As I rested my head on the window glass and shut my eyes, picturing in my mind Dee's smile and her dimple and wondering when I'd ever see her again, the same nasty voice interrupted my thoughts.

"Where ya headed, sonny boy?"

I couldn't believe my ears. Should I answer? Not knowing what to do, I shut my eyes again and pretended I hadn't heard him.

"Hey, you."

I opened my eyes, and slowly turned my head toward him.

"I asked you a question. Where are you going?"

Might as well answer. "Cornell University. It's in Ithaca,

New York."

The guy guffawed like I'd said the dumbest thing in the world.

"Jesus, I know where Cornell is." He paused and looked me up and down. "I'm a sophomore at Cornell," he said, making it sound like he was the King of Siam. "What year are you in?"

"First year," I answered.

"Jesus," he hooted. "A miserable frosh."

I wondered for a second whether he knew any swear word except "Jesus." I turned away and looked out the window again. The train, now clear of the city, picked up speed, the wheels clicking, the car swaying and bumping over the rough roadbed. The faint wailing of the whistle from the engine reached my ears, and the jangle, jangle, jangle of a bell as the Black Diamond Limited rumbled through a grade crossing.

"Hey, frosh, you'll have to wear a little white beanie with a red topknot, you know that, don't you?" This guy persisted in pestering me. I'd read the freshmen rules. They seemed silly, and I'd planned to see how things went before deciding whether to pay any attention to them.

"Yeah," I said.

"Yeah," he mocked. "Yeah, yeah, yeah." He turned the pages of his newspaper and started looking at a column of numbers in the business section.

I reached in my mackinaw pocket and pulled out a copy of *Life* that Uncle Dan had given me. I turned to a page showing a picture of Jesse Owens winning the 100-meter dash at the Olympics in Berlin in 1936, more than a year ago. I remembered Uncle Dan saying how the talk in Germany about a master race got squelched, at least for a few weeks, after Jesse won four gold medals. The next page showed a picture of Adolf Hitler reviewing a bunch of troops wearing steel helmets, with rifles fitted with bayonets on their shoulders, goose-stepping along. Hitler wore a plain brown uniform. He stood rigidly on a platform decked out with a bunch of flags, his jaw jutting, his right arm thrust out. I remembered Uncle Dan saying over and over again that we'd have to fight another war unless someone stopped that maniac.

"Hey, frosh, I see you're looking at a photo of Hitler. What do you think about him?" The nosey guy's close-set eyes stared at me, his eyebrows pointed upwards, waiting for an answer. I looked back at the magazine for a couple of seconds. I remembered what Dee had said about her relatives in Germany who had disappeared—probably murdered by Hitler's thugs or stuck in work camps like thousands of other men, women, and children, just because they were Jews. I kept staring at the picture. I didn't like what I saw: the little black mustache, the bulging eyes, the jutting jaw.

The guy broke into my thoughts. "Personally," he said, "I think he's doing a hell of a good job, getting rid of all those hebes." I looked over at his smirking face.

"Hebes? What do you mean?"

"Jesus! Kikes, yids, schmoes. What the hell do you think I mean?"

I guess my face must have shown I still didn't catch on, because his face wrinkled up in disgust. "Jews, for God's sake."

I could feel myself getting warm all over. I didn't know what to say, so I decided to keep my mouth shut. I kept looking at the picture, wondering if other Cornell students talked that way about Jews. He kept on yacking like he'd read my mind. "We don't have anything to do with that kind at Cornell," he said, real smug. "They have their own fraternities and sororities." He smirked again. "Some of the Jew broads have big boobs, but that's the only good thing I can say about them."

"Why don't you shut your filthy mouth, Harry."

The voice startled me. I glanced up to see a girl holding on to the back of the guy's seat. She'd come up the aisle from the rear of the car without either of us noticing. Her angry eyes made me think she wanted to kill this guy. Harry, I guess that was his name, looked like he'd been caught with his hand in the cookie jar. The smirk disappeared and his face changed color.

"Take it easy, Betty," the guy whined. He looked over at me, obviously embarrassed. "Don't talk to me like that in front of this frosh."

"You take it easy, buster," she said. "And try to confine that kind of talk to your miserable fraternity brothers." Harry snorted and opened up his paper, pretending like she wasn't standing there.

I stared at the girl, wondering how she had the nerve to speak up like that. She smiled at me, a nice smile, showing even-white teeth, but no dimple. Her dark curls, just covering her ears, reminded me of Dee, although she was taller than Dee, nearly as tall as me, and I'm six feet. Her deep blue eyes smiled at me. She was kind of skinny, but wiry, probably a good athlete, maybe played basketball.

"Has this dope been hassling you?" she asked. Another snort from Harry. But he kept his head buried in his newspaper.

"Uh, no," I replied. "I guess not."

"I'm Elizabeth Marshall," she said. "Mind if I sit down with you?" She smiled again. "My friends call me Betty. And it's too bad I'm not Jewish, since my boobs aren't all that great." She grinned, glancing down at her tan blouse.

My face must have warmed up, because she laughed, a nice laugh. "Don't mind me. I guess I'm a little too brash at times. I'm really harmless." She slipped into the seat beside me, and held out her hand. "What's your name?"

I took her hand. "Bill Creelman," I answered. I decided to drop "Billy," although Mom and Dad and Uncle Dan still called me that. So did Dee.

"Well, Bill," she said, "so you're going to be a Cornellian?"

"Yeah," I said after hesitating for a couple of seconds, beginning to be ashamed of being a freshman.

"What school?"

"College of Agriculture," I replied.

"An Aggie. Jesus. I might have guessed. I can almost see the hayseeds." Harry had stuck in his two cents' worth again.

"Harry Dobson, if you don't knock it off, I'm personally going to kick your butt from here to Ithaca, New York," Betty snapped. "I'm an Aggie, too," she said. "One of a handful of coeds majoring in animal husbandry." I must have looked impressed, because she quickly went on to say it wasn't all that great. "You have to pick a major in your junior year, and that's what I did...last year. My dad keeps a herd of Aberdeen Angus as sort of a hobby, and I've worked every summer since I was twelve, getting to know about breeding and raising beef cattle. I've learned a lot at Cornell."

This news impressed me. A rich girl who liked farm work. "So, you're a senior," I managed to say.

"Yep. And we seniors know how to handle puffed-up sophomores." Her voice rose. "Like J. Harold Dobson, a would-be big man on the campus from the Main Line, you know, in Philadelphia. Hey, Harry," she called over, "what's the J stand for? Jesus?"

He glared at her but went back to his paper without saying anything.

She turned back to me. "I hope you like Cornell. It's a wonderful school. Although," she added, "I am a bit prejudiced."

"Why is that?" I asked.

"Well, if you really want to know, I'll tell you." She laughed. "And even if you don't want to know, you'll have to listen anyway. My mom and dad met at Cornell. My grandfather graduated in 1872, the first four-year class. My great grandfather was a member of the first faculty in the English Department. Also a bunch of aunts, uncles, and cousins attended Cornell. And, to top it off, my Uncle Phil is Dean of the College of Arts and Sciences."

"That's amazing," I said. None of my relations had ever attended college. My mom and dad graduated from high school, and that ended their education.

"But enough about me," she said. "Now let's hear something about you. For starters, where do you hail from?"

I explained about living on the tiny dairy farm in Harford County, Maryland, but that I lived now with my Uncle Dan in Bethlehem.

"Why did you pick Cornell?" Betty seemed really interested. I felt at ease for the first time since leaving my folks and Dee.

"I didn't pick Cornell. Cornell picked me."

Her eyebrows went up. "What on earth do you mean?"

I told her about my baseball scholarship. Hoping I wasn't bragging, I mentioned I was captain of my team at Bethlehem High School, and the leading pitcher.

"That's really great." Betty exclaimed. "We've needed some good pitching for the past three years. Our freshman team won only three games last year, and the varsity didn't do much better."

"Jesus. Don't tell me that this hayseed and my brother are going to be teammates." Harry butting in again.

"What are you gabbing about now?" Betty asked.

"I'm gabbing about Steve, that's what I'm gabbing about. He went up last week for orientation. He's been meeting with the freshman coach and working out." Harry's lips curled into a sneer. "He's paying his way, not taking any handouts."

I guess I'd about had enough from J. Harold Dobson, because I started to get up. I don't know what might have happened if Betty hadn't grabbed my arm and pulled me back. "You really are a fool, Harry. What do you get every week but handouts from your old man. You've never earned a thin dime in your whole life. Everything's been served up to you on a silver plate." She squeezed my arm. "Don't let him get you down," she said. "He's been spoiled rotten by his doting papa, who owns a couple of banks in Philadelphia, and his loving mama, who's in the rotogravure every Sunday."

"Well, you haven't exactly suffered," Harry said. "With all the loot your old man manages to spare you, not to mention the convertible you drove around on campus last year. Which reminds me," he went on, "how come you're stooping to go by train instead of driving up? Did poppa Marshall's Chevy dealerships go broke?"

"Well, if you must know," she replied, "I earned the dough for that car. And I'm picking up a brand new Chevy in Elmira next week." She grinned. "Another red convertible that poppa Marshall arranged for me to get." Harry grunted. "With a white top. Our school colors."

Another grunt.

Then she snickered. "Too bad you've been grounded for speeding."

That shut Harry down. At least for now.

"I'm a sports nut," she confided. "I love them all. Women don't have any chance to compete at the varsity level. Everything is run by guys, even though Cornell's been a coed school from its beginning." She turned toward me. Her blue eyes sparkled and widened as she spoke. "My sorority has a basketball team, and I've been the center for the past couple of years. Guess why?" she added with a wry grin. "My height's good for basketball, bad for dating."

"What is a sorority?" I asked timidly, worrying about a put-down.

But Betty just shrugged. "Oh, it's a bunch of coeds who live in a house together on campus. It's like a club. You have to get invited to join. All the sororities have names with Greek letters. Mine is Kappa Alpha Theta. No Jews. Not because we want it that way. But that's just the way it is far above Cayuga's waters. Fraternities are the same thing, except only men belong." She shot a glance at Harry. "If you want to call them men. Most act like brats."

Harry glared back, but said nothing.

She jerked her head toward him and lowered her voice. "Now Harry there is a stuck up Phi Delta Theta. No Jews in that fraternity. His chapter would be kicked out of the national organization if it took in a Jew." I must have looked worried that Harry might overhear her, even over the squeaking and rattling of the car, because Betty's voice dropped even lower. "It's hard to believe, but last Spring Day weekend, a couple of fraternities hung swastikas from their windows." She pointed to my open *Life* magazine. "You know, those flags that Hitler and his gangsters wave all the time."

"You mean those fraternity guys like what Hitler's doing?" I whispered, thinking of what Harry had said.

"Oh, not all of them," she replied, "but enough of them to make life miserable for a lot of good people." She sighed. "You'd be amazed at the amount of anti-Semitism there is at Cornell. It makes me sick. I wanted to transfer to another university, but my mom and dad begged me to stick it out. Cornell has one of the best ag schools in the country."

"Anti what?" I asked.

"Oh, anti-Jews, I guess is the best way to explain." Her voice dropped. "I'm sorry. I get carried away at the injustice of it all. Over what's going on in Germany, what's going on in Italy, what's already happened in Spain. The whole world's going nuts."

I thought about "All Quiet On The Western Front," the movie I saw when I was fourteen—a depressing film about hand-to-hand combat with bayonets, about soldiers getting hung up on barbed wire and dying in the mud. "Do you think there'll be another war?" I asked.

Betty breathed in and seemed to drop into a trance for half a minute, then shook herself, as though coming out of a bad dream. "Unless England and France do something to stop Germany from re-arming." She shut her eyes. "Unless that miserable Hitler's stopped, and soon. Yes, I think there will be another war."

Just what Uncle Dan said, I thought. And I'd probably have to go to war. I'd hoped deep down that a stammer I used to have might keep me out of the military service if war came, but it had just about disappeared after speech therapy from a guy in my high school. I shuddered. I'd never be in the Army. Never. No hand-to-hand combat for me.

Betty took my arm again. "I'm sorry to run on like that. Let's talk about something else. Where are you going to live?"

When I explained that my dorm was called Cascadilla Hall, she burst out enthusiastically. "That's a great old building just off the campus in College Town. It's right across the road from Cascadilla Falls. You'll drop off to sleep every night listening to the wonderful sound of rushing water."

Neither of us spoke for about ten minutes. I leaned my head against the window and had started to doze, when I heard Betty's voice. "Look Bill, I'm going back to my seat. I've got some pre-assigned school work to do." She smiled and held out her hand. I took it. Her grip was firm. "How about coming to dinner at my sorority house some evening after you get settled? I'd love to hear how you're doing. Maybe I can give you a few pointers." She grinned. "At least I can give you a good meal." She stood, smiling down at me, waiting for my reply.

"Well, gee, thank you, B...." Should I call her Betty? I wondered. She seemed so much older than me.

She picked up on my problem. "I told you my friends call me Betty, and I hope we're friends."

"Well, thanks. I'd like that very much. How do I get in touch with you?"

Betty opened her black purse, pulled out a scrap of paper and a stub of a pencil, and wrote on it. "Here's the telephone number of the sorority. If you don't call me within a month, I'll track you down at the dorm." She grinned wickedly. "Even if women aren't supposed to be there."

CHAPTER 3

The iron cot squeaked and groaned as I rolled over on my right side, shifting my position for at least the twentieth time. The ceaseless tick, tick, tick of the clock reminded me that at 10 o'clock in the morning I had my first prelim, a written examination in the chemistry lecture course given in a huge auditorium in Baker Lab. The classes would have been as dull as dishwater, except for the comical showboating of Professor Browne, who got almost as many laughs as Jack Benny. But there was nothing funny about the way I felt now. I knew I'd flunk the exam.

I squeezed my eyes shut to block out the fear of failure, desperately hoping that somehow I'd fall asleep. Instead, images of the past few weeks began creeping through my mind like a movie in slow motion, with the first scene being the train's arrival at the Ithaca station. I managed to lug my two suitcases from the train and drag them to the platform. As I stood there, scratching my head and wondering what to do, Betty hollered for me to join her at the taxicab stand. She offered to share a cab. Lucky for me. I'd have never been able to climb the steep streets leading up to the campus with my luggage. I had no idea how to get to Cascadilla Hall any other way.

Harry stood behind us while we waited for a cab. He guffawed when I told Betty my destination. "What a dump!" he hooted. "Too bad you won't be rooming in the Baker Dorms where Steve's living." Harry puffed up like a toad. "He's got a room in Baker Tower."

I'd read that the Baker Dormitory, especially Baker Tower, was much ritzier than Cascadilla, but also twice as expensive. We didn't have that kind of money to pay those prices. Anyway, I felt pretty sure I didn't want to live close to Steve Dobson, not if he was anything like his blow-hard brother.

My first sight of Cascadilla Hall had increased my anxiety. The drab four-story building looming up in the dark looked more like a prison than a college dormitory. But after six weeks I'd grown to feel at home in the old building. I lived in a large third-floor room. No roommate. Although the furniture didn't look so great, it filled my needs—a beat-up wooden desk and straight-back chair, an amber-shaded floor lamp, a scarred brown four-drawer bureau, a second straight chair, and the narrow bed on which I now tossed and turned. The closet was plenty large enough to hold my mackinaw, my one good suit, a raincoat, four pairs of slacks, a flannel bathrobe, my sneakers, two pairs of shoes for every-day wearing, moccasin slippers, and my prize possession—the leather flight jacket Uncle Dan wore in France. A gray mat covered the center of the wooden floor below a 60-watt bulb, dangling from the ceiling by a black cord. The window looked out over Cascadilla Place. Beyond a stand of elm trees, Cascadilla Falls tumbled and roared, lulling me to sleep every night. Just like Betty said it would.

The huge white-tiled bathroom shared by the eight students on my floor was 50 feet down the hall. A pay telephone hung on the wall just outside the bathroom door. I'd called Uncle Dan after I got settled in and talked to him and then to Mom and Dad. They said Spike was okay. I missed him. My best friend. I heaved a big sigh now, thinking how homesick I was when I first got to Cornell. I was really blue after talking to Mom and Dad and Uncle Dan. Couldn't help it. My thoughts drifted back to the Sunday evening, the day before classes started, when I ventured out to take a look around the campus. I got goose bumps now, remembering the view from the Library slope of Cayuga Lake, spreading for miles into the distance, shimmering in the setting sun. As I gawked at the beautiful scenery, wishing someone, maybe Dee, could have been with me to share my excitement, the Library Tower chimes suddenly burst into sound. I wondered why they were playing "Maryland, My Maryland." We lived in Harford County, Maryland, before the bank took over our tiny dairy farm. At every high school assembly, the students stood and sang the State's official song. I learned later that Cornell's Evening Song had the same tune. Every evening the chimes from the Library tower rang out the familiar melody. And every morning at about 7:45, except Saturdays and Sundays, the chimes pounded out the "Jennie McGraw Rag," a raucous banging of the bells up and down the scale. I had 8 o'clock classes four days a week, and the racket sure helped wake me up.

One of the assistant chime masters told me the history of the sixteen bells in the Library Tower. Someone named Jennie McGraw gave nine of them to Cornell when the university first opened for business in 1868. A year later, the great tenor bell that struck the hours was given to the university by Mrs. Andrew Dixon White, the wife of the first president of Cornell. Six more bells had been added.

The one morning a week I didn't have an 8 o'clock class, I waited table for breakfast at the Kappa Sigma fraternity house, about a ten-minute brisk walk from Cascadilla Hall. I also waited table at the fraternity for lunch and dinner every day of the week. The food was not all that great, but my meals were free, so I didn't complain. Coach Tatum had lined up that job for me. Coach Tatum didn't coach the freshman baseball team. Fred Feese, an Agricultural Economics grad student, handled that job on the side. He was the star pitcher for the varsity team last year, so I hoped to learn a lot from him.

Going to classes and working was tough. I had courses in English, botany, animal husbandry, agronomy, and chemistry. I liked all my teachers except the English instructor, Richard Printz. The students called him "Dickie Bird" behind his back. He treated the girls like queens, and most of the boys like dirt. It made me sick the way he sweet-talked the coeds, especially Madeline McDaniel, a pretty blond, blue-eyed girl, who had Dickie Bird wrapped around her little finger. Madeline showed up late for class most of the time, and it never failed that, when she was not in her front-row seat by 9 o'clock sharp, Dickie Bird started pouting and whining and fretting, and complaining over and over, "Where is Miss McDaniel?" Once, after class, I heard him ask her if she liked the way he dressed.

I hadn't made any good friends. The closest, I guess, was a guy on my floor at the dorm, Erwin Redding. Erwin came from a town in New Jersey called Hohokus. I thought at first he was kidding me. He was about my size, maybe a little shorter, with a round face and wide-apart brown eyes. His straight black hair, parted on the left, as often as not hung down over black, bushy eyebrows. Erwin always looked to be in need of a shave. A mechanical engineering major, he loved to practice his skills in doing calculations on his slide rule for my benefit. Even though a junior, he hadn't tried to lord it over me.

Unlike most of the guys I met, Erwin didn't seem to be what Betty called anti-Semitic. The bad-mouthing of Jews really upset me. A few days ago, while walking in the quadrangle behind a couple of guys, one of them had pointed toward a group of students just about to enter Goldwyn Smith Hall and had hollered, "Hey, get a load of those kikes headed for Goldberg Schmidt!" And Rick Carson, who lived on the second floor of Cascadilla, hung a swastika on the door of his room, just to upset Felix Weinstein, who rooms across the hall.

The recollection of Dee and her relatives in Germany and what Hitler had done to them kept bothering me. I held my tongue, because if I let those bigots know how I felt about the way they talked and the cruel things they did, it probably would lead to a fight. I wondered how Betty felt about all the bad-mouthing of Jews. I hadn't telephoned her. Trying to get up my nerve.

Another thing. I've never heard such swearing in all my life, not even during times when the neighboring farmers helped fill our silo. None of the guys on my floor could say anything without using a bunch of four-letter words. And the way they carried on about girls was really stupid. I tried not to listen, but in the bathroom, when I toweled off from a shower or brushed my teeth, I couldn't help hear them hollering back and forth about the small "boobs" of such and such a girl, or snickering about how another "broad" would be a great lover.

I must have finally dozed off because a pounding on the door and a voice yelling startled me awake. "Hey, Bill, Bill. Get your butt out of the sack. Some bimbo's on the horn for you." I recognized Erwin's crude voice.

A bimbo. A girl? I sat up, trying to shake out the cobwebs. A glance at the Baby Ben told me it was nearly 8:30. Who would be calling me? My mom? Maybe something bad had happened.

"Bill, for Christ's sake. Are you dead or something?" Erwin shouted even louder.

"Okay," I yelled, "I'll be right there." I slid out of bed and stumbled to the closet. I slipped into my bathrobe, stuck my feet into my slippers, and opened the door. Erwin stood there, hands on hips, leering at me.

"Well, Bill, this is a first. I didn't think you knew any babes on campus. You been holdin' out?"

Pushing past him, I rushed down the corridor to the telephone. The receiver dangled from the cord, swinging back and forth. I reached down and pulled it to my ear. "Hello. Hello." I gasped, nearly out of breath from worry and running.

"Hi, Bill, it's Betty."

Betty! Betty Marshall. I couldn't even speak.

"Are you okay?" she asked.

I had to clear my throat a couple of times before I could talk. "Yeah, I'm fine," I finally choked out. "I thought it might be bad news from home."

"Oh, sorry. Didn't mean to alarm you." She laughed, a soft, friendly sound. I could picture her smile. "I heard the frosh are taking their first prelims today, and I just wanted to wish you good luck. I know you'll knock it dead."

I couldn't even think for what seemed like a year. Finally I managed to get some words out. And my stammer came back, the first time in more than six months. "GG GGosh BB BBetty..." Then a thrill and a feeling of confidence shot through me. I would knock the exam dead. I got control of myself. "Thanks very much, Betty. I really appreciate it."

"My pleasure, Bill." A silence followed, and I thought she might have hung up, when she spoke again. "How about that date we had for dinner? How come you never called me?"

I suddenly felt warm all over. Sweat popped out on my forehead. "Well," I said hesitantly, "I wait table at the Kappa Sig house. I don't know..."

"Oh, come on," she chided. "I happen to know that the frat house waiters get at least one evening off a month. So, don't give me that excuse."

She was right. I hadn't missed any dinners yet, and I knew I could get permission from Chuck Randolph, the head waiter, to skip one. He wouldn't object. He was a good guy, even if he was a senior.

"Can I call you after I check it out? I have your number."

"Well, okay," she replied. "But try to come on a Wednesday night. That's when we have steak. You deserve the best."

CHAPTER 4

"Wonders will never cease!" Mr. Bentley, my chemistry lab instructor, stared at me and then at the blue prelim book he clutched in his hand. His furrowed brow and puzzled frown and slowly shaking head made me wonder what I'd done now. I had made a mess of my laboratory course in more ways than one. I just couldn't get the hang of it. My experiments almost always failed miserably. Just last week, I created an uproar when I had stupidly held a test tube containing liquid ether over a Bunsen burner, thinking I could speed up a reaction. The tube had exploded. In a panic, I hurled the remnants of the tube across the room. Tiny fires broke out where drops of ether had fallen.

"I beg your pardon?" was all I could think to say to Mr. Bentley.

"I said wonders will never cease." Another head shake. "I just don't understand how in the world you, of all people, managed to get a ninety-eight on this exam."

My mind went blank for a couple of seconds. A ninety-eight! I reached out and took the prelim book. Yes, there it was. Professor Browne had written "good work!" next to that wonderful grade.

"Give it back. Let's see what you missed."

I complied, and he thumbed through the exam book. "Oh, for God's sake. You screwed up on the atomic numbers and weights of carbon and antimony. Cost you two points. You'd have a perfect paper but for that."

I silently wondered when, if ever, I'd need to know that bit of fascinating information. Maybe on a radio quiz show.

Mr. Bentley smiled and patted my shoulder. "Nice going, Bill. It's the highest mark any of my students got. You'll certainly exempt the final examination if you keep that up." He sighed. "See if you can put some of that brainpower to work for me."

I stumbled out of class in a daze and headed down the concrete steps to East Avenue, longing to share my feeling of exhilaration with someone. But who? The guys in the dorm could not care less. Probably say I cheated. I had ten minutes to get to the Plant Science Building for my botany class. One of my ambitions had been to try to make Dr. Petry look me squarely in the eye when he answered a question. So far, no luck. He would stroke his graying goatee and gaze over me or through me or around me. His uncanny ability to avoid eye contact while lecturing or when speaking to a student one-to-one was a frequent and weighty topic of discussion.

"Hey, Bill, congratulations!" I swung around. Steve Dobson strode toward me, holding out his hand. For the second time that morning, I felt speechless. I'd seen him in the chemistry lecture class. The seating was alphabetical. Students with last names beginning with the letter D sat strung out in the row behind my assigned seat. And I caught sight of him a couple of times in the gym chatting with Fred Feese, the freshman baseball coach, sucking around, I learned to my disgust, hoping to be the first-string catcher. He hadn't bothered to speak to me, and I had avoided him like the plague. Spring practice would be soon enough to have to deal with Harry Dobson's little brother. I could only pray that we would not be battery mates.

The hand I took felt clammy and limp. I wondered for a second how he could hang on to a baseball, much less throw one with any velocity. He was about Harry's height, but bigger and stronger looking. His hair was jet black, soft and wavy, curling up at the back of his neck. His eyes were a deep brown, his face olive-tinged. He was a good-looking guy, I had to admit. The girls probably loved him. I couldn't help feeling self-conscious when I noticed his clothes. Steve's blue, pin-striped suit, polka-dot bow tie, and white shirt, sporting a monogram on the pocket, next to Uncle Dan's leather jacket and my khaki slacks made me feel like the country boy I was.

"I heard you really killed that chemistry exam," Steve said. His smile seemed too friendly. He pulled a cigarette from the breast pocket of his jacket and stuck it between his lips.

"Uh, yeah, I guess so," I replied.

"Jesus, I really messed up," he moaned. "Mind if I walk with you for a while? I don't have a class this period." He lit the cigarette with a silver lighter, sucked in, then exhaled a puff of blue smoke.

I didn't particularly want to have anything to do with him, but couldn't think of a way to turn him down. "I guess not," I finally said. "I'm headed for the Plant Science Building."

He looked puzzled. Being in the Arts and Science College, he probably had never been on the ag campus.

"It's just across the ag quadrangle from Warren Hall," I explained. I doubted that he was any more enlightened, but he fell into step with me without asking any questions, and we started up Tower Road. I decided to let him do the talking. I didn't have anything to say to him anyway.

Steve cleared his throat a couple of times as we passed by the Veterinary College Building. "I got a fifty-eight in the goddam prelim," Steve snarled. "A lousy fifty-eight. That bastard Browne has it in for me, I know damn well he has." His face reddened. "He hates my brother. And he's taking it out on me."

"How come?" I finally asked.

"Oh, the no-good s.o.b. flunked him last year." He snorted with glee. "Good old Harry politely handed his final exam paper to Professor Browne and suggested that he take his protons, neutrons, and electrons, and stuff them up his ass one at a time." Steve cackled. "That really cooked big brother's goose. He was on probation for the rest of the year. Ineligible to participate in any freshman activities."

I had nothing to add to this conversation. The idea that a student would even think of talking to a professor in that way lay beyond my imagination. We pushed ahead in silence, on past Roberts Hall, and stopped in front of the Plant Science Building. I admired once more the flowers planted along the edge of the walkways leading up to the building— purple, pink and blue asters, yellow and rust-colored chrysanthemums, and a few hardy red roses hanging on in spite of cool weather, all carefully tended by the horticulture students. Last week, I overheard one of them shout to his fellow gardener, "Hey, Jack, did you know you can lead a horticulture, but you can't make her think." Jack had burst out laughing. Erwin Redding explained to me later what the guy meant.

Steve looked around uneasily, then tossed his lighted cigarette butt into a rose bush. "I just thought I'd get acquainted with you," he said. "Harry told me he bumped into you on the train, and he said you're here on a baseball scholarship."

"Yeah, " I replied. I couldn't think of anything else to

say. I just wished he'd go away. What did he want from me, anyway?

"Well," Steve went on, "I guess you know I'm going out for the team." He waited for a reply, but I just stared at him. "I'll wet my pants if I'm put on probation and can't play," he muttered. "And if I don't straighten my ass out in chemistry, I'll be sitting in the grandstands."

"I hope not," I lied.

"Look," he said, real friendly, "maybe we can get together at Zinks this Saturday and split a pitcher of suds." He giggled. "I hear you're a pitcher. A pitcher for a pitcher." His eyebrows lifted. "What do you say?"

I didn't need to lie this time. "Thanks, but I don't drink. Anyway, I don't have any money to spend on beer."

"Well," he said, the smile returning. "I've got plenty of dough. My old man sends me a hundred bucks a month to spend any way I want. They serve cokes at Zinks. The drinks will be on me."

The Library Tower began to chime the hour. "I've got to go," I said hurriedly. I turned and rushed up the walk to the front door.

"I'll get in touch with you later, Bill," he yelled, maybe you can come to dinner at the Phi Delt house some evening. Save you a few bucks."

I didn't even look back.

During most of Dr. Petry's lecture on the miracle of photosynthesis, I kept thinking of my prelim grade in chemistry. What had Mr. Bentley said? I'd exempt the final examination if I kept on getting high grades in the lecture course. Not have to take the final. That would save hours of studying and would give me a chance to bone up for my final in English, my weakest course. I wish I'd read more good books. The only book we owned on the farm was the bible, and Mom made sure I read that. I had to learn some parts by heart, like the twenty-third Psalm. Every month or so I'd get a mystery from the Belair Library, maybe a Sherlock Holmes story, and a few adventure stories, some of them about the Civil War. But that was about it. Dickie Bird and a couple of his favorite students, girls of course, constantly talked about Charles Dickens and Mark Twain and Robert Louis Stevenson like they were pals. And poetry! Dickie Bird loved to prance back and forth in front of the class, reading poetry, pretending he was on the stage. He always leered at Madeline McDaniel when he came to verses about love or women's bodies. One day he was reading from a long poem called "The Eve of St. Agnes." When he reached a line that said something about Madeline's fair breast, he licked his lips and smirked at Madeline McDaniel. I knew he picked out that part on purpose. I wanted to vomit, and I think all the other students did too, including Madeline. Anyway, I wished I knew more about good books and good poetry.

I escaped from botany class without being called on. A good thing. My mind had been elsewhere. I'd have to borrow a classmate's notes. The Library Tower started in chiming 11 o'clock. I had to be at the Kappa Sigma house at 11:30 to set up for lunch. Thank goodness it was all downhill to 600 University Avenue. But uphill back to the ag campus, and I had to be at the animal husbandry barn by 2 o'clock to attend a class on judging sheep.

I thought about the Kappa Sigs as I hurried down the Library slope. They were a pretty decent bunch of guys. The members loved to sing. I liked that. Almost everybody at Cornell seemed to burst into song at the drop of a hat. The school songs were wonderful, starting with the "Alma Mater" and ending with the "Evening Song." There was a bunch more, including the "Crew Song" and the "Song of the Classes," and one that started, "A soldier loves his general's fame, the willow loves the stream, a child will love his mother's name, the dreamer love his dream." I broke out into goose bumps every time I heard it.

After dinner ended, the Kappa Sigs stood and sang one of their fraternity songs, something about drinking to Kappa Sigma and the crescent and the star. And then, as the brothers strolled from the dining room and headed up the stairs to the huge living room, they sang, "Wait 'til the Sun Shines, Nellie." It was a pleasure to clean the tables and set up for breakfast, listening to the guys harmonizing.

I wished I could sing with a group. I'd have loved to sing in the men's glee club. But...oh well. Anyway, I wouldn't have time to rehearse, I told myself a hundred times, not with a full schedule of classes and two jobs. And baseball practice would start in March.

Judging sheep was no fun, especially when it came to measuring the width of a part of the ewe's rear end. Most of the class did not come away "unsullied," Professor Evans' laughing description of the embarrassing event each time a student suffered the humiliation of being peed or pooped on. I just got out of the barn, thanking my lucky stars that I was unsullied, when I heard a girl's voice behind me calling my name. "Bill, wait up." I stopped dead in my tracks and turned around. Betty Marshall ran toward me, clutching a brown knapsack. I hadn't seen her since the taxicab dropped me off in front of Cascadilla Hall my first day at Cornell. Her flushed face indicated she'd rushed to catch up. Her eyes sparkled and the tips of her dark curls, tied back with a red ribbon, danced up and down, reminding me of Dee. The blue denim overalls looked good on her. She stopped in front of me, breathing hard, and gripped my arm. "Bill, how did you make out in your chemistry prelim?"

My expression must have startled her because her face froze. "You did okay, didn't you?" she asked anxiously. It made me feel good that she cared.

"Yeah," I replied, a silly grin on my face.

"Well?"

"I got a ninety-eight."

"Oh, Bill, that's wonderful." She threw her arms around me. We were head to head, and I smelled a slight trace of the barnyard in her hair. I'm sure she got a whiff of sheep from me. Betty pulled back and grasped my shoulders. "Bill Creelman, we've got to celebrate. Right now." She glanced at her wristwatch. "It's just after 4 o'clock. We can get a Coke in the Willard Straight cafeteria." She laughed, a tinkling sound up the scale. "And I'm buying!"

We walked along Tower Road in silence for a few minutes. Why was Betty being so nice to me? I couldn't figure it out. She must have a dozen boyfriends. Her fresh open face with freckles scattered around was real pretty. And yet...I glanced sidewise at her. She was tall and kind of skinny and didn't have much in the way of boobs. I felt warm all over, thinking how crude I'd become, even to think that way. Was that what Cornell had done to me?

"Have you ever been there for a concert?" She pointed toward Bailey Hall.

"Uh, no." I paused, embarrassed. "I've only been there once, when the men and women's glee clubs put on a free show a week after classes started." The truth was, I didn't have money to spare to go to any concerts.

"Oh." We walked on in silence. "Well," she finally

said, "the Rochester Symphony Orchestra is performing this Saturday. How about being my guest?" She looked over and smiled. "It's a great program. Beethoven's Fifth Symphony, one of Mozart's violin concertos, and a Schubert string quintet. The best kind of selections for someone who's not had much chance to hear good music."

She had me tagged. I'd sure never had much of a chance to hear good music, only once in awhile on the radio when we visited Mom's relatives in a suburb near Baltimore. They always tuned in to a station playing classical music and then drowned out most of it with their gabbing with Mom and Dad.

"Well, what do you say?" she asked, breaking into my thoughts. "The seats are in the balcony, first row, the best place to be. You can see the entire orchestra, and the acoustics are terrific."

Acoustics. Another new word.

She must have noticed my wrinkled brow and dumb expression, because she patted my shoulder. "You've got a lot to learn, Bill."

I felt insulted for a second, but her smile and bright eyes told me she'd not tried to embarrass me.

"All I mean is the music sounds great. Now, how about it? Will you escort me to the concert on Saturday?"

I had another hot flash. What would the guys in the dorm say? Would they make snide remarks because I was going to a concert? With a tall and skinny girl? But it sounded a lot better than hanging out at Zinks with Steve Dobson. Oh, to hell with them. I didn't care what those jerks thought. To hell with them. Then it came over me that more and more I was thinking and using swear words. Hearing foul language all the time had begun to wear off on me. Dad and Uncle Dan probably wouldn't mind. But what would Mom think? And Dee?

"Thanks," I finally said. "I'd love to escort you to the concert." I glanced at her quickly. "You'll be my first Cornell date." We reached East Avenue and then stood waiting while an R.O.T.C. company marched by, each student in a wool gray uniform, wearing black leather boots, and carrying World War rifles at shoulder-arms. We watched in silence until the unit cleared the intersection. Then Betty took a deep breath. "Thank goodness coeds don't have to go through that." She glanced at me. "What about you? Do you have to put on one of those monkey suits and play soldier?"

I shot a glance toward the enormous structure overhanging the campus. Drill Hall, where male freshmen attended R.O.T.C. classes one afternoon a week. "Yeah," I replied. "I hate it. Our drill instructor gleefully tells us every session that he's fattening up us poor turkeys for the next war."

"Don't talk like that!" Betty's eyes widened with apprehension. "I couldn't stand to lose another friend," she said, whispering. She seemed to choke up. I wanted to ask her what she meant. What friend had she lost? And when? And how? But she grabbed my arm and started down the street, running, pulling me along. "Come on," she cried. "Let's get to the Straight before the place crowds up."

CHAPTER 5

"Do you have a girlfriend, Bill?" Betty Marshall glanced over at me as she asked that question, then back at the road as we zipped along in her brand new Chevy convertible with the top down. Just as she told Harry on the train, she picked up the flashy vehicle in Elmira the first Saturday after classes started. And just as she described to Harry, the body was a brilliant red, the top a dazzling white.

The acrid smell of burning leaves at the side of the highway leading up the west side of Cayuga Lake, was carried on the warm Indian summer breeze that ruffled Betty's dark curls. I'd just been thinking that her windblown hair reminded me of Dee, when she tossed that question at me out of the blue. I took a quick peek at her. She held her head high and tilted back, her eyes fixed on the road, lips drawn in like she had something on her mind. Both hands gripped the steering wheel, her knuckles showing little white splotches.

We'd become pals over the past couple of weeks. She was the only real friend I had at Cornell. We went to the concert at Bailey Hall and afterwards drove to Buttermilk Falls State Park, where we sat in the car with the top down and stared at the falls after dark, marveling at the film of water like a huge white curtain covering the rocks. We talked about the program, about Beethoven's Fifth Symphony, Mozart's Third Violin Concerto, and The Trout, a piece written by Schubert. She seemed anxious to know if I enjoyed the music. I had. And I told her so and thanked her for taking me to such a wonderful performance. She reached over and squeezed my hand.

Betty had invited me to dinner at the Kappa Alpha Theta house the Wednesday after the concert. Erwin Redding nearly split a gut laughing when I told him. "You know, they call it the cat house," he informed me, a smirk on his ugly puss. I wanted to punch him.

It had taken me nearly an hour to get dressed in my one suit. I must have worked on the necktie for at least ten minutes before I got the ends to come out even. Then my hair kept falling down over my forehead no matter how many times I brushed it back. I wanted to look good and not embarrass Betty for inviting me.

The dinner made up for my worry. Fruit cocktail, sirloin steak, French fries, green beans, avocado and tomato salad, topped off with a chocolate sundae. I'd never tasted food like that in my whole life. Betty's sorority sisters treated me like a king, insisting that I sit at the head of the senior table next to Betty. She hadn't told me she was the president of her sorority. Just like the Kappa Sigs, they sang before, during and after dinner. They persuaded me to memorize one of their sorority songs to pay for my dinner—the girls all shouted, laughing up a storm. I had to stand and sing the song before they let me eat my dessert. It went like this:

I pity the others who aren't in Theta;
I pity them through and through.
I pity the Eskimo way up north
And the Zulu with his pet kangaroo.
I pity the Hindus and I pity the Chinese,
　Way across the sea.
I pity my father and my brother and my uncle
　'Cause they can't be a Theta like me!

Needless to say, I made a fool of myself. But Betty and her sorority sisters stood and clapped like they'd lost their minds when I finished. I wished Dee could have been there, to see and talk with those cheerful and friendly girls. I wondered if she belonged to a sorority at Muhlenberg. Probably not. Probably cost lots of money. One thing Dee didn't have much of.

After dinner, we gathered in the living room for coffee. The cups and saucers had red and blue flowers painted on them. An older lady they called the housemother joined us. Mrs. Case. I liked her right off the bat. She looked like a mother. But not like Mom. My poor mom had one good dress she wore to church and church socials. She'd never had her hair "done." She washed it from a bowl every Saturday night before bed with Ivory soap. Mrs. Case's elegant blond hair, showing a few gray streaks, was pulled neatly to the left. She stood and sat erect, stiff. But my first impression that she was unfriendly evaporated when she smiled, which she did most of the time.

We finished the coffee by 9 o'clock, and I was thinking I'd overstayed my welcome, when Betty asked Mrs. Case if she could drive me to Cascadilla Hall. I had to guess from Betty's need to get permission that the house mother kept close track of her charges. Anyway, Mrs. Case said it would be okay.

Betty had driven slowly past Beebe Lake, and then, instead of heading down East Avenue, continued on University Avenue, and turned into Central Avenue and stopped the car in back of McGraw Hall, with the Chevy facing west. She turned off the motor, and we sat for about a minute in silence. "I wanted you to see the lake and West Hill at night from up here," she finally said. "Come on, hop out. Let's walk down the slope to get away from the street lights." As we made our way down Library slope in the dark, she reached out to grab my hand—to keep her balance, I guessed. We'd gone about half-way down the hill, when she stopped. "Look over there at the lake and the house lights on the hill," she whispered. "And look at that sky. There are millions and millions of stars in the Milky Way alone. Isn't it awesome?" It was awesome—the moonless and cloudless autumn night; the Milky Way, an immense river of light.

"Oh, look!" she gasped, "a shooting star!" A pinpoint of light streaked across the western sky, flickered once, then disappeared. Betty's eyes shown with excitement as she turned toward me, her lips parted, her breathing rapid. "God!" I thought, "she's beautiful!" My own breath quickened, and a thrill swept through me, overwhelming me for a moment. Then a pang of guilt hit me. What would Dee think? We stared at each other for what seemed like an hour. I turned hot, then cold, wondering what was going on. Finally, she took a couple of deep breaths, then turned and started up the hill, walking fast. "Come on, Bill," she called over her shoulder. "Got to get you back to the dorm. Don't want you late for that 8 o'clock tomorrow." Well, *that* was a letdown. I hadn't expected to be treated like someone's kid brother.

I saw Betty soon after that. She was leaving the Animal Husbandry building as I entered. She gave me a bright smile. "How about driving out to Taughannock Falls Sunday afternoon?" she asked. "I'll scrape together some sandwiches and Cokes, and we can have a picnic. What do you say?"

Well, I had agreed quickly enough, my heart pounding, but I had to promise Chuck Randolph that I'd handle two breakfasts next week in return for missing the noon Sunday dinner, one of the two big meals of the week at the Kappa

Sigma house. And now we were on our way, with that question hanging in the air like a World War barrage balloon: Do you have a girlfriend?

Thank goodness Betty's eyes remained fixed on the road ahead and not on my face, which had to be showing my confusion. I don't know why I felt so flustered. I had a simple enough answer. And so I cleared my throat a couple of times and told her the truth. "No."

Her head turned toward me for a split second, then turned back, but not before I saw the warm glow of her smile. "Not even in Bethlehem?" she persisted.

I shook my head. "No, I'm afraid not."

She chuckled. I noticed her grip on the steering wheel had relaxed. She pushed the gearshift into neutral and slowed to a stop. We reached the entrance to the park. "Nothing to be afraid of, Bill." she said. "But I am surprised, a good-looking guy like you."

Good-looking! No one, not even Mom, ever called me good-looking. My face is spattered with freckles, my eyes are a funny blue-green color, and too far apart. My school pals, even some of the girls, called me carrot top, and I couldn't keep my hair from hanging straight down over my forehead. My teeth bothered me most. When we played "spin the bottle" at school parties, I worried that the girls would be put off by them. But come to think of it, none of them had seemed to mind. And Dee hadn't said anything when she gave me that birthday kiss. Not even a wisecrack.

Was Betty pulling my leg? I stole a look at her, but she seemed serious enough. She eyed me up and down, a half-smile on her face, then shifted to low gear and headed the Chevy into Taughannock Falls State Park. We pulled up to a spot that gave us a terrific view of the falls. A rushing column of foaming white water cascaded straight down for more than 200 feet, crashing into a large pond, sending spray high into the air. We stared for several minutes.

"This place was once covered with ice," Betty finally said. "Hard to believe." She pointed to one of the park pavilions. "We had a terrible flood here a couple of years ago. Just dumb luck that a bunch of kids partying over there didn't drown." She turned off the engine. "Come on, give me a hand," she cried out. "You grab the basket and I'll bring the blanket."

We brushed away hundreds of acorns, then spread a

soft pink blanket between two gigantic white oak trees, still bearing enough foliage to cut off most of the early afternoon sunlight that speckled the brownish green grass with light and dark splotches. Dressed in a wool red turtleneck sweater, a red and green plaid skirt, and red wool socks that reached to just below her knees, Betty looked much younger than twenty-two. She told me her age without my asking, not that I ever would be that nosey.

I whistled in amazement when I got a look at all the food she fished out. Cold cuts of roast beef, ham and turkey breast along with tomatoes, celery stalks, lettuce, pickles, potato salad, and a loaf of rye bread. Two slabs of chocolate cake rounded out the feast.

"Where did all of this come from?" I asked.

"Well," she replied with a giggle, "if the truth be known, I raided the Theta house pantry." She nodded toward the dishes, cutlery, and glasses laid out on the blanket. "Borrowed them, too. My only contributions are the Cokes and this thermos, which is mine, all mine." She waved the container over her head, sloshing the contents back and forth. "So, thank you, Kappa Alpha Theta."

She sat cross-legged, reached for a bread knife and began constructing sandwiches. "Maybe I'll make you warble that ditty we taught you before I let you eat. Sing for your supper?" She glanced up, eyebrows raised.

"I'd rather starve than go through that again," I muttered, only half-joking.

But she did not insist on torturing me, and I did not starve. We soon polished off every crumb of food and drank every drop from the thermos. I lay back on the blanket and closed my eyes. The rush of the waterfall seemed far away, and I might have dozed off if I hadn't had so much on my mind. I wondered again why Betty was being so nice to me. And how I felt about her. I not only didn't have a girlfriend, but I'd never had one. Dee was the only girl I'd ever given a second thought to...except for Betty. But Dee had lorded it over me most of the time, making me feel like a young kid, embarrassing me. And yet, she was wonderful, helping me search for Spike after I was sure he'd been killed. I never would have found him if it hadn't been for her. Not in a million years. And I did lie awake some nights, thinking about her, squirming when I recalled over and over again that one kiss. And that dimple.

Then I got to wondering if Betty might want to be my girlfriend. She lay on her back next to me, so close we almost touched. I could hear her breathing, real steady, like she was asleep. Why would a senior want to bother with a freshman? I felt myself getting warm all over. How dumb could I be? She must have a boyfriend, either at Cornell or in Philadelphia, or both places. But I'd never seen her with a guy on campus; had never seen her with a girlfriend, for that matter, except at her sorority house.

I opened my eyes and stared at the sky. A couple of buzzards wheeled fifty feet overhead. They'd spotted their dinner, probably some poor mangled rabbit run down by a Cornell student barreling up the road to keep a date at Wells College.

"A penny for your thoughts, Bill."

I glanced over at Betty. Her face turned toward me, no more than a foot away, her lips curved upwards in a half-smile. Immediately my guard was up, I felt caught, and I couldn't answer for a few seconds.

"Well...well, I guess I was wondering if you have a boyfriend." I looked away quickly, flustered that I'd asked such a personal question. It just popped out. But, I thought, she hadn't hesitated to ask me if I had a girlfriend.

Betty's reaction startled me. The smile vanished instantly; her eyes widened and filled with tears. She turned her head away and lay on her back with her hands behind her neck, staring at the sky, now empty except for wisps of white clouds miles above the earth. Her lips trembled ever so slightly. I pushed myself up, leaning on my elbow, and stared at her. I couldn't imagine what had upset her. And she was upset. No doubt about that. "Gee, Betty," I whispered, "I'm sorry I was so nosey. I didn't mean to trouble you." I choked up for a few seconds. "You're my best friend at Cornell. The last thing in the world I want to do is to hurt your feelings."

She looked at me, the smile back, her eyes glistening. She brushed her hand across her face, then reached over and grabbed my hand. "You didn't hurt my feelings, Bill." She breathed a sigh. "But I guess I am a little upset." She lay back again on the pink blanket. I didn't say anything, thinking she might want to get something off her chest. The last thing she needed was to have to answer some dumb questions. So I lay back, too, and waited for her to explain, if she wanted to. During the long silence that followed, I became conscious of the soft roar of the falls and the distant cries of red-winged blackbirds. It was all so peaceful. No one should be upset on such a day.

Finally, she did start to talk, looking straight up, and I listened without interrupting. "Bill, I've been sort of flying under false colors. I guess you think I've been flirting with you, and I can't blame you for that." She paused, reached again for my hand and gave it a quick squeeze, then let go of it. "Even if I'm much too old for you."

At least, she hadn't said I was too young for her. That was something.

"All I want is for you and me to be good friends. I don't want to be your best friend at school or anywhere else. You're such a great guy. I know you'll find a girl you like much better than you like me." She paused. "If you haven't found one already."

I thought of Dee. She was older than me, too. I never thought of her as being my girlfriend. And I was sure she didn't think of me as her boyfriend. A friend, yes. But that was it. Or was it?

"I'll never have a boyfriend or fall in love," she said. "Never again."

I came close to interrupting her then but managed to control the urge. I did glance over, and I saw that her eyes had closed, lips drawn back real tight.

"I was in love, really in love, for more than two years with a Cornell student. We met at the Junior Week dance in our freshman year. He cut in on me, and, well..." She breathed in again. "Well, we fell in love at first sight, as they say. He was an Agriculture Economics major. His family owned a huge muck farm near Batavia. Hundreds of acres. Grew vegetables like crazy. He was supposed to take over the management when he graduated. He was the only son. He had two younger sisters." She started talking rapidly, mechanically. "His father was killed when Jack was just starting his junior year. He was driving a tractor down a steep grade, when it overturned. He wasn't able to jump clear and was crushed to death. That was bad enough. Jack worshipped his dad. But then his mother nearly drove him crazy after that, insisting that he had to be admitted into Phi Kappa Phi, had to get highest honors, had to excel in everything he did. He was doing okay until she started pressuring him."

Betty was silent for such a long time I wondered if

she'd told me everything she was going to. I was about to say something, I don't know what, when she started talking again. "I guess she didn't nearly drive him crazy, she actually succeeded, because when Jack didn't excel, when his grades fell off, when he didn't get into Phi Kappa Phi..." Betty was silent again for at least a minute, then began speaking in a monotone, bitterness creeping into her voice. "He strolled along the path to the Suspension Bridge one beautiful moonlit night last May and..." She took a deep breath. "Jumped into Fall Creek Gorge."

I was so stunned, I couldn't speak.

"Damn Mrs. Virginia Randolph!" Betty shouted. "I hope she goes to hell and rots there!" She sat up and turned toward me, her eyes wild, like she'd gone crazy. I still couldn't think of anything to say. Why would a guy kill himself, I wondered. Just because his mother was tough on him. That didn't seem like a good reason, or any reason at all. I couldn't even think of a reason. My mom had been plenty tough on me. It had never even crossed my mind to kill myself. I always thought later that I deserved what I got when I wouldn't do things Mom wanted me to do. Anyway, we always made up real fast. She loved me and I loved her. That was the important thing. Maybe Jack Randolph's mother didn't love him.

Betty's face relaxed a bit. She reached for my hand and squeezed it, then let go. "Look, Bill," she said, "I'm sorry I sounded off like that. But..." She shrugged and stared out at the falls, then began speaking again in a low tone of voice, like she was talking to herself. "I want a guy for a friend, someone nice I can talk to and listen to and go places and do things with. But I don't want to fall in love again, not ever as long as I live." She looked up and smiled a half-smile. "I liked you right off the bat on the train. You're so different from the other guys I've met at Cornell since Jack..." She gnawed on her lower lip, then went on, speaking without any expression on her face. "You're smart and honest and interesting. I admit I've been selfish. I like to help people, and I think I can help you and really want to help you by taking you places you've never been, to concerts and the theatre, and teaching you about music and literature. Jack loved classical music and good books. We went to concerts together. We listened on Saturday afternoons to the Metropolitan Opera performances. We read nearly all of Shakespeare's plays out loud. We loved to take parts in the plays. We read Middlemarch and Vanity

Fair and Tom Jones, and all of Jane Austen's books, and most
of Charles Dickens's works, and at least a dozen of Trollope's
novels. How I miss all of that." She sat up suddenly. "God, he
was such a romantic. I thought for a couple of scary weeks he
was going to rush off to Spain, to fight Franco and his Fascist
mob, or at least drive an ambulance. Stories about the awful
atrocities committed by those barbarians drove him wild."

I felt dizzy trying to understand her. I'd read a little about
Franco, and how he murdered men, women and children who
opposed him. I hadn't thought much about his dirty deeds
until Hitler and Mussolini stuck their noses in. Even then, the
killing in Spain seemed a long way off. And I'd never heard
of any of the books or authors she rattled off, except Dickens
and Shakespeare, when Dicky Bird and his favorite female
students yacked about them in English class. I knew about
the Metropolitan Opera's Saturday afternoon broadcasts, but
it never occurred to me to listen to them. Anyway, I didn't
have a radio.

Betty took a deep breath and kept talking. "We joked
about merging his family's muck farm and my dad's beef
cattle business after we graduated. He'd raise the food for our
Aberdeen Angus." She smiled at this. "Feed them bushels
of spinach and onions. We had endless discussions about
how the Nazis and the Fascists would take over the world
unless someone stopped them. Jack was sure another war
was coming. And so we decided to get married and have at
least one child before civilization caved in around us. We
planned to have a wedding in Sage Chapel, the Saturday after
commencement, and a huge reception at the Ithaca Hotel."

She looked over at me. "I hope you don't mind me letting
my hair down like this. To tell you the truth, I haven't been
able to talk to anyone this way about Jack. We didn't let my
folks in on our plans, though they knew we were close, so I
haven't felt like burdening them with my troubles. I'd cut off
my left arm before saying anything to that mother of his, and
I never could relate to either of his sisters. I don't have any
close friends, except a few of the girls in the sorority, but..."
Her voice trailed off for a few seconds. "I feel more comfortable
talking to a man about things like this. And..." She drew in
a deep breath. "You're my man, Bill." She grabbed my arm.
"More like my psychiatrist, I guess."

CHAPTER 6

"Hey Bill, wait up."

It was Steve Dobson yelling at me. I hadn't exchanged more than a half-dozen words with him since we walked up Tower Road to the Plant Science Building nearly two months ago. I swung around, and there he was, about fifty yards away, running toward me, waving his hand, with two other guys right on his heels. I reached midway between the statues of Ezra Cornell and Andrew Dixon White in the quadrangle, headed for the Library to study for my final English examination next Wednesday. An early December gale blew the powdery snow in great swirls, making me appreciate the overcoat and wool scarf and gloves that Uncle Dan had given me when I was home for Thanksgiving.

When the rushing figures drew closer, I recognized Harry Dobson, but the other guy was a stranger. The three of them surrounded me, pounding their gloved hands together and stamping their feet, gasping and blowing out steam from the cold. I couldn't help noticing they wore identical black overcoats with fur collars and black fur hats, like they were in uniform.

"This is Brad Keane, and I guess you know my brother, Harry," Steve said. "We'd like to talk to you if you have time. Maybe we could go to the Willard Straight cafeteria. Okay?"

It wasn't okay. I had no use for Steve or Harry, and I didn't like the looks of Brad Keane. He'd drawn his fur cap down over his ears, nearly covering his face, all blotchy red either from the cold or too much boozing, but not hiding his long, pointed nose or thin lips that curled down in what looked to be a permanent frown. Cold and unfriendly dark eyes stared right through me. He only jerked his head when Steve introduced us. I checked an instinct to give him a polite hello and nodded back without saying anything. Harry just stood watching with a silly grin on his face.

"Well," I said, "I don't know. I've only got a couple of hours to study for an exam, then I've got to get down to the Kappa Sig house to wait table."

"Oh, come on, Bill," Steve said.   He actually looked worried and even scared. "It's real important. We'll only keep you a few minutes. I promise."

"Yeah, Bill," Harry chimed in, "we'll even buy you a beer."

"Bill doesn't drink," Steve said.   Then he half-smiled. "Maybe a hot chocolate."

I couldn't for the life of me figure out what they wanted of me. It crossed my mind for a split second that they might ask me to pledge their fraternity. Steve and Harry were Phi Delts and maybe Brad was, too. No way I could join. The few fraternities that had made an approach dropped me like a hot potato upon learning I had no money. But that couldn't be it. Rush week had come and gone months ago. Then, I thought, why not at least listen to what they had to say. A cup of steaming hot chocolate topped with whipped cream sounded good on this wintry day.

The chimes from the Library Tower began sounding the preliminary notes leading up to striking the hour. As the huge bell began tolling four o'clock, I glanced around at the three faces confronting me. Steve, all eager and expectant, Harry still wearing his silly grin, Brad, cold and repulsive. I took a deep breath, a sigh to let them know I wasn't happy about going with them. "Okay," I said, "maybe for fifteen minutes."

"Great," Steve shouted, and slapped my back. I resisted the urge to punch him in the nose, then walked swiftly toward Willard Straight, with the three of them plunging along behind me in single file.

"Let's sit over there," Steve said, waving his hand at the far corner of the cafeteria. The few other students who had ventured out on this frigid, blustery day lounged at separate tables scattered around the dining room. Steve seemed to want to be as far away as possible from them, and so we threaded our way between tables to the one he had pointed out. The rattling of dishes and clinking of glasses and cutlery in the kitchen announced the preparation of the evening meal by student food preparers and waiters.

Harry and Brad and I sat in silence while Steve hurried off for the drinks. Harry kept fidgeting and squirming in his chair, and gazing around the room as though he either expected someone to join us or was worried about the four of us being seen together. Brad leaned back, staring at the ceiling, his face expressionless. He'd removed his black coat and hat, and I noticed for the first time his lean and sinewy build, like that of a long-distance runner. Without the fur hat that had covered most of his face, I could see he was a good deal older than most undergraduates, maybe twenty-five. He still hadn't said a word to me.

"Give me a hand, Harry." Steve approached the table with a tray loaded with a cup of hot chocolate and six steins of beer, the foam overflowing onto the tray. Ordinarily, I would have helped distribute the drinks, but this time I just sat there and let Steve and Harry pass around two steins for each of them, and the hot chocolate for me. Steve hung his coat over the back of the chair, pulled off his fur hat, and sat down across from me. It was his move, so I waited, pretending to examine a watercolor of the Library Tower on the wall behind him. He shifted uneasily for a few seconds, then coughed twice. "Well, Bill, how are things going?" he asked in a friendly tone of voice.

"Not bad," I replied, giving him no opening.

The three of them simultaneously raised their steins to their lips, took a swallow of beer, and simultaneously lowered the steins to the table, like a military drill. A silence followed, while I sipped the hot chocolate, wondering again what they were up to. Why were they so anxious to talk to me? And in private.

Maybe because I glanced at the clock on the wall a couple of times, Harry cleared his throat and start talking. "You know, Bill," he said, "Brad's going to coach the freshman baseball team." He nodded toward Keane, who continued to study the ceiling.

This was stunning news. "What do you mean?" I asked. I'm sure my voice reflected my surprise. "I thought Fred Feese was the frosh coach."

Harry let out with a cackling laugh. "Well, he was, but he ain't no more. He's dropped out of the Ag. Economics program. Already headed for home. His father's had a heart attack and is in real bad shape. Fred's got to help take over the management of a hick farmer's grange near Rochester. Coach Tatum asked Brad to take over. Brad will finish up his graduate work in corporation finance next June."

A bunch of thoughts raced through my mind. Fred Feese had been a good friend, and I had looked forward to learning a lot from him. We'd talked about pitching and the kind of team he hoped to field. He'd told me a couple of times he planned to build the pitching staff around me. He'd said there would be room for only two catchers on the squad, and he had mentioned that Steve was being considered for one of the two positions, but doubted that he would make the team. I wasn't too unhappy about that.

Brad Keane might not feel the same way about me. Would my scholarship be affected? It could be lost altogether if I didn't at least become a starter on the team. Goodbye, Cornell. I glanced at the three pairs of raised eyebrows and three pairs of eyes fixed on me. They obviously expected some kind of response. What's going on? I wondered. Why are they making such a big deal of telling me this? What did they expect me to say? I decided to leave, and fast. I finished the hot chocolate and stood. "Well, I've got to get going. Thanks for the drink." I pulled on one of my gloves.

The three exchanged startled glances. Harry jumped up and confronted me. "Hold up, Bill, don't be in such a rush. We need to talk to you about something." He pushed me back to the chair, just hard enough to cause me to sit down again.

"I don't get it," I said. "What do you guys want from me?"

"We want your...How should I phrase it?" Harry paused, a smirk on his face. "Let's just say we want your cooperation."

Steve giggled. "Yeah, that's a good word. Cooperation. Says it all."

I glanced at Brad Keane. His cold stare was all I got back. Cooperation? I felt baffled.

Harry cleared his throat. "We heard you exempted the final chemistry exam. Is that right?"

My bafflement increased. "Well, yes, I did. So what?" I added, doing my best to sound defiant.

Harry shot a glance at Steve, then continued. "Well, my stupid little brother has made such a mess of chemistry that, if he doesn't pass the final with a reasonably decent grade, he'll be put on probation."

I'd heard about Steve's having a rough time in chemistry, but I hadn't thought much about it and didn't care. The three of them seemed to be waiting for some response, but I couldn't think of a thing to say. I hitched forward to the edge of my chair and stared at Harry.

"And, I imagine even you can figure out what that will mean. The poor slob will be ineligible for the freshman baseball team, and that will make all of us very, very unhappy." He nodded toward Brad. "Especially Coach Keane."

If Harry wanted me to cooperate with him in some undisclosed manner, he sure was going about it the wrong way. "Look," I lied, "I'm sorry Steve's having a rough time. But there's nothing I can do about it." Then, it suddenly came over me what they were driving at. I heaved a sigh of relief. They wanted me to help Steve prepare for the exam. Maybe I could even earn some extra money. "Do you want me to tutor Steve in chemistry? Is that how you want me to cooperate?"

A snort from Brad Keane, the first sound from him during the entire conversation. He rolled his eyes and resumed his study of the ceiling.

"Jesus." Harry's favorite word. "No, we don't want you to tutor him for Christ's sake. Nobody could fill his empty skull in time. The exam's scheduled for next Monday, and it's Friday already."

I sat frozen in the chair, unable to figure out what Harry could be driving at.

"For crying out loud, Harry," Steve cried out, "why don't you just tell him what we want him to do, instead of screwing around?"

"Okay, okay." Harry looked at me. "What we want you to do is take Steve's exam for him."

My mind went blank for what seemed like forever. My face felt as though I'd stuck it in an oven. I wasn't sure what I just heard, so I asked: "Do you mean, you want me to take the final chemistry examination for Steve?"

"That's it." Harry leaned close to me, and began speaking in a low voice. "It be a cinch. At least a hundred and fifty people will be taking that exam in a huge assembly hall, monitored by a half-dozen grad students who don't know you from Adam. They'll never realize Steve's not there. You needn't worry about your handwriting. You can print the exam. We don't want any super-high marks. That would look suspicious. You could make enough mistakes so Steve'll get no more than an eighty. That would get him a passing grade in the course."

I opened my mouth to speak, but Harry raised his hand and continued at the same rapid pace. "But for God's sake, don't sit near people in your lab class. They know you exempted the exam and might wonder why the hell you're there. Come in a few minutes late. Pick a spot near students you've never seen before." He stopped, raised his eyebrows, and waited for my response, which wasn't long in coming.

"I couldn't do that," I said. "I be kicked out of school if I was caught. So would Steve."

"You better damn well give this some serious thought, Creelman." This warning came from Brad Keane, along with a cold, fishy stare. "We need Steve for the team. He's by far the best catcher in the group."

I knew this wasn't true. Not after what Fred Feese had told me. What was going on here? What was in it for Brad Keane?

"And," he added, "for your information, Creelman, a couple of outstanding high school pitchers have registered for next term and will be eligible to play."

This had to be a lie. Feese wouldn't have kept that information from me. This guy Keane must have an axe to grind. Brad Keane wanted to have Steve on the team for some reason that had nothing to do with his catching abilities. And I figured he probably was malicious enough to keep me off the team if he didn't get his way.

Harry seemed a bit upset at Keane's threatening attitude. "Look," he said, "just think it over, Bill, and let us know your answer by six o'clock Sunday afternoon. You can give me a call at the Phi Delt house."

My prospects for the future floated through my mind in the moments that followed. Brad Keane held my fate in his hands. He could find some excuse for refusing to let me pitch, even if his story about the two super-stars was made up out of whole cloth.

I should tell them to go to hell.

And yet...

CHAPTER 7

I peered once again through the early morning gloom at the Baby Ben. The radium dial showed the time to be ten minutes of seven. I hardly slept all night.

The previous day, after leaving my tormentors I headed for the library, but I couldn't even open a book to study; I just stared straight ahead for about an hour, trying to sort out my thoughts. I wished I'd had the nerve to tell them to go to hell. But I chickened out, mumbled something—I don't remember what—and dashed out of the cafeteria.

"Talk to you Sunday," Harry had yelled after me.

During dinner, I spilled hot tomato soup on George Simpson's coat. I was that upset. George just laughed it off and asked for another napkin to mop up. But Chuck Randolph blew a fuse. He threatened to kick me out of the dining room and furlough me for a month. If that happened, I'd either go broke or starve to death. Chuck calmed down when George came to my defense. George, a first-year law student, winked at me when Chuck caved in. "I just won my first case, Bill." He laughed. "You can forget about the fee."

Lying on my cot in the darkened dormitory room, I groaned out loud. What should I do? Should I report Harry's proposition? But who could I report it to? And who would believe me? Harry and Steve and Brad would lie, and they'd say I was crazy. It would be my word against theirs. Three against one. Why should anyone believe me and not them?

Should I cave in to them? If I did, what were the chances of getting caught? Harry was right. A mob of students would be taking the exam, with only a few monitors. It would be easy to find a seat surrounded by strangers. I had only a handful of acquaintances in the chemistry class. Anyway, everyone would be worried sick about the exam and not thinking about who was in the room. And I could print instead of writing, or print some and write some, slanting words back, instead of using my normal script. If I took the exam, my worries about not making the team and being forced to leave Cornell would be over.

That sounded good to me.

For about three seconds.

What would Mom and Dad think, if they ever found out? And Uncle Dan? And Dee? And Betty?

What would I think of myself?

Sweat burst from every pore. Maybe I should take a walk to the Suspension Bridge and put an end to my misery. I wanted to laugh. Just a short time ago I mentally criticized Jack Randolph for killing himself, wondering how anyone could do such a stupid thing. And now...I sat up abruptly. A hot shower might help me think through this mess. While I was toweling off, I decided to ask Uncle Dan for advice. Dad's and Mom's feelings might be hurt. But I couldn't trust their judgment. They hadn't been around all that much. Uncle Dan would tell me what to do. I was sure of that. They'd be up by now, even on a Saturday, probably eating breakfast. I had some quarters for calling home in an emergency. This qualified as an emergency. My whole life depended on doing the right thing. I pulled open the top drawer of the bureau and counted my change. Seven quarters. A dollar and seventy-five cents. That should be good for at least ten minutes.

After pulling on my moccasins and slipping into my robe, I traipsed down the empty hall to the telephone. Most Saturday mornings were like a morgue. Nearly everybody slept in. No exception today. Before lifting up the receiver, I thought for a moment of calling person-to-person, then changed my mind. Mom and Dad would really be upset if they thought I didn't want to talk to them.

I placed the call through the operator, after dropping seventy-five cents into the coin box for the first three minutes, and waited while the bell at the other end rang, shifting my weight from one foot to the other. I counted eight rings and was about to hang up, when a breathless voice answered, a woman's voice.

"Hello, hello. Who's calling?"

"Mom, it's me, Billy," I replied. "Can I..."

"Oh, Billy, darling," she shrieked, "I'm so glad you called. We haven't heard from you in ages. Foster," she called out, "it's Billy, calling all the way from Cornell University."

Actually, I had written my weekly letter home last Saturday. "A letter should have got there a couple of days ago," I said hurriedly. "Look, Mom, I need to talk to Uncle Dan for a few minutes, then I'll talk to you and Dad."

I might have been speaking to a brick wall. Mom went rattling on in her high-pitched, excited voice. "We've been worried about you. We read that there was a blizzard in Western New York. Are you warm enough? Did you get the wool scarf we sent you? I knitted it myself. Are you getting enough good food and plenty of sleep?"

"Mom," I pleaded, but there was no stopping her.

"Spike's missed you so much. He's standing here next to me, wagging his tail. He heard me say your name. Spike," she called out, "Spike, it's Billy. Say hello. Come on, bark. I've stuck the receiver next to his ear, Billy."

I nearly died. Then I heard the familiar woof, woof of my best friend." Tears spurted. I hadn't realized until now how much I missed him.

"Hi, Spike," I yelled. "Good boy. Good boy."

"Jesus Christ, what the hell's going on out there?" I glanced over my shoulder and Erwin Redding stood in the open door of his room, loud and threatening, bleary-eyed, looking like a convict in his horizontally striped blue and white pajamas.

"I'm trying to call home," I shouted back.

"Well you don't have to make so damn much racket," he hollered. "The way you're yelling they can hear you without the phone. How the hell's a guy supposed to get some sleep."

"Please deposit fifty cents." The operator demanded more money. I reached into my bathrobe pocket, fished out two quarters, and dropped them into the coin box.

"Mom, can I please talk to Uncle Dan."

"Billy, Billy, how are you?"

It was Dad.

My mind went blank for a few seconds.

"Dad, I'm fine, I really am," I finally said, "but I..."

"We really miss you. We talk about you all the time."

"Gee, Dad, I miss all of you too. I really do. I'm calling to ask Uncle Dan a ques..."

"Dee dropped by last weekend. Wanted to check on Spike and Dan. She asked about you, too. She's as pretty as ever. I really am fond of that gal. Smart as a whip."

"Please deposit fifty cents."

I only had two more quarters. I knew I couldn't explain

to Uncle Dan the situation and get his advice in the time I had left.

As the last coin jingled into the coin box, Dad rattled on and on about Dee. "She's getting all A's at Muhlenberg. She's president of her class, even though she's a woman. That never happened before."

I was glad to hear about Dee and pleased that she even thought about me. "Tell her hello from me, when you see her again," I said. "And tell her to drop me a line."

"What did you want to say to Uncle Dan, Billy? He's just come in the house from shoveling the walk. We had ten inches of snow last night."

A feeling of despair overwhelmed me. No time to explain my problems and get an answer from Uncle Dan. At least not before six o'clock tomorrow evening. Unless he telephoned me. "I've run out of change, Dad. Can you ask Uncle Dan to call me back at..." I squinted, looking for the number. I couldn't believe it. Someone had scrawled over it with red ink. It was obliterated.

"I'm sorry, your time is up." The operator again. "I'll try to call later," I shouted hurriedly. The line went dead. Now what, I wondered. I gripped the receiver for a few moments, then slowly lowered it into the cradle. Should I try to borrow some change from Erwin and call back? Then I thought, Erwin's so damn nosey. He'd insist on knowing why I wanted to telephone home before lending me the money. As I leaned against the wall, trying to figure out what to do, it came over me like a flash. I didn't need to talk to Uncle Dan. I knew what he'd say. He'd say tell them to go jump in Cayuga Lake and hope they can't swim. That would be his advice. But what about my scholarship? What about Cornell? What about my life?

"Hey, Bill." Erwin peered through the half-open door of his room. "Did you get things settled at home? I hope everything's okay. Anything I can do?"

To my surprise, he seemed genuinely concerned. I hesitated a few seconds. "Well, thanks, but I guess not. I thought they could help me solve a problem, but I've pretty much decided they can't."

"Yeah, I know what you mean. I never get any decent advice from my folks. Have to rely on friends." He gave me a half-smile. "Well, good luck." The door closed with a click.

Have to rely on friends. One of my best friends in the

world lived only a mile or so away from where I stood. It didn't take me more than ten minutes to get into warm clothes and pull on my R.O.T.C. boots, rush down the stairs, and step through the dormitory doors into the bitter cold morning. Off to the east, brilliant streaks of red, orange and green shot upward through the dark sky. As I crunched along the sidewalk past Myron Taylor Hall, I wondered if the few visible stars helped sailors in the middle of the ocean figure out where they were. The bell from the Library Tower tolled eight times as I reached East Avenue. I'd gone tearing out of the dorm without thinking of the hour. Too early to bother Betty with my problem. I hesitated for a few moments, then plodded on toward Hoy Field. A blanket of snow covered the baseball playing field, sparkling and shimmering in the first light from the gigantic red ball balanced on the horizon. I pushed the wire mesh gate open with an enormous squeak and trudged through the deep snow to the bleachers. I scraped off an area in the first row and sat down. The College of Architect students had carved out a six-foot-tall ice sculpture of a ballplayer on the spot of the pitcher's mound. A Cornell baseball cap sat rakishly on the frozen head, a glove attached to his right hand. The southpaw leaned forward slightly, staring toward home plate.

Would I ever be on that spot? Would I ever pitch for Cornell? My thoughts returned to Harry's proposition and the scary consequences if I refused. It seemed unfair to be in a mess because I was at the top of my chemistry class—an accomplishment to be proud of, not something mean or dishonest. A sudden puff of cold air shook me from my reverie. I'd catch pneumonia if I sat here much longer. I retraced my steps, carefully placing my feet where I'd stepped before, pulled the gate closed, and strode toward my destination. I was soon opposite Baker Lab, the scene of my scholastic success, then crossed Forest Home Drive, and started over the bridge across Fall Creek. When I reached the middle, I leaned against the stone parapet and gazed somberly in the direction of the Suspension Bridge, where poor Jack Randolph had drawn his last breath.

Memories of the picnic with Betty near Taughannock Falls and her tragic story flooded my mind. We agreed to get together after dinner every Saturday and also Sunday afternoons for a few hours. Sometimes we studied in the Library. Other times, in decent weather, we drove to a spot in the country where we parked and took long walks. When we weren't studying, we talked incessantly or took turns reading aloud from books. We finished *Great Expectations* and four of Shakespeare's plays. We went to a couple of concerts at Bailey Hall. Betty insisted on paying. She did let me take her to the movies. We saw "The Informer," about the revolution in Ireland, and how Victor McGlaglan ratted on his buddy just to get money to spend on his girlfriend. The revolutionaries bumped off his buddy, and also Victor McGlaglan when they finally caught up with him. Maybe I should have taken Betty to a more cheerful movie, but she said she liked it a lot.

Betty had talked a lot about what she'd be doing after graduating next June, managing her dad's farm, raising and feeding Aberdeen Angus beef cattle until they grew big enough to be turned into sirloin steaks. I thought about our pathetic little dairy farm in Harford County, Maryland, and how we had so few cows, we even gave them names, like they were pets.

Helen Rogers and Sis Martin bounced through the door of the Theta House as I started up the shoveled walk between mounds of snow. I was practically adopted by the sorority since making a fool of myself with my warbling. I was invited to their fall dance, but I wasn't about to go. Or so I thought. The invitation said "black tie." Betty begged me to accept, saying it would be okay to wear my one suit, and that she'd look out for me. When I dug in my heels, Betty said she wouldn't go either. And so I gave in. What else could I do? Betty did stick with me most of the evening, and I had a pretty good time. She persuaded me to dance with her when the orchestra played a real slow number. No one laughed, even though I must have stumbled over her feet at least six times. I guess no one paid any attention to me. Why should they? A Theta pledge with short black curly hair and black sparkling eyes asked me to dance with her. I almost agreed because she reminded me of Dee, but I lost my nerve and mumbled something about the music being too fast for me. She giggled and grabbed a guy all dolled up in a tuxedo by the elbow, and they went spinning off across the floor.

"Hi, Bill!" Helen called out as she and Sis rushed by me, "If you're looking for Betty, she's in the study drinking coffee and chatting with Mrs. Case. Go on in."

"Okay, thanks," I called back.

Betty glanced up in surprise at my tap on the half-open door leading into the cozy study where, so Betty had confided, Mrs. Case often listened sympathetically to sad stories of failing grades, faithless sweethearts, family problems, and other tales of woe from her charges. No tale of woe this Saturday morning, judging from the smiling faces and spirited discussion I had interrupted.

"Bill, come in. What a nice surprise. Take off your coat. Have some coffee." Betty's dazzling smile and invitation warmed my heart and boosted my spirits.

"Yes, Bill," Mrs. Case chimed in. "Take my chair. I've got to get into the kitchen and check on the lunch menu." The housemother bustled from the room before I could protest. I stood for a moment, flustered at the rapidity with which we were left alone. Betty wore a red and green plaid wool shirt and blue denim trousers, her soft dark hair tied back with a red band. She looked more like a teenager than a sophisticated college senior. Her smile lingered. Pleased to see me. As always.

"Do you mind using my cup?" she asked. "Or I can get one from the kitchen?" She made a motion to rise.

"No, no, that's fine," I said.

"Two teaspoons of sugar and a splash of cream," she said. Another quick grin. "I remember."

I sank back into the deep easy chair Mrs. Case had vacated and watched as Betty poured the steaming black coffee from the pot, and then added the cream and sugar. She leaned over and handed the cup to me. "Okay, my friend. To what do I owe this unexpected pleasure of your company? Did we have a date this morning?"

"No." I took a long sip from the cup, the hot fluid warming and strengthening my body. I stared for several moments at the cup, following with my eyes the outlines of the Kappa Alpha Theta insignia.

"Well?" Her eyebrows raised. The smile vanished. "Is something the matter?"

I looked up at her for an instant, then glanced down again at the cup. I started asking myself questions. Why did I bother Betty with my problems? What could she tell me? What could she do, anyway? She's not my mother or my sister. Why was I here? I placed the cup and saucer on the side table and stood up. "Look, I'm sorry I bothered you." I started to reach for my coat. "I'd better get going."

Betty shot out of her chair. She stood facing me, eye to eye, angry eyes flashing. I'd never seen her like this before. She pushed me hard in the chest, and I fell back in my chair.

"Look at yourself" she snapped, "don't come in here on a Saturday morning acting like you've lost your best friend and then tell me you're sorry and that you'd better get going." She glared at me for a few seconds, then sat down again. "Now, just what the hell is the matter?"

I folded my arms on my chest and stared at her, trying to collect my thoughts. I cleared my throat twice, then began talking. "I need someone's advice." I stopped and waited. But she only stared at me. "I need someone's advice," I continued, "and I guess you're the only person I know at Cornell whom I can trust to tell me the right thing to do."

Betty's eyes remained fixed on me, her face expressionless.

"You know I have a baseball scholarship."

Betty nodded.

"If I don't make the team, I'll lose my scholarship and have to leave school."

Now Betty smiled. "There's no chance you won't make the team, if that's what's worrying you. No way. I read the clippings you gave me. You'll be the top starter on the frosh team. I'd bet my dad's farm on that."

I'd shown her some clippings from the *Bethlehem Star* after she'd badgered me about my pitching record in high school. It embarrassed me to have her bring that up. I waited while she poured me another cup of coffee and added the sugar and cream, glad to have the extra time to think about what to say next. "You know I exempted the final exam in chemistry."

She nodded slowly, a puzzled expression on her face.

"Yeah, sure, I know that. And I think it's terrific. But what's that got to do with baseball?

"Everything," I answered abruptly. "Every damn thing."

"What do you mean? What are you driving at, Bill? Stop talking in riddles. Just what in the world is the matter?"

I took a deep breath and launched into my story, speaking mechanically. "A guy named Brad Keane is going to coach the freshmen team. Fred Feese had to drop out of graduate school. His dad's real sick. Keane and Harry Dobson and Steve Dobson are big buddies. Steve's failing chemistry and will be ineligible to play on the team if he doesn't get at least an 80 on the final exam. They want me to take the final for Steve. If I don't agree, Brad Keane as much as said I won't make the team. The exam is Monday morning. They want me to let them know what I'm going to do by tomorrow evening."

The silence probably lasted a minute, maybe less, but it seemed like an hour to me. During the entire time, Betty did not take her eyes off of me. I stared back, wondering what she thought and whether I'd made a mistake telling her what had happened.

Betty let out her breath slowly. "So, what's your problem?"

I couldn't think of a thing to say. I thought I'd made the situation pretty clear.

"Bill," she said, "you don't have a problem. Those idiots have a problem, and they're going to have a much bigger problem by the time I get through with them." She paused and smiled. "Unless they back off."

"Why would they back off?" I asked.

"Because I'm going to have a little chat with Brad Keane. I know all about that arrogant character. He's been sucking around Harry Dobson's father for a year, trying to get a job with one of Harry Senior's Philadelphia banks after he gets his master's degree. Times are tough and jobs are hard to come by. Brad figures if he can work it so little Steve's eligible to play, he'll have a great chance of landing that job with old man Dobson."

So that was it. I thought there was something fishy, that there had to be more to it than Keane just wanting Steve on the team.

"Gee, Betty, I wondered what was going on. But what can you do? Why would Keane pay any attention to you?"

"He'll do more than that. He'll stand at attention and then roll over and play dead when I break the news that my Uncle Phil is Dean of the College of Arts and Science, and that Uncle Phil would not be happy to learn that one of his grad students is involved in this kind of hanky-panky."

CHAPTER 8

"I finally got Keane on the phone. You won't believe it. He'd been to Sage Chapel for church services. That miserable sinner in church. The poor slob must have nearly died after I said my piece. You never heard such bluster and baloney." Betty chortled. "Allowed as how you were a lying hick that didn't know which way was up. I wish I could have seen his ugly mug."

"Gg gg gosh Betty. What else did he say? Is he going to kk kick me off the team?" My stammer was back.

"Oh, don't worry." Betty reached over and patted my hand. We were seated at a table in the Willard Straight cafeteria, the same one where I was propositioned to take the chemistry examination for Steve Dobson. Betty had left a message at the Kappa Sigma house to meet her after Sunday lunch. Why I didn't spill more soup on one of the Kappa Sigs, I'll never know.

"He didn't say much of anything," she went on. "I did most of the talking."

"Yeah, but what did you say to him? How do I know he won't fix my wagon somehow? Keep me riding the bench? Make me lose my scholarship?" My voice must have been an octave higher than usual.

"Because I told him calmly in words of one syllable that if he messed you up, I'd have a little chat with Uncle Phil and abruptly end his career at Cornell and his chances of working for Harry's daddy." Her eyes sparkled. "Yeah, I actually threatened him. Can't remember when I've had so much fun."

"But he must have said something about my playing or not playing for the team."

"He just yelled a nasty four-letter word and slammed down the receiver." She grinned. "You know, the word that describes what we try to avoid stepping in when we're in the barnyard?"

I stared into the half-empty coffee cup, my heart sinking into my boots. I couldn't believe that Keane would back down. I'd never make the team, never graduate from Cornell. Betty must have sensed my mood. "Come on, Bill," she said, "you have no problem. I promise you." Her voice became serious. "I wouldn't lie to you. Ever. Cross my heart." She did just that.

I felt my eyes tear up. I'd become a regular crybaby. Did I deserve such a wonderful friend? I stared at the ceiling, trying to hide my emotions from her. "Thanks," I managed to mumble. "I wish I could tell you how much I appreciate what you've done." I glanced at her. Her lips parted slightly; her eyes shone. A feeling of warmth surged through my entire body. I'd wondered before and now I wondered again—was she more than just a pal? I'd read a couple of love stories in a magazine Erwin Redding had given me. "Read these, country boy," he'd said, an ugly leer on his face. "They'll stir up the old libido." I looked that word up the next time I went to the library. The stories seemed kind of silly, and they hadn't stirred up anything. Betty took a deep breath, pushed back her chair and stood abruptly, then unexpectedly ran her hand through my hair. That was a first, but, I had to admit, something my mom might have done.

"You're more than welcome, Bill. I'm really happy I could help. And it was a pleasure to stick it to sleazy Keane." She paused, a faraway look in her eyes. "I wonder what Steve Dobson will do now? I hope the bum flunks the exam and gets put on probation. We maybe could stir up enough dirt to get all three of them kicked out of school. But..." She paused. "Maybe we couldn't. Anyway, we'll hold our ammunition in reserve just in case Keane tries anything fancy."

She glanced at the clock on the far wall. "I've got to dash," she said hurriedly. "Let's have another reading session soon. We have to finish *Pickwick Papers*. It gets even better. And more comical."

I watched her until she disappeared through the cafeteria doors. A twinge of disappointment struck me. She hadn't looked back and waved. We'd started doing that when we parted company. We'd turn after walking fifty feet or so, look back and wave. It had become a ritual. Back in my room, I fretted for a half-hour, wondering whether I'd imposed too much on Betty. Why hadn't she waved to me? Four strokes from the Library Tower roused me from my childish concern. Our friendship couldn't rise or fall on such trivial nonsense. I reached for the volume entitled *Great Poems of the English*

Language and started thumbing through the pages. I needed to study for the miserable English exam and try to wangle at least a B grade out of Dickie Bird. All of the A's would go to his favorite coed students. I no sooner settled down at my desk, when I was startled by three sharp raps on the door.

"Come in," I shouted.

The door opened. Erwin stood in the doorway, attired in filthy khaki trousers and a greasy Wells College sweatshirt. He'd donned slippers, but bare hairy ankles showed where socks should have been. A heavy black growth of beard made him look ape-like. I started shaving once a week only a few months before. Erwin shaved every day—except Saturdays and Sundays. A smile on his round face contrasted with his menacing appearance. "Just wondered whether you solved your problems, whatever they were. Can I come in?" The smile widened.

I glanced reluctantly at my poetry book. Dickie Bird expected his students to know by heart at least one of the classical English poems. I'd selected John Masefield's "Sea Fever." But I could memorize it later. Erwin and I had never had more than a few casual conversations. Betty had urged me to make friends with some of the guys. But I hadn't had the time. Or the desire, for that matter. I waved him to the only decent chair and swung around to face him after he sprawled in it. He raised his eyebrows, waiting for my reply. "Well, yes. I did. At least I think I did."

"What's going on? Anything I can do?"

I wondered. Should I tell him about Harry's proposition. No. Better not. Just tell him part of the story.

"Well, I just learned that Fred Feese won't be coaching freshmen baseball. He's been replaced by a guy named Brad Keane."

"Brad Keane. That turkey." Erwin rolled his eyes in disgust.

"How do you know him?" I asked.

"He's a grad student, and I had the misfortune of suffering through a lecture he gave in my corporation finance course. Part of his graduate training. The idiot tried to explain what arbitrage was all about, and he got his tail so tangled up, he didn't know whether he was afoot or on horseback."

Another strange word. But I didn't ask for an explanation, not even how to spell it. "Oh?"

"Yeah, what a dope. We never saw him again. Professor

Martin wised up after that." Erwin looked at me inquiringly. "But so what if he's going to coach frosh baseball. How does that affect you?"

"Well, I got word that he had a couple of buddies trying out for pitching slots, and that he might favor them over me even though he knows they can't pitch as well as I can." I felt uncomfortable, blowing my own horn. But what I said was at least partly true.

"How the hell did you solve that problem so fast?"

My face must have turned red, because Erwin persisted. "Come on, Bill, what did you do? Bribe the guy?"

I jumped from my chair and would have taken a swing at Erwin, I'm sure, if he hadn't raised both hands. "Sorry, Bill, only kidding. Don't get bent out of shape. Just tell me what happened."

I sat back and thought for a few seconds. Might as well spill the whole story. What harm could come of it? And I proceeded to do so. He listened in silence, shaking his head in disgust a couple of times during my narrative. When I was done, I waited for his reaction. But not for long.

"Those three sleazeballs should be kicked out of school," he muttered. "But I guess I can understand why you and Betty don't want to take it any further, at least not now." Erwin yawned and stretched. A leer spread across his face. I knew what was coming. "What's the story with you and Betty? Are you making out with her?"

I had learned enough to know what he meant, but I was determined not to get angry at him. "No. We're just good friends." I laughed nervously. "She's older than me, anyway."

Erwin sniffed in disbelief, but went no further with his third degree about Betty."Have you ever had a girlfriend?" he asked. "Ever gone steady with anyone?"

I thought of Dee. She was the closest to a girlfriend I ever had. I never mentioned Dee to anyone at Cornell, not even Betty. I don't know why. Maybe I thought Betty might be jealous. How stupid can you get? As for guys like Erwin, I worried that they would make cracks about her being Jewish. Then I thought for a few moments. I never heard Erwin make any snide remarks about Jews. Maybe I could tell him about Dee. "Well," I finally said, "there is a girl I like a lot, who goes to Muhlenberg College in Allentown, Pennsylvania."

Erwin's eyes lit up. "Tell me about her."

"Well, her name's Delores Feldman. Everyone calls her Dee. We had an adventure together awhile back. She helped me find my dog, Spike, after we got separated from each other. She was wonderful! But..." I sighed. "She's older than me, too."

I waited. Again I knew what was coming.

"Feldman. Is she Jewish?"

"Yeah, she is," I said. I tried not to sound defensive. "Do you have a problem with that?"

"No, no, no. Not at all." He chewed on his lower lip. "It's just..."

"Just what?"

"It's just that there's so damn much anti-Semitism at Cornell. A bunch of Nazis. It's pitiful. If you ever invited her for Junior Week or Spring Day weekend, jerks like Harry and Steve Dobson would make life miserable for you...and her."

I laughed out loud. "Invite her? How could I do that? I don't have the money to pay for the dance and all the other stuff that goes on. And, anyway, she might not come even if I did invite her. And, anyway, where would she stay if she did come? Neither of us has the dough to pay for a room. And she'd have to buy her meals. It just wouldn't work."

"B.S. if you'll pardon my French," Erwin exclaimed. "Why wouldn't she come? The weather's spectacular in May. I heard they've lined up Glen Gray and his Casa Loma Orchestra for the Spring Day dance. It'll be a blast. Chances are she wouldn't even have the pleasure of meeting Harry. Or his little brother," he added.

Erwin jumped to his feet, his eyes shining with excitement. "I've got a great idea. I bet your pal Betty would put her up at the KAT house and feed her as well."

"But wouldn't I need to wear a tuxedo?" I asked. "I don't have one, and I don't have the money to rent one."

Erwin eyed me up and down. "Stand up," he said.

I rose slowly to my feet, wondering what was going on.

He positioned himself next to me. We were side by side. "You're an inch taller than me," he announced. "But we weigh about the same."

"So what?"

"So, you can borrow my tux. I won't need it. I'm off to Wells for their annual spring frolic that weekend. Lots of beer. Lots of women. Lots of fun." Another leer. "And who knows? Maybe lots of loving."

My mind whirled. Dee here at Cornell. But would Betty wonder why I didn't ask her to go to the dance? Then I remembered her telling me she'd never attend another Spring Day dance or Junior Week dance. Too many memories of Jack.

"But what about Molly?" I asked. "Aren't you going to invite her up for Spring Day weekend?"

Erwin had shown me a full-length picture a couple of weeks ago that had nearly knocked my eyes out—a side view of a gorgeous girl, with hands on her hips. Her blond hair hung loosely and partially covered a sweater at least one size too small. Her shoulders and head tilted back, her chest thrust forward prominently displayed the curve of her breasts and even showed the outline of her nipples, much to my embarrassment. The narrowed eyes that stared into the camera mocked and challenged the photographer.

"I've been in love with this bimbo ever since we were in the fifth grade at Hohokus Elementary," Erwin had proudly announced.

Bimbo. I couldn't get over it. How could anyone call someone he's supposed to be in love with a bimbo?

Erwin flushed and stared uneasily at the floor for a few seconds. "Well, she's got other fish to fry that weekend. Been invited to Dartmouth for some kind of goings-on in Hanover." He deliberately pronounced Dartmouth like it's spelled, emphasizing "mouth."

"Of all weekends," he moaned. "Molly's and my favorite orchestra and our favorite singer coming to Cornell. And they'll play our favorite song."

I thought for a second he was going to cry.

"What singer and what song?" I asked curiously.

"Kenny Sargent, singing 'Under a Blanket of Blue,'" was his gruff answer.

I didn't tell Erwin that I'd never heard of either Kenny Sargent or his and Molly's favorite song, and had barely heard of Glen Gray's orchestra.

"Oh, well, to hell with her," he said cheerfully. "I'll find some Wells College broad and forget all about Molly Turner."

"How can you forget someone you love so easily?" I asked.

"Well, she doesn't seem to have any trouble forgetting me," he muttered.

He swung toward the door. "Look, I don't want to talk

about it." He glanced at his wristwatch. "Anyway, I've got to get back to the books." He shuffled toward the open door.

I suddenly remembered. "Hey, we've got a game with Dartmouth that Saturday, the same day as the dance."

"Great." Erwin exclaimed. "I hope you kick hell out of their butts." He paused. "Has your friend, Dee, ever seen you pitch?"

"No. She's a terrific pitcher herself. She'd have been the star of her high school team if they let girls play."

"So, you'll pitch a no-hitter against the Dartmouth frosh and be a big hero. No telling what goodies she'll give you for that."

"Holy smokes, Erwin, you really have a one-track mind. Do you think the only thing girls are good for is...?" I couldn't think of how to say it.

"Yeah. That's all. Loving. That's what it's all about, country boy."

I shouldn't have been surprised at what he said. But I was. I heard guys on the high school team tell stories about what they'd done with girls. Locker-room talk. I never believed any of it. It couldn't be true. I couldn't imagine Dee or Betty letting any guy mess around with them. One false move and they'd be missing a couple of teeth. The look on my face must have given away my thoughts, because Erwin started to laugh, an irritating cackle.

"Don't tell me you're a virgin," he sneered.

I could feel the flush spreading across my face.

"Don't answer," he said. "Anyway, I already know the answer." He waved his hand and was gone.

I slowly closed the door, then reached for the open book of poetry and started reading aloud, pacing across the room.

"I must go down to the seas again, to the lonely sea and the sky. And all I ask is a tall ship and a star to steer her by." I shut my eyes and tried to visualize a tall ship. A four-master under full sail, plunging through the rolling ocean swells, green water cascading across the deck, a stiff breeze in my face, the smell of salt in my nostrils. I dreamed of going to sea ever since reading *Two Years Before The Mast*. Uncle Dan had given me the book for my eighteenth birthday. It was heavy going, but I loved it. If war ever came, that's where I'd be. On the ocean.

CHAPTER 9

"Dear Billy." That's how the letter from Dee started, to my disgust. I'd invited her to Cornell for Spring Day weekend, and I'd told her she could stay at Betty's sorority house for free and also eat some meals there. I'd explained that Betty was a friend, and had gone on about what a great weekend it would be, and that the frosh baseball team would be playing Saturday morning, and there'd be a terrific dance that night with a terrific orchestra, and a lot of other stuff about the weekend, trying to talk her into coming. I'd signed the letter "Bill," hoping she'd take the hint, but no such luck. Anyway, "Billy" was better than "Billy Boy." She'd soon learned I hated that name after she'd used it a couple of times. The letter was so short, I was sure she turned me down, but she hadn't. I read on.

"Thanks for the invite. I'll be on the Black Diamond Express on May 13. It gets to Ithaca at 5:30 p.m. Can you meet me?

As ever,

Dee

P.S. Who is this Betty Marshall anyway?"

Who is Betty Marshall? Why would Dee ask that question? I thought I explained in my letter who she was. I glanced up at a calendar advertising the Cornell Book Store. In two weeks Dee would be right here on the Cornell University campus. I never thought it could happen until Erwin had come up with his brainstorm. Betty had jumped up and clapped her hands when I timidly mentioned what Erwin had suggested. "Oh, Bill, that's great," she said. "She can bunk in with me. It'll work out just fine. Elly will be gone that weekend." Elly Bahret, Betty's roommate, lived in Albany. She took off most weekends to see a senior at R.P.I. I'd never talked to Betty about Dee, and naturally she bombarded me with questions. Where did I meet her, how long had I known her, where did she live, where did she go to college, how old was she, what did she look like, was she short, was she tall, was she thin, was she fat, was she pretty, was she my girlfriend, and on and on.

I told her about how Dee had helped me find Spike after we'd been separated, how she lived with her sister and her husband and was a junior at Muhlenberg College in Allentown, and about her relatives in Germany, who disappeared.

"So, she's Jewish," Betty had said, matter-of-fact like.

I nodded.

"She'll never hear from her relatives again," she said. "Never. Those thugs have dumped them in a concentration camp or slaughtered them, or both." She ranted on. "What fools the French and British and Americans are. Letting those murdering Nazis get away with what they're doing. They're systematically killing off the Jews. They've already taken over Austria and no one's lifted a finger to stop them. It's so easy to see what's going to happen. Next it will be Czechoslovakia, then Poland, then France, and finally England. Hitler and his flunky, Mussolini, will pick them off one at a time, like shooting ducks on a pond, while they and we sit around wringing our hands. Then the murderers will come after us."

Everything she said was true. The Germans and the Italians and the Japanese had stirred up trouble all over the world, overrunning countries and killing innocent people. It seemed like the world faced the outbreak of another terrible war less than twenty years after the war to end all wars had ended. I wondered for the fiftieth time if I'd ever have to fight in a war, where people actually killed other people. After a guy has been killed he is as dead as George Washington or Abraham Lincoln or Julius Caesar. Like he never lived. And maybe millions of people would die because a bunch of timid fools sat around and twiddled their thumbs. It was like sitting on the front lawn having a tea party and watching your house burn to the ground.

But now was no time to worry about such depressing things. I read the letter again. I couldn't wait to give Betty the news. The sound of the chimes from the Library Tower striking the three-quarter hour drifted through the open window of my room, not quite drowned out by the roar of Cascadilla Falls. I looked at my watch. We planned to meet in front of McGraw Hall at five, fifteen minutes from now, and study on the lawn of the quadrangle for an hour before I had to be at the Kappa Sig house to set up for dinner.

I crammed the letter in my shirt pocket, grabbed my

book bag, and rushed from the room, slamming the door behind me. I reached the street in record time and narrowly avoided being struck by a Ford pickup truck as I darted across College Avenue. "I'll get you next time, college boy," the driver hollered. I waved. Nothing could upset me. Dee was coming to Cornell.

"Your friend is jealous, Bill."

Betty smiled and waved Dee's letter at me. I quickly spotted her, seated on a blanket, back supported by the trunk of one of the huge elm trees, now bursting with green leaves, that filled the quadrangle.

I stared at her. "What do you mean?"

"I mean she's jealous. Didn't you read the postscript?"

"Yeah, but..."

"Yeah but, yeah but." Betty smiled, then held the letter up. She pursed her lips and frowned. "Who is this Betty Marshall, anyway?" she asked in a demanding tone of voice. Then glared at me.

"That's not the way Dee feels," I protested. "Why would she be jealous of you? I told her you're my best friend at Cornell."

"Oh, Bill." Betty took a deep breath. "That's why she's jealous. She'd rather your best friend at Cornell wear trousers and smoke a pipe and play on the freshman baseball team."

"Well, she's agreed to stay with you at the sorority," I pointed out. "She can't be all that upset."

"Maybe she's coming up here to get a look at me, scope out the competition."

"Competition." My mind whirled. Why was Betty talking like this? I could only stare at her.

She reached over and patted my hand. "I'm just pulling your leg, Bill," she said. "She's probably just curious. From what you've told me about her, she's a wonderful person, and I'm sure I'm going to like her." She paused. "I just hope she likes me."

"She'll love you." I felt my face warming up. I felt funny using the word "love" when I talked to Betty. Every now and then, especially when I couldn't get to sleep, I wondered if I loved her. Then thought of Dee and asked myself over and over, can a guy love two girls at the same time? I didn't remember anything in the Bible that talked against that. And Mom had read aloud from the Bible often enough to come across that rule if there was one. Erwin claimed that he and Molly Turner were in love, and yet she was going to Dartmouth instead of coming to Cornell for Spring Day weekend. I finally decided, I really didn't know what it was like to be in love with a girl. Maybe someday I'd find out. To my relief, Betty changed the subject to something I could talk about.

"So how's it going on the team? Are Brad Keane and Steve Dobson acting like the jerks they are?"

"Well, Brad tries to get Steve into the games, but his problem is that Ken Sterns is twice the ballplayer Steve is, and everyone knows it. He's a much better catcher, and he's batting over 400. Steve only plays in the late innings if we've got a big lead."

"Where are the Big Red frosh in the league standings?"

"We're tied with Dartmouth. We've both won twelve and lost two. The championship game will be played on May 14 on Hoy Field, just before the varsity's game."

"And Dee will be here to watch you pitch. That's wonderful.

I shrugged. "Only if Keane lets me pitch."

"What do you mean? He has to let you pitch. You're by far the best."

My record was the best, both in games won and lost and in earned-run average, and so Keane's hands had been tied. Larry Scott was a close second. He and I had carried the entire pitching staff during the season. But Keane still had it in for me. He made that clear enough by not talking to me unless he had to, and by never smiling at me. Even the other players gossiped about the difference between the way he treated me and the way he treated Larry. Everyone except Steve Dobson.

"He doesn't have to let me pitch," I replied to Betty. "He probably will start Larry Scott." I paused. "And I'll bet he also starts Steve. It's the last and most important game of the season, and his mom and dad will be there."

"Steve Dobson, that cheating little sleazeball," Betty grumbled. "How did that wimp pass the chemistry exam, anyway? That's what I'd like to know. And with a high enough grade to avoid going on probation."

"Someone took it for him, that's for sure," I said. "I bumped into Harry the day after grades were posted. He couldn't resist telling me I wasn't the only smart guy in the freshman chemistry class."

"Well, he'll bust out sooner or later. That'll be my bet. If not this year, next year. His cheating ways are bound to catch up with him." She started singing softly, the first verse of the Song of the Classes, ending with, "I soon will be busted right out of Cornell." She turned toward me and smiled."But you. You'll never have to worry about that. I'm so proud of you. An A in all subjects last term, except one."

The "except one" was a C+ in English. True to form, Dickie Bird had reserved his quota of A's and B's for his favorites, all of whom wore skirts and belonged to sororities. He scrawled "Sorry, too much competition" on the self-addressed penny postcard I left with the final exam papers. I dropped by his office three or four times, hoping to find out the reason for my low grade, but he never was there, or so I was told by the buxom female grad student who screened his visitors. I finally gave up.

Betty glanced once more at the letter. "May 13. That's a Friday. Friday the thirteenth. I better drive you to the station. Keep you from having bad luck."

I angled the rear view mirror of Betty's Chevy down to look at my hair for the twentieth time. I'd combed it back again and again, but it persisted in flopping over my forehead. We'd been in the station parking lot for a half-hour, and it was still only five o'clock. Betty had lowered the top. Now she leaned back, stared upward at the cloudless sky and took a deep breath. "What a heavenly day," she cried. "And it's going to last the entire weekend with a full moon tomorrow night." She looked at me, eyebrows raised. A mischievous smile flickered across her face. "Great weather for romancing, wouldn't you agree, Bill?"

I felt too nervous even to let that remark bother me. Another thirty minutes to go—assuming the train would be on time. It usually arrived on schedule. But today, I was sure it had been wrecked. My imagination ran a bit wild. Maybe Dee had been hurt. Maybe she was somewhere alongside the tracks, bleeding. Maybe... "Should I check the station master to see if the train's going to be on time?"

"You just did that twenty-five minutes ago. It was on time then, and that's what he'll tell you again. So please relax or you'll have a stroke."

"But suppose there was an accident since then. Maybe I'd better check." My voice felt strained.

"Oh, come on Bill, let's talk about something else. Who's going to pitch tomorrow? Has Keane made up his feeble mind?" She leaned against the door and turned in my direction.

"Well," I replied, "he had planned to start Larry, but guess what?"

She frowned thoughtfully. "He's finally recognized that you're his most reliable pitcher." She paused. "Although it would be hard to believe he had that much sense."

"It's not that. Larry is at this very moment stretched out on a bed in the University Infirmary on Buffalo Street, running a fever."

"Don't tell me the poor guy's got the measles."

An epidemic of German measles had been raging on the campus. An article in the *Cornell Sun* called it rubella. I'd never heard that word used for measles.

"That's what the doctor said." I laughed out loud. "You should have heard Keane moaning and cursing. He called a team meeting and said he guessed he'd have to start this hayseed against Dartmouth. He just jerked his head in my direction. Didn't even look at me."

Betty clapped her hands gleefully. "Thank you, German measles germs." she cried out. "I'm really excited. And Dee will be, too."

"There's a downside, though," I said.

"Well?"

"Steve's going to catch."

"Why, for goodness' sake? What about Ken Sterns? I thought he was the team's ace catcher."

"Because Ken and Larry are roommates in the infirmary, along with five or six other measles patients."

Betty was silent, a puzzled look on her face. I wondered what she was thinking. She soon let me know. "Can you and Steve work together for an entire game? You two have never done that, have you?"

We never had. Steve had been brought in a couple of times in late innings, when I was pitching. He was a real pain in the neck, wanting to call all the pitches and grumbling when I disagreed. But there were no open arguments. Only nasty remarks on the mound after I refused to throw the pitches he called for. I had no doubt that he wanted me to look bad. Even though he knew my most reliable pitch was my fast ball, he invariably called for a curve in a tight situation.

"No, not for a full game." I replied. "But, we'll just have to..."

A wail from far down the tracks interrupted me. The Black Diamond was early. I stared frantically at Betty, my mouth hanging open like a flytrap, my lips quivering like I was going to cry.

"Pull yourself together, Bill," she urged. "You've got to make a good impression on our visitor."

Within a couple of minutes, the huge engine rumbled slowly into the station, the brass bell clanging. Two Pullman cars passed by, and then the engine shuddered to a squeaking halt. Silence followed, except for the swishing of steam from between the gigantic wheels. I froze, unable to move a muscle. "Dee will be in one of the coaches near the end of the train," I finally managed to blurt out.

Betty pushed my shoulder. "Well then, go on and meet her. I'll wait in the car."

I mentally thanked Betty for her thoughtfulness. I wanted to be alone when I first saw Dee. Slamming the car door behind me, I dashed through the parking lot to the platform, then elbowed my way through a throng of passengers, mostly girls, some gazing anxiously around, others chatting and laughing with their weekend dates. I was momentarily disconcerted when I spied Harry and Steve reaching out for the luggage of two girls, each dressed in smart-looking gray suits, who emerged from one of the Pullman cars. I hurried by, glad that they didn't notice me.

The platform alongside the cars looked empty. After a moment of panic, I saw her descending the steps of the rear coach, lugging a large suitcase. She turned and gazed at me, hands on hips. She wore a green sweater and brown pleated skirt under a tan raincoat. A large brown purse was slung over her shoulder. Her dark hair, grown longer than I remembered, hung loosely to her shoulders, making her look younger, like a teenager. Her eyes sparkled and a smile lit up her face when she caught sight of me. And there it was. The heart-stopping dimple that had softened me up dozens of times when I was irked about something she'd said or done. She held out her arms as I rushed toward her. My hug was returned with equal vigor. I smelled the freshness of her hair. She never wore perfume, one of the many things I remembered and liked about her.

Dee pushed me back and looked me up and down at arms length. "You're looking great, Billy, really great."

I'd have to say something about her calling me Billy. But now wasn't the time.

"Well, gg gee, thanks." I cleared my throat a couple of times. "You're looking kind of great yourself."

We stared at each other. I'd forgotten how pretty she was. I felt proud that she would be my date for the entire weekend, would watch me play baseball, and that I would escort her to the Spring Day dance.

"Well, Billy, what do we do now? How do I get to your friend's sorority house?" The question brought me down to earth.

"Betty's here. She's going to give us a ride up to the Theta House. She's got a new Chevy convertible," I added, then suddenly felt self-conscious, thinking about Betty's saying a couple of weeks ago that Dee was jealous of her.

Dee whistled. "A new convertible. She must be loaded. Is she both rich and pretty?"

My face must have shown my reaction to that comment, because Dee reached up and touched the top of my head. "Sorry, Billy, I'm just teasing. I really am anxious to meet Betty Marshall. You know I'll like any friend of yours." She strode toward the station. "Come on, we don't want to keep her waiting."

I grabbed the suitcase and staggered after her. She must have packed nothing but lead, I thought. How could clothes just for one weekend weigh so much? She glanced over her shoulder and laughed at my efforts to keep up with her. "Brought some books, Billy, just in case I got bored." Then she stopped, turned back and reached for the handle, covering my hand as she did, sending a chill up my spine. "Just teasing again. I have a couple of tough exams on Monday and needed to study on the train. I know I won't be bored. Here, let me help."

We dragged the suitcase up the platform until we reached the edge of the parking lot, now almost empty. I could see Betty's face turned in our direction. I whistled and waved. She waved back, started the engine, and the Chevy moved slowly forward and stopped at the edge of the sidewalk. Betty left the car and walked toward us.

"So this is Dee." She held out her hand, smiling as she did. "You are even prettier than our friend let on. I'm really glad you were able to come, and I'm looking forward to getting acquainted."

Dee glanced at me, then turned back to Betty. She seemed about to speak, when a raucous shout interrupted her.

"Hey, country boy."

I looked up. A green Pontiac sedan stopped about thirty feet away. Harry's ugly face peered from the driver's window.

"Think you can handle two women and still be in shape for tomorrow's game?"

A burst of laughter floated from the rear seat. Steve Dobson. With the brothers were the two girls I noticed earlier on the platform, their faces taut and angry, probably embarrassed by their dates' crude behavior. Before I could respond, the Pontiac shot across the parking lot and was gone.

"Just who the hell was that?" Dee demanded to know.

Betty grasped her hand. "Just a couple of prime jerks. Please don't pay any attention to them. Come on," she urged, "we ought to get going. Don't want to be late for dinner. You and Bill are guests of Kappa Alpha Theta tonight." She looked over at me. "But Bill has to get to bed early to be ready for the big game."

Chuck Randolph had given me the weekend off. I wanted to kiss him when he said it would be okay. I knew I'd have to pay him back later, probably serve breakfast for seven straight days, but that didn't bother me. Just so I could spend as much time as possible with Dee.

"Hop in back with the suitcase, Bill. Dee can sit up front with me." I obeyed, and we zoomed out of the parking lot and tore up Buffalo Street toward the campus. As we passed by the infirmary, I thought about Larry Scott for a few seconds, a little embarrassed when I realized I didn't feel at all sorry for him. As Betty had said, "It's an ill wind that blows no good." She had to explain what that meant.

Betty and Dee chatted away like they'd known each other forever. I strained to hear what they were talking about. Betty asked Dee what she was majoring in at Muhlenberg. "Languages, mainly German," she said. "I took German all through high school. With another four years in college, I'm hoping to get a job in Germany after graduation that requires speaking and writing German. Maybe as an interpreter. I don't know."

Betty looked thoughtful as we waited for a traffic light to turn green. "Bill says you have relatives in Germany."

Dee laughed. A bitter laugh. She stared straight ahead, her face showing no emotion. "Yeah. Whether below or above ground, we don't know. They'd probably be better off dead."

The Chevy moved ahead slowly, inching along behind a line of traffic, then turned left on Stewart Avenue. "Are you thinking about trying to find them?"

Dee's head turned abruptly toward Betty, a look of surprise on her face. "Hey, you're pretty smart," she said.

I nearly died, hearing this. I couldn't believe Dee would try to do something so stupid. But I didn't dare say anything. Not now. Not in front of Betty. Maybe when we were alone.

Betty drove in silence after that. Just stared ahead. I figure she had some of the same kind of thoughts I had. Dee twisted around and smiled. "Spike says hello. Also your mom and dad and Uncle Dan. They all miss you very much."

"Is everyone okay?" I asked.

She hesitated and the smile disappeared. A feeling of dread crept over me.

"Well," she said, "Spike's got a couple of lumps under both front legs. We took him to the vet. He said to just watch them and see if they grow."

"Is that bad?" I asked. I tried to keep my voice from shaking.

Another silence, and then she spoke. "It's bad if they're malignant, but the vet says, even if they are, they'll develop very slowly at Spike's age. He said he wouldn't advise cutting them out, no matter what."

My thoughts raced back all the way to Montana, when Spike was a puppy and first learned how to round up the sheep. Then that awful time when we lost each other. If it hadn't been for Dee, we never would have found him. What if Spike died? The excitement and happiness I felt just a minute ago disappeared, and I settled back in the seat, feeling nothing but gloom.

"Hey, Bill," Betty cried out, "snap out of it! There's nothing you can do about Spike. Just keep your fingers crossed and hope for the best. Meanwhile, have fun."

CHAPTER 10

I became dimly aware of the ringing of a distant bell, at first persistent and high-pitched, then slower and slower and lower and lower, like an old-fashioned phonograph that needed rewinding. It couldn't be morning already! I opened one eye, peeked at the Baby Ben, and groaned. Eight o'clock. I hadn't slept at all, or so it seemed. After Betty and Dee dropped me off at Cascadilla Hall, I went straight to bed, just as I'd promised. But I couldn't promise I'd sleep.

"Don't worry about anything, Bill," Betty had called out, as I entered the building. "Yeah, Billy, get a good night's sleep," Dee hollered. "You'll need all your strength for tomorrow. Like Betty says, just try not to worry." She smiled and blew a kiss. I waved half-heartedly and ducked through the door.

Don't worry. Did anyone else in the world have so many worries? I couldn't even figure out which was my most worrisome worry. I shut my eyes tight, trying to arrange them in order of importance. At first the leading worry was tomorrow's game, then Spike's lumps, then whether Dee and Betty would get along, followed by how I felt about Dee, then how I felt about Betty, then how Dee felt about me, then how Betty felt about me, then whether I could tie the black bow tie I had to wear with Erwin's tuxedo, then whether it would become untied at the worse possible moment, then whether I'd make a fool of myself at the dance, stumbling all over Dee's feet.

My mind had drifted off to fretting about final examinations coming up in less than two weeks. At least there'd be no Dickie Bird to pull down my average. And there'd be no classes for a week before exams. Plenty of time to study. Then I had to go to the bathroom. I dragged myself out of bed and trudged all the way down the hall, not bothering to put on my bathrobe. I noticed a light under Erwin's door. The engineering college examinations started next Monday. When I returned to bed, I decided that Spike was my only really big worry. But nothing could be done about that. I made up my mind to telephone home tomorrow to find out how he was doing. I must have dropped into a deep sleep after that, because the next thing I knew Baby Ben was ordering me out of the sack.

The freshman game was scheduled to start at 10 o'clock, followed by a game between the Cornell and Dartmouth varsities. Keane had ordered us to report to the field house an hour before game time. "For a pep talk," he said. I sure didn't need it. Not with Dee in the stands.

It took me only a half-hour to shower, dress and rush over to the College Town diner, where I managed to swallow a cup of coffee and choke down a Danish, my stomach in knots. I hadn't been so nervous since just before our championship game in Bethlehem. But we won that one, I reminded myself. I pitched a three-hit shutout. In the last of the ninth, Bobby Bernstein, our catcher, crushed a ball far out into center field and scored the only run of the game with an in-the-park home run.

And we'll win today.

The weather couldn't have been more magnificent. A beautiful spring day at Cornell. I felt the sparkling clearness of the air and marveled at the deep blue of the sky. Fleecy white clouds drifted to the west like a squadron of sailing ships, pushed along by a soft breeze. Dozens of thickly planted purple and pink azaleas bloomed in the front yard of the Kappa Alpha house. The fraternity's Golden Lab stood guard on the front porch.

The Cornell campus teemed with dogs of all kinds and descriptions. I was astonished when a tri-colored mutt wandered into one of our early chemistry lectures, and after looking over the array of students, located his master and settled down for a nap at his feet. "Pray join our somnolent company." Professor Browne had bowed, as he extended that solemn invitation; then he continued his lecture on basic chemical reactions.

I soon grew accustomed to the comings and goings of man's best friend to and from our classrooms. I patted and spoke to all of them. It helped keep me from being too homesick for Spike. "Hi Casey," I called out. The Golden Lab wagged his tail. A good omen.

And I felt good. My arm felt good. Dee would be watching me pitch. My fast ball would be on fire. Humming "March on Cornell," one of my favorite songs, I strode briskly along

Campus Road toward Hoy Field, named after Davey Hoy, the legendary Cornell registrar. I caught sight of a dozen gaudy fraternity floats lined up for the Spring Day parade, one of the rowdier events of the weekend, so I was told. Lots of beer, lots of risque banners and posters. But lots of fun. It was going to be a fun weekend. I could hardly wait for the game to start.

"Hey, Creelman, don't be in such a rush."

Steve Dobson. The last person in the world I wanted to see. Calling me Creelman. Steve drew up alongside me, panting. Beads of sweat popped out on his forehead. I knew he had to be out of shape with the wild night life he led. Guzzling beer. Closing down Zinks practically every night. Chasing women. I overheard the Kappa Sig freshmen talking about him. "He's been banned at Wells College," Bill Kruse had proclaimed to his fascinated audience. "Dragged the sweater clean off the Dean's niece at a drunken picnic. No bra. Good idea, but bad choice," he solemnly added.

And now the slob stood right next to me, wanting to talk, for some reason. "Who was the chick with you and Betty Marshall?" he asked.

I glanced quickly at him, my face warming up. The leer reminded me of his obnoxious brother.

"I don't know any chicks," I retorted.

"Don't give me that kind of crap, Creelman. You know who I'm talking about. The one at the station. A sexy chick if I ever saw one. I'd like to meet her. I heard she's Jewish. But I don't mind with jugs like that."

I guess I'd had about enough of Steve Dobson. Maybe I was wrong, but I couldn't help saying what I said: "Why don't you go straight to hell, Dobson."

He stopped short. His jaw dropped in amazement. I walked away from him. Fast. My heart pounded. I'd never spoken to anyone like that before. Never had the nerve. Footsteps rapidly approached. He came up alongside me again. "Wow. Our country boy using bad language? Naughty, naughty. What will Betty Boop say when she finds out?"

I stopped short and confronted him. "Look, you miserable jerk." I'm sure my voice trembled. From anger, not fear. "Just keep your filthy mouth shut about my friends."

His mouth hung open. I guessed he wanted to say something, but no sound came out, just heavy breathing, a startled look in his eyes.

"Screw you, Creelman," he finally snarled. "Screw you and screw that kike chick of yours, too, and I hope you don't enjoy it."

I didn't even think. I swung. My fist landed squarely on the point of his jaw. A tingling feeling shot up my arm. Steve Dobson crashed to the ground on his back, like a sack of flour had fallen on him from a hundred feet up. Fortunately for him, he landed in a grassy plot next to the sidewalk. Surprise swept over me. Surprise that I hit him. And surprise that I flattened him. I'd been in only one fistfight before, and that was when I knocked down a guy who'd tried to stop Dee and me from saving Spike's life. I watched as Dobson rolled over and sat up. He looked wildly around, rubbing his jaw that was now turning red and starting to swell, probably not so much concerned about what had happened, but whether anyone had seen him get knocked off his feet. No one had. Campus Road was nearly empty of people.

"I'll get you for this, you little bastard," he gasped. "I'll get your ass."

"Any time, Dobson. Just let me know when and where." I hoped I sounded more confident than I felt. After all, I had taken him by surprise. Maybe it wouldn't go so well next time. I could hear him muttering and cursing as I strode off, rubbing and flexing my knuckles, surprised at how hard his jaw was. The Library Tower stroked the three-quarter hour— fifteen minutes to go before the team meeting was supposed to start. I'd have to put on my uniform. I'd probably be late. But so would Steve.

Brad Keane had already assembled the team when I slipped into the training room and elbowed my way to the rear. I leaned against the wall to listen to what he had to say. The ends of his thin lips seemed to curl further down than usual. I'd never seen him smile. Even after we won a game, he showed no appreciation, at least not to me or to anyone in my presence. I decided that his lips had been frozen in a downward arc for so long a time, he probably couldn't smile even if he wanted to. But, then, I bet he forced a smile when bootlicking Steve Dobson's father.

"Where's Steve?" he demanded. "He's got to start today." The cold blue eyes surveyed the room. I groaned inwardly. I'd hoped and prayed that somehow a miracle would instantly cure Ken Stern. I dreaded having Steve as my catcher even before today. But now.

"Here I am."

Steve ambled into the room, and quickly sat down on a wooden bench out of Keane's sight. He wore shin guards and a chest protector. Three white strips of tape covered the point of his jaw. He must have been tended to by Art O'Brian, the varsity's trainer. He noticed my stare and raised his right fist, the middle finger extended. I didn't show any emotion, just casually looked back at Keane, trying to act as cool as a cucumber. I hoped I looked cool, because I didn't feel that way at all. The excitement must have heated me up. Someone should open a window, I thought. Then I noticed all six windows and the door were wide open. Steve must have really riled me. Or maybe it was pre-game tension.

"Okay, guys," Keane began, and then went on to proclaim how important winning the game was to the team and to Cornell. Like he was Knute Rockne, or something. It turned my stomach, the way he carried on. I was sure he was really thinking how important the game was to Brad Keane. Mr. Dobson the banker would be in the stands, watching his youngest son play. A Cornell victory might just nail down that job. The room was as quiet as a tomb for about five seconds after Keane finally stopped haranguing us and disappeared into Coach Tatum's tiny office, probably to get some final words of wisdom.

Most of the guys rolled their eyes and shook their heads in disgust. Not Steve Dobson. Steve must have decided he would try to take charge. He rose to his feet and stood on the bench where he was sitting. But by the time he got set to say something, the team had broken ranks. A few sat on benches, leaning over and tying their shoes; others painstakingly oiled and massaged their mitts; about a half-dozen headed for the bathroom. One last chance before the game started. The rest of the team shuffled toward the open door leading to the field, the clatter of spikes on the concrete floor echoing from the walls and ceiling of the training room. I waited to hear what was coming.

"Listen up, you guys. I've got something to say."

The players massaging their mitts stopped what they were doing and looked up at Steve, obviously surprised. The rest of the team paid no attention at all. Most had left the room.

"Wait a minute!" he shouted. I couldn't imagine what he

wanted to say, but it didn't matter because he never got to speak.

"Hey, Steve!" Whitey Jones called out, "What happened to you? Did your Wells girlfriend's daddy punch you out? Or did you stagger into an electric fan?"

"Yeah, Stevey baby," Larry Ferguson urged, "tell us all about it. What poor unfortunate female did you get caught messing around with this time? Or did you get drunk and fall down the stairs?" A burst of laughter erupted from the few guys still in the room, but not from me. I must have smiled a little, because Steve jumped from the bench and blocked my way to the door leading to the field. His voice shook. I could just barely hear what he said, but it was distinct enough. "I hope you lose the goddam game."

CHAPTER 11

"I'd jerk you out if I had anyone to replace you!" Brad Keane's face resembled the color of a new brick chimney. He rushed to the mound after I'd thrown a fast ball a foot wide of the plate, making the count three balls and two strikes on Turkey Simpson, Dartmouth's leading hitter. I stared toward home plate without answering, massaging my elbow. It had started aching in the seventh inning. Steve strolled toward the mound, taking his time. Just what I didn't need. More stupid suggestions from that dope. I had to shake off at least four signs every inning. He kept calling for a curve, when I wanted to throw a fast ball. He complained to Keane between innings, and Keane had ordered me to follow Steve's signs, which I refused to do. I'd wreck my elbow for sure if I threw a bunch of curve balls. I kept thinking about Steve saying he hoped I'd lose the game.

I gave up three scratch hits and walked only three guys, two in the eighth inning. A double play had ended that threat. We were hitless so far; we hadn't connected solidly more than three or four times, and each time the ball had been smacked directly at a Dartmouth fielder. We were unable to figure out Clint Heyd's slow curve ball and sinker. Everyone, including me, kept over-swinging, trying to kill the ball. I suggested to Keane that we try bunting. He told me to mind my own business.

Now the game was a scoreless tie, with two outs. Johnny Caskey, Dartmouth's right fielder, stood on third base because Chuck Gruen had stumbled going after a routine fly ball and had to chase the ball to the wall. Steve started talking when he was two yards from the mound. He kept his mask on, another of his habits that irritated me. "Maybe you can get this hick to throw a curve ball," he complained to Keane. "Look where his great fast ball has got us." He leaned over and spit on the ground, just missing my left foot.

"Look, goddam it, Creelman," Keane hissed, "I told you to throw curves when Steve calls for them. So do it."

I stared between Steve and Keane, massaging the ball for

a couple of seconds before answering. "Steve better not be looking for a curve ball on the next pitch."

Keane's eyes popped open wider. "Why you little..." Whatever he was about to say was cut off by the umpire, who joined us. "Okay," he growled, "let's end this cozy tea party. Play ball." Keane stalked off, leaving Steve and me on the mound. He spit again, this time spraying one of my shoes. "I see your hebe friend's in the second row rooting for you. If you want to make her unhappy, just throw your miserable fast ball." He headed back toward home plate before I could even think of anything to say. I'd been hot before, but now I felt like I'd walked into an oven.

Turkey Simpson knocked the dirt from his spikes with his bat, then stepped into the batter's box and set himself for the pitch. Steve crouched down, held out his mitt, and extended two fingers of his left hand, the sign for a curve.

I shook my head.

He shoved the mitt directly under Simpson's bat and flexed two fingers twice in rapid succession.

I shook my head again.

Simpson stepped out of the box. "What's wrong, Creelman?" he shouted. "Can't make up your feeble mind? It won't matter. This one's going bye-bye."

"Play ball, dammit, unless you want to forfeit the game." That command and threat came from the exasperated umpire.

I stepped off the mound, reached down for some dirt, rubbed it between my fingers, then glanced past the first baseman and spotted Dee in the second row, squeezed in between Betty and Erwin Redding. She was dressed in a tan skirt and sweater; a green ribbon held back her hair. We exchanged smiles when I took the mound for the first time, but that had been it. Now I caught her eye. She nodded and held up her right hand, the index finger extended. Fast ball.

The crowd had been rowdy throughout the game, mostly on account of the spontaneous parties that had erupted after members of the ATO and SAE fraternities had rolled in several kegs of beer. Now a rhythmic clapping began, accompanied by chanting in a sort of singsong, "Dartmouth's in town tonight, run girls, run." Whistles and raucous shouts of encouragement followed that musical effort.

"Breeze it by him, Bill!"

"He swings like a rusty gate!"

"Send the poor slob back to Hanover!"

"This turkey's ready for the axe!"

Boisterous gobbling sounds poured from the bleachers.

I stepped back on the rubber and glanced over at third. Caskey had a short lead, not enough to try a pick-off attempt. He lunged forward, then stopped dead in his tracks. He wasn't about to try to steal home. Not with a full count and the team's heaviest hitter at bat. I gripped the ball as tight as I could, took a full windup and let go with probably the fastest and toughest pitch I'd ever thrown—straight as an arrow.

Simpson swung so hard that he fell to the ground from his own momentum.

"Strike th..." The umpire swallowed his words. The ball had torn through Steve's mitt and rolled toward the stands. Simpson scrambled to his feet and dashed to first. Caskey raced down the third baseline. I rushed to cover home plate. Steve tossed his mask aside and quickly caught up with the spinning ball. "Throw it. Throw it." I screamed. He looked toward first, and hesitated a split second, just enough to do the damage. He hurled the ball into my glove, but Caskey slid under my outstretched arm in a cloud of dust.

"He's safe." the umpire hollered.

Dazed, I could only stand at home plate and stare at the ball, still clutched in my right hand. Keane's shouts and curses were not quite drowned out by the groans and catcalls from the spectators. "You really screwed that one up, country boy. Throwing a fast ball when I expected a curve. Coach Keane ought to kick your butt off the team." Steve stood in front of me, sneering, as he knocked the dust off of his mask.

"Look, Dobson, I know what you're up to. Now get the hell back to your position before I deck you again." I swung around and strode back to the mound. One more batter to be disposed of to end the inning. Gregg Henderson stepped into the batter's box, the crowd now silent, in contrast to the boisterous shouts that had greeted Turkey Simpson's arrival at the plate. Steve's two fingers signaled for a curve. I went into a full windup, ignoring the runner, who took off for second base. I reared back and threw the next fastest ball of my career. Henderson swung and sent a pop fly toward first. Ken Smith backed up a few steps, and latched on to the ball for the third out.

I walked slowly toward the bench, my head down, wondering what obnoxious words would be directed my way from Keane. Russ Kent, our center fielder, trotted past me. "Not your fault, Bill," he said. "Steve screwed it up."

"Thanks," I mumbled, not feeling any better.

To my surprise, Keane said nothing, just gave me a dirty look.

I sat at the end of the bench and glanced at the batting order. Joe Cribb would lead off, followed by Mike McGarry. Then, to my dismay, I saw that Steve would be batting third. His average for the season was a shade under 200. Today, he'd struck out and had popped to first base.

Cribb selected a bat from the bat rack and started in the direction of the batter's box. He got only a couple of yards away when Keane called to him. "Wait a second, Joe." Cribb stopped and looked back. Keane hurried up to him, put a hand on his shoulder, and whispered something I couldn't hear. Joe looked puzzled for a second, then shrugged and continued toward home plate.

"What's the story, Brad?" Steve asked.

"I told him to take a hit. That's one way we can get a base runner."

"Isn't that cheating?" The words were out of my mouth before I knew it.

"You are a wimp, Creelman." Keane snarled. He turned away, a disgusted look on his ugly face. Steve snickered, but he managed to keep his mouth shut. The crowd again began its rhythmic clapping and chanting, accompanied by whistles and shouts of encouragement.

Joe Cribb always crowded the plate, but now he stood even closer than usual. Clint Heyd looked him over, then threw a slow curve that caught the inner edge of home plate. Joe's bat remained on his shoulder. Another slow curve, but this time Joe leaned even further toward the plate. He seemed to try to pull back ever so slightly, but the ball broke sharply toward him and made contact with his left hand.

"Take you base." the umpire shouted.

Well, the Dartmouth coach came barreling out, screaming and hollering that Joe had got himself hit on purpose. The umpire plain ignored him and started brushing off home plate with his little whisk broom. The crowd whistled and hooted and hollered all kinds of insults, until the coach, after blowing off steam, finally marched back to the Dartmouth bench, kicking dirt as he went.

Mike McGarry reached for a bat, then glanced at Keane. "Want me to take a hit, coach?" he asked.

Keane shook his head. "No. We won't get away with it a second time. Just get on base, for Christ's sake."

But McGarry failed miserably. After swinging twice at empty air, he fouled out to the first baseman.

The crowd began to chant over and over again, "We want Ed. We want Ed." They wanted Ed Roberts to bat. I prayed that Keane would send him in to pinch-hit for Steve. Roberts couldn't field well or run fast, but he could hit. He knocked in the winning run as a pinch hitter in three of our games. Also, he batted right-handed, and, since Heyd was a southpaw, had a better chance to get on base than did Steve, who swung from the left side. If the game went into extra innings, Al Crawford could take over Steve's position. He was a backup catcher in high school. But I should have known better. No way would Brad Keane take the youngest son of his future boss out of the game.

"Keep it alive, Steve," Brad called out.

Steve reached for a bat from the rack and pounded it on the ground a couple of times. He straightened up, then began rubbing his jaw, all the while hatefully staring at me. I noticed that the strips of tape had turned a brownish-gray from the dirt and dust. He veered off and walked toward me. When he reached a spot no more than a foot away, he stopped and looked me up and down for a couple of seconds, like I was some kind of ugly reptile. A nasty grin spread across his face. "I've got you over a barrel, wouldn't you say, country boy?" Before I could think of a reply, he swung around and strode toward the batter's box. Mingled boos, groans, and half-hearted applause greeted his arrival at the plate. "Hey, butterfingers, did you learn to catch at Vassar?" Hoots of laughter followed that shouted insult.

Steve glared in the direction of the unknown heckler, and raised the middle finger of his left hand—his favorite crude gesture, I decided. The jeers and taunts increased in volume. "Come on Steve, bring me around," Joe Cribb called from first base. He clapped twice, took three steps off the bag, and leaned in the direction of second base. Steve turned his attention toward Clint Heyd, waved his bat a couple of times, then set himself for the pitch.

Heyd took a full stretch, and his arm whipped sharply downward, as though a fast pitch was coming.

A knuckler. The ball floated toward the plate, looking the size of a pumpkin. Let it go. Don't swing. Those frantic pleas tumbled through my head. But Steve, expecting a fast ball, swung mightily. The ball barely grazed the head of the bat and dribbled toward third base. "Run it out. Run it out." The team jumped up in unison, shouting frantic instructions to Steve.

What happened next seemed like a movie scene in slow motion, with the camera panning from point to point as the scene developed. Heyd rushed for the spinning ball. Joe Cribb and the Dartmouth shortstop dashed toward second. The Dartmouth first baseman wildly waved his glove. But Heyd whirled and hurled the ball to second, the hardest he'd thrown all day. The Dartmouth shortstop grasped the ball, his foot grazing the bag a split second ahead of Cribb's slide. In a flash, the white sphere streaked toward first base. Out of the corner of my eye, I saw the infield umpire's thumb jerk upward.

But where was Steve? He wasn't even in the picture. Then he appeared. Still more than five feet from first base. Loafing.

"You're out." The fateful shout came from the home plate umpire, who'd made the trip down the first base line nearly as fast as Steve's leisurely journey. A groan erupted from the entire team. Brad Keane slumped back on the bench, despair written all over his face. I almost felt sorry for him.

"What in the world are those things on your face?" Dee's dark eyes narrowed, as she peered closely at me, her face only inches from mine.

After listening to Keane's screams of rage and Steve's feeble excuse of how he slipped as he started toward first; and after they both shouted that it was all my fault anyway; and after I showered and dressed, we borrowed Betty's convertible and had driven to Taughannock State Park, with the top down, not staying to watch the varsity game. We parked a few feet from where Betty and I had picnicked, an event that I decided not to mention.

I asked Dee to drive. I felt done in, much more drained than usual after a game. My face was hot, and my neck felt swollen, as we whipped along the west side of Cayuga, Dee's foot heavy on the gas pedal. I remembered the times she drove me in her beat-up Pontiac when we were searching for Spike. Now I stared at her, wondering what she was talking about. "What do you mean?"

"I mean, what are those spots?" She opened up her purse and took out her compact. She flipped it open and held up the tiny mirror. "Take a look!"

I squinted at the mirror. Red spots. Two red spots on my forehead, about three inches apart, two on my left cheek, and one on my right cheek.

"Unbutton your shirt," she ordered.

"Whuh, whuh. What do you mean?"

"Oh, come on," she urged, "don't be a prude. Let's have a look." She reached over and began unbuttoning my shirt. I shut my eyes, not knowing what to think.

"Oh ho. What do we have here?" My shirt hung open. I opened my eyes and slowly looked down. A dozen red spots were scattered across my stomach.

German measles.

CHAPTER 12

"Steve ought to be hung by his thumbs, then drawn and quartered." Gil Stern's reaction to my account of the dismal game. My narrow iron bed stretched in between his cot and Larry Scott's bed. The three of us were the last remaining German measles victims, confined to the fourth floor ward of the dreary infirmary overlooking Buffalo Street. Larry disagreed. "That would be too damn kind," he growled.

I told the sad story just the way it happened, not omitting my refusal to follow Steve's signs. I did hold back mentioning a couple of uneasy thoughts—like if I'd thrown curves I might have struck out Caskey, and if I hadn't punched Steve, maybe he'd have tried harder to get to first base ahead of the ball. The duty nurse, whose grim expression reminded me of Keane, abruptly stopped our conversation by sticking a thermometer in my mouth. Any hope for sympathy from that quarter had been rudely shattered when she snatched the doctor's admission form, which revealed that I was in truth afflicted with German measles.

"Oh, God, another one," she muttered. "Give me strength!"

Larry and Gil must have given her a rough time.

Now she stood menacingly next to my bed, glaring down at me. "Keep it under your tongue," she ordered. "I'll be back in three minutes."

"Keep that diabolical instrument on top of your tongue," Gil advised. "You'll never get out of this hellhole until your temperature's been normal for 24 hours. Just being in this dump's given me a damn fever. Thank God, Larry and I are out of here tomorrow morning." He shot a glance at the open door through which the nurse had disappeared. "But don't let the dragon lady catch you. She'll chew your butt out. Florence Nightingale, she is not."

I rolled the thermometer on top of my tongue, then shut my eyes and wallowed in my misery, imagining what I was missing. I'd fantasized all kinds of exciting happenings. Holding Dee in my arms as we swayed to Glen Gray's romantic music. She closing her eyes and draping her arm around my neck, and me drawing her close, like I'd seen couples do at the Kappa Sigma dances when I helped tend bar. After the Spring Day dance, driving along the lake in Betty's convertible under a full moon with the top down. Then slow down and pull the car over and park in one of the scenic views. We'd sit back in the seat and gaze up at the starry sky and breathe in the smell of the trees and nearby fields. After a minute or so, I'd reach over and grab her hand. She looking at me and I looking at her. My heart would first stop beating, then pound like thunder, wrapped in each other's arms and kissing.

"Let's have it."

The dragon lady loomed over me, her hand outstretched. I quickly pulled the thermometer from my mouth and handed it to her. She studied the instrument for a full 15 seconds, frowning as she turned it first one way and then the other in the half-light. She leaned over and placed her open palm on my forehead. "You feel warm, but your temperature's only a fraction above normal." She examined the thermometer again, her lips pursed. Finally, to my relief, she shook it vigorously. "Maybe you got heated up during the game," she said. "I'll take it again before dinner."

"Congratulations, Bill," Larry said with a laugh. "You learn fast. Keep up the good work and you'll be out of here by this time tomorrow."

A lot of good that would do me, I thought. Dee's train left at 4 o'clock tomorrow afternoon. I lay back with a long sigh and closed my eyes again, this time not fantasizing, but wondering if anyone in the whole world felt as miserable as I felt.

"Hey, Bill, how the hell are you?" The raucous greeting shook me back to reality. I looked up into the smiling face of Erwin Redding. My mouth dropped open, and I stared at him, amazed to see him standing at the foot of my bed. I noticed he must have shaved sometime between the end of the game and now. Unusual for a Saturday.

"Hey, I have the measles. You'd better get out of here."

Erwin's smile broadened. "I had the German measles two years ago when I was a sickly little freshman, just like you," he said.

"I sure wish I had them before. What a kick in the teeth." I took a deep breath, then introduced Erwin to Gil and Larry.

"Your guy did a hell of a good job," Erwin said. "Would have won the game for sure if it hadn't been for that stupid catcher screwing things up."

Gil shrugged. "The silver lining is that stupid Stevey will bust out for sure, so the team won't have to put up with him next year."

I suddenly remembered what Erwin's plans had been. "I thought you were headed up the lake for the Wells frolic this weekend."

"Oh." He paused. "Oh well, what the hell. I changed my mind." A frown replaced his smile. "No, that's not true. I've been stood up." He barked out a laugh. "But to hell with her. I didn't come here to talk about that broad." He shifted from one foot to the other. His frown deepened. I waited, wondering what was on his mind. He cleared his throat twice, then finally spoke, his voice a bit husky. "I thought maybe I could take Dee to the dance tonight, since you obviously won't be able to make it." The smile returned.

Erwin take Dee to the Spring Day dance. A wave of guilt swept over me. I'd been feeling so sorry for myself I hadn't even given a thought to what Dee would be doing, with me lying here in the infirmary. "Gosh, Erwin, that would be wonderful." I reached up and grasped his hand. "You're a real pal."

"Oh well. Actually, it might be fun. I just feel terrible that you're going to miss everything."

"I'll feel a lot better knowing someone's looking after Dee." I paused. "Maybe you'd better give her a call and ask her. She's staying at the Theta house."

Now he looked worried. "Actually, I've already asked her, and she said it would be fine. She'd love to go to the dance with me."

The wind spilled out of my sails, hearing that things had already been arranged, and Dee apparently happy about it all.

"Oh."

"Yeah." He glanced at his wristwatch. "I'd better get back to the dorm and get cleaned up and dressed." He looked distressed for a couple of seconds, then added, "Betty and her have invited me to dinner at the Theta house before the dance."

Another blow.

Erwin waved to Larry and Gil, then headed for the door. He turned and gazed back at me. "I'm really sorry you won't be wearing the tux tonight. You looked terrific in it. Dee would have loved it." Then he was gone.

I'd tried on the tux and had admired my reflection in Erwin's full-length mirror for about ten minutes, while he applauded enthusiastically. Just about a perfect fit. I only needed to push the trousers down about an inch to cover my socks. I couldn't wait for Dee to see me looking so elegant. But...it wasn't to be.

Gil's harsh voice shattered my reverie. "I wouldn't trust Erwin Redding with my woman for ten seconds."

"Yeah," Larry chimed in, "did you notice his sneaky smile, and the way he wouldn't look you in the eye? That guy's bad news."

Sweat broke out on my forehead, like I really was running a high fever. I groaned aloud. I couldn't think of anything to say. Gil must have seen the look of misery on my face, because he quickly tried to reassure me. "We're just trying to give you a hard time, Bill. Just kidding around. For God's sake, don't take us seriously!"

But I did take them seriously. Dee and Erwin together at the dance. Erwin's arms around Dee. Erwin and Dee under that full moon. Erwin and Dee driving along Cayuga Lake, pulling over to the scenic view, stopping, gazing at the stars. And then...

I tossed and turned, trying to get comfortable. But sleep wouldn't come. I'd like to think because of the fever I knew I was running. The dragon lady had popped the thermometer in my mouth before dinner, and also before the lights were turned out at nine o'clock. Following Gil's and Larry's advice, each time I held it under my tongue for about thirty seconds, then had rolled the instrument to the top of my tongue. Each time she mumbled her surprise when she examined it, turning it this way and that, frowning all the while. But the main reason for staying awake was knowing that Dee and Erwin were together. I even hoped it would rain so at least there'd be no moon. That hope was tossed into the ash can around eleven o'clock when moonlight streamed through the dingy window next to Larry's cot, lighting up the ward like it was midday.

I slipped out of bed and pulled one of the folding chairs

close to the window, quietly so as not to awaken Gil and Larry. I sat and gazed upward into the black sky. There it hung. A huge splotchy yellow ball. I remembered how I read in the Rootabaga Stories written by a guy named Sandburg that the moon was made of green cheese. I knew that couldn't be true. But I wondered what it was made of, and whether it would be possible to fly to the moon some day—not on a giant moth like Dr. Dolittle did, but maybe on a rocket.

I planned to phone Uncle Dan to ask about Spike but didn't get a chance before the doc in the clinic rushed me to the infirmary. Then the dragon lady had turned me down flat when I asked to use the telephone. I made the mistake of telling her I needed to check up on my dog. She seemed to think that was the dumbest idea anyone could possibly have. Maybe I should have told her I wanted to talk to my mom and dad.

I suddenly felt lonely. And homesick. It just swept over me like a blanket. I wished Spike were here. My best friend. He would comfort me. He'd have stuck by me; not gone off to a dance with someone else. If only people could be like dogs. Dogs never let you down. No matter what. Always showing their love; always eager to please. Just say the word. Dogs were all the good things Boy Scouts were supposed to be. And more. I must have dozed off in spite of myself, because the next thing I knew, the dragon lady was shaking my shoulder.

"What are you doing out of bed? You'll get pneumonia with that fever." Her rasping voice grated on my ears.

"I don't have a fever," I mumbled, as I climbed back into bed.

"We'll see about that," she muttered. She shoved the glass instrument once again between my lips. This time she stood alongside the bed, her arms folded, glaring down at me. After about the usual thirty seconds, I pretended to straighten the thermometer and managed to get it on top of my tongue without her noticing. After a few minutes, she reached down and retrieved the instrument from my mouth. The same routine followed. Much mumbling and head-shaking and pursing of lips and holding the thermometer up to the light.

"Well, it's 98.7," she finally announced. You're just about cured." A grim smile appeared then disappeared in an instant. "Thank the Lord."

My hopes leaped skyward. If the dragon lady was so anxious to get rid of her patient, maybe I could persuade her to discharge me before Dee's train left. "Please, can I leave this morning?" I hated myself for begging.

"You can leave at 5 o'clock if your temperature is no higher," she retorted, not giving an inch.

While all of this was going on, Larry and Gil had been in the bathroom, showering and dressing, laughing and singing all the while. Now they appeared, grinning and chuckling. You'd have thought they'd just won the Irish Sweepstakes. Gil bowed from the waist to the dragon lady, like he was addressing the Queen of Sheba. "We'll remain for breakfast, Madam, and then we're very much afraid that we must leave your palatial establishment."

"Humph."

The dragon lady stalked from the ward, her starched skirt swishing as she went. She obviously resented having to serve meals to us, muttering and sighing each time she delivered our trays. She should have been a prison guard instead of a nurse. The scrambled eggs were runny, the toast cold, and the bacon lined with fat. I had no appetite, so didn't much care. My face felt flushed from the fever I managed to hide. At least the coffee was hot, even if bitter. I felt much livelier after drinking two cups.

Larry pushed aside his tray, a disgusted look on his face. "I bet you wouldn't even feed this swill to the pigs on your farm."

I managed a smile. "We didn't have any pigs."

"Well, you know what I mean." He glanced at his wristwatch. "Look, Gil and I talked it over, and we'll stick around for awhile this morning to keep you company. We hate to leave you alone with that dragon."

We carried on a desultory bull session for a couple of hours until we finally ran out of things to gripe about. As Gil and Larry got up to leave, I was startled by the sound of loud voices from the hallway, like some kind of an argument was going on. One of the voices belonged to the dragon lady. The other was a male voice. Suddenly, a second female voice chimed in.

Dee.

And Erwin.

"We've both had the stupid measles," I heard Erwin say. "So don't worry." They must have won the argument, because there they stood in the doorway. Dee and Erwin. With huge grins on their faces. Dee's soft black hair fell loosely to her shoulders. She wore a green a red plaid skirt and a soft green turtleneck sweater. She looked like a million dollars.

"Billy, how yuh doing?" she called out.

Why did she have to call me Billy in front of Larry and Gil? I could tell by their smirks that they made mental notes to embarrass me at the worst possible time.

"Uh, okay," I mumbled.

Dee pulled a chair next to my cot and sat down, while Erwin ambled across the room and stood next to her, hands in pockets, rocking back and forth on his heels, the grin, now a bit sheepish, still on his face. I didn't like his looks. Before I had a chance to stop her, Dee placed her palm on my forehead.

"You're as hot as a furnace!" she exclaimed.

I glanced apprehensively toward the door leading to the next room. No sign of the dragon lady. "Please, don't talk so loud," I whispered. "I'm trying to get out of this dump. I'll be here forever if the wicked witch thinks I'm running a fever."

Dee quickly pulled her hand back. "Oh, Billy," she whispered, "I'm so sorry. But please don't rush it. You'll just make yourself worse."

I felt better already, seeing the look of concern on her face. "I'll be fine, really." I looked over at Gil and Larry, interested observers, staring first at Dee, then at Erwin. Dee's eyes focused on the two of them. "Are you going to introduce me to these two handsome guys?"

I groaned inwardly. There she went. Torturing me again. But I complied. She held out her hand and favored Gil and Larry with her dazzling smile, dimple and all.

"It's terrible that the three of you missed the dance," she said. "It was marvelous." Her eyes shone with excitement. "Wasn't it, Erwie?"

Erwie.

"Yeah, I guess so," Erwin mumbled.

"Guess so. That's not what you said last night," she cried out. "Or I should say, early this morning. You raved about the dance, Glen Gray, Kenny Sargent, Pee Wee Hunt. Everything. And I agreed. Don't you remember?"

"Oh, sure." He laughed, a high-pitched, squeaky laugh, more like a giggle.

Erwin's face turned a dark pink. I noticed he'd obviously

shaved. And on Sunday morning. His eyes shifted uneasily in my direction. He licked his lips, then looked toward Dee for help. But none came from that quarter. She sat there, rambling on as bubbly as ever, raving about the dance, about the campus, about the Library Tower bells, about the weather, about Cayuga Lake, and on and on.

Gil and Larry seemed hypnotized. Erwin couldn't keep his eyes off of her either. I tried to put my mind in neutral, and I gave only short answers when she asked me questions. I just wished they'd go. Leave me to my misery. Let me die in peace.

"What time is it, Erwie?"

Dee's question aroused me from the depths of self-pity.

"Nearly eleven fifteen," Erwin replied.

Dee jumped to her feet. "We've got to go. The brunch starts at noon."

Brunch. One more fun event I'd miss.

Erwin cleared his throat a couple of times. "Betty invited me to the brunch at the Theta house," he explained. "I wish it were you, instead of me," he added hurriedly.

Dee patted the top of my head. She gazed at me for several seconds, then suddenly leaned down and planted a kiss on my forehead. "I feel terrible that your weekend was messed up, Billy," she whispered. "Thanks a million for inviting me. I'll write. I promise." She was leaving. I descended once more into the pits. When would I ever see her again? Erwin interrupted my mournful thoughts.

"So long, Bill," he said. "Don't worry about Dee's getting to the station. Betty said she'd drive us. Hope I'll see you back at the dorm tonight." They crossed the room and vanished through the door without looking back.

Drive us.

A long silence followed their departure. Gil and Larry stared at each other for a few seconds, then looked down at me. I shut my eyes and groaned aloud. Why didn't they leave?

"Hey, Bill." Larry stood next to my cot, a worried look on his face. "Are you okay?"

"Yeah, I guess so," I mumbled. Then I let out a huge sigh, in spite of myself.

Larry frowned and scratched his head. "Is Dee your girlfriend? Are you two going steady or something? If so, I'm sorry Gil and I joked about you and her yesterday."

His questions made me stop to think. I'd have to answer "no" to both of them. She wasn't my girlfriend. We weren't going steady. Then why was I acting so stupid? Why was I so jealous? "No," I finally said. "No, we're just good friends." I paused for about five seconds.

"She's really too old for me."

CHAPTER 13

I stared at the ceiling for more than an hour after Gil and Larry waved so long and headed back to the campus. To freedom. Lucky guys. Sweat ran down my cheeks. My head ached. I finally closed my eyes, hoping to sleep. But Dee's and Erwin's grinning faces kept sailing by. Then the word "brunch" swept toward me, getting bigger and bigger and bigger as it floated past. I sat up and caught sight of a thermometer on the side table. The dragon lady had forgotten to retrieve it in the confusion that accompanied Gil's and Larry's departure. I reached over and popped the instrument under my tongue. After a couple of minutes, I held it to the light. I groaned. The red line sat between 100 and 101 degrees.

"Well, what's it now"? The dragon lady's raspy question startled me. How had she slipped into the room so quietly?

"It's normal." I gave the thermometer three or four violent shakes.

"Wait. Hold up. Let's have a look." She hustled forward, snatched the instrument from my hand, and shoved it back in my mouth. It slid easily across my tongue, and I prayed that I could fool the old dragon one last time. After a couple of minutes, she jerked the thermometer out and held it to the light, while I held my breath. She pursed her lips, frowned, looked over at me, stared again at the instrument, then shrugged.

"Well, it's still 98.7," she said grudgingly. "Looks like that's normal for you. I guess you can leave any time."

Any time!

"What time is it now?" I burst out. Dee's train left at four. Maybe I could see her before she left. My spirits soared.

The dragon lady heaved a big sigh, like I'd asked her to lend me five dollars. She dragged a beat up pocket watch from under her uniform. "Nearly one thirty," she snapped. "You'll have to eat lunch before you leave," she added.

"I don't want any lunch," I cried out. "I'm not hungry. I've got to get out of here."

"The rules say I got to feed you lunch, and that's what I got to do, so you're going to eat it. Now get up and get your clothes on." With those snarled remarks, the dragon lady stomped from the room.

I eased out of the cot and sat on the edge for a few seconds, then stood and shuffled across the room toward a closet where I'd left my canvas bag and the clothes I'd worn when Dee and I drove out to Taughannock Falls after the game. Was that ten years ago? The room began to sway. I grabbed the open closet door and held on. I heard the dragon lady throwing my lunch together, muttering all the while. I couldn't let her see me like this. She'd order me back to bed quick as a flash. I yanked my clothes off the hangers, took a deep breath, and hurried into the bathroom. She wouldn't follow me there. I sat on the edge of the tub until my head cleared, then slowly struggled into my clothes. I pulled a comb from my bag, then stared into the mirror above the sink. A ghost stared back. The circles under my eyes looked like they'd been painted with charcoal. Drops of perspiration stood out on my forehead.

I splashed cold water on my face, then ran the comb through my hair sticking out every which way, grabbed my bag, kicked open the bathroom door, squared my shoulders, took another deep breath, and walked briskly toward the door of the ward.

"Just a minute, young man. Where do you think you're going?" The dragon lady stood next to my cot, holding my lunch tray. I nearly tossed my cookies when I saw what she had in store for me. A bowl of clam chowder, chipped beef on toast, and a glass of milk. Probably warm. I rushed on by, and before she could put the tray down I reached the hallway, hoping I wouldn't pass out before I made it to the stairway.

"You come back here." The dragon lady's voice rose an octave. "Come back here. Come back here." I still heard her shouts from halfway down the stairs. I burst through the front door on Buffalo Street, nearly blinded by the bright sunlight. I could smell the purple and white azaleas blooming in the front yard of the infirmary. A soft breeze cooled my face. For a few seconds, I felt like a human being. Then I started trudging up Buffalo Street, one of the steepest in Ithaca, and headed for the entrance to the campus.

It took me more than an hour to struggle as far as Eddy

Street. I had to stop at the end of every block for three or
four minutes. I tried thumbing a ride for awhile, but only a
few cars tore by filled with guys and girls, grinning from ear
to ear, talking excitedly, probably raving about the wonderful
weekend and the terrific Spring Day dance. I cursed my bad
luck each time I sat down to rest.

As I staggered up to the entrance of Cascadilla Hall,
I heard the sound of the Library Tower bell striking three
times. Only an hour before Dee's train left. I'd hoped to get
to the dorm in time to take a shower, get into some decent
clothes, then catch a bus to the station. I'd never make it in
time now.

Unless!

Unless I phoned a cab to take me to the train station. I
pulled out my wallet. Three dollars. Plenty of money for the
fare. I had at least one nickel for the call in the top drawer of
my bureau. The climb up the stairs seemed to take another
hour. I stopped at each landing to get my breath. I finally
reached the third floor and staggered down the hall to the
door of my room. Fishing the key from my pants pocket, I
opened the door, and stumbled in. The dreary, stuffy room
seemed like heaven compared to that hellhole infirmary . I
dropped my bag to the floor, hustled across the room, and
raised the window. The rush of air cooled my face and lifted
my spirits. I looked back and noticed an envelope on the
floor that someone must have slipped under the door. I
picked it up. A letter from Mom. Special delivery. But I
had to get going. I laid the envelope on the bedside table. It
could wait.

I glanced at the Baby Ben on the bedside table. I did a
double take. The hands showed the time to be eleven thirty.
Then I realized that, of course, it had stopped. I quickly set
it for a little after three, then scrambled over to the bureau,
opened the top drawer and retrieved a nickel for the phone
call. No time for a shower. I hurried down the hall to the
pay phone. Wonders will never cease. The phone was not
being used. As I passed Erwin's door, I pictured him and
Dee at the station together. Someone had posted the cab
company's telephone number on the wall next to the phone.
Thank goodness. I'd never used a cab in Ithaca before. Or
anywhere else, for that matter. I dialed the number.

Busy.

Cold sweat broke out all over. I thought for a second I

would pass out. Until that awful buzzing noise hit my ear, I'd forgotten I still had a fever. I laid my head against the phone box and shut my eyes. I counted slowly to thirty, then picked up the receiver from the cradle and dialed again.

"Ithaca Cab Company." The most welcome three words I'd ever heard. "I'm at Cascadilla Hall, and I need to get to the station to catch the 4 o'clock train," I shouted. I seldom lied. But, this was an emergency, and I figured I'd be forgiven. Even Mom would understand.

"Well, buddy," the voice replied, "we can't have a cab there for another twenty minutes. We're busy, you know, even if it is Sunday. All you college kids..."

"Please. Just get a cab here as soon as you can. I'll be out front."

I slowly hung up the receiver and again rested my head on the phone box. My legs felt like dishrags. After a couple of minutes, I managed to stumble into the bathroom. I filled a sink with cold water and stuck my face in it for as long as I could hold my breath.

Twenty minutes later, I sat in the back seat of a rickety 1932 Chevrolet sedan that passed for a taxicab in Ithaca, barreling down Stewart Avenue. "Can we make the four o'clock?" I leaned forward anxiously.

The driver's eyes stared at me in the rear view mirror. They looked dubious. Then he shrugged. "You have ten minutes. You can pray either that the train's late, or we make every traffic light, or both."

I sank back and stared out of the window. We'd never make it. No way. But just then a bunch of thoughts raced through my mind. Hadn't I already decided that Dee was too old for me? Or had I? What's the big deal? Was this what people called love? Or was my fever making me think strange thoughts and do strange things?

"Where's your luggage?"

The question startled me. My lie was catching up with me. Might as well tell the truth.

"I need to say goodbye to someone."

"Girlfriend?"

"Sort of," I mumbled. His eyes again glanced up at me through the rearview mirror. "None of my business," he finally said. "I'll do my best to get you there." The cab shot forward but came to a screeching stop, throwing me forward, when the light on Seneca Street turned red. From then on, the entire lighting sequence worked against us. After what seemed like forever, we pulled in front of the station. Just as the line of cars began to move.

Too late.

"Sorry."

I forced a smile. The cab driver did seem truly sorry. The rumble of the cars reached my ears as the train picked up speed. Two toots of the horn announced the Black Diamond Express's approach to the first grade crossing beyond the station. And then the last car disappeared around the bend.

All the anticipation, excitement, and hopes I'd had just a few days ago, looking forward to being with Dee, rushed through my mind. It was like a magic wand had been waved bringing her here, and then, in a flash, waving her gone. She might as well be in Timbuktu, not just a half-mile down the tracks. A swarm of students streamed in front of the cab, shouting back and forth. I watched them glumly for a few seconds. Betty and Erwin suddenly emerged from the station door, looking so darn happy, laughing and chattering away. I ducked my head, pretending to look for something on the floor. They were the last people in the world I wanted to talk to.

"Take me to the dorm, please," I urged the driver. My face must have looked like I'd lost my best friend because the driver said he wouldn't charge for the ride back. "I'm headed in that direction, anyway," he said, when I protested. "Gotta pick up the old lady and get her to the church social by five o'clock. She's on the food committee. Can't be late. She baked ten loaves of bread and five lemon meringue pies. Best baker in Tompkins County. Wins prizes every year. That's why I'm too darn fat." He ran on and on, probably trying to take my mind off my woes. I shut my eyes during the ride to the dorm, feeling hot all over. Then I thought how I had stupidly risked getting really sick just to see Dee for a couple of minutes at the most. She didn't care two cents for me. That was for sure. I began to feel sorrier and sorrier for myself. Then wondered again. Why? Why couldn't I accept Dee as a good friend? Like before. She was the best pal a guy could ever have. My mind went back to the time when Dee and Spike and I got tangled up in the riot at the Bethlehem Steel plant. When we helped Uncle Dan beat off the goons hired by the company to break the strike.

I smiled.

"Hey, you look like you're feeling better." The cab had stopped in front of the dorm. The driver stared at me through the rearview mirror.

"Yeah." I paused. "Yeah, I really do. Thanks very much. I appreciate your bringing me back."

The climb to the third floor didn't seem quite as exhausting as before. I couldn't wait to get in bed. I hadn't eaten any lunch. But I wasn't hungry. I didn't want food. I needed sleep. When I opened the door to my room, a gust of wind blew an envelope from the bedside table. Then I remembered. A letter from Mom. Special delivery. She hardly ever wrote. Every now and then a postcard. But nothing more. I picked up the envelope and tore it open. A bill fluttered toward the floor. I grabbed it in mid-air and stared in amazement. Twenty dollars. I'd never even seen a twenty-dollar bill before. It took me a few seconds to recover from my surprise. Then I looked at the letter. It was in Mom's scrawl. I sat on the cot and started reading.

Dearest Billy:

Spike is very sick. Doc Browning says he's got the cancer real bad, and won't last more than two or three weeks.

Dad and your Uncle Dan and I thought you should be told this because you always said Spike was your best friend.

He's not in pain because of pills Doc Browning gives him.

Your uncle Dan is sending 20 dollars so you can take the train home and back to school if you can come.

I'm sorry to tell you this. I know it will upset you.

Lots of love,
Your Mom

I stared at the letter until the words got all blurry, then read it again real slow, hoping I'd misunderstood Mom. But there it was. In my mom's own handwriting. She'd written his name twice and said he was my best friend.

And so Spike was going to die. I'd thought about his dying. Especially when I couldn't sleep. I knew it had to happen someday. I'd been lucky all my life. None of my family had ever died—Mom or Dad or Uncle Dan. Not any of my close friends like Dee or Marion Grafton or Jim Huff, or guys on my high school baseball team. Bradbury Emerson was killed when he fell off the Conowingo Dam and landed in the Susquehanna River. He tried to walk along the parapet after taking a dare from a bunch of kids who drove over there late one Saturday night after guzzling home brew. But he wasn't a close friend. He was a couple of years ahead of me in school. I saw him in the lunch room and the gym and places like that. But we didn't say more than "hi" to each other. Bradbury's body never turned up, even though they dredged the river for more than two weeks. I remember wondering whether he might be still alive when they had a memorial service for him at the little church in Scarborough. I read in a magazine on magic that Houdini once escaped from an airtight tank filled with water.

I tried to figure out what I should do. What could I do? Suddenly sweat broke out all over my body. Even my hair felt wet. I lay back on the bed and tried to think. The next thing I knew it was pitch dark. I was as weak as a kitten, but cool. No fever. It must have broken when I started sweating and while I slept. I turned on the table lamp next to my cot and peered at the Baby Ben on the side table. Nearly 11 o'clock. I'd slept for more than six hours.

Then it hit me like a ton of bricks. Spike was going to die. A huge wave of despair crashed over me. The best time to cry is when you're alone. And that's what I did for about five minutes. Real quiet. When I ran out of tears, I took off my clothes and slipped into my bathrobe. A shower would make me feel better. Then I'd try to figure out what to do. While the hot water nearly scalded me, I suddenly thought of how Betty had lost the guy she loved. Jack Randolph. Gone forever. Nothing could be any worse than that. But she had coped with her grief, even though she would never forget him. I felt better. Even stronger. If Betty could do it, so could I. That's what Spike would want. But I'd never forget my best friend.

CHAPTER 14

The train shuddered, lurched ahead for about a hundred feet, then ground to a sudden stop, causing the few impatient passengers, standing in the aisle, to grasp the end of the seats to hold their balance and keep from falling. "That clumsy fool ought to go back to school and learn how to drive a locomotive." This caustic observation came from a well-rounded, overweight woman, looming above me. She complained constantly ever since the Bethlehem cars had been hooked onto the train that had originated in Philadelphia: the conductor couldn't say for sure that the train would not be late arriving in Ithaca, the dining car too crowded, her lamb chops undercooked, the food bill unreasonable, the ladies room occupied for too long a time, the heat insufferable, and on and on. Cigarette and cigar smoke filtering from the smoking car into our car caused her to emit a persistent racking cough.

She wore an elegant pink silk dress that persistently hitched up a few inches over her enormous rear, defying her repeated clutching and tugging. Despite the warmth, she wore a brown fur neckpiece draped across her shoulders. The top of her straw hat looked like she tried to start a flower garden there. Tree-trunk legs were planted firmly on the floor of the car. She glared toward the exit, red jowls quivering, eyes bulging, waiting, I imagined, to berate the first unlucky railroad employee that appeared on the scene. I mentally compared this old battle-axe with Mom, who, along with Dad and Uncle Dan had come to the station to say goodbye. Mom had never owned a fur piece in her life. She had only two Sunday dresses she ordered from the Montgomery Ward catalogue.

Mom had learned to love Spike after all of us finally got together to live with Uncle Dan. I told her how he rescued me during the labor riots, when Buck was about to choke me to death. She cried for nearly an hour after Spike died. I had to comfort her. That was good for me; it gave me something to think about after losing my best friend. This old cow probably hated dogs.

"You there. Get my bag down."

My daydream halted abruptly. I looked up to see bulging eyes fixed on me, her fat stomach within inches of my nose. Beads of perspiration rolled from her forehead across her nose and hung for a moment before dropping to the floor. A pudgy finger pointed to a huge green suitcase in the luggage rack. I felt like telling her to jump in the lake but didn't have the nerve. "Yes, ma'am," I mumbled. I reached up, grasped the giant case, then nearly went sprawling to the floor from its weight.

"Be careful, for God's sake." she shouted. "That bag cost nearly a hundred dollars."

Now I wanted to tell this old hag to go to hell. But, instead, I meekly deposited the green monster on the floor in front of her, wondering why people like me seemed to always knuckle under to people like her.

"Find a redcap and tell him to come back here and help me," she ordered, then pursed her lips. "Or maybe that no good, cheating son of mine has deigned to spare an hour of his valuable time to meet me." She glared at me. "You," she rasped, "do you know Steve Dobson?"

Steve Dobson. Could this be Steve's mother? I must have looked like the village idiot, because she let out a huge sigh. "For God's sake, are you deaf, dumb or both? Do you know Steve Dobson?"

I was stunned for a second. I wanted to lie. But couldn't. "Yy yeah," I stammered. "Yeah. I know him."

"Well," she said, "if you see him in the station, tell him to get his tail in here and help me with my bag before this damn train pulls out and carts me all the way to Buffalo. If he's not there, send a redcap."

I grabbed my canvas bag and scurried to the front of the car and down the steps, wishing the train would take off with Mrs. Dobson aboard. No sooner had my feet hit the platform than I heard the familiar nasal voice. "What are you doing here, hayseed?" There stood Steve, lolling against the wall of the station, clutching a lighted cigarette, wearing brown slacks and a white sweater with the red "C" he received for playing on the freshman baseball team. I was entitled to wear the letter but didn't want to spend the money to buy a sweater just for that.

I ignored the question. To hell with him. "Your mother

wants you to give her a hand with her suitcase," I said. "She's in that car. About in the middle." I nodded toward the car I just left.

"My mother," he mocked. "Mama comes all the way from Philadelphia by herself just to see her little Stevie." He dropped the cigarette and ground the butt into the wooden platform. "I wish the damn train had dropped into the Susquehanna." He snickered. "But that wouldn't have helped. She'd probably have floated 'til someone pulled her fat ass out of the river."

I'd never heard anyone speak about their mother that way, or anywhere near that way. But I didn't say anything. It was none of my business. I thought how sad it was that Steve and his mother, with all their money and possessions, seemed to hate each other. As I hurried down the platform, I wondered if he and his father also hated each other. And what about Harry?

"Hey, Bill." Another familiar voice. But this one so welcome. Betty. I nearly dropped my teeth. How did she know I was on the train? She strode toward me, dark curls dancing and sparkling in the afternoon sun, her blue eyes staring a little apprehensively. Probably worried how I felt about Spike.

"How did you know I was on this train?"

"Well," she said, "I know you have an animal husbandry exam tomorrow. That's my department. So I figured you'd be back today." She held out her arms. I dropped my bag, and we exchanged a long hug. The soft hair that brushed my cheeks smelled like all outdoors. I shut my eyes, feeling like I'd come home.

"Oh, Bill," she murmured, "I'm so sorry about Spike. I never saw him, but I know he meant so much to you."

It took me a couple of seconds to calm myself. I didn't want to cry in front of Betty. So I gave her an extra squeeze before pulling back. "Thanks. He was my best friend. I'll never forget him." I picked up my bag and we started walking up the platform. "Only good thing is, he didn't suffer. The vet loaded him with painkillers. He licked my hand, then just shut his eyes and went to sleep. We buried him in my Uncle Dan's back yard, right next to the grape arbor along the fence." I smiled. "Where he used to relieve himself when Uncle Dan wasn't looking."

"Why don't we ride for awhile, then I'll take you to the

dorm," Betty said.

That was fine with me. So before long, we were driving up the west side of Cayuga in Betty's convertible, with the top down, headed toward Taughannock State Park. She looked straight ahead, the wind blowing her hair back. I admired her profile, and for the hundredth time I wondered whether I was in love with her. Could a guy love two girls? I'd read about that sort of thing but never thought it was possible. Now I just didn't know.

She gave me a quick glance, and a smile broke out. "What are you staring at? See something you don't like?"

My face felt as hot as an oven. "No, nothing. Never." Not when I'm looking at you, I thought, wishing I had the nerve to say it out loud. I frantically tried to think of something to talk about, then remembered Mrs. Dobson.

"You know, Steve Dobson's mother was on the train. And Steve met her at the station. What do you suppose she's doing here?"

"I don't have to suppose," Betty said. "I know why she's here. Wait 'til we get to the falls, and I'll fill you in."

We drove in silence until we reached the park. Betty eased the car into a space, switched off the ignition, and turned toward me. "Steve Dobson's on the verge of being kicked out of Cornell University," she said, "and Mama's trying to put a stop to that. Can't stain the family escutcheon, you know. She doesn't give a damn about her baby boy."

"What happened?"

"Well, it seems that Stevie did get someone to take the chemistry exam last term, and that someone was a coed, and that someone and little Stevie got in a fearful row, and when that someone got jilted by Stevie, she spilled the beans."

"Who was it?"

"I don't know her name. Since my Uncle Phil's going to make the final decision, he told me that much and no more." Betty smiled grimly. "But from what he said, Miss Someone may have known her chemistry but failed a couple of other courses. She left campus before being busted out. But Steve's fighting to stay in school, and Mama's charging to the rescue. So she thinks."

"What do you mean by that?"

"I mean there's no way that Uncle Phil is going to let that cheating jerk stay in school. He's out of here."

All sorts of thoughts rushed through my mind. Gone

was the guy who gave me so much grief. No more Steve Dobson on the baseball team to worry about. No more snide remarks. Betty broke into my thoughts. "How is Dee?" she asked. "What is she up to these days and what are her plans?"

I explained that Dee was concentrating on her German language studies and how she was really getting good at reading and speaking German, and she hoped to land a job in Hamburg after she graduated next June, working for the State Department or doing translations for a private company. "She's going to try to locate her relatives if it's the last thing she does. They haven't been heard from for nearly two years, and then only a letter mailed six months before, the contents blacked out by the censor so much that it was nearly illegible."

I thought about my last meeting with Dee just after Spike died. We didn't say much about Spike. We didn't have to. I tried to talk her out of going to Germany, but she wouldn't listen. I didn't tell her that my big worry was her being Jewish, and how the Germans were shipping Jewish people to concentration camps, and even murdering them. But she didn't have to be told. She knew.

"I admire her courage," Betty said. "I don't think I'd have the guts to do something like that." Her voice filled with tension. She seemed to be speaking to herself. "The whole world's gone nuts. That murderer Franco has taken over Spain with the help of that puffed-up Italian toad. Hitler's the worst of the bunch. He's swallowed up Austria. And Czechoslovakia will be next. You watch." She breathed deeply, then seemed to relax. She turned to me with a smile. "Let's talk about something more cheerful. Like Bill Creelman's plans. What are you going to do this summer?"

That was another problem. I explained to Betty that I hoped to work at the Bethlehem Steel plant, but jobs were scarce, and the union wasn't about to let someone like me work during the summer when dozens of its members were unemployed. Betty leaned back and closed her eyes. I glanced over at her after a few minutes. I thought she'd fallen asleep, when she sat up suddenly and looked over at me. "I've got a great idea!" she said. "You can work on Dad's beef cattle farm this summer. He'd love to have someone like you. He hires at least three Cornell Ag students each summer, but usually city boys who've had no farm experience and need to earn their farm credits in order to graduate. Maybe we'd put you in charge of them since you know all about farming." Her eyes sparkled. "And I'm starting to work as assistant manager right after graduation. I'd be your boss. How do you like those apples?" I couldn't think of anything to say. I must have looked like a fool, because Betty burst out laughing. "Come on. That's not the worst thing that could happen to you. I'm really a kind taskmaster. All I demand is hard work ten hours a day, six days a week, and we even pay twenty dollars a week. Plus room, board, and laundry. When you're not cleaning the barns or hauling feed or scything fence rows, you'll sleep in a shack with two or three other college students. But the good news is that your Sundays will be your own. You might even be asked to eat dinner with us."

My turn to laugh. "I worked harder than that with no pay at all. And at least I won't have to do any milking. So please don't try to scare me." I opened the door and stood next to the car, my elbows on the door, leaning toward her. "Look," I said, "it would be wonderful to work for your dad. And you," I added quickly. "But how do you know he'd hire me?"

"He'll do anything I ask him to do, within reason, that is. And this is reasonable." She reached over and patted my hand. "And it will be nice for me to have you around all summer."

CHAPTER 15

I spent the happiest summer of my life working at Inthered Acres. It took me awhile before I learned where the name Inthered came from. I pronounced it like it was "Inthird" one day. Betty laughed up a storm. "It's IN THE RED," she hooted. "Dad loses a ton of money on this operation. But don't worry about him. Inthered Acres is a corporation connected to Dad's automobile business. His lawyer came up with some kind of tax gimmick so the losses from the beef cattle business can be deducted from the profits his company earns. He's made a bundle despite the Depression. It's all legitimate."

So I decided not to feel sorry for Mr. Marshall.

Just as Betty had warned, I put in ten hours a day, six days a week, with every Sunday off. I unloaded fifty-pound bags of feed from trucks, mixed the feed, fed the young steers, cleaned out the barns, and did a lot of other chores. But it was a breeze compared with the work on our poor little dairy farm in Harford County, Maryland. No milking. No haying. No cutting corn. No chopping wood. No confinement in the superheated silo. Best of all, indoor toilets and electric lights. And to top it off, I was paid twenty dollars a week.

Betty worked just as hard and long, but in a different way. She spent hours every day in the office. Mr. Marshall let her run the business. He put all his trust in his daughter, and it was easy to see why. She graduated from Cornell with the highest honors in June, the shining star of the Animal Husbandry School. She also excelled in the farm management courses she took from Professor Warren.

Betty was the best boss a guy could have. Not just to me, but to the other Cornell Ag students and the regular hired hands. Everybody loved her. You could tell from the way their eyes lit up when she came by. Always had a smile and a cheerful word. Always stopped to chat and really seemed interested in knowing what you were doing and how things were going. She never failed to compliment someone if he'd done a good job. That made us work even harder.

The other Cornell guys kidded me a lot about Betty. But I didn't care. They kept hinting that we were having some kind of love affair. I never denied it. I just grinned when they questioned me about whether I had "made out" with her, sometimes using cruder words and suggestions. It was fun to keep them excited and guessing. But they were way off base. We had what I read about in a couple of books Betty loaned me. A platonic relationship. The word sounded silly to me at first. But our relationship was anything but silly. We never ran out of things to talk about. Music. Books. Poetry. The beef cattle business. Baseball. Her favorite team was the Philadelphia Athletics. History. Politics. She loved Mrs. Roosevelt and read her newspaper column, "My Day," like it was the Bible. She'd argue with anyone at the drop of a hat in favor of President Roosevelt, which surprised me, because her parents and ninety percent of their friends and relatives hated the President. They were always cursing him, even though the country seemed to be coming out of the Depression, so I read, and the Marshalls and all their acquaintances were making piles of money, driving around in Packards and Cadillacs and taking luxury ocean liners to Europe. Betty kept wishing and praying that the President would do something about "that Nazi murderer," her way of referring to Adolph Hitler. She reminded me of Uncle Dan.

She did treat me differently from the other Cornell guys. I'd have to admit that. We spent every Sunday together. Either visiting historical places like Valley Forge, where we marveled at how George Washington and his troops could survive the terrible freezing weather, or driving to Philadelphia for a symphony concert, or to Robin Hood Dell, a beautiful outdoor amphitheater near Philadelphia, where we picnicked and listened to all kinds of music. Even jazz. We invented a musical game. One of us would hum the opening bars of a piece, like the second movement of a Beethoven symphony, and the other had to identify what was being hummed within thirty seconds or lose a point. She usually beat me at first, but I got better as the summer went along.

We even drove to Bethlehem one Sunday in August and spent the day with Mom and Dad and Uncle Dan. The first thing I did was show her where I buried Spike alongside the grape arbor. "Spike was the smartest dog I ever knew," I confided to Betty. "Smarter than most people for that matter." She gave my arm a squeeze. I knew she understood. She knew me better than anyone in the world.

Betty had made a big hit with Mom and Dad, but most of all, Uncle Dan. They had talked for more than an hour about what was going on in Europe and Asia, about Hitler taking over Austria and threatening Czechoslovakia, about Mussolini throwing his weight around, about Japan taking over Manchuria and now beating up on China. "There's going to be another war," Uncle Dan had said over and over. "And the U.S. better damn sight get ready, 'cause we're going to be dragged in again."

Betty had got real excited. "I couldn't agree with you more," she said. "My dad and his crowd keep hollering that we should stay out of it. Not get involved." She paused. "But we're bound to be involved if Hitler's not stopped."

"We should pass a draft law now," Uncle Dan had muttered. He glanced quickly at me, then looked away. "Much as I hate the thought of young guys like Billy getting mixed up with a war. But if we wait, it'll only get worse." He sighed. "And the stupid English and French better get off their butts before it's too late. Hitler will pick them off like ripe cherries. One at a time. And eat them for breakfast."

I turned hot all over, hearing talk like that. The last thing in the world I wanted was to be a soldier in a war. Like those poor soldiers in "All Quiet On The Western Front." I shivered at the thought of hand-to-hand combat, with guys stabbing each other with bayonets, and clubbing each other with rifle butts. Or getting hung up on barbed wire. Or being gassed. Bleeding and dying in the mud.

Am I a coward? I kept wondering.

Even though it seemed like anyone my age with no money only had a horrible war to look forward to, more than once Betty wanted to talk about my "future." What did I want to do when I graduated from Cornell.

Did I want to be a farmer?

No!

A doctor?

A softer no. But no.

An economist?

Too nutty.

A teacher?

Maybe.

A writer?

Don't make me laugh.

A lawyer?

Never thought about it. Sounded like fun.

We had one of those conversations the last Sunday evening of my stay at Betty's home, swinging back and forth in the glider on the front veranda. It was early September, and I used some of my hard-earned cash to take Betty to dinner at a country inn near Norristown. I planned to leave for Bethlehem the next morning and spend a week with Mom, Dad, and Uncle Dan. I kind of hoped to see Dee. But she wrote me only twice the entire summer. She told me how busy she'd been, going to summer school, taking advanced courses in German reading and writing. She was determined to go to Germany after graduation next June and find out what had happened to her relatives. She mentioned seeing Erwin, who spent a couple of weekends in Allentown, and going dancing with him. To be honest, she didn't just mention him. She wrote a lot about him and what a good time they had together.

After our discussion of my "future" that last night at Inthered Acres, I worked the conversation around to Dee and Erwin. I knew Betty could set me straight in my thinking. "Dee's always been honest with you, Bill," Betty reminded me. "She's a wonderful person, but there's no use bashing your head against a brick wall. Just accept her as a good friend. Probably your best friend now. Don't do anything to wreck that friendship."

I reached over and grabbed Betty's hand. I couldn't help it. "But Dee's not my best friend." I swallowed hard. "You're my best friend, Betty. And always will be." I swallowed hard again, and stared out over the meadow toward the huge white barn looming through the dusk. I'm sure my voice shook, but I wanted Betty to know the special way I felt about her.

"That's the nicest thing I've heard in a long time, Bill," she whispered. Then before I could think, she leaned over, grabbed the back of my neck, and kissed me squarely on the lips. I nearly passed out. "That's for being such a great guy, and also for being my best friend for nearly a year." She took both my hands and turned toward me. Her eyes gleamed in the half light. "You have made me feel good about life again. Brought me out of my depression." She leaped to her feet. "Why, you've made a new woman out of me." She burst out laughing.

"Bill Creelman, I've got your future all figured out. You should be a psychiatrist."

CHAPTER 16

I've thought a lot about that kiss, and Betty looking down at me, a big smile on her face, and my heart pounding. I stayed awake a bunch of nights, tossing and turning, wondering what might have happened between us if I was a couple of years older, or she was a couple of years younger, or if Jack and she had never met, or if, if, if... And then I'd kick myself back to reality. For one thing, if Jack hadn't been a part of her life she never would have taken any interest in me. But...I'd heave a big sigh and try to get back to sleep.

I grew up a lot that summer, working for Betty's father and spending those wonderful hours with her. When I returned to Cornell in the fall of 1938, I missed her every day for the first three or four months. No one to cheer me up when I was down. No one to share new discoveries in books and music. No one to tell my dreams to. Finally, the pangs of loneliness subsided, and I was able to put our relationship in what I hoped was a sensible perspective. I guess.

The years that followed at Cornell were uneventful without Betty. I studied hard and got good grades. I continued earning my scholarship pitching baseball. I made a few friends and started dating, nothing serious, just some fumbling around. I was mostly just getting through it and looking forward to when my real life would begin. I worried about the escalating war in Europe and what might happen to me if America got involved. Then my senior year arrived, and the future spread out before me.

I wrote to at least twenty-five companies and state and federal agricultural agencies for a job during the fall and winter of my senior year. My grades were high enough to get into Phi Kappa Phi, and so my hopes were also sky-high. I must have worn out the hinges of my mailbox at Cascadilla from opening and shutting the little metal door, even when I knew the mailman hadn't come yet. Time after time I fished out an envelope with trembling hands, only to be disappointed. "Sorry, we are not hiring." "We regret to inform you that our budget does not permit..." "Try us next year." The same old story.

I fully expected a rejection when I stared at an official envelope from the United States Department of Agriculture. I'd written to six Department of Agriculture offices in various parts of the country. Four turndowns so far. This postmark showed Washington, D.C., April 1, 1941.

April Fools' Day!

But this wasn't an April Fools' joke. I had to read the letter three times before I finally believed it.

> Dear Mr. Creelman:
>
> We are pleased to offer you the position of Junior Marketing Specialist at an annual salary of $2,000 with the Fruit and Vegetable Division of the Agriculture Adjustment Administration at our headquarters in the South Building, Washington, D.C.
>
> If you wish to accept this offer, please so advise Mr. Irving Hasbrouck, Personnel Officer, Room 2020, at the above address, and report to him at 9 a.m., May 26, 1941.
>
> We look forward to a long and mutually satisfactory relationship with you.

Two thousand dollars a year! More than $165 every single month. I would be rich.

Then my elation dropped like a ton of bricks. May 26. Graduation exercises were scheduled for June 6. Mom and Dad and Uncle Dan were coming. Betty had written, saying she couldn't wait to see me get "that sheepskin." She'd be there with bells on. But I didn't think about putting up an argument. Jobs were too hard to come by... Especially ones that paid such an enormous salary. I'd have to get my sheepskin through the U.S. Mail. I did wonder how long my job would last. The Army might have something to say about that.

And so, after taking my last exam and a quick visit to Bethlehem, I road a Greyhound bus to Washington, where I'd managed to rent a room with two meals a day from a French couple who lived on 44th Street in Foxhall Village, a quiet area not far from Georgetown with tree-shaded streets lined with English-style row houses, each sufficiently different from the others to make the architecture of the neighborhood interesting and attractive.

Now my biggest problem was the draft. I was classified 1-A. It said so on a little brown postcard the local draft board had mailed to me. I even had a number. 7756. All of my friends from college worried themselves sick about the draft. A few dreamed up strange medical problems, hoping they'd be classified 4-F. It didn't work. A couple of them had managed to evade the draft by getting appointed as F.B.I. agents. Gil Stern even got married. I'd hoped my stammer would disqualify me from the military service. No such luck. Anyway, it had almost disappeared. And so a bunch of draft board doctors decided that I was physically fit to put on a khaki suit and learn how to kill other guys, and how, hopefully, to lower the chances of their killing me. It wasn't a happy future. For starters, buck privates in the Army got paid, like the song went, "twenty-one dollars a day, once a month."

Since I was headed for the armed forces unless Hitler threw in the towel, which wasn't about to happen, I'd tried everything I could think of to avoid being drafted. I wasn't against going into the military service as long as everyone else had to go. I just didn't want to be a buck private in the Army. There weren't many other options. The Army Air Corps and Naval Air Corps turned me down because of my history of stammering. Colonel Vandergrift, a Marine officer who lived next door, urged me to enlist in what he called "The Corps." He couldn't wait for the U.S. to go to war. A dream come true for him. He even offered to drive me to Quantico. But I politely declined. Too much like the Army.

Paul and Marie Michel, my landlord and landlady, kept moaning and griping about the United States not getting mixed up in the awful war that began in Europe on Labor Day weekend in 1939. I wouldn't forget that day. I was visiting Bill Kruse, one of the Kappa Sigs, who lived in St. David on the Main Line near Philadelphia. I worked all summer for the Railroad Perishable Inspection Agency in the Manhattan Produce Yards between Newark and Jersey City, inspecting watermelons shipped in boxcars from the south. My pay was a fantastic $125 month. I was so excited when I opened the letter offering me the job, I ripped it in half.

Bill and I had become good friends. He didn't look down his nose because I had to work while attending college. Like those jerks Harry and Steve Dobson. He invited me that Labor Day weekend to his home before starting our junior year at Cornell. I was a bit flustered at first when Erwin Redding showed up, along with one of Bill's friends from his Wayne High School days. Erwin had a job with the Baldwin Locomotive Works after graduating from Cornell. Bill's father was a vice-president, and Erwin's boss. I thought that seeing Erwin would upset me on account of his taking a fancy to Dee. But it didn't. He told me what I already knew, that she sailed for Germany after graduating from Muhlenberg in June of 1939 and was working in Hamburg with the U.S. Consulate. She wrote me a couple of times, and I could tell by reading between the lines that she was worried sick about the goings-on in Germany. I thought about her quite a lot, but it wasn't love, I finally decided. Erwin and I agreed that she was a wonderful girl and pal and started toasting her with our beer steins, with each toast getting more and more garbled. I started drinking beer after inspecting watermelons all day long in the steaming hot boxcars. The hottest summer ever. So "they" said.

We were sprawled around Bill's living room, telling jokes, gossiping, and guzzling Pabst Blue Ribbon, when the music from the radio broke off, and some guy, real excited, said that German Panzer Divisions had attacked Poland. Tanks and infantry were swarming across the border; Stukas were divebombing Warsaw and other Polish cities. A few hours later, the announcement came that a British ship, the Athenia, carrying 1,400 passengers had been sunk by a U-boat off of Scotland, with the loss of 112 lives, including 28 Americans. The awful news threw a huge wet blanket over the party atmosphere. Erwin and I talked a lot about Dee.

"She's Jewish," Erwin kept saying. "What's going to happen to her? What will those Nazi bastards do to her?"

"But she's an American," Bill said. "She'll be okay. She can come home if things get too hot over there."

I disagreed. "But she won't. The only reason she's in Germany in the first place is to hunt for her relatives. I know Dee. She'll stay there until she either finds them or learns they've been murdered."

The struggle in Europe had gone from bad to worse, with all kinds of hot and heavy debate among the politicians as to whether the United States should get involved. I didn't know what to think. In my heart, I knew we probably would be drawn into the war. Just like the last time. But I hated the idea. After a lull, which the stupid newspaper and radio reporters called the "Phoney War," Hitler's blitzkrieg had skirted the Maginot line, which the French generals promised would be impregnable, and swarmed through Denmark, Norway, Belgium, Luxembourg, Holland, and France.

I learned a lot about geography from reading and hearing about repeated disasters suffered by the British and French. Montevideo, River Plate, Scapa Flow, Narvik, Trondheim, Bergen, Ardennes Forest, Boulogne, Calais, and other strange names. In May of 1940, we hung around the radio in Willard Straight Hall for what seemed like forever, crossing our fingers and biting our nails, while we listened to accounts of the miraculous evacuation of British and French troops from Dunkirk. Less than a month later, Paris had fallen, and newsreels showed masses of German infantry goose stepping through the Arch of Triumph and along the Champs Elysees, with crowds of French people just standing there, sad-eyed men and women looking like they'd been run over by a truck, wiping tears from their faces. And then there were the film shots of Hitler strutting like a bantam rooster after the French generals threw in the towel in the same railroad car where the Germans surrendered in November 1918. I guess no one in France or England or America or anywhere else in the world dreamed that only about twenty years later there would be another gigantic killing spree. And for what? The big shots started the wars, then ordinary guys like those poor soldiers in "All Quiet On The Western Front" were forced to fight in it. To get themselves killed or maimed. Ruined forever.

Some good news came late in 1939, when the battered German pocket battleship Graf Spee was chased into Montevideo by British and New Zealand warships, where she was scuttled by her crew after the Argentina government refused asylum. Then, in 1940, we listened to heartening reports of the Royal Air Force's beating back the German Luftwaffe, shaking up Hitler so much that he called off the invasion of England. I broke out into goose bumps listening to the broadcasts from London about the Battle of Britain, particularly Churchill's defiant and inspiring talks. I loved the way he pronounced "Nazi." Like he was spitting out a piece of rotting meat.

But then came the worst blow of all. Or so it seemed to me at the time. In September of 1940, the 16th to be exact, just after I started my senior year, President Roosevelt signed the draft law. Uncle Dan said he'd help pay my expenses if I wanted to study for a master's degree. That would keep me out of the service, so he thought. But I couldn't do that. My baseball scholarship was ending, and my tuition and expenses would have been too much of a burden for him.

Well, it came at last. Monday, May 26, 1941. Mom always called big days in people's lives "red-letter days." I never knew why, or whether the letter was the kind you wrote or a letter in the alphabet. I don't think she ever had a red-letter day, unless it was when she married Dad. Anyway, today was the day I started my first job after graduating from Cornell, and I guess that qualified. Because I, Bill Creelman, was about to enter the South Building of the United States Department of Agriculture and go to work as a government official. My big boss was Henry A. Wallace, Secretary of Agriculture. I kind of doubted that I'd see much of him. The building, about as ugly as a building could be, was called the South Building because it was south of the main Department of Agriculture building. Constructed of some kind of drab brick, the building was five stories high and occupied a huge area between 12th and 14th streets in the southwest part of Washington, taking up more ground space than any other building in the city. The main Agriculture Building, where the big shots worked, was white and beautiful and looked more like a huge chateau than a government office building.

No one had told me what I would be doing in my new government job. I'd taken courses in Agriculture Economics, but I didn't know whether that qualified me to be a marketing specialist, "junior" or otherwise. Wanting to make sure I got to work on time, I set my trusty Baby Ben for 6:30. I rustled up some toast, orange juice and coffee, and slipped quietly out of the front door so as not to awaken the Michels. I walked briskly up 44th Street, then headed along Reservoir Road, feeling at first like a million dollars this beautiful May morning. The magnolia and the forsythia blossoms had come and gone, but white and red and purple azaleas and red and yellow tulips had taken their places. But my worries soon descended with a dull thud as I trudged along. There was no possibility that a junior marketing specialist would be classified as essential to the war effort and avoid the draft. If only the war would end. But how could it end without Hitler and Stalin and Mussolini taking over all of Europe? Only the British kept fighting. But everything had gone wrong. One disaster after another. It seemed like no one in the U.S. gave the British a chance of beating back the Germans. What would happen when Great Britain was occupied? That bastard Hitler wouldn't be satisfied. He never had been before. Why should he be now? He'd catch his breath, build more tanks, airplanes, and warships, then come after us.

I boarded a streetcar on Wisconsin Avenue and rode to 14th and Pennsylvania Avenue, where I got off, and hoofed it the rest of the way to the South Building, as nervous as I'd ever been. Even before a big game. I kept telling myself I was an important government official. A Junior Marketing Specialist. I didn't much like the sound of "junior," but I was stuck with the title. At least for now.

I used the extra time by walking around the block until five minutes before nine, trying to calm my nerves. Finally, I took a deep breath and entered the building. A uniformed guard slouched down in a chair behind a desk in the lobby reading the sports page of the *Washington Herald*. I noticed the headline. "Senators Lose Fourth Straight." He didn't seem impressed when I told him I was a Junior Marketing Specialist and announced that I had an appointment with Mr. Hasbrouck. Only muttered that room 2020 was on the second floor and jerked his thumb toward a bank of elevators.

After cooling my heels in an outer office for a half-hour, I was admitted into the presence of Irving Hasbrouck, a prissy-looking guy, who gave me a fishy handshake and waved toward a chair. He was about 5 feet 4 inches tall, with short sandy hair and rimless glasses, about forty years of age, too old for the draft. I couldn't help noticing his brown suede shoes with tassels. He handed me a two-page form and a ballpoint pen.

"Fill this out and sign it," he ordered. "Make sure all the information is accurate," he added. "Then I'll take you to Mr. Collins."

"Who is he?" I asked. I'd never heard his name before.

Mr. Hasbrouck let out a sigh, like I'd asked to borrow a cigarette, which I wouldn't anyway, because I don't smoke.

He compressed his lips. "Spencer Collins is the head of the vegetable section. He's a Senior Marketing Specialist. You'll occupy the same room with him and Ted Armstrong. Ted's an Associate Marketing Specialist."

That really got my attention. A Senior Marketing Specialist earned at least $5,600 a year. And Ted Armstrong must be pulling down $4,800. Maybe more. I thought about my mom and dad, who probably hadn't seen that much money in their entire lives. Uncle Dan probably made about $3,000 a year, and I'd bet he worked a lot harder and longer than either Mr. Collins or Mr. Armstrong.

"Do you know what I'll be doing?" I asked timidly.

"I have no idea," he huffed. Another sigh. "I just don't understand why we need any more people in vegetables. Just makes more work for me." He smoothed back his hair. "I had to find a desk and chair to cram in that room. Also another file cabinet."

I stared at him. Did he expect an apology? Then I realized who he reminded me of. Dicky Bird. The same prissy voice. The same impatient attitude toward everyone but his special favorites. He'd probably hoped my job "in vegetables" would be given to one of them.

CHAPTER 17

My job "in vegetables" turned out to be disappointing, to say the least. I worked maybe two or three hours a day on dull and tedious marketing agreement programs supposedly designed to help raise prices on a bunch of vegetable crops, including California lettuce, Florida watermelons, Idaho potatoes, and shallots produced in Colorado by second-generation Japanese farmers whose last names, to my embarrassment when I read them aloud to one of the secretaries, always seemed to end in "shita." Mr. Collins did his best to give me interesting assignments, but his options were limited. I had the strong feeling that neither he nor Ted Armstrong needed any help, and that they must have wasted many fretful hours trying to figure out things for me to do.

Mr. Collins was a neat guy, though. He surprised me just after lunch one day, when he and I'd been alone in the office. Ted had called in sick. He cleared his throat and, when I looked up from across the room, beckoned to me, a conspiratorial look on his face. When I approached his desk, he whispered, "Let's sneak out and see Gone With the Wind. It's playing at the Uptown."

I read that great book, as had millions of others, and had followed the arguments and controversy over who'd play various roles, particularly Scarlett O'Hara. The movie had recently premiered, and I was dying to see it. And so I didn't think twice before agreeing with his plan, and we played hooky for the rest of the day. Mr. Collins' and my big secret brought us closer together.

In addition to lack of work, I had another problem. My landlady, Marie Michel. She insisted that I call her Marie. I'd begun to spend too many not so fretful hours thinking, sometimes dreaming, about her. Marie was just over five feet tall, maybe thirty years old, but with as much pep as a girl in her teens. A hundred pounds of energy, with curly black hair that bounced when she walked. Built like a brick outhouse, Erwin would have said. She talked rapidly with a delightful accent. More often than I'd like to admit, I had the urge to hug her. Especially when she greeted me enthusiastically after work, dragging me to the living room sofa and insisting on knowing all about my day. I'd resisted the impulse. So far. Usually she produced glasses filled with some kind of red wine, which we sipped while I babbled away.

She squealed with laughter when I confided one evening after three glasses of the red stuff how Mr. Collins had asked me to prepare the official United States cabbage crop report for 1941. I didn't know whether to laugh or cry when he dumped that one on me. What did I know about cabbage? Professor Work, our Vegetable Crops professor, had spent two hours discussing that dull vegetable, and we planted seeds in small flats out at the greenhouses. Even transplanted them to larger flats later on. Whether they lived or died the students never found out. I was forced to memorize that the cabbage genus was <u>Brassica</u>, the species was <u>B. oleracea</u>, and the variety was <u>capitata</u>. Knowing those vital facts helped me get an A on my Vegetable Crops exam. I also recalled that cabbage was biennial and suffered from all kinds of horrible diseases. Such as club root and yellows. I never dreamed that I would put that exciting information to any practical use.

"But, Beely," Marie cried, "what on earth did you say to Monsieur Collins?" For some reason it didn't bother me that she called me Beely. The opposite. I wondered why, remembering how upset I was when Dee called me Billy. Maybe the French accent. Or the dancing black eyes. Or the dazzling smile. Or the pert nose. Or the perfume. I don't know.

"I just said okay. What else could I do?"

"How were you able to write theese report about the cabbawges?" Her eyes widened. She waited expectantly, as though the most important news in the world was about to be announced.

"Well, I decided to go to the Department library and check out the 1940 Cabbage Crop Report, and start from there."

"But, Beely, that was brilliant. Then what?" She held her breath, the even row of white teeth clamped on her lower lip.

"Well, I decided it would be unusually dry next year in the Pacific Coast states. So I reduced the 1941 crop by fifteen percent. Then I predicted fabulous weather in the northeast, the kind that any intelligent cabbage would have to love, and increased the crop by fifteen percent over 1940. My crystal ball then told me that the growing conditions would be about the same in the southwest as last year, and so no significant change in production. However," I said, "I regret to inform you that abnormally insidious outbreaks of the yellows and club root will do their dirty work in the Midwest, reducing the crop by twenty percent in that region. But you and the rest of the world will be happy to know that the south should be about the same cabbage-wise in 1941 as it was in 1940."

Marie clapped her hands. "Bravo, Beely. You are a genius."

She raised her glass in salute and took a sip.

"Or maybe more like God," she said.

"Well, thanks," I said. "Could I have another splash?"

Marie stretched back and grabbed the decanter from the side table. I couldn't help noticing how her blouse tightened across her breasts, and how the tiny nipples pressed against the white fabric. Maybe I was getting tipsy.

She poured out the wine and replaced the bottle on the table. With the same effect. Marie turned back toward me, her face flushed, her eyes alight.

"Did you actually write about theese fabulous vegetable?"

"Wrote the report and submitted it to a bunch of stuffed shirts sitting around a huge oak table in an even huger conference room," I replied.

"What did those important people say to you? Were they happy with your predictions?"

"Well, yes. But you'll never believe what happened. I was told to show up at three o'clock, which I did. I walked in and stood at attention in front of those big shots. All of them were staring at copies of my report. It was really scary. The head man said they read the report and were happy with it. What a relief. But then, as I was about to leave, one of the guys told me in a real stern voice to wait a minute."

Marie gasped. "Was something wrong?"

"I thought the cat was out of the bag. All my cabbage predictions were going to be shot down in flames. I just held my breath and waited. Maybe prayed."

Marie edged anxiously toward me. "But what did the old gentleman say?"

"Well, all he said was something about every time Mr. Creelman made a comparison between 1941 and 1940, he said 'compared to.' He should have said 'compared with.'" I swallowed my drink. "And that was it," I said triumphantly. "I promised to make those important changes, and I was out of there in two seconds. Happy to be alive."

"Oh Beely, you are magnifique! Vive le cabbawge!" With those inspiring words, she leaned over, kissed me smack on the lips, then rushed into the kitchen, leaving my heart beating like I'd just run six times around the bases.

I couldn't shake that episode from my mind during the next few months, and I wondered more than once if I was falling for Marie. I kept seeing that smile and feeling that kiss when I should have been thinking about my work. On a couple of occasions, Mr. Collins looked at me real funny, and asked if I was okay after he had to explain an assignment two or three times. What was the matter with me? Every time a girl treated me nice, I seemed to think I was in love with her. God knows, she really was too old for me. And married. To Paul. Whom I liked a lot. And who liked me. Even if he did sort of drive me nuts talking about the war in Europe, he was a nice guy, and didn't seem to mind the way Marie made a big fuss over me. At least I hoped not. But she made me nervous.

I felt like a heel, but I did try to avoid being alone with Marie, especially when Paul was home, which he often was. Instead of joining her on the couch, I mumbled an excuse about not feeling well, or having to meet some of my vegetable colleagues to play poker. Fred Todd lived in a shack on the banks of the Potomac River just above Key Bridge, where we gathered on numerous occasions to play five-card stud and consume quantities of beer from a barrel furnished by our host. And so poker had been a fairly legitimate excuse.

Marie quickly sensed my standoffishness and resented it, I was sure of that, because often there would be a chill in the air when I got home from the office even if Paul was still at work. Instead of greeting me enthusiastically the way she used to, there were times when she barely spoke, or she disappeared upstairs without saying a word. Just a nasty look. Once in awhile, like when we were at breakfast Sunday morning, I'd turn my head toward her suddenly and catch her staring at me. Her face would turn red, and she'd jump from the table and head for the kitchen, muttering in French, no doubt some choice expletives intended for me. Banging of pans would often follow.

So I was startled when I got home from work one Friday evening about an hour later than usual to be greeted by Marie at the open door, wearing a blue satin robe over what looked to me like pink silk pajamas. Her face was flushed, her eyes lit up like 100 watt bulbs, her tantalizing curls held in place by a blue ribbon. She'd been at the wine bottle. No doubt about that.

"Paul was called to New York theese afternoon," she announced. "Very important beesiness. Something to do with the Free French. He's been going crazy trying to get into the action, as he calls it. Moi, I call it keeling. But I can't seem to talk him out of commeeting suicide." She drew me through the door. "But let's forget about him. He won't be back 'til tomorrow."

"Whuh, whuh, whuh," was all I could say.

"I'm cooking a beautiful French meal for you, Beely. We will be alone together. Vous et moi." She pouted. "I'm tired of you being mean to Marie." She unbuttoned my jacket. "Take theese thing off, and loosen your tie."

"Whuh, whuh, whuh," I barely managed to gasp again.

"Oh, relax, Beely. I'm not going to eat you for dinner." With those words, she patted my cheek, whirled and disappeared into the kitchen, where she started rattling dishes, leaving me standing in a daze, like I'd been pounded on the head.

"You can freshen up if you want," she called out. "Then we'll have a cozy veesit."

I stumbled up the stairs to my room, my head spinning. And I hadn't had anything to drink. What was going to happen? Was Marie going to try to seduce me? I was twenty-two years old, and, although Erwin Redding would never have believed it, still a virgin. What a stupid word. Virgin. All I could think of when I heard or saw the word was a woman. Specifically, the Virgin Mary. How could a man be a virgin? I'd never come close to losing my virginity, if that was the word to use. Maybe a few wild thoughts about Dee and Betty. Wondering what it would be like to...I hated the descriptions used all the time by bragging guys in bull sessions. Dozens of obscene words and phrases.

I read in novels about people turning hot and cold, then hot again. For a few seconds I was sure I was going to pass out. Then I thought I'd just stay in my room. Hide out until tomorrow morning. Or maybe sneak down the stairs and through the front door while Marie busied herself in the kitchen. Walk to Georgetown and grab something to eat there.

"Beely. Beely. What ever are you doing up there? My coq au vin will be ruined. And the champagne will get too warm." Marie's impatient voice floated up the stairs.

Coq au vin! Champagne! God!

I rushed into the bathroom and took a look at myself in the mirror. Wild, frantic eyes stared back. I ran my hand through my hair which was practically standing on end, then filled the sink with cold water, and immersed my head completely until I ran out of breath. After wiping my face, I shut my eyes and started counting to ten.

"Beely Creelman. What in the world are you doing?"

She was there. In the doorway. Hands on hip, eyebrows raised, lips compressed. The look on my face must have told her something about my state of mind. I don't know. Anyway, she flashed a smile, grabbed my hand, and pulled me out of the bathroom, down the stairs into the small dining room, through the French doors leading to the screened porch, and pushed me down on the sofa. Although it was mid-November, the air was balmy, like Indian summer. The aroma of burning leaves in front of the neighbor's house confirmed that fall had arrived; Thanksgiving was not too far away. I had lots to be thankful for. Except Spike was dead. I'd never forget him. And I had the Army to worry about.

"We'll have our champagne here," she announced.

I started to struggle to my feet.

"No. Just sit and relax."

Relax?

Marie swished back to the kitchen, her satin robe brushing against my knees as she went by. She reappeared twenty seconds later, walking carefully, clutching a small silver tray on which she balanced an open bottle and two glasses nearly filled with an amber fluid. "Pouilly Fuisse, Beely, the finest French champagne one can get in theese country nowadays. Paul's been hording six bottles for special occasions. He won't mind if we steal one leetle bottle from his treasure."

"God, I hope he never finds out," I mumbled, more to myself than to Marie. But no use dwelling on that possibility. Instead, I focused my fascinated attention on the hundreds of bubbles streaming upwards from the stems of the glasses and breaking the surfaces of this exciting fluid.

"A votre sante, my cher Beely." Marie extended her glass. I did likewise. They gave off a delightfully ringing ting as they made contact. She smiled as she sipped, her dark eyes seeming to bore clear through me. The fuzzy liquid felt alive as it passed over my tongue and down my throat. So this was champagne. Its romantic reputation was more than deserved. I emptied my glass and instinctively held it out to her.

"Only one more for you," she said, as she poured a refill. "Not too fast. Champagne must be cherished. Like a special lover."

I felt myself warming up again.

"And we're having burgundy with our coq au vin," she continued. "I want my Beely to enjoy every tiny theeng."

Enjoy everything I did. A four-course meal. First, white radishes and sweet butter. Next, the promised coq au vin, attended by fresh garden peas and thinly-sliced fried potatoes, washed down with two glasses of burgundy, followed by an endive salad with romaine lettuce and a creamy sauce. I wouldn't have admitted it to Marie, but I enjoyed her home-made rolls the most. She complained that she couldn't get the kind of flour she used in France. "Because of theese horreeble war," she explained. But the rolls were as crunchy and tasty as the best Mom ever made on the farm.

When I swallowed the last delicious morsel, I started to rise, holding on to my empty plate.

"Non, non, non." Marie exclaimed. "You weel not enter my kitchen. Just sit. I'll bring the creme brule and demitasses and then we'll have a liqueur to help digest our food."

Crème brûle. Demitasse. Liqueur. Those weren't even English words. I wondered what Mom and Dad and Uncle Dan would think if they knew how I feasted tonight. And with a fascinating and sexy French lady who couldn't seem to do enough to make me happy.

I'm not sure what I expected would happen after we polished off the creme brule, which must have been made in heaven, sipped our demitasses, and consumed tiny glasses of a liqueur called Drambuie, which tasted like I imagined gasoline must taste but did leave a warm spot in the pit of my stomach. By that time my vision blurred and my tongue became twisted, and I'm sure that most of what I

was saying or trying to say to Marie probably made no sense
at all to her. After much yacking about the little dairy farm
in Harford County, and what a wonderful friend Spike was,
and how he was the best friend I ever had, and bragging
how I pitched Cornell to three winning baseball seasons, and
spouting out some mournful tales about Dee and Betty that
I can't remember, Marie dragged me from the dining room
table to the screen porch, where we sat on the sofa, and
then she started in talking. Getting back at me, I guess. In
fact, it seemed to me like she never did stop jabbering. All
about growing up and attending a convent school in a place
not far from Paris called Soissons—she had to spell it for
me— how she met Paul while visiting Algiers after finishing
school, how he was posted to that exotic North African town
for five years and was just completing his tour of duty in
some diplomatic position for the French government, and
how they ran off to Paris and lived together until six months
before war started in Europe, then were married by a justice,
and how the generals and political bigwigs kept promising
everything was going to be okay because the Germans could
never ever break through the Maginot line, but that turned
out to be a bunch of boolooney (as she called it) when the
Germans bypassed that useless fortress and swept through
the Ardennes Forest into The Netherlands and Belgium,
where the horreeble panzer divisions and Stuka bombers
proceeded to pulverize everything in front of them. Her two
brothers, Philippe and Louis, were captured by the pig Boche
and probably were dead. Her mother and father still lived
in Soissons, in occupied France, probably starving to death.
She and Paul managed to escape to Calais, then depleted
nearly all their cash to persuade the owner of a battered
and leaky fishing vessel to transport them across the
English Channel to Southampton. Then Paul, because of his
diplomatic experience, was able to organize a Free French
group in London, and after a couple of months, the two of
them were sent to Washington, where Paul spent most of
his time pestering politicians, trying to get the United States
into the war. He even attended a meeting at the White House
with President Roosevelt, although forty or fifty others were
there and he never got to speak to the President. And on and
on and on.

    Her low, intense, hypnotic voice finally sent met into a
trance, in which I imagined I was urging President Roosevelt

to give more destroyers to Great Britain, and maybe make Paul an admiral in the U.S. Navy. Then Falla showed up, violently tugging at a red-and-black-plaid leash Mrs. Roosevelt struggled to hold on to. I was patting the little Scottish terrier, and telling the President and Mrs. Roosevelt about Spike, and what a smart dog he was, when, suddenly, I was aware that someone was shaking my shoulder and calling my name.

"Beely. Beely. Are you awake? Did I put you to sleep?"

My eyes popped open. Marie peered down at me. Why was her head rotating slowly in full circles? And why did she have four eyes? I started to rise, but fell back, my legs too wobbly to stand.

"My poor Beely," she said. "I'll have to get you to bed."

It vaguely crossed my mind that this was it. Bye-bye virginity.

But I needn't have worried. If I was worried. Later, I was kind of disappointed. Marie hauled me to my feet and led me to my room, where she pulled back the covers and sat me down on the side of the bed. She unlaced my shoes, pulled them off, kissed the top of my head, turned off the light, whispered "Bon nuit, cher Beely," and was gone.

CHAPTER 18

"A telegram for you, Monsieur Bill." The voice was that of Paul Michel. The day was Sunday. The time was 10 o'clock in the morning. I stayed sprawled out in bed nearly all of Saturday after my adventures of the night before, with Marie fussing around me, straightening the bed covers, replenishing the ice bag, and plying me with aspirin and hot coffee every two hours, acting like a nurse and not the lover I fancied she was going to be.

Paul returned from New York in mid-afternoon on Saturday. Things must have gone well with him in New York. He radiated good humor. Marie had tried to wangle some information out of him about his New York meetings, with no success. "Secret business," was all he'd say. But his enigmatic smile upset Marie, I could tell. "Paul's going to get into theese fight if it keels him. And it probably weel," she moaned while adjusting the ice bag on my throbbing forehead.

The wiry little Frenchman with typically Gallic features and fierce mustache thrust the brown envelope under my nose. I was seated in the breakfast room overlooking Glover Park. It was a beautiful morning. I guess. I couldn't be sure, being only half-awake and still the worse for wear. As I stared at the envelope, I wondered for a second if Paul had the notion that something was going on between Marie and me. But then I thought, they are French. And I heard and read that the French had pretty loose ideas about married people messing around. So perhaps he didn't care. Or maybe he knew his wife well enough to figure that the last thing in the world she wanted was a fling with me. Anyway, nothing had happened between Marie and me. Almost, maybe. But I wasn't even sure of that.

The telegram was from the Western Union office in Philadelphia. Dated November 16, 1941. I glanced at the name at the bottom. Erwin. Why would he be sending me a telegram? I read it.

```
BILL.  JUST HEARD ON RADIO U.S. NAVY
OFFERING ADMINISTRATIVE NAVAL RESERVE
ENSIGNS COMMISSIONS TO RECENT COLLEGE
GRADUATES.  APPLY NAVAL HEADQUARTERS NAVY
YARD WASHINGTON.  GOOD LUCK. ERWIN
```

"Wow!" I couldn't help shouting.

"Q'est-ce que c'est? Bill," Paul at times rattled off French expressions even though he spoke English better than I did, and knew I didn't understand his language. I did figure this question out, though.

"Wow! Wow! Wow!" was all I could manage in response.

Marie looked in from the kitchen, where she was rustling up fried eggs and sausages.

"Beely, what is theese wow business? What is theese important messawge?"

I could only grin like a Cheshire cat, so she rushed over and snatched the telegram out of my hand. Her brow furrowed as she read. Then she looked up with a frown. "Does theese mean you may be leaving us? I wouldn't like that. Non. Not one bit."

I glanced hastily at Paul. He didn't seem concerned about that remark. Just reached over and grabbed the telegram from Marie. He read it twice. "Well, Monsieur Bill," he said,. "this may be the break you've been looking for. I'll drive you to the Navy Yard tomorrow. The sooner the better."

"I'd better check in with my office first," I said. "They may not want me to take the time off."

"Bull sheet, if you'll pardon my French," Paul snorted. The Navy Yard is going to be mobbed with applicants when the word gets out. Get your derriere down there demain. Tomorrow. Au plus vite!"

Paul was as good as his word, rousting me out of bed at 7 o'clock the next morning. Usually Marie cooked our breakfast, always cheerful, full of energy and sparkling conversation. But not this morning. A feeling of disappointment crept over me. I really wanted and needed her encouragement this fateful morning. Paul drove the white 1940 Dodge sedan down Foxhall Road, through Georgetown, heading for 8th and M streets, in the southeast part of Washington, the location of the Navy Yard. "Did you know, Bill," he said as we rounded Dupont Circle, barely avoiding crashing into a streetcar headed the wrong way, "that the Navy Yard is the oldest Navy facility in your country?"

I guessed he was trying to take my mind off my worries. Might as well go along with it, so I said I wasn't aware of that interesting bit of information.

"Oh, yes," he went on, kind of smug, I thought, "the father of your country ordered it to be established. Many of your famous ships were built there before the War of 1812."

"I didn't know that," I was forced to reply. Embarrassed. It crossed my mind that Paul knew more about American history than I did, and I knew nothing about French history. I was full of information about vegetables, though.

"Oh, yes," he said again. "I did a lot of reading and talking to my American friends about your country when I worked in Algiers. Your countrymen were my best friends."

Now I was really getting irritated.

"And the Navy gun factory was established in the yard in the 1880's, and has produced many, many guns of all sizes for U.S. warships." Well, the history lesson went on for the entire trip. I learned more about John Paul Jones than I really cared to know, even though he was the first American Navy hero. And, after all, I did hope to join the Navy. We finally reached the entrance to the Navy Yard on M Street. I sat frozen. Fearful. Afraid to get out of the car.

"Come on, Bill," Paul urged, "you don't want to be late." He patted my shoulder. "You'll do fine."

A Marine sentry stood stiffly at attention at the entrance to the yard, saluting smartly as several cars driven by uniformed Navy officers passed through the ancient arched gate.

"Why don't you ask him where you should go?"

I did, and I received directions in a courteous manner to the "Administration Building, right over there, the one with the white columns. Proceed to room 102 on the first floor, Lieutenant Gullickson's office. The office opens at zero eight hundred, sir."

Sir! That really bucked me up. I could just feel those ensign's bars. Zero eight hundred must mean 8 o'clock. Ten minutes from now. Trying to look like the officer I hoped to be, I squared my shoulders and strode down the street, up the concrete steps between the columns, and into the building. A second Marine, seated at a small table, answered my inquiry by pointing to a sign jutting from an office door about twenty feet down a wide corridor covered with brown linoleum. The sign read "POTOMAC RIVER NAVAL COMMAND ADMINISTRATION." I rattled the doorknob. Locked. But at least I was the only applicant. Or was I? For just at that moment, a guy who looked to be about my age hurried through the front door of the building and spoke to the Marine, who gave him some kind of reply and pointed in my direction.

Competition. He was bound to be on the same mission I was on. As he headed my way, I gave the interloper the once-over. A skinny guy about 5 feet 9 inches tall, he couldn't have weighed more than 125 pounds. But, nevertheless, his close-cropped brown hair, square jaw, and aquiline nose gave him a distinct military appearance. As he drew near, I was struck by his jet-black eyes. I was glad I wore my almost-new gray suit and had acceded to Marie's plea before going to bed last night to "wear a white shirt and tie, Beely; you have to make a good impression to get into theese Navy," because my rival, or so I thought of him, was neatly turned out in a dark, pinstriped suit, white shirt, and red-and-blue-striped necktie. (University of Pennsylvania colors) I softened my instinctive hostile feelings a bit when he smiled broadly and held out his hand.

"Hi, I'm George Dugan. You're probably headed for Lieutenant Gullickson's office just like me."

I couldn't help smiling back as I grabbed his hand, which was large, firm and calloused. Maybe a farm boy too. "Yeah," I said. "My name's Bill Creelman. I just heard about this deal yesterday, and I'm hoping the news hasn't spread too far."

"Me too." George sighed. "I've tried every damn way possible to beat the damn draft, except slicing my damn wrists, and this may be my last chance."

I couldn't help laughing. "Join the club. I know this is my last chance."

"I just gotta get in the damn Navy," he muttered. "Gotta. I practically grew up on the damn water. Been around boats all my damn life. The damn Army will kill me."

"I don't know the front end from the rear of a boat," I said, "but the Navy sounds a hell of a lot better than the Army."

A long silence followed. He probably wondered, as did I, who would be the first to apply for an ensign's commission.

I was here before him, and my name began with a C and his with a D. So, logically, I should go first. My thoughts were interrupted by George's voice.

"Look, Bill," he said, "you were here first, so why don't you go in ahead of me. I'll wait a few seconds and follow."

His generous offer softened me up. Again. This guy should be a diplomat. I thought for a moment, then had an idea. "Let's toss a coin." I fished a quarter from the pocket of my jacket and, without waiting for a possible objection, flipped the coin in the air, caught it with my right hand, slapped it down on the back of my left hand and covered it. "Heads or tails?"

George pursed his lips. "That's damn nice of you, but I wouldn't feel right if I won the toss."

"No, go on! Call it," I urged. "It probably won't make any difference in the long run which of us goes in first."

"Well." He hesitated. "I usually call heads and win, so I'll call tails."

I uncovered the coin. The overhead neon light shown down on the American Eagle.

"Tails it is," I said. As I backed down the corridor a few feet, the office door was flung open. A young man dressed in a blue sailor's uniform— I guess he was a bluejacket— peered out at George. "Come in, sir," the sailor said. "If your applying for a commission in the Naval Reserve, Lieutenant Gullickson will see you right away."

George turned, winked, gave me a thumbs up, and disappeared from my view. I looked anxiously down the corridor toward the Marine guarding the front door, fervently hoping no one else would show up and possibly push ahead of me. But all was clear. I waited a minute or so, then entered the Administration office. The sailor sat behind a desk, cluttered with file folders and loose papers. A tag on his blouse identified him as B.F. Stubbs, Yeoman First Class. I hoped he wasn't occupied with applications for ensigns' commissions. Behind him I spied a closed door with the name R. J. Gullickson painted in black on the frosted glass. Yeoman First Class Stubbs rose as I entered.

"I'd like to apply for a commission in the Naval Reserves," I said as boldly as I could.

"Well, your at the right station." Stubbs smiled. He seemed friendly. "You'll have to wait. Lieutenant Gullickson has just started interviewing another applicant." He pointed to an upright wooden chair. "Please have a seat."

I sat down, wishing I hadn't been so weak-minded as to let George go ahead of me. Especially after he suggested that I go first. But there must be more than one commission to be handed out. So I decided to relax. At least try.

"You can save some time by filling out this application form while you wait, sir." Stubbs handed me a pencil and a two-page form entitled "Application for Commission in U.S. Naval Reserve." "Just fill in the blanks in pencil, and I'll type a smooth copy."

The simplicity of the form surprised me, considering what was at stake. My future, as they say, hung in the balance, to go one way or the other depending on the decision of a Lieutenant R.J. Gullickson, whom I'd never even heard of until a few minutes ago. Either a buck private in the Army or an officer in the United States Navy. With a gold stripe. Either life in the mud or life on the ocean.

And then it suddenly crossed my mind that I knew nothing about ships or anything else connected with the Navy. I'd never even been in a canoe. I couldn't swim a stroke. No swimming pools on the farm. I'd probably get as sick as a dog the moment I stepped aboard a Navy vessel. What was I thinking?

But I couldn't retreat now. So I studied the form for a few minutes, then methodically began filling in the blanks. Just as I handed the completed document to Stubbs, the door to Lieutenant Gullickson's office opened. George shut the door behind him, then stood there, staring at the floor, frowning. He did not look happy.

"How did it go?" I asked anxiously.

"Well, it went okay up to a point." He paused. "Only thing Lieutenant Gullickson questioned was my damn weight. I have to weigh at least 135 pounds, and I know damn well I'm barely within ten pounds of that."

George sighed. "And I've got to return in two weeks for a damn physical examination. If I pass, I'm in. If I don't, I'm out." Then the infectious grin appeared. "Mama Dugan has to beef up her little boy. If anyone can do it, she can." He reached out, and we shook hands. "Good luck," he said. "I'll probably see you back here in a couple of weeks."

"I think we can work up a commission for you."

Lieutenant Gullickson smiled at me.

Was I dreaming?

He studied my application, put a couple of questions to me about my general health and my ROTC training at Cornell, asked me to step on the scales in the corner of the room, and then uttered those magical words. Lieutenant Gullickson stood and held out his hand. "Report back here two weeks from today at 0800," he said. "We'll put you through a thorough physical. Meanwhile we'll check out the references you gave us."

I shook hands. Then, emboldened by his friendliness, I asked when I might have to report for duty if everything went well. I explained that I'd have to give my boss some kind of notice that I was leaving the Department.

Lieutenant Gullikson glanced up at a wall calendar. "Well, two weeks from today is 1 December. Things will move pretty fast after that. My best guess is that you'd be ordered to report to headquarters, Potomac River Naval Command on or about Monday, 15 December. Headquarters are in the building next door," he added.

I mumbled my thanks, opened the door and entered the outer office. Stubbs was busily signing a stack of papers. He didn't look up as I passed by him and slipped into the corridor, still dazed by the sudden turn of events.

CHAPTER 19

"Beely, why don't you take a walk? Do something theese lovely Sunday afternoon. Don't just lie there on the couch listening to a seely football game. Come on, put on your topcoat. I'll go with you."

Marie was right, of course. The day was gorgeous, the sun shining brightly. Just the kind of day to be outdoors. And it would be fun to walk with her. I didn't care who won the stupid game. Two professional football teams, the Washington Redskins and the Philadelphia Eagles, were playing in Griffith Stadium, the home of the Washington Senators, my favorite sports team nowadays. The only football game that aroused any interest in me was the annual Thanksgiving Day game between Cornell and the University of Pennsylvania, always played in Franklin Field in Philadelphia. I managed to get to one game my senior year at Cornell, along with more than 75,000 screaming fans. Cornell's football team had astonished the sports world in 1939 and 1940 by being voted either number one or number two among all college football teams in the country.

I'd been as jumpy as a cat on a hot tin roof ever since being sworn in as an ensign in the U.S. Naval Reserve, waiting for December 15, one week from tomorrow, when, as predicted by Lieutenant Gullickson, I was ordered to report for "such mobilization assignment as determined by the Commandant, Navy Yard, Washington, D.C." I was impressed to read that my orders were issued at the direction of Admiral C.W. Nimitz, Chief of the Bureau of Naval Personnel. Exactly what assignment the Commandant of the Navy Yard had in mind was unknown to me. Certainly not sea duty, with my total lack of experience. Anyway, I was almost sure that no U.S. Navy ships were attached to the Navy Yard.

When I showed no interest in Marie's sensible suggestion, she made a little face, stuck her tongue out, and hurried upstairs where she and Paul had been sorting out and organizing his Free French files. Paul had become more and more active in distributing Free French propaganda, and also

more and more distressed as the horrible news of German
and Italian aggression continued to pour in from Europe.
He frequently cursed the Senators and Congressmen he
called "pig-headed isolationists," who were determined to let
England fight alone, always backing up their view by quoting
George Washington's ancient warning to avoid "entangling
alliances," as if even that great man could have figured that
no one like a murdering Hitler would come along more than
150 years later to threaten the whole world.

I kept telling myself I did not want to fight in any war.
But then I wondered. What would it be like to have a bunch
of German thugs ordering this country around? Killing Jews.
Throwing innocent civilians into prison camps. I tried to
concentrate on the radio announcer's description of the game,
but my attention soon wandered. I didn't know which team
was winning and didn't care. I finally shut my eyes and smiled,
recalling how pleased I was to bump into George Dugan at
my swearing in ceremony, which consisted of signing a paper
accepting the appointment as an Ensign in the Naval Reserve
and swearing to support and defend the Constitution of the
United States against all enemies, foreign and domestic. He'd
already completed his papers, and, as soon as he caught sight
of me, announced that he was now an ensign in the United
States Naval Reserve.

"I probably will outrank you," George had said, laughing up
a storm. And then, grinning from ear to ear and bubbling over
with enthusiasm, he related in gory detail the trouble he'd had
reaching the minimum required weight for his acceptance in
the Naval Reserve. "Damn, it was a close call!" he exclaimed.
"All the credit goes to dear old Mom. She really came through,
even though she hates the thought of her little boy going into
the service and off to the damn war. I had exactly two damn
weeks to gain about ten pounds. She stoked me with food
and drink swarming with calories. Two eggs in a glass of
Cocomalt three times a day. At least six damn bananas a day.
All kinds of miserable fattening foods. On the day when I had
to step on those damn scales, I started drinking water as soon
as I woke up. Mom drove me to the Navy Yard, and I polished
off a quart of water from a damn thermos bottle on the way.
When I got to the Administration Building, I drank from the
water fountain until my damn tonsils started floating."

George had reflected on his great adventure. "Thank
God," he continued, "when I got to the Administration Office,

the first thing they asked me to do was step on the scales. If I waited any longer, I'd have started peeing and flooded the damn joint."

George had paused for effect, his eyes gleaming. "ONE HUNDRED AND THIRTY- SIX POUNDS," he shouted. "A pound to spare."

"How in the world did you get through the rest of the physical examination?" I marveled.

"Oh, I told the doctor that I had to go to the head and asked to be excused." George laughed. "There was no problem. I stood at the damn urinal for about ten minutes, or so it seemed. I drained my damn bladder, and then I waited and drained it again. What a relief. But..." Another grin. "It was worth it. And guess what," he announced, "I've been ordered to the Local Defense School in Boston to report no later than December 8 for training for sea duty. God, I'm so damn excited. What a break."

I pondered that surprising news as the radio announcer proclaimed the end of the first quarter of the game. George getting training for sea duty, and me getting assigned to the Navy Yard. A shore-based bastard. I'd heard that expression. Couldn't remember where or when. I didn't like it. No. Not a damn bit, to use George's favorite adjective. I finally managed to doze off. I was between sleep and awake when the radio announcer's voice, loud and excited dragged me back to the real world.

"Ladies and gentlemen, we interrupt this broadcast to report that the White House has just issued a bulletin stating that just before 2 o'clock Eastern Standard Time the United States Navy installation at Pearl Harbor was attacked by Japanese torpedo and dive bombers. The extent of damage to warships and the number of casualties are unknown at this time. We will inform you of further details when additional information becomes available." I sat up as though I'd been hit by a bolt of lightning. Pearl Harbor. I'd never heard of any place called Pearl Harbor. I rushed to the foot of the stairs. "Marie! Paul!" I shouted, "the guy on the radio just said that the Japanese have bombed Pearl Harbor."

They were down the stairs in a flash and dashed to the radio. But all we heard was that the Eagles were on the Redskins' ten-yard line, first down. "Those idiots," Paul growled, "talking about a miserable football game when the whole world may be caving in."

"Maybe they don't know anything more," Marie suggested.

"Then why don't they find out?" Now Paul paced the floor, running his hand through his hair, jerking on his mustache. In a frenzy.

"Where is Pearl Harbor?" I asked.

"It's in Alaska, I believe," Marie ventured. "At least I theenk so."

"Non! Non! That's Dutch Harbor. Maybe the Philippine Islands." Paul screamed in exasperation. He strode into his study and flipped through the huge *Webster's International Dictionary* that lay open on his desk. Marie and I hung in the doorway, hardly daring to breathe. Paul stopped turning pages, then ran his finger down a column of words. He seemed to freeze. His face turned white. Then red.

"My God! Pearl Harbor's in Hawaii. Oahu. How did those yellow bastards get that far from Tokyo?"

Hawaii. I thought. Thousands of miles from Japan. How did they do it? And without warning.

"Ladies and gentlemen."

We rushed back to the radio.

"The White House has just announced that losses of warships and naval personnel at Pearl Harbor from a surprise Japanese attack which included low-level bombing and strafing is severe. Hickam Field and Ford Island have also been heavily bombed and strafed, with substantial losses of aircraft and military personnel. All officers at or above the ranks of commander in the Navy and Coast Guard, and lieutenant colonel in the Army and Marine Corps have been ordered by the President to proceed immediately to their stations."

"Your country is at war!" Paul shouted, his eyes nearly jumping out of their sockets. For a few seconds I thought he was going to cry. He sat down slowly on the couch and reduced the volume of the radio. Now his eyes were really on fire. Like he'd gone temporarily crazy. But he spoke quietly, his voice quivering. "This is a great day for France, Marie and Bill. A great day for England. A great day for the world." He paused and stared at the ceiling. Then spoke again. Exultantly. "December 7, 1941, is the beginning of the end for the Nazi butcher and his Fascist jackal."

CHAPTER 20

Throughout the night and into the next morning, a fever of excitement and apprehension swept the country, particularly the residents of the West Coast. Rumors of doom and destruction abounded. The Pacific fleet was gone. Obliterated. Hundreds of aircraft were lost or damaged beyond repair. The Hawaiian Islands were defenseless. Jap infantry and tanks were pouring onto the beaches of the Big Island. The Aleutians had been invaded. Enemy aircraft carriers had launched an attack on San Francisco. Scores of planes with the rising sun insignia on their wings, the dreaded Zeros, had been spotted headed toward Seattle. So the rumors swirled and expanded.

There was good cause to worry about the Japanese onslaught, when almost overnight Guam had been occupied by Japanese troops, and Great Britain's supposedly unsinkable battleship, the Prince of Wales, and the battle cruiser Repulse had been sunk after repeated bombing attacks, with the loss of hundreds of British sailors and the loss of an enormous amount of prestige by the British Navy.

All the news was not bad as far as Paul was concerned, for he became delirious with joy when, within a few days following the Pearl Harbor disaster, Germany and Italy declared war on the United States, and the United States declared war on Germany and Italy. "France will rise again! Vive La France!" he kept shouting. Then Marie and I would be subjected to repeated phonographic renditions of the Marseillaise.

I was swept up with his enthusiasm and the wildly angry radio broadcasts and news accounts. I couldn't wait to go after those "yellow-bellied bastards." But I was forced to wait. "No, no, you needn't report until December 15 as previously ordered." So Lieutenant Gullickson had responded to my telephoned patriotic offer to report for duty to the Commandant of the Navy Yard on the day following the date that President Roosevelt had proclaimed to the world would live in infamy.

A bit of a letdown. I guess the war effort would have to get along without me. At least for a week. And so I went about the business of complying with the required dress code. Blue, white, and khaki uniforms; ensign's bars and shoulder boards; a visored hat with blue, white, and khaki covers; two black neckties; six white shirts; six pairs of black socks; and a pair of black shoes. All paid for out of a uniform allowance provided by the United States government. To top it off, I became the proud owner of a sword. With "Ensign William Creelman" etched on the steel blade. I couldn't imagine ever wielding it in battle. But just possessing that elegant weapon made me feel like an officer. And a gentleman.

Marie nearly swooned, or pretended to, when I paraded around the living room in my blue uniform with the single broad gold stripe and a gold star on each sleeve. "You are so handsome, Beely!" she kept exclaiming. "The ladies will adore you."

I tried to explain that my purpose in wearing the uniform was not to attract girls, but I did feel kind of excited by her unrestrained enthusiasm.

And so off to war I went. Not romantically as it occurs in the Hornblower books, where the newly commissioned ensign spots his ship gracefully riding at anchor in the harbor, is then propelled across the water by able-bodied seamen in a long boat, the salt spray stinging his face and flushing his cheeks, and is piped aboard as he climbs the ladder to the quarterdeck to salute the colors. My far-from-nautical conveyances were a streetcar and bus, which deposited me at the Navy Yard gate. I will say that, to my huge gratification, the Marine sentry snapped to attention and saluted smartly as I strode through the arches. My ROTC experience at Cornell came in handy. I did know how to salute and return a salute. Also, although I wouldn't have admitted it to anyone, I practiced before the full-length mirror in my bedroom.

It didn't take long after reporting to the office of the Commandant of the Navy Yard for disillusionment to set in. I don't know what I expected, with no naval experience or training, but I did not expect to be the Assistant Personnel Officer of the Receiving Station at the Navy Yard. I didn't even know what a Receiving Station was, but I soon learned that it "received," "processed," then "shipped out" sailors to U.S. Navy establishments far more directly connected with the war effort than the station to which Ensign William Creelman had been assigned.

The Receiving Station headquarters were in a four-story, yellow brick building, probably erected shortly after what was now referred to as the first World War. In a one-story structure across the street were located the ship service store, a barbershop, a dry-cleaning establishment, and a cafeteria, all operated either by enlisted personnel or civilians, and theoretically under my direct supervision.

The offices in the main building were small and crowded with furniture. In my exalted position, I shared a room with Chief "China" Dalton, an old salt with thinning gray hair, who walked with a limp. Hash marks on the sleeves of his uniform showed he'd served at least thirty years. I figured I now knew what the term "weather-beaten" meant, because he surely fit that description. He greeted my arrival on the scene as his "superior" with raised eyebrows, I'm sure, but soon became a great friend and advisor. When I first met him, I "sirred" him. I learned later that he served on the China station during the 1930s.

My work as Assistant Personnel Officer was tedious and boring. I spent hours briefly scanning orders directed to enlisted men, then signing my name in spaces designated with check marks by Chief Dalton. Once a week I "inspected" the facilities across the street, not having the foggiest notion of what I was doing or how I would detect any possible inadequacies. My demoralization was intensified by the unfortunate fact that my immediate superior was a horse's ass, and of no help to me whatsoever in my efforts to learn something about my various assignments. In fact, the opposite. Although only himself a reserve lieutenant junior grade, one rank above ensign, Mr. Fraley acted toward me and other subordinates as though he was Admiral of the Fleet. Mean. Vicious. Nasty. Snide. Malicious. Those were only a handful of the printable descriptive terms, usually followed by the word "bastard," used by any individual, civilian or naval, having the misfortune of serving under this misfit.

Mr. Fraley took great delight in pointing out the slightest error or deficiency that caught his attention, first chewing out the unlucky perpetrator then gleefully taking me to task in the privacy of his office for not having detected the flaw, no matter how trivial. It galled me that I had to take his petty criticisms lying down. But that was the Navy. Or so I thought at the time.

The frustration and disgust of all were magnified upon witnessing how Mr. Fraley sucked up to his superior officers. "Look at that shit-eating grin!" I overheard Chief Dalton mutter to himself, as Mr. Fraley greeted the arrival in our office of the commanding officer of the Receiving Station for some kind of consultation about the operations of the personnel office, from which I was excluded.

Taking pity on me, I guess, after several frustrating months the Chief suggested that perhaps correcting the examination papers of enlisted men seeking increases in ratings would add some variety to my life. "We'll keep it between you and me, sir," the Chief confided. "His royal hind ass would burn my butt if he found out I talked you into lowering yourself to take on this kind of task. And yours, too." he added

I gratefully accepted his offer, which involved plowing through a stack of multiple- choice examinations one day a week. It troubled me to note that I, an officer, could not possibly have passed the examination from seaman to any of the third-class ratings. Maybe that's why I started thinking about becoming a real Navy officer instead of a high-paid clerk all dressed up like one.

For some reason, I can't think why, I decided to learn the International Morse Code. Chief Dalton came to my aid again. He'd been a signalman at some point during his long career and was still an expert at sending and receiving messages by blinker. He dug up an elementary communications manual, and I began to memorize the code. Dit dah (• –) is A; dah dit dit dit (– • • •) is B, and so on through the alphabet to Z, which is dah dah dit dit (– – • •).

After a couple of weeks I felt confident enough to try my skills on the Chief. One evening after the office closed, we armed ourselves with flashlights and commenced sending messages back and forth. I will have to confess that my first message was as follows:

```
  • • – •  • – •  • –  • – • •  •   – • – –
         • •   • • •
              • –
• • • •   – – –   • – •   • • •   •   • • •
         • –   • • •   • • •
```

(FRALEY IS A HORSES ASS)

Chief Dalton grinned, acknowledged receipt of the message (dit dah dit), but did not confirm or deny my opinion.

The blinking-light sessions continued for several more weeks until one evening, after we had a spirited exchange as if between a tanker and a destroyer regarding the problems arising from refueling at sea in heavy weather, the Chief announced, "You're as good at this as I am, sir. No use continuing the lessons." He laid aside his flashlight and wheeled his chair to a metal cabinet against the wall next to the single window of our office. He opened the double doors, reached down and fished out four small flags. "You might as well learn semaphore," he said. "You never know when it will come in handy."

Chief Dalton stood and pointed the flag in his left hand straight down and positioned the other flag 45 degrees to the right. "That's the letter A," he said. He moved the flag in his right hand upward until it extended straight out at a 90-degree angle. "That's B." And we were off again with more lessons, waving our flags at each other every evening for another three weeks, interspersed with blinker communications, just so I wouldn't forget.

After a flag-waving session on a Sunday afternoon, when I had the duty as officer of the day, Chief Dalton reached into his briefcase and pulled out several volumes. The first was a battered copy of the U.S. Navy Regulations. "We call these 'rocks and shoals,'" he solemnly informed me. "Stay clear of them at all times. If you run afoul of these regs, your next stop is a court-martial. You need one of those like a hole in the head. Even if you are acquitted."

He handed me a small blue volume, equally shabby. "The Watch Officer's Guide." "This you won't need unless you're lucky enough to draw sea duty." Chief Dalton sighed. "Something I'll never get again. Too damn old and decrepit." He grinned wryly. "I'm what they call a metallic sailor. Silver in my hair, gold in my teeth, and lead in my ass."

He followed up that profound pronouncement by handing me two larger volumes. "Now these babies will teach you how to navigate a ship anywhere in the world, in channels and harbors, and along the coast where you can see objects to fix your position, and also when you're out of sight of land and need the heavenly bodies to help you figure out where you are." He chuckled. "You'll be lucky if you're within ten miles of your fix, even in good weather."

The large faded brown volume was entitled "American Practical Navigator—Bowditch." A smaller blue volume was entitled "Navigation and Nautical Astronomy—Dutton." My mind boggled as I turned the pages of Bowditch, filled with charts, diagrams, and mathematical formulas, looking for all the world like a trigonometry text. A subject I never mastered in high school and, fortunately for me, not required by the Cornell College of Agriculture. "God, I'll never be able to figure this out," I moaned.

"Well, it's not as bad as it looks," Chief Dalton said. "All the mathematical calculations have been done for you. You just have to learn how to use the tables." He reached over and turned to the back of the book where, sure enough, there were nearly three hundred pages of tables filled with figures.

Chief Dalton crossed the room to his locker and opened the double doors. He pulled out a wooden case, opened it, withdrew a strange-looking instrument, and handed it to me. "If you're going to be a navigator, you gotta know how to use this."

The blank look on my face drew a laugh from the Chief.

"It's a sextant," he said. "It measures the altitude of the sun, the moon, the stars, and the planets." He retrieved the instrument. "Here, let me show you." Chief Dalton walked to the window and raised the sash. The mid-afternoon sun, shining dimly through the haze, hung above the Navy Gun Factory overlooking the ball field, where a company of sailors engaged in close order drill, wheeling and turning to the shouted commands of a Marine sergeant.

"At sea you need a horizon to take a sight," Chief Dalton explained. "You look at the sun or a star through this piece that looks like a telescope, then bring the index arm down until the sun or star touches the horizon in the clear glass on the left. Then you read the degrees through this little mirror, and that tells you the altitude of the celestial body you're looking at. You need at least two star sights to get a fix. Three's preferable. Sun sights are used at sea to get a line of position," he added.

The Chief pointed the sextant out of the window. "I'll bring the sun down to the top of the gun factory," he said. "We'll pretend its the horizon." He moved the index arm down a short distance, then handed the instrument to me. I looked through the telescope, and sure enough, I could see the sun touching the top of the historic brick building.

"God, I'm totally confused as to how this thing works," I said, "and how you can figure out where the hell you are from using this gadget."

Chief Dalton retrieved the sextant, carefully restored it to its case, and placed it on the upper shelf of the cabinet. "You can't figure it out, sitting here. You gotta learn the fundamentals in a training course, then practice what you learned at sea. On a ship."

CHAPTER 21

2 September 1942

Dear Bill:

Wanted to let you know that I've graduated from Local Defense School and am headed next week for Submarine Chaser Training Center in Miami. The training at Local Defense was terrific. We learned the basics of piloting, celestial navigation, gunnery, and communications. Got some "sea duty" out of Boston Harbor on YMSs. The instructors are mostly petty officers who really know their stuff. SCTC, as they call it, is supposed to be much more advanced. We'll get training at sea on subchasers and learn to operate sonar, which is the underwater gizmo used to detect submarines. I'm so damn excited!

You really ought to apply for training at Local Defense. Maybe we'll be shipmates someday.

Regards

George

Well, that really tore it. George Dugan's letter arrived in the Saturday mail delivery. Marie nearly died when I read it to her and Paul after dinner, and announced that first thing Monday I was going to request a transfer to Local Defense School. "Oh, Beely," she pleaded, "Don't even think of doing such a seely thing. I beg of you. You have a safe job now. Why do you want to risk your life on one of those Navy ships? You can't even swim."

"I can't sit on my can and let everyone else fight the war for me," I argued. "I'm nothing but a clerk. Any woman could do my job." I went on hastily, seeing the nasty look Marie gave me. "Sorry. I didn't mean it that way. But the truth is, anyone with a missing leg could handle every stupid detail I've had in the Navy. And I'm supposed to be an officer. Besides, I'm really fed up with Fraley. He's getting more and more critical. He even had the gall to tell me to get a haircut. What a bastard. I'm afraid I'll punch him in the nose someday, and then I'll end up doing ten years in Portsmouth."

"Bill's right," Paul chimed in. A now familiar look of longing passed over his face. "I can't wait until I'm actually fighting for my country instead of spending my time wheedling stupid politicians." He glanced quickly at Marie. "And, if things go the way they promised me in New York, I'll get my wish. And soon."

Marie sighed and made a little face. "You never tell me anytheeng about what goes on in New York with your mysterious friends. But I can tell what's happening. You can't fool Marie. I'll lose all my men before theese awful war is over," she moaned. "I just know it." Brushing her hand across her face, she jumped up from her chair, hurried into the kitchen, and began rattling dishes in the sink.

Paul shrugged. He smiled ruefully. "My poor Marie's had it tough. Her brothers captured by those butchers, her mother and father probably just barely existing if they're still alive." He shrugged. "And now she worries sick about you and me." His face hardened. "But they can't win. It's too horrible even to think. We must stop them." He stood and clapped his hand on my shoulder. "Make your request, Bill! Your country needs you. Marie's just got to understand."

"What makes you so sure you'd be worth a damn on shipboard?" This sarcastic pronouncement emanated from Lieutenant Junior Grade Charles Fraley, as he reclined in his swivel chair, huge black shoes plunked down on the battered wooden desk cluttered with at least a dozen requisitions I'd left for signature, his hat at a rakish angle, my request for transfer to Local Defense School clutched in his hand.

"I believe I could learn, sir," I replied.

"You learn. Don't make me laugh. The way you've fouled up around here." He gave me a snotty look. "You can't even make the cash in hand add up to the weekly receipts from the laundry."

His nasty reference was to one occasion when I miscounted the station laundry's cash receipts by ten dollars.

"Well, sir, that only happened once. Anyway, I'm sure I'd be much more interested in the courses taught at Local

Defense School than the unimportant assignments I've had
here. I think I'd do a better job."

Fraley glared at me for a few seconds, his cheekbones
coloring, then snarled, "Well, Creelman, I think your attitude
needs one hell of a big improvement. I guess you're just too
green to realize that my office performs a vital function on
this station, funneling hundreds of sailors a month through
to their next wartime assignments. Someone's got to do that
important job. And like it or not, I'm very much afraid you
and I are stuck with it."

"But, sir," I urged, "anyone ineligible for military service
can do what I've been doing." I hesitated. "Even a middle-
aged woman." I didn't think Marie would mind my so
qualifying this sexist observation.

Marie may not have minded, but there was no doubt that
Lieutenant Junior Grade Fraley minded very much indeed.
Now his beefy face turned as red as the proverbial beet. His
feet crashed to the floor, or I should say the deck. "That
remark comes damn close to amounting to insubordination,
Creelman. You can feel very lucky if I don't put you on
report."

What came over me, I'm unable to say. There are events
in life that really are turning points. This surely had to be
one of them. I guess I'd had it up to my ears from Mr. Fraley.
I heard a voice. Was it really mine? The voice said, "Put me
on report, sir, I want you to do that." Yes, it was my voice,
for Mr. Fraley's faced turned an even deeper crimson. He
pushed back his chair and bounced to his feet. "Get out
of my office, Ensign Creelman. Now. And take this with
you." He flung my request for transfer. I caught it in mid-
air, turned and walked stiffly from his office, through the
double doors, down the concrete steps, and onto the street,
my mind in a whirl. Now what?

A familiar figure emerging from the ship service store
caught my attention. Chief Dalton. My trusty mentor would
help me figure out what to do. "Chief," I called out, "Could
I talk to you for a few minutes?"

"Of course, sir," was the friendly response. He saluted.
"Why don't we take a walk on the parade ground." That was
the new name for the ball field. We fell into step together,
while I recounted my meeting with Fraley and the climactic
challenge that I tossed at him.

"Good for you, sir," Chief Dalton said with great

enthusiasm. "Someone should have called that phony's bluff long ago."

"But now what?" I eyed him anxiously.

"Now you take your request to the exec. He'll give you a fair hearing."

"Lieutenant Commander Bauer? He's regular Navy. He won't listen to a greenhorn like me. He'll kick me out of his office."

"No, no, he won't. He's first-rate. Most of the regular officers are. It's some of these reservists, not you, sir, who think they're the greatest things that ever walked the planet. Put the stripes on them and overnight they turn into little Napoleons. Fraley's one of those. I guarantee that Mr. Bauer'll give you a fair hearing."

"What's he like?" I asked. "I've only seen him a couple of times. Fraley never includes me in any meetings with him."

"Boots Bauer is a really decent guy. He was given a medical discharge back in the mid-thirties but was recalled to active duty after Pearl. Just between the two of us he's got a terrible drinking problem. Before being assigned to Personnel, I worked in an office next to his. I've seen him stagger in on a Monday morning looking like he encountered a wildcat, face full of scratches from his girlfriend's talons, heavy beard, eyes looking like two piss holes in the snow, if you'll forgive my French."

I stopped walking and stared in amazement at the chief. He pulled up and swung around toward me. "How does he function during the day?" I wondered.

"Well, he first goes to the cafeteria, where Gus gives him a huge tumbler filled with gin, which he tosses down the hatch, then he heads for the barbershop, where Mario shaves him and massages his face with some kind of oil, and then good old Boots struts over to his office, rubs his hands together, and shouts to his chief yeoman, "Okay, Chuck, let's get to work." Chief Dalton smiled. "The guy's incredible."

"You think he'll listen to me?" I asked doubtfully.

"He will." The chief glanced over my shoulder. "Look, there he is now, headed for his office. Go after him... sir," he added.

Turning, I saw the executive officer striding purposefully toward the Station Headquarters. His military bearing and quick step belied the dissolute life described by Chief Dalton.

"This will be a good time to see him," the chief urged. "He's bound to be free for the next half-hour." I think my friend would have given me a physical as well as verbal push if I hadn't been his "superior" officer.

"Thanks, Chief," I said. "I'll take your advice."

Chief Dalton's "good luck, sir," followed me as I raced across the street and up the steps to the third floor. Mr. Bauer was just entering his office as I emerged from the stairwell into the corridor. I rushed after him and managed to enter the outer office right on his heels.

"Good afternoon, Chuck," his raspy voice shouted. "How're they hanging?"

"First-rate, sir," was the response.

I was trying to analyze that question and answer, when Mr. Bauer turned and caught sight of me. Despite his erect posture, the executive officer's ruddy complexion, bloodshot eyes rimmed with dark circles, and paunch straining against his trousers only too clearly exposed the telltale signs of dissipation. "And good afternoon to you, Mr...." He paused. "I do know you, don't I?"

"Yes, sir, I'm Ensign Creelman, assistant personnel officer of the Station. We met a couple of times, when you visited Mr. Fraley's office."

"Oh yeah, that prima donna," Mr. Bauer muttered.

To say that I was encouraged would be one of the great understatements of the last ten years.

"Come in, come in." He waved to a straight-back chair. "Take the lead off."

Mr. Bauer walked to a steel cabinet, fished out a silver flask, unscrewed the top, raised it to his lips and swallowed deeply. "Cough medicine," he explained. "Been having a nasty cold for the past week."

"Oh, I'm sorry, sir," I said.

"Thanks. It's been a bitch."

He rubbed his hands together and smiled.

"Okay, Mr. Steelman, what's on your mind?"

"It's Creelman, sir," I said meekly.

"Never could remember names," Mr. Bauer grumbled. He coughed, a deep racking sound. "Oops, need more medicine." Another long swallow ensued. "Well?" His eyebrows raised. "And what can we do for you?"

I took a deep breath. This was it. "I'd like a transfer to the Local Defense School in Boston, sir. I very much want sea duty after I'm trained for it." I'd done it. And it wasn't all that difficult.

"Good for you, son!" he exclaimed. "God, I wish I could get back into it." He emitted a huge sigh. "But I'm stuck at this station. Just a damn paper pusher. Beached." He swiveled around and stared out the window behind his desk. "Last tour of duty I was exec of the Hensley, one of the old four stackers," he mused. "China station, South Pacific, North Atlantic, Caribbean, you name it. She went everywhere. Talk about seaworthy. We rode out a typhoon in the Philippines, and a hurricane off Cape Hatteras. God, I'll never forget when she rolled 60 degrees. We were headed for Davy Jones, I was sure of that." There was a long silence, so protracted that I finally cleared my throat.

Mr. Bauer swung around in his chair, a mournful look on his face. "There's nothing like being on a ship at sea, Mr. Creelman. Nothing. I'd give my left testicle to be back aboard the Hensley depth-charging those miserable Japs. I envy you, my boy. I envy you."

"But, I'm not at sea yet, sir," I said. "Nor am I even at a training school."

Mr. Bauer pounded the table, causing the empty flask to rattle along the desk. "Well, get your ass up to Local Defense School. What the hell are you waiting for?" He must have caught sight of the paper clutched in my hand. "Is that your request? Hand it here."

I passed it over to him.

He frowned as he read the application. "Why isn't Fraley's endorsement on this?" he asked. "He's supposed to approve this kind of request before it gets to me."

"Well, sir." I stopped.

"Well, what?"

"Well, sir," Mr. Fraley refused to approve the request."

"Why in the name of God would he do that?" Mr. Bauer asked.

"Well, sir, he said that my work was of great importance to the war effort and that I should continue in my present position."

"Jesus Christ on a crutch!" Mr. Bauer shouted. "That stupid, arrogant asshole." Mr. Bauer pushed back his chair, jumped to his feet and strode to the outer office. "Chuck, get on the horn and call that idiot Fraley and tell him to get his butt over here. On the double."

"Aye aye, Mr. Bauer," the chief responded, a grin breaking

out on his weather beaten face.

I nearly had a heart attack on the spot. What would happen to me now? What would Fraley say? What would he do to me?

"The executive officer would like to see you in his office," Mr. Fraley. The voice was that of the chief yeoman. "No, he said immediately. I would put off getting that haircut for the time being, sir."

"What an utter jerk," Mr. Bauer muttered to himself. I can't say I disagreed with his observation.

We waited for a little more than three minutes in complete silence, broken only by the clicking of the chief yeoman's typewriter.

"You wanted to see me, Commander?" It was Fraley. And it was so typical of him to address a lieutenant commander as commander.

Fraley suddenly took notice of me.

"What are you doing here, Creelman? Why aren't you attending to your duties?"

"Mr. Creelman is here with my permission, Fraley," Mr. Bauer snapped. "Hold it," he went on, as Fraley's mouth dropped open. "Mr. Creelman wants to transfer to the Local Defense School. I guess, being relatively new in the Navy, he didn't realize that he needs your endorsement. I think it's a splendid request. I plan to approve it, but I need your signature before I take it to the skipper." Mr. Bauer thrust the request toward Fraley, who first looked at me, with hatred in his eyes, then took the paper, placed it on the desk, reached for the pen that Mr. Bauer handed him, and scratched his signature in the line next to the words "Endorsement No. 1."

"Okay, Mr. Creelman, I'll take this to Captain McDermott when I meet with him this afternoon. Your transfer will be processed within the next ten days or so."

The hatred in Fraley's eyes intensified. His cheeks bulged, and I thought for sure that he was about to burst out with some kind of lie about me, but then I guess he decided to wait and get his revenge until he had me at his mercy. The executive officer must have sensed the situation, because his next words were like a cool shower descending on a poor wanderer in the Sahara. "In the meantime, Mr. Creelman will be assigned temporarily to my office until his orders come through from BuPers."

CHAPTER 22

I'd read how young guys at the start of the Civil War and the First World War, as the politicians and military big shots were now calling the war that was supposed to end wars forever, worried themselves sick that the fighting would stop before they'd have an opportunity to get themselves killed or maimed for the glory of their country. No chance that this would happen to me. I worried more that the British would be brought to their knees by starvation and lack of military equipment, and the Allied merchant fleets would be sent to the bottom of the Atlantic by Admiral Karl Doenitz's wolf packs before I sailed off to war. It was a frequent sight to witness from Long Island or Boston and numerous other spots along the East Coast a red glow over the horizon from a torpedoed ship on fire. Newspapers and radio broadcasts bombarded us with stories of millions of tons of cargo bound for Great Britain destroyed and hundreds of sailors drowned or burned to death. Bad news from Europe and the Pacific outweighed the good news, such as it was, mostly about the British managing to contain, then push back the Desert Fox in Egypt. Was I stupid to give up my safe job at the Receiving Station? Marie had no doubts.

"You are a fool, Beely," she informed me. "You will only end up feeding the feeshes."

Ten days had passed since I regaled Marie and Paul with the story of the Fraley confrontation and Boots Bauer's enthusiastic response to my transfer request. Captain McDermott had signed on. Now I nervously awaited arrival of official orders from the Bureau of Naval Personnel. The dinner dishes were washed and dried, and the three of us had gathered in the den for the nightly news broadcast. The subject of my transfer had arisen once more after listening to the usual depressing worldwide accounts from war correspondents, with Marie's inevitable recriminations.

"Bill's doing the right thing," Paul told her firmly. "And what's more," he added, "we're going to have two heroes right here on this street." Paul's reference about the "other" hero was to Major General Vandergrift, our next-door neighbor who tried to persuade me to join "The Corps" and who commanded a division of Marines on Guadalcanal. Reports of the slaughter that ensued during the invasion and partial occupation of that steamy South Pacific island confirmed the soundness of my decision not to join the leathernecks.

"It ees better to be a live coward than a dead hero, ees all I have to say," Marie responded.

"Well, I'm not going to be either, so don't worry about that," I tried to reassure her. "At least I won't be a coward." Or would I? How could I be certain? Is a guy who goes batty under the strain of combat a coward? That didn't seem fair. How would I react to being shot at? Or to being on a ship in the middle of a typhoon or hurricane? What would a coward do? How would he act? He'd have someplace to run and hide if the enemy was shooting at him. But on a ship there is no place to run. No place to hide. Then I wondered. Is being afraid cowardly? No. That couldn't be right either; otherwise the armed forces would be filled with cowards.

I shook myself out of my daydream and glanced at Marie. "Anyway, it's too late to back out. Chief Dalton checked with a former shipmate assigned to BuPers. My orders have been cut and should reach me in the next day or two."

NAVY DEPARTMENT
BUREAU OF NAVAL PERSONNEL
Washington, D.C.

15 September 1942

From: The Chief of Naval Personnel
To: Ensign William Creelman, D-V(S), USNR
Via: COMMANDANT, NAVY YARD, WASHINGTON,
D.C.
Subject: Change of Duty.

You are hereby detached from duty as Assistant
Personnel Officer, Receiving Station, Washington, D.C., and
from such other duty as may have been assigned you. You
will proceed immediately, via rail transportation, to Boston,
Massachusetts, and upon arrival report to the Commanding
Officer Naval Training School (Local Defense), Receiving
Station, Commonwealth Pier, South Boston, Massachusetts
for temporary duty under instruction.

RANDALL JACOBS
cc: CO NTS (Local Defense)

"Congratulations, Mr. Creelman." Lieutenant
Commander Bauer smiled as I read through the document,
my hands trembling. "Give those miserable Japs or Nazis
hell, whichever you have the good luck to tangle with."

"Thanks, sir," I mumbled. "And please thank Captain
McDermott for his endorsement."

"He envies you. We all envy you, my boy. Except that
beachcomber across the street," he added. I had turned to
leave his office, when he called out to me. "Do you know
where you'll be living in Boston? No quarters are furnished
with this assignment."

"Well, sir," I replied, "I thought I'd look around when I get
there. Take a look at the newspaper ads. I'll have a whole
day to report to the school."

"No, no, no!" he growled, "the town is chockablock.

You'll have a hell of a time finding housing in one day or even one week." He gave me a tight smile. "You've got to be forehanded if you want to succeed in this man's Navy, Creelman. Your problem isn't exactly earthshaking, but you should have solved it a long time ago."

My embarrassment must have shown through, because his tone softened. "I think I can help you out, if you don't mind living in Brookline. My twin sister's got a house there. Plenty of room. She's alone for most of the year. Her husband's a regimental commander on Guadalcanal. Lucky bastard. Her son's training to be a Navy pilot in Pensacola, and her daughter, my favorite niece, just started her senior year at Vassar. She'll be getting home rarely, if at all."

"Well, gosh, sir, that would be terrific. But will she want a stranger boarding with her?"

"Oh, yeah, I'm sure Peggy would love the company. I know she's lonely. She told me so. And she'll appreciate the extra money."

He tore a sheet from a notepad on his desk, scribbled a few lines, and handed me the paper. "Here's her name, address, and telephone number. Brookline's a suburb of Boston," he informed me. "You can walk a couple of blocks to the Brookline station from Peg's place. The train will carry you to South Station, and then you have a short bus ride to Commonwealth Pier. Whole trip won't take more than an hour. I'll give her a call this evening, when I know she'll be home. She spends a good deal of her time at the Red Cross office in Boston. I'll have Chuck call you and let you know it's okay."

I read information on the sheet of paper. "Margaret Evans, 604 Beacon Street, Brookline, Mass. Phone number— Revere 5430."

He held out his hand. I shook it and thanked him again. I hurried past the chief yeoman, who gave me a thumbs up, and headed for my old office, hoping to find Chief Dalton, and hoping not to bump into Fraley. I was lucky in both respects. The seasoned old-timer stood as I entered my old office. "I'm off to the war, Chief," I exulted. "Well, almost. Anyway," I rushed on, "I've got my orders. I'm Local Defense School-bound."

"Good sailing, Mr. Creelman," he said. "You'll do great. You already have a leg up with your knowledge of blinker, piloting, and celestial navigation."

"I'll never forget what you did for me, Chief." I felt all choked up. I shook his hand and left before I made a fool of myself. Next stop, home, to give Marie and Paul the good news.

"Marie. Paul." I shouted their names as I rushed into the living room, leaving the front door wide open in my excitement. Silence. I hurried into the kitchen. No Marie in her frilly apron, busily preparing the evening meal, sometimes laughing and joking, but not so much recently. Not since she started openly fretting about her husband's secretive behavior. I checked the study, the room where Paul had looked up the location of Pearl Harbor in the dictionary that fateful Sunday. Empty. The huge volume was still open to the page on which Paul had frantically run his finger.

Where were they? I couldn't figure it out. I walked to the foot of the stairs and looked and listened. Only the methodical ticktock of the grandfather's clock standing in the corner of the living room could be heard. Nothing else. Marie and Paul's bedroom door was closed. "Paul! Marie!" I called out, a little more tentatively than before. "Is anyone home?" The bedroom door opened.

"Oh, Beely!" Marie stood framed in the doorway at the head of the stairs. I could tell she'd been crying. Her eyes were red, her dark hair tousled. She wore her blue satin robe, the very one she wore the night of the gourmet dinner, following which I managed to drink myself into oblivion. And, yes, the bottoms of the familiar pink silk pajamas brushed her bare feet.

"What's the matter, Marie? What's wrong? Are you ill? Where's Paul?"

"Oh, Beely. Oh, Beely." She shut her eyes, then opened them. Paul's gone."

I couldn't think of what to say for a couple of seconds and then didn't do much better when I finally managed to speak. "Gone. What do you mean gone? Gone where? When? Why?"

"Oh, Beely, all those questions," she sobbed. "All those seely questions." She ran her hand through her hair. The tears started to flow.

I didn't know what to do. I'd never had to cope with a crying woman. The nearest, I guess, was when Betty told me about Jack. But Betty wasn't practically undressed at the time. It did seem to make a difference.

"Please come and comfort Marie," she pleaded. Two arms stretched out toward me.

"Oh, Marie, I better not come up there." My voice shook and sounded hollow in my ears, like I was in a deep well. And, it crossed my mind, I was in deep and about to sink below the surface unless...unless what. Where could I go?

"Why not?" she asked impatiently. She brushed her hand across her eyes. "Paul is not here. He's gone. He came home at noon, packed two suitcases, kissed me on both cheeks, like I was his sister, madly screamed Gibraltar, Gibraltar, walked out the front door, climbed into a taxicab, said he'd write, and then he was gone. I don't know why he's gone to Gibraltar, if that's where he's gone, or when he'll come back. If he ever does." She actually stamped her foot. I'd read about that happening, usually when women were mad about something, but had never seen it. "I want you to comfort Marie. Now!"

Well, I had that same feeling I'd had before of my whole life passing by. In the space of only a few seconds, I guess, I thought of Mom, Dad, Uncle Dan, Dee, Betty, Erwin, wondering what they would think if I started comforting Marie. I guess I must have been ascending the stairs while those thoughts chased each other around in my mind. The next thing I knew, Marie grabbed me by the arm, pulled me through the door and pushed me on the bed. I didn't resist, I'll have to admit, when she yanked off my shoes, pulled off my jacket, undid my tie, unbuttoned my shirt, pulled it off, unzipped my trousers, pulled them off, and practically ripped my shorts before she managed to drag them off, too. Only my socks remained. As the Navy saying goes, I definitely was "out of uniform."

Later I thought about the day, the hour, and even the minute I lost my virginity forever. Never to be regained. Marie did all the work, if you call it work. I wondered how comforted she was in the short space of time the whole thing took. To say I was embarrassed would be an understatement. I did think it was kind of ironical that after it was all over Marie started comforting me.

"Don't worry, Beely," she said, "you were queek, but so is Marie."

I didn't have the slightest idea of what she was talking about.

"And I am very comforted. Merci."

She kissed me, shut her eyes, and, to my amazement, fell sound asleep.

CHAPTER 23

Hundreds of uniformed men and a sprinkling of uniformed WAVES and WACS crammed the main concourse of Union Station, either rushing toward the exits or waiting patiently at the gates, many chatting with husbands, wives, and children who came to say farewell to their loved ones, maybe forever. I edged toward gate 13, my two medium sized suitcases scraping against the legs of my future fellow passengers as I squeezed by. I was determined to get a seat and not be forced to sit on one of my bags until some of the passengers disembarked in Baltimore or Wilmington or even Philadelphia. And God knows, I didn't want to be seatless until 6 o'clock the next morning when the train was scheduled to reach Boston. And so I hustled down the platform and scrambled aboard the first passenger car, already more than half-filled.

After swinging my cases into the overhead rack, I tossed my blue Navy raincoat on top of them and took a seat next to the window. I removed my hat, brushed the blue cover and polished the visor with the palm of my hand, and placed it in my lap. Leaning back and shutting my eyes, my mind wandered to Marie. She'd prepared a salad lunch for the two of us without mentioning the GREAT EVENT, just as though nothing unusual had happened. She looked like death warmed over, moaning sadly about Paul leaving her and maybe never seeing him again.

After I helped Marie with the dishes in silence, she turned and held out her hand. "I'll say au revoir now, Beely. Please take care of yourself, and write to me. Thank you for being so sweet." She brushed her lips across my cheek and hurried up to her bedroom. I didn't try to see her again. I packed, took one last look at the comfortable room I'd occupied for many months, carried my luggage downstairs, and left the house, quietly shutting the door behind me.

I opened my eyes and stared out the window. It was dark now. Sailors and soldiers thronged the platform, a few preferring to remain in the arms of their girlfriends or wives for just a few more precious minutes, rather than making sure they found seats on the train. What a mess of everyone's lives the damn war was making, I thought. Hundreds of thousands of new widows and orphans. Thousands of crippled and maimed men and women. Jobs lost. Careers cut short. Educations disrupted. Families split up. But at least everyone was involved. No one wanted out now. Not after the sneak attack on Pearl Harbor. Not after the barbarous way the murderous Japs had mistreated American and British prisoners. Not after the word got out that German U-boats had surfaced and machine-gunned lifeboats crammed with women and children. A sudden bump and the squeaking of moving wheels jolted me out of my morbid thoughts. The train passed by the end of the platform and moved slowly through the rail yards. I thought of the time, years ago, when Black Jack, Spike, and I had slipped into a boxcar in the Philadelphia yard to catch a ride to Bethlehem, where I hoped to find Uncle Dan. I shuddered, remembering how we were attacked by Pop and Buck, and Spike had accidentally fallen from the moving freight car trying to protect me. It had all worked out okay. With Dee's help. But. Tears started in my eyes. Spike was dead. The smartest and best dog in the whole world. He'd always be in my heart.

"Mind if I join you, sir?"

I looked up. A tall, rangy sailor stood in the aisle, his sea bag at his side, his white hat squarely on his head, his double-breasted woolen peacoat slung over his shoulder. He looked to be about 30 years old. A half-dozen ribbons spread across his blue uniform, with two Bronze Stars, and the Purple Heart. I blushed inwardly, realizing that I couldn't even wear the pre-Pearl Harbor ribbon that had been authorized for those in active service before December 7, 1941. His insignia showed him to be a bosun's mate, first class.

"Please have a seat," I replied. I felt like standing in the presence of this authentic hero.

He managed to squeeze his sea bag in the rack across the aisle, and sat down, his peacoat on his lap. "I guess I'm lucky to find a seat, sir," he said. "The train is really full."

I murmured an agreement, then wondered what in the world we would find to talk about, assuming my seatmate wanted to talk.

"My name's Johnson, sir."

"Mine's Creelman," I responded. "Glad to meet you."

We shook hands.

"Where you headed?" I asked after a couple of minutes of silence. That seemed safe enough. Then I wished I'd picked another subject. I'd feel foolish if he asked the same question of me.

"Philadelphia Navy Yard, sir. I'm assigned to new construction. A tin can."

"Was your last ship a destroyer?" I asked.

"No, sir." He paused. "In fact, this will be my first destroyer."

My curiosity was aroused. "What other kinds of ships have you served on? If you don't mind my asking?"

"No, sir. Not at all." He let out a deep sigh. "First a battlewagon, then a light cruiser. I was on the Oklahoma when the Japs hit Pearl. Bastards. She went down, and then I was assigned to the Pittsburgh. I was aboard her during the start of the fighting on Guadalcanal. I took a flesh wound in the shoulder the second night after the Marines landed. Nothing serious, but the medics shipped me off to Honolulu. After getting patched up, I was shipped back to Frisco, and from there to the Receiving Station in Washington. And now off to Philadelphia. I'm hoping to be assigned to the Atlantic fleet. The Pacific is for the birds. Too damn hot, if you don't mind my saying so."

I laughed. "No, I don't mind." I glanced over at him. "I ought to tell you, I've never even set foot on a Navy vessel. I've been stuck at the D.C. Navy Yard Receiving Station since a week after Pearl Harbor."

"Well, it's guys like you who'll win the war," he said. "Our Navy couldn't pull this one off without the reserves."

A long silence set in, while my new friend leaned back and soon seemed to be asleep. God knows, he was entitled to all the rest he could get. A low wail from the engine up ahead told me we were approaching a grade crossing, which was verified by the clanging of the warning bells as we rumbled through. I looked out as the train entered a tunnel. We began slowing down and soon ground to a halt in Baltimore's Pennsylvania Station.

Johnson roused himself and took a look around. "Baltimore!" he exclaimed. "That's close to home. I was born and raised in Belair, Maryland, not too far from here. You probably never heard of it."

Well, that was a surprise! "Belair. I lived on a farm only about ten miles from Belair. Near Scarborough." That bit of information started us into a prolonged discussion of Harford County, Maryland. He finished his senior year in Belair High School just as I was entering Scarborough High. His dad owned and operated an Esso filling station. Johnson went to work for him after graduation but got the wanderlust and enlisted in the Navy in 1938.

"When did you get assigned to the Oklahoma?" I asked.

"I picked her up in Frisco in June of '41. We operated out of Pearl Harbor until the big day." He stopped. Another big sigh.

"Would it bother you to tell me about it?" I asked. "I can understand if you'd rather not. But I didn't even know where Pearl Harbor was when the Japs attacked. I've never figured out how they were able to get there without being detected, or something."

"You and thousands of others," he said. Then he went on. "No, I don't mind talking about it. I lost hundreds of shipmates. But it's better to get it out of your system. I think. I don't know. I'll never forget what happened. I'll never forget my buddies who died. I'll never forgive those goddam Japs. Those sneaky bastards." He glared upwards at the ceiling of the car. I thought for a few minutes that he changed his mind, that he couldn't bear to talk about that tragic day. But he finally spoke in a low steady voice, with hardly any inflection, a monotone.

"We were moored outboard of the Maryland. I left the shower and had finished dressing to go to breakfast and planned to go to church on board. I was wearing my whites and looked like a million bucks. General quarters sounded. I thought at first it was a drill. But then I heard the roar of aircraft, real low, followed by terrible explosions. Someone yelled over the intercom, 'Man your battle stations, this is no shit!'" Then a huge explosion rocked the ship. I learned later we were hit by a torpedo from one of the Jap aircraft. I was thrown to the deck and lay stunned for about fifteen seconds. Then we were hit again. I ran up the ladder and managed to reach the main deck. Just then a third torpedo hit us about amidships. We started taking on water and began listing to port. I scrambled up the deck to the starboard side of the ship. Then I heard the order to abandon ship. Well, I didn't know what the hell to do. I couldn't jump overboard.

So me and a bunch of other guys just hung on as best we could. Then we got hit again, and she started rolling over, with us scrambling and sliding down the starboard side so we wouldn't be thrown into the water. We ended up on the bottom of the ship. Then the Arizona blew up in front of our very eyes. It was a nightmare." He stopped for a moment, then went on, his voice even softer. "I couldn't stay where I was, so I took a deep breath and jumped from the bottom of the ship as far out as I could and landed in the water along with dozens of my shipmates. A tug picked us up after we treaded water or hung onto debris for about fifteen minutes. It seemed like fifteen years. My beautiful white uniform was black with oil. I looked like hell. And I felt like I'd been through hell."

"I can't imagine going through anything like that," I said. "You guys will never be forgotten."

"Wanna bet?" he asked sarcastically. "We'll be forgotten soon enough. Just like the veterans of the last war. My dad got screwed out of his bonus by our government." I thought of Black Jack and his telling me about the bonus march to Washington, and how he and his veteran buddies and their wives and kids had been driven from the city by tear gas ordered by none other than Colonel Douglas MacArthur, the same Dugout Doug who promised the country that the Philippines could be defended, and who ran to safety when the going got tough, leaving Skinny Wainwright and his other comrades behind to surrender his troops to the Japs. They were probably dead by now. Starved or murdered.

Soft snores told me that Johnson had really dropped off after completing his story. That seemed to be a good idea, and soon I dreamed of Paul chasing me around the Receiving Station drill field, brandishing a pitchfork. Thank goodness, I was awakened before he caught up with me by a loud voice proclaiming "Philadelphia, all out for Philadelphia Pennsylvania Station."

"Well, it was nice riding with you, sir," Johnson said, as he shrugged into his pea- coat and slung his sea bag over his shoulder. Maybe our bows will cross again before this mess is over."

"Thanks," I replied. "I hope so. Good luck to you."

He, along with half the passengers in the car, made his way down the aisle and out the door onto the platform. He saluted as he walked past my window. What a great human being, I thought. How could we lose the war with guys like him on our side.

A Marine corporal and three Navy seamen boarded the car, found empty seats, and immediately sacked out. The train sat for at least thirty minutes, the engine panting and sighing, before grudgingly starting to move down the tracks and out of the station area. With the additional room, I was able to use my raincoat as a pillow and lie back, feet stuck under the seat ahead, my hat shielding my eyes from the overhead lights. Next stop Newark. Or so I thought.

"North Philadelphia. North Philadelphia next." The conductor wandered down the aisle, announcing that unexpected news. Once more the engine slowed and ground to a halt, a shudder passing up the entire length of the train. We'd never get to Boston on time at this rate. A group of bluejackets, probably in their teens, pushed and shoved their way down the aisle, laughing and joking, having the time of their lives, or so it seemed. They scattered to the empty seats, hoisted their sea bags into the luggage rack, and continued shouting to each other, every noun modified by the ubiquitous adjective that, overnight, seemed to have appeared in the vocabulary of all naval enlisted personnel, at least the younger ones.

Suddenly I was conscious of a figure standing in the aisle next to my seat. A Navy officer. I glanced up and found myself staring into the beefy face, now a bit jowly, of...I could hardly believe my eyes. Harry Dobson!

"You're not Bill Creelman, are you?" Harry's voice reflected the same shock and amazement that I felt.

"Yeah, that's me," was all I could think to say.

"Christ! I haven't seen you since Steve busted out of Cornell. When was that? 1938?"

"Yeah. 1938. I guess. Or 1939. I dunno." I was totally confused by Harry's sudden appearance. I could hardly talk in a straight sentence. I remembered now that he lived in his family's mansion on Philadelphia's Main Line while attending Cornell. Not far from Betty's home. I never liked the guy. He was only slightly less obnoxious than Steve. But, I thought, maybe he'd changed for the better. Maybe not the horse's ass he used to be.

Harry heaved a large shiny leather suitcase up into the overhead rack, tossed a smaller matching case onto the seat opposite mine, pulled off his overcoat, then, to my dismay, sat down next to me. A single gold stripe on each sleeve told me that at least he didn't outrank me. That would have been too much to bear.

"Where are you headed?" he asked.

"South Boston. Local Defense School."

"Jesus. So am I."

I couldn't think of one thing to say in response to that appalling news. It didn't matter. The way he rattled on made it clear that he wasn't interested in my thoughts on the subject. "Jesus. My dad was able to pull enough strings to line me up with a permanent shore assignment in the Philadelphia Navy Yard. Or so I thought. Then my job was abolished, and I had to scramble. I mean scramble. I hated the thought of sea duty, but it was either Local Defense School or a transfer to Honolulu, and from there God only knows where, probably the South Pacific, where the goddam fighting's going on, maybe assigned to a Navy transport as assistant supply officer. Screw that. Local Defense School was the lesser of the two evils. I figure by the end of two months' training Dad will be able to fix something up with the Navy brass that'll keep me in the good old U. S. of A."

My head whirled from this diatribe. The leopard's spots do not change. That's for sure. Once a jerk, always a jerk. I remained silent while Harry reached in his pocket, extracted a Lucky Strike pack, fished out a cigarette and lit up. He blew a cloud of smoke toward the ceiling and went on yacking about his cushy shore job, the women he chased after, and how he even asked one of the "broads" to marry him, to have a better chance of landing a safe job, but the "bitch" had turned him down. He couldn't figure out why.

"By the way," he informed me, "Steve never did get a college degree."

Harry waited for me to comment, but I had none to offer. "No way Stevey could get a commission. He tried like hell to avoid the draft, but the best he could do was enlist in the Navy." Harry snorted with glee. "The poor little fart's a seaman, assigned to some kind of small craft under construction in Newport, Rhode Island. I think he told Dad it was an antisubmarine warfare vessel, or something like that." Harry dropped his cigarette to the floor and ground it out with his foot. "By the way, I've got some news about your friend Betty Marshall."

That did arouse my interest.

"Yeah? What's the story on her?" I asked. "I've kind of lost track."

"You won't believe this, but Betty joined the WAVES. She's in London on the staff of some admiral, and get this, she's a one-and-a-half striper. Lieutenant (j.g.) Betty Marshall. She outranks you and me!" Harry guffawed.

I couldn't figure out the humor.

"Jesus. Can you beat that? We'd have to salute if we bumped into her. Saluting a woman. What kind of damn Navy is this, anyway?"

"I wouldn't mind that," I said. "I'd be proud to salute her."

"Well," Harry sneered, "I just hope to God I never bump into her. If I see her coming, I'll run the other way. You can be damn sure of that." With that typically snide remark, Harry deserted me for the seat across the aisle. To my great relief.

After a few minutes, just as I had dozed off, he called over to me. "Wanna share a cab to Commonwealth Pier?"

I had a good excuse to refuse, thank goodness. I phoned Commander Bauer's sister after receiving word from his chief yeoman that she'd "love" to take me in as a boarder. She gave me directions from the Boston train station to her home in Brookline by bus and a short walk. I was all set.

CHAPTER 24

17 October 1942

Dear George:

Local Defense School is as great as you said it would be. I reported here for duty about a month ago and it's been eight hours a day instruction and four hours a night studying ever since. As you know, since you've been through it, we're concentrating on piloting, celestial navigation, and communications so far. Next week they're adding an intensive course in ordnance use and maintenance along with all the rest. We've been out in small craft up to Gloucester and around Halibut Point and back six times already. That's when it really gets hairy, particularly the piloting. We act as officers of the deck, and the instructor doesn't get involved unless the ship's about to run aground or is headed for the minefield. So far so good for me, although at least a dozen of the guys have really screwed up, especially a horses ass I knew at Cornell. He'll never make a deck officer. That's for damn sure. I guess the best part is that I have yet to get seasick although we've hit some nasty weather, especially last week working our way into Boston Harbor in a gale with a terrible following sea. You know all about that though.

I'm way ahead of the rest of the class on piloting and communications, especially blinker. I drive the rest of the guys crazy the way I read the blinker messages in class and when we're at sea. A chief at the Receiving Station in Washington taught me everything I know. We haven't had a chance to try out our celestial navigation skills except in the classroom. One of the guys ended up in the Indian Ocean! It's great fun.

I've already let it be known at the school that I want to transfer to SCTC when I leave here. I have a pretty fair chance. By then, of course, you'll be long gone from there, and probably commanding your own ship.

Drop me a line when you get a chance. I'm rooming and boarding with a terrific lady. She treats me like her son, who is about to get his wings as a Navy pilot. She has a daughter, Eleanor, whom I haven't seen, but judging from the dozen or so pictures scattered around the house, is really gorgeous. I'm hoping she'll be home from Vassar College for a weekend so I can meet her.

All the best,
Bill

It was late Saturday afternoon when I finished writing George. He sent me a couple of short letters from Miami after I let him know I took his advice about Local Defense School. In the second note, he asked if I'd ever been to the Merry-Go-Round Bar in the Copley Plaza Hotel. "Lots of fun and lots of girls searching for handsome naval officers," he wrote. Mrs. Evans had been trying to get me to take a break. "Relax, Bill," she urged, "you need a little R&R. If my daughter can ever catch a ride home with one of her classmates who's saved enough gas coupons, I'll make her introduce you to some of her friends. If any are left in town," she added mournfully. "This damn war. When's it going to end?" She didn't expect an answer, and I couldn't have given her one, anyway.

"I think I'll grab the bus downtown, mail this letter, and then drop in at the Copley Plaza," I announced to Mrs. Evans.

A delightful grin spread over her face. My landlady was maybe fifty-three years old, about five feet three inches tall, with one of the best figures I'd ever seen, especially the legs. It was hard to decide on her greatest attraction. Probably her hair, which was naturally and beautifully gray, falling in silky waves to just below her ears. A close second would have to be her smile, which broke out frequently despite the absence of her husband and two children. Despite the war. I wasn't sure about the color of her eyes. Maybe hazel. Anyway, they sparkled a lot. Her features were perfection—a small perky nose; pliable lips, thin but not too thin; even white teeth; and a softly rounded chin. But it was the composite of all those attributes plus a vibrant personality and great sense of humor that made her so alluring. And to top it off, she was as smart as a whip. I could easily imagine falling in love with her, if...if what? If I were twenty years older, I suppose. It was hard to believe that this trim, vigorous person was Boots Bauer's twin sister. But she assured me it was true, commenting that twins of different sexes often don't resemble one another physically. I had to take her word for it. She didn't hint that her brother's dissolute appearance and his lack of success in the Navy stemmed from overindulgence in alcoholic beverages, gin in particular.

"Oh, that's great, Bill!" she exclaimed, when I revealed my plans for the evening. "Should be a fun crowd down there tonight. Grab a seat at the Merry-Go-Round Bar. Order a pitcher of beer and have a ball." That smile again. "But don't fall off. And don't forget to take a flashlight. You'll be walking home from the bus in the blackout."

She stood in the doorway, smiling and waving. I waved my flashlight and trudged off to catch the bus for downtown Boston. I couldn't help thinking what a rough time she was having, with her husband in the middle of the slaughter on Guadalcanal. No word from him for nearly two months. Not knowing if he was alive, dead, or in a jungle hospital. We listened to the 11 o'clock broadcast every night together. Her spirits never dampened, no matter how rotten the news.

After dropping my letter to George in a mailbox in front of the Post Office Building, I struggled through the mob of soldiers and sailors jamming the sidewalks and finally reached the Copley Plaza Hotel, one of Boston's finest, so my landlady had said. It was early enough on a Saturday evening that I quickly found a seat on the famous Merry-Go-Round Bar. Taking my landlady's advice, I ordered a pitcher of beer.

About ten couples occupied the circular floor, dancing to music pouring from Buck Bingham and his Back Bay Boys in the style of Glenn Miller. I noticed a left-handed tenor banjo player. Now the ten-piece band belted out "Chattanooga Choo Choo." I could never hear that particular number without recalling my journey, under orders from the Chief of Naval Personnel, to Chattanooga on the Chattanooga Choo Choo, and from that city traveling in a battered and ancient black passenger car, with soot streaming through the open windows, to Mont Eagle, where I was met by the grieving father, mother and fiancée of the late Ensign Marion F. Johnson, Jr., whose "remains" in the form of ashes rested in an urn contained in a box wrapped with brown paper held in place by a length of cord, and driven to Sewanee, where Marion had attended the University of the South, graduating the previous year at the top of his class, then easily passing the rigorous naval pilot physical examination, following which he trained at Pensacola, excelling in every respect, winning his wings, then promptly killing himself at age 22 while attempting to land his aircraft in a dense fog at the Jacksonville Naval Air Base. After attending the church service crowded mostly with old men and women of all ages, flinching at the armed guard's volley of three rifle shots practically in my ear, followed by the melancholy notes of taps, and presenting to the dead hero's mother the neatly folded flag for which her only child had so tragically died, I reversed my course, arriving back at Union Station a few minutes before midnight of the same day I left on that sad mission.

"On your feet, Ensign!"

The barked command startled me from my reverie. I looked up into the grinning face of a lieutenant junior grade. I couldn't have obeyed if my life depended on it, I was so stunned. I just sat in my seat, my mouth hanging open like I'd seen a ghost.

Erwin Redding!

"Well, I'll forget it this time," he chuckled. "But don't let it happen again." He sat across the table from me and stuck out his hand. "It's great to see you. What in God's name are you doing in Beantown?"

"Local Defense School," I replied. "I'm trying to learn to be a real sailor. Been here about a month."

"Terrific!" Erwin grinned. "Join the club. I'm attending the Armed Guard School. Pronounced Aaamed Gaaad in this crazy town," he added. Then he frowned. "How come I've never bumped into you before? We're right there on Commonwealth Pier."

"Beats the hell out of me," was the best explanation I could offer.

"I see you're well into the suds," he said, glancing at my now half-filled pitcher. "I need something stronger." He craned his neck around the room, finally catching the eye of a waiter, who hurried over. "A double Old Grand Dad on the rocks, and bring us some pretzels."

"Yes, Lieutenant."

"God, I've been promoted," Erwin muttered as the waiter

hurried off.

I asked Erwin when he'd finish training.

"I've got another two weeks, then I'm out of here," he said. "I'll probably be assigned to some beat-up merchant ship, then it'll be off to Europe in a slow North Atlantic convoy, praying that the weather's so damn lousy that Hitler's U-boats won't be able to blow us to kingdom come."

Erwin was not kidding. I could tell by his grim tone. I counted my blessings I wasn't among the poor buggers being trained to supervise gun crews assigned to tankers, troop transports, and cargo ships. Great Britain's lifeline.

Our waiter was soon back with Erwin's bourbon and a basket of pretzels. "Well, here's to a quick end to this frigging war." Erwin raised his glass and took a sip. I did the same. "Fat chance, though," he said. "We're getting the crap beat out of us all over the world." He stared moodily into the amber contents of his glass. "This war has royally screwed up my life," he moaned. "I had a great job at the Baldwin Locomotive Works. Just got a promotion, and then the goddam draft started breathing down my neck. So I jumped into the frying pan instead of the fire." He gave a disgusted snort. "With my training at Cornell and my job at Baldwin, I thought I'd at least get assigned as an engineering officer on a decent-sized ship. But that's the stupid Navy for you. If I'd asked for armed guard training, they'd probably have assigned me to a battlewagon." He downed his drink and signaled the waiter for a refill.

"Sorry to subject you to all my troubles," he said. "But I'm really..." He stopped short. "I've got something that'll interest you." He reached into his jacket pocket and fished out an envelope, opened it, and handed me a letter.

I instantly recognized the tiny, vertical handwriting. "From Dee?"

"Yeah. From Dee. What a neat gal. Go ahead and read it." Seeing the doubt in my expression, he hurried on. "Don't worry, it's not a love letter. We're pals. That's all."

I unfolded the two sheets of paper and started reading.

"Dear Erwie."

I stopped, recalling how upset I was when she called him Erwie that horrible morning in the gloomy infirmary on Buffalo Street, a thousand years ago. I read on. She managed to get out of Germany in late November of last year and rented a flat in London, not far from St. James

Park, only three blocks from her job with one of the overseas information services. She hadn't located any of her relatives. They were shipped off to labor camps in Austria. At least it wasn't Siberia. There were rumors of massacres of Jews by the Nazis, and she'd given up hope that they survived. London was better than Germany, but not all that great. Bombing raids nearly every night. She spent too damn many hours in bomb shelters. Ducking at every near miss. Like a scared chicken. The British people were fantastic. Always joking and laughing. Hitler would never conquer them. No way. She bumped into Betty Marshall. Betty looked terrific, all dolled up in her blue uniform with her gold braids. We had a wonderful reunion at a pub on the Strand. She loves her job. Loves her boss. Not in a romantic way. He's more like an uncle than a big shot vice admiral. We talked about the time I stayed at her sorority house at Cornell when I went up to see poor Billy, who got the measles after that idiot Steve Dobson lost the ball game."

Another memory. I wasn't likely to forget that weekend. I glanced up at Erwin, who was watching me, an amused look on his face. "I thought you stole Dee away from me," I said. "Not that she was ever mine to begin with."

"I'll level with you, Bill, I didn't even kiss her. That weekend or any other time. It was great fun. For me anyway. She seemed to spend most of the time worrying about you. So what the hell." He shrugged. "I was tempted to make a pass at her, but didn't, and I probably would have had my head knocked off if I had."

"Well, gee," I mumbled, "I guess I was a little jealous." Little jealous! I was bent out of shape. I kept reading. "I don't know whether you remember my talking about my brother-in-law, Sid, who was a sports writer for the *Bethlehem Star*. Well, he's with the Associated Press in London. Sends dispatches to the U.S. for home consumption. We have lunch every other week or so. He's a terrific guy. I have to admire him for volunteering for his assignment, which is a heck of a lot more dangerous than writing a column in a hick town in Eastern Pennsylvania."

I shut my eyes and thought about the time Dee and I had visited her sister and her husband, Sid, in Bethlehem, when we were still searching for Spike. She was wonderful. I'd have lost him forever if she hadn't come along and insisted on trying to find him. Erwin was right. What a neat gal. The letter went on to say she enjoyed her work despite the bombs and the lousy food and the lousy weather. She hoped the war would be over soon but knew it wouldn't. "We've got to cross the channel and catch that bastard Hitler, then string him up by his testicles." Dee never did mince words.

I handed the letter back, slightly put out that I hadn't heard from her for more than a year. Maybe the old feeling of jealousy was still hanging around. I don't know.

"How's your love life, anyway?" Erwin wanted to know. His face one big leer. I knew that question would be asked sooner or later.

"Non-existent."

"Oh, don't give me that crap! A good-looking Navy officer like you." He snickered. Looking and sounding like the Erwin of old. "Don't tell me you're still a virgin."

My face must have given me away, because Erwin could tell even in the darkened room that I was thrown off guard by the question.

"So. It's happened. At last. Tell your Uncle Erwin all about it."

"There's nothing to tell," I lied. No way I'd let him in on my personal life. Marie didn't deserve being the subject of a bull session.

"Oh, well, I don't believe you. But what the hell. It's none of my business."

"I'm hoping to meet my landlady's daughter one of these days," I said. "She's a knockout, judging from what her mother says and the photos I've seen of her."

"Well here's to the landlady's daughter." Erwin raised his glass. "She couldn't find a nicer guy."

That compliment, coming from Erwin, left me speechless.

"I mean it. Despite being a country bumpkin and as naive as hell, you are a good guy and a good friend." He raised his glass. "Cheers."

Down the hatch went his second double bourbon.

The rickety Boston Transit bus geared down as it trundled along a darkened Beacon Street, past the Boston Commons and the Public Gardens through the Back Bay area, the ancient vehicle's partially covered headlights barely illuminating the road ahead. There was little traffic—only a few approaching vehicles, their headlights also masked and dim. I peered through the stained window toward where I knew the Charles River to be, but that historic body of water was invisible in the darkness that enveloped the city. Blackout regulations were scrupulously observed. Violations brought heavy fines. Was this where the patriot Paul Revere crossed the river with muffled oars? No. The Charlestown shore and the Old North Church were far behind the rumbling bus. The stirring poem ran through my mind.

'Twas the eighteenth of April in '75, hardly a man is now alive who remembers that famous day and year!

Another century. Another war. Or the beginning of another war. I shut my eyes and thought about the visit with Erwin. All in all, it was a good evening, reminiscing about Cornell. About living in the ancient Cascadilla Hall. The chimes from the Library Tower. Dee and Betty. Too much beer, though. And too much booze for Erwin, who became maudlin, lamenting his forthcoming duty as an Armed Guard officer. "I'll never get through this frigging war alive," he kept repeating. At one point he smiled. "But maybe you'll protect me, Bill. Maybe we'll be in the same convoy, and your escort vessel will sink the frigging submarines trying to blow my ass to hell."

My stop didn't arrive any too soon. Two pitchers of beer and only one trip to the head. As the saying went, my kidneys were floating. I bade the driver a goodnight, leaped from the bus, activated my flashlight and hastened toward my home away from home. To take my mind off my problem, I commenced singing one of the songs rendered by Buck and his Back Bay Boys, striding along and waving my flashlight in time to the so-called music.

Roll out the barrel, we'll have a barrel of fun!

Roll out the barrel, we've got the blues on the run!

And so on.

Mrs. Evans' house loomed through the darkness. At last. I quickened my steps. But I wasn't going to make it! No way. I ducked behind an elm tree on the front lawn, unzipped my trousers, and proceeded to relieve myself. To my great relief.

"Is that you, Bill?"

I froze. My landlady's voice. I adjusted my clothes and

stepped from behind the massive trunk. She stood in the open door, barely visible in the gloom.

"Watering the lawn, eh?" Then a trilling laugh. "Well, when you gotta go, you gotta go."

I couldn't remember when I'd been that embarrassed.

A second figure appeared behind her. "Who's out there, Mom?"

"Oh, it's only Bill, my tenant. The young and handsome naval officer you've heard so much about."

At that point I could only hope that a sudden tornado would cause the giant elm to come crashing down on me, putting me out of my misery forever. But no such luck.

"Come on. Come on. Meet Eleanor, down from Vassar until Monday morning."

I shuffled toward the two of them. Eleanor's grin put me a bit at ease. "I've looked forward to meeting you," she said. "Mom spends half her letters saying how lucky she is to have such a nice tenant."

"Well, I'm the lucky one," I managed to mumble.

"I've got a nice fire in the den," Mrs. Evans said. "Come on in, and let's have a chat and a nightcap."

After I requested and received a glass of water instead of a nightcap, I covertly watched Eleanor as she mixed two Tom Collins, then dropped the red cherries into the glasses with a splash. She was slimmer and taller than my landlady, maybe 5 feet 6 inches. Not quite the perfect figure, but close enough. The quick smile was like her mother's and also revealed perfect teeth. Her skin was smooth, her complexion slightly tanned. The lips were a bit fuller than her mother's. Maybe too much lipstick. Brilliant red. Her dark short wavy hair revealed pearl earrings. Her eyes were wide apart. I guessed they were hazel. Hard to tell. And her voice. What a voice. Visions of Jean Arthur in "Mr. Smith Goes To Washington" ran through my mind when she spoke. She sat and raised her glass to me. I noticed she wore brilliant red fingernail polish. I wondered if it was supposed to match her lipstick. "Mud in your eye."

"And yours." I frantically searched my mind for something to say. Finally, I asked, "How was the trip?"

"Terrible!" She sighed. "Ten hours in a five-year-old Chrysler with only one pit stop in Springfield. And I've got to reverse the procedure Monday." That smile again. "But it's worth it seeing Mom."

"Well, Eleanor, your old mom appreciates it." Mrs. Evans finished her drink and stood. "I've got to hit the sack," she said. "Why don't you two get acquainted." She reached the door, then swung around. "I managed to beg, borrow and steal three tickets to the Symphony Hall concert tomorrow afternoon after Eleanor telephoned me from Springfield," she said. "Koosey's conducting. It's a wonderful program. Tschaikowsky's Fifth and Beethoven's Emperor Concerto with Vladimir Horowitz at the keyboard. Can't beat that. Goodnight all." With that announcement and a nod to Eleanor, she vanished.

I glanced at Eleanor uncertainly as she sipped her Tom Collins. "I know a little bit about Horowitz," I finally said. "But who is Koosey?"

"That's the snobbish way old-time Bostonians and reviewers refer to Serge Koussevitzky, the conductor of the Boston Symphony Orchestra. Not to his face," she added.

"Oh" was all I could manage to say about that bit of news.

"He's world-famous, straight from Russia," she said. "A bit too stuffy for me. I don't go much for the long-haired junk, anyway. Art's my big interest."

My mind flashed to Betty and how much we'd enjoyed that long-haired junk together.

After divulging that information, Eleanor stood and walked to the fireplace, where she retrieved a beech log from the wood basket and tossed it onto the fire. The flames shot up the chimney with a delightful crackling sound. The brown turtleneck sweater and matching skirt neatly fitted the curves of her attractive figure. Now my mind shot back to Marie. And her voluptuous body. "I love a wood fire," Eleanor murmured.

I studied my landlady's daughter again as she stared into the flames. Her profile revealed a perfectly shaped nose I hadn't noticed before. The photographs had not lied. She turned toward me, an anxious look crossing her face. "By the way, you don't have to take in the symphony tomorrow. It probably would be a gigantic bore for you. Don't feel you have to go. Maybe we could go to a movie," she added after a quick glance at me.

"No, I'd love to go," I said. "Anyway, your mom's gone to a lot of trouble. We shouldn't disappoint her." With that, I started yacking about Betty, and how she'd introduced me to the classics, and how much I learned from her, and all about the summer on her dad's beef cattle farm, and how smart she was, and now she was a lieutenant (j.g.) in the WAVES, stationed in London.

"Is she your sweetheart?" Eleanor asked when I finally finished my declamation. The brilliant red lips drew up in a frown.

The question took me by surprise. And yet it was a perfectly natural one. I had raved on about Betty with enthusiasm.

"Oh, gg gosh, no," I finally said. The stammer was back. "She's a wonderful friend but not my girlfriend. She's too old for me, anyway."

"Well, who is? A good-looking guy like you must have a girlfriend. Maybe more than one."

My face must have matched the glow from under the logs because without waiting for any answer, she stood abruptly and placed her empty glass on the mantel. "Sorry. I'm always asking direct questions." She smiled. "Maybe we'd better turn in." She held out her hand. "It's been wonderful to finally meet you. I'm really glad you're staying here. Mom says you're great company, not that you have much extra time with your tough schedule."

I took her hand. It was small, soft and firm. She looked directly into my eyes, a half-smile on her face. My heart began to pump, and for just a half a second I was sure she was asking to be kissed. I felt the stirring that Marie aroused. "Well, thanks," I mumbled, losing my nerve, "she's about the nicest person in the world." A funny, warm, dizzy feeling swept over me. "I dd don't have a girl friend," I finally stammered out.

Her smile broadened. "Good," she whispered, "I like that."

CHAPTER 25

"And let's be thankful that Daddy's safe and sound." Eleanor raised her head and smiled at her mother, whose hazel eyes glistened with tears.

"Not only safe and sound, but on his way to Washington for assignment to General Marshall's staff," my landlady exulted.

"And the proud wearer of the Silver Star, and now a one-star general," Eleanor cried out.

My head swiveled back and forth like I was at a tennis match as mother and daughter exchanged excited comments and observations. I stood and extended my beer stein. "I'd like to propose a toast to General Evans," I announced.

The two women rose and lifted their wine glasses.

"To a hero of the Guadalcanal campaign and the husband and father two brave and wonderful ladies."

"Here, here!" my audience responded enthusiastically.

Mrs. Evans remained standing after we'd toasted her husband. She glanced at Eleanor and me, then spoke quietly: "Now, let's raise our glasses to General Eisenhower and his brave soldiers in North Africa." The world had been electrified and the Germans dumfounded when, a few weeks earlier, Allied troops supported by a huge armada landed on the coasts of Algeria and Morocco near Casablanca. Hitler responded immediately by occupying all of France. My thoughts had turned to Marie. Alone, without Paul, she must have been devastated by that awful event. I wondered many times what had become of Paul; what mission could have carried him off so swiftly and so secretively, without any advance warning to Marie.

We sipped our drinks, somewhat subdued now. How fortunate we were to be able to celebrate Thanksgiving in a safe and comfortable home instead of in the African desert, or the jungles of Southeast Asia, or on the storm-swept ocean, or in war-torn Great Britain. Our somber reflections could not last long, however. A banquet fit for a king and queen lay spread before us on the candle-lit dining room table—a small but elegant browned turkey, serving dishes overflowing with mashed potatoes, sweet potatoes, green beans, French onions, and home-made rolls, to be topped off by the pumpkin and apple pies baked the evening before by Eleanor, only a few hours after her long and tiring journey from Poughkeepsie.

We gorged ourselves, of course, and, after washing and wiping the seemingly hundreds of dishes, glasses, and cutlery, retired to the den with coffee and chocolate mints in front of a crackling fire in the den. Eleanor glanced at me from a reclining position on the sofa, looking more enticing than ever. Until yesterday, I hadn't seen her since she departed for Vassar that Monday morning after the unforgettable concert at Symphony Hall. Unforgettable mostly because of her. She grabbed my hand at the start of the last movement of the Emperor Concerto and held on until the climactic finish, with me in a nervous sweat, desperately hoping my palm wasn't too clammy.

"Well, Bill, what do you have to be thankful for?" she asked.

I thought for a few moments, then said, "I guess in addition to my mom and dad and Uncle Dan being okay, I'm most thankful for completing training at Local Defense School and getting my orders to SCTC."

Her lips drew in. "I'm not sure I like the idea of your learning how to do battle with submarines," she said.

"Oh, Eleanor, don't frown and don't begrudge Bill his new assignment. How can he become the Navy hero I know he's going to be without learning to navigate a ship?" My beautiful landlady blew a kiss in my direction. "But," she went on, "I think Bill should be even more thankful that he has ESP."

"What in the world are you talking about?" Eleanor asked.

"Tell her, Bill. Tell Eleanor how that rotter Harry Dobson nearly got you thrown out of school, if not worse."

Eleanor's eyes widened like saucers. "For goodness' sake, please tell me," she cried.

"Well, I guess I did sort of have ESP, at least this once," I said. I placed my empty coffee cup on the side table next to my chair and started my recital. "Dobson was a complete washout at school. Spent most of his time chasing women. He barely passed piloting and celestial navigation, and our communications course totally confused him. He couldn't conn a ship without nearly running aground or coming within inches of slamming into the dock. He was a mess, except, for some unknown reason, he liked ordnance class and did fairly well. The jerk was nuts about guns of all shapes and sizes. We were issued an ordnance manual, each with its individual number, with a 'confidential' classification. We had to sign for our manuals and were warned to guard them with our lives. One day I left mine at the bottom of my unlocked locker underneath a pile of notebooks and papers while attending a fire-fighting demonstration." I shut my eyes, recalling my stupidity. "It seemed a safe thing to do. But it was dumb. I know that now."

"What in the world happened?" Eleanor asked.

"Well, I came back from the demonstration, opened my locker, reached under the pile of stuff, but..." I took a deep breath. "It was gone!"

"Gone!" Eleanor's expression must have been the same as mine when I made the awful discovery.

"Yeah. I didn't know what to do. I was frantic. I could visualize a court-martial followed by a tour in Portsmouth. I walked over to a window at the end of the locker room and stared out for about five minutes, agonizing, wondering whether I should report the loss to the captain. Then I heard someone entering the room. It was Harry. He seemed startled when he caught sight of me. I don't know why I confided my troubles to him, but I did. When I told him I couldn't find my ordnance manual, the look on his face started my ESP ticking. He turned red, seemed flustered, and began blustering, saying gosh, that's too bad, are you sure it's lost, maybe you left it in your room in Brookline, and stuff like that. I suddenly knew he took my manual. I just knew it."

"Did you say anything to him?" Eleanor asked breathlessly.

"No. He'd have denied taking it. I decided to tell Cliff Mills, our platoon leader, about my suspicions, then have him tell me in Harry's presence just before navigation class began that the captain wanted to see me in his office. While I was gone, I'd search Harry's locker. None of the lockers had locks. Shortage of steel, I guess." I paused while Eleanor's mother refilled my cup from the silver coffeepot.

"Go on, for goodness' sake." Eleanor leaned forward in

her chair.

"Well, to make a long story short, Cliff and I carried out the plan. I went to Harry's locker, opened it. A canvas bag was lying there. I was certain the manual was in the bag. I unzipped it. And..."

"And what?" Eleanor gasped.

"And there at the bottom of the bag under the front section of the *Boston Globe* was my manual. Number 15467."

"What in the world did you do? Did you report that terrible person?"

"No. I didn't want to ruin his career. Although he sure didn't care if he ruined mine. I replaced the manual in the bag and rejoined my platoon. He couldn't wait to see me after class. He wanted to know why the captain had ordered me to his office. What had happened? Was I in trouble? I told him a yeoman had seen him take the manual from my locker and reported it to the captain. He blanched, saying things like it was only a joke, that he was going to give it back to me, and on and on. He wondered whether he should give some explanation to the captain, but I told him I'd given assurances that it was only a joke between him and me. We walked to his locker, and he handed me my manual." I raised my coffee cup. "Thank God for ESP!"

"Amen!" Eleanor practically shouted her agreement.

My landlady rose, yawned, stretched and headed for the door. I noticed that she frequently arranged to leave Eleanor and me to ourselves. Or was it Eleanor that did the arranging? I wasn't sure. Did I care? I wasn't sure of that, either.

"Well, to be corny, all's well that ends well. Thank goodness." She yawned again. "I'm going to take a nap. Why don't you two make your plans for tomorrow."

Eleanor had suggested we take a bus into town and do some sightseeing. "You can't leave this historic town without at least visiting some of our famous landmarks," she said. "Let's get going early, start with the Museum of Fine Arts, then head for the Old North Church for a look-see, catch Paul Revere's House and Faneuil House, and wind up for a late lunch at your favorite spot at the Copley Plaza, where there's plenty of beer."

I felt a bit warm, hearing that remark.

We managed to leave the house before nine the next

morning and spent a couple of hours examining the huge variety of art at the Museum of Fine Arts. Eleanor seemed particularly fascinated with the ancient Egyptian, Greek and Roman art. "I'm majoring in fine arts at Vassar," she explained as we passed through the massive doors out to the sidewalk. "You'll have to take a look at some of my artistic endeavors."

"What are they like?" I asked.

"Mostly watercolors of scenic views. Mountains, rivers, lakes, farms, stuff like that. They're at school. I'll bring them home after I graduate next June. Then you can take a look at them." She stopped short. "Oh, hell, you'll probably be on some Navy ship fighting this horrible war." Her voice choked. She gave me a quick look and brushed her hand across her eyes. "You will take care of yourself, won't you?"

"Gg gosh, yes. Of course I will." I was shaken. She really seemed to care.

Eleanor hastened toward the street. "Let's grab that bus," she called out. "It'll take us close to the Old North Church."

We spent about twenty minutes looking around the church and reading the literature about its historic past, took brief tours of Paul Revere's House and Fanueil House, then made our way to the Copley Plaza Hotel. The timing was perfect. Exactly 2 o'clock. Unlike that unforgettable Saturday night when I bumped into Erwin and consumed the infamous pitchers of beer, the Merry-Go-Round Bar was only half-filled with a much quieter clientele, mostly middle-aged or older civilians. Instead of Buck and his Back Bay Boys, a four-piece stringed ensemble made up of moonlighting members of the Boston Symphony Orchestra, decked out in swallow-tail coats and striped trousers, struck up a Strauss waltz as we sat down.

"The Blue Danube. How wonderful!" Eleanor exclaimed. Her enthusiasm was contagious. "Shall we waltz?" She looked at me eagerly.

"You'll have to teach me."

She rose, skipped out onto the dance floor and held out her arms. Had anyone ever looked so absolutely gorgeous? There she stood in her trim, green suit that seemed to highlight her eyes, now sparkling with excitement. Her dark hair reflected the dimmed overhead light—all of that loveliness topped off by a broad smile of anticipation.

Well, my waltzing left a lot to be desired, but it was worth the stumbling and apologizing just to hold Eleanor in my arms. Her body felt as soft and yet as firm as I imagined. Her hair brushed against my lips. No perfume. I liked that. My mind whirled when she kissed my neck as the great waltz ended.

After resuming our places at the table, we sat silently for more than a minute. I'd never forget the Blue Danube Waltz. That was for sure. I stole a glance at her. She seemed to be studiously examining the menu. That flustered me, until I noticed she held it upside down.

The rest of the afternoon passed in sort of a haze as far as I was concerned. As we disposed of our shrimp salads, just right after yesterday's feast, Eleanor talked about Vassar. I learned that its founder was Matthew Toddingham, who hailed from somewhere in England and became a big wealthy beer man in Poughkeepsie. Irreverent students sometimes referred to the philanthropist as "Two Ts" which helped them remember how to spell his first name.

After I described some of the highlights of my four years at Cornell, Eleanor recalled aloud the Poughkeepsie Regatta and her rides each June during the past three years along the Hudson River on the crowded boat train, filled to capacity with drinking and cheering students. For reasons she couldn't now recall, she always rooted for Cornell. "Maybe because it was the closest of the participating colleges to Vassar," she speculated. She gave me one of her quick looks. "I'm glad I did, now. Not that it did much good," she added, "poor Cornell never won much."

"Not like the good old days, or I should say the good old, old days, when our varsity, junior varsity, and freshmen crews under Coach Courtney, the Grand Old Man of Cornell rowing, swept the water year after year at Poughkeepsie and at most other regattas." I imparted with pride that ancient lore I learned from Betty, who'd been so informed by her uncle.

After a respectful silence honoring that earthshaking bit of rowing history, Eleanor glanced at her watch. "Oh, I guess we better go," she sighed. "I've had the best time in months."

We made some small talk after finding a seat at the rear of the bus. I could think of nothing to say that made any particular sense. Eleanor pointed out the enormous shell near the Charles River where, she told me, the Boston Pops orchestra performed free concerts in the summer before the blackout. "It's so romantic on a beautiful moonlit night," she said dreamily. I received another quick look. "Someday, maybe...after this awful war." She stopped, and leaned back in her seat, her eyes closed.

My mind raced. Maybe this really was it. Was I in love with her? Or was it the war? I wished I could consult with Erwin, but he was probably somewhere on the broad Atlantic. And anyway, tomorrow I'd be Miami-bound. And anyway, what could he tell me? He'd probably respond with one of his lewd suggestions. I tried to analyze my feelings. First there was Dee. I must have thought I was in love with her. The way I felt during that awful Spring Day weekend. But... but this was different. I didn't know exactly in what way. I could just feel the difference. Then, I thought, what about Betty? I'd never forget her. She changed my life. Maybe she was more like a loving older sister. But I never had a sister. So how could I know?

I glanced sidewise at Eleanor. Was she asleep? No. She shot a quick glance at me, smiled, then closed her eyes again. My heart started pumping. My mouth felt like sandpaper. Should I say something? Tell her I love her? Did I love her? How could I know? I turned cold, then hot, then started to perspire. I dragged a handkerchief from my pocket and mopped my forehead. No. I'd never have the nerve. Not in a million years. But if I didn't say something now, I'd never get up the courage later on. Probably wouldn't have another opportunity before I shoved off. But maybe that was just as well. No. To hell with it. It was too big a step. Or was it? I shut my eyes in an agony of indecision.

"Look, Bill, we've got to settle something before you leave tomorrow."

My eyes popped open. Eleanor sat straight up, turned partially toward me, her lips compressed.

"Wh what dd do you mean?"

"I mean we've got to settle how we feel about each other." She placed her hand on the back of mine. Her blue eyes seem to bore into me. "I mean I think I've fallen in love with you, and I need to know how you feel about me before... before you go off and get yourself killed."

No, I wasn't dreaming. She said it. A wave of exultation swept over me. This wonderful person said she loved me. I was sure that's what she said. I could feel the tears starting. How could I help but love someone who loved me? "Oh, Eleanor, I'm crazy about you," I finally managed to gasp.

She raised her hand, clasped it around my neck, pulled my head toward her, and we kissed. She abruptly pushed me from her. "Then come home safely!" Another quick kiss.

"That's an order, Ensign Creelman."

CHAPTER 26

"Gentlemen, when we're done with you, you'll be the best trained antisubmarine warfare officers in the world, and I personally want each one of you to kill at least one murdering Nazi bastard, and, if you're lucky enough to get the chance, blow at least one Nazi submarine to hell."

Captain E.F. McDaniel, the commanding officer of Submarine Chaser Training Center, stood rigidly on the elevated porch, hands on hips, glaring through horn-rimmed spectacles at the fifty officers packed in front of the two-story, yellow stuccoed-structure that passed for the school's Administration Headquarters.

"Take a look at that lifeboat!" He thrust his leather riding crop toward a battered thirty-foot open boat that lay partially on its side about ten yards away. "Take a close look!"

The entire group of officers edged forward in unison.

"Do you see those holes?"

We edged even closer. The weather-beaten planking had been riddled with dozens of holes from bow to stern, each circled with red paint.

"Those, gentlemen, are machine gun bullet holes," he shouted. "This lifeboat was filled with women and children from a Dutch passenger vessel torpedoed by one of Hitler's gutless commanders, just hours out of Antwerp. The miserable bastard surfaced, then proceeded to murder every last soul in cold blood. Every innocent woman. Every innocent child."

All eyes turned back to Captain McDaniel. A huge silence hung over his audience.

"Don't ever forget what you've seen here." He saluted. "Good luck. And good hunting." Our commanding officer wheeled and disappeared through the headquarters' door.

"Holy buckets! Is that guy for real?" Cliff Mills stared at me, his eyes popping.

"Beats the hell out of me," was the best reply I could come up with.

Cliff and I had been seatmates on the DC-3 Eastern

Airlines flight from Boston to Miami, and now we were roommates, billeted at The Mirimar, a three-story Spanish-style hotel surrounded by royal palms, situated near the corner of Biscayne Boulevard and 84th Street. We became close friends after what we called "the Dobson incident." A tall, lanky blond Texan from Houston with a typical Texas drawl, his piercing blue eyes seemed to bore straight through you when he spoke. His military bearing and unflagging observance of Navy rules and regulations reflected four years of training at Texas A&M University.

"Most of my classmates are in the Army," he told me. "I thought the chow would be better in the Navy." A grin followed that remark.

I learned that Texas A&M was in College Station between Houston and Dallas, closer to Houston. Cliff was engaged to his college sweetheart, a "beautiful Dallas gal." He and Helen hoped to get married between graduation from SCTC and a shipboard assignment.

A wave of anxiety swept over me upon boarding an SC for our first training exercise at sea. Surely this tiny vessel was not expected to operate in the mighty ocean. The SC 512, one of more than a dozen SCTC training ships, like all subchasers of its class, was only 110 feet in length, with a wooden hull and superstructure. Its armament consisted of a 40 millimeter gun forward of the pilothouse, two 20 millimeter guns on the flying bridge and two amidships, rockets, called "mouse traps," for some unknown reason, to be launched from bow racks, and depth charges to be dropped from the stern and propelled outward from K-guns, one on each side, during an attack on a submarine. The heart of the SC 512 was the pilothouse, the location of the radar monitor, the sonar recorder, the gyrocompass, the wheel, and the engine telegraph. That small space was jammed during our simulated submarine attacks with the student captain, the radarman, the sonarman, the helmsman, an engineroom operator, the instructor, and a half-dozen other students pressing in, awaiting their turn to blast a submarine to hell.

The single mast rose from just forward of amidships, topped by the radar dome, a short distance above the crow's nest. Two diesel engines turned twin screws that propelled the tiny craft at a maximum speed of 15 knots. The principal mission of SCs was to protect coastal convoys from submarines and to defend harbors from hostile infiltration by underwater saboteurs, E-boats, or any other means. The normal ship's complement consisted of the captain, the executive officer, the third officer, and a crew of twenty-three.

But operate in the mighty ocean the hardy little ships could. And did. Dozens of SCs were engaged in the task of escorting convoys in the Caribbean and along the eastern coast of the United States. Others had sailed to Europe to join the armada that supported the North African landings, along with the two larger classes of antisubmarine warfare vessels, the PC, a 173-foot steel ship, and the Destroyer Escort, DE, the size of many of the older destroyers. Officers of these vessels, the vast majority without any previous experience at sea, came from the civilian population, most having completed training at Submarine Chaser Training Center. The mission of Submarine Chaser Training Center was, within a space of two months, to qualify the inexperienced landlubbers to assume the role of executive officer of an SC, or a more junior position on a PC or DE. It was hoped that eight hours of class, afloat and ashore, six days a week, plus additional hours of study would suffice to train students to be seagoing officers.

The main differences between the curriculum at SCTC and Local Defense School were the many more hours spent at sea, conning the ship; making simulated runs on submarines, using the sonar echoes from differing gradations of water temperatures or a school of fish to serve as targets; participating in flag signal and blinker exercises with other SCs; piloting, using lighthouses and other shore objects as navigational aids; and, during twilight or just before sunrise, attempting to fix the ship's position from star sights. Once again, Chief Dalton's instructions gave me a leg up on my classmates when it came to communications, piloting, and celestial navigation.

An important maneuver that our instructors would not allow us to perform was docking the ship, the danger of wiping out the side or bow of an SC being too great. Instead, each student officer was required repeatedly to attempt to bring the ship alongside a buoy set adrift in the ocean. I watched with admiration and awe as the little ship's captain, time and time again at the end of a training session, skillfully brought the ship alongside the dock unscathed, no matter how stiff the breeze or swift the current. A "one-bell landing" was the pinnacle of docking achievement.

My greatest achievement at SCTC, or so I thought, was to acquire an apparent immunity from seasickness. "Get your butt to the lee side, and hang on to your hat," the instructor would shout each time one of his charges turned sickly green and commenced emitting strange gurgling sounds. Then there would be the rush to the rail, the awful retching, followed by the halting return of the now ashen-faced victim of the rolling sea.

The Christmas season was tough on all of us. No liberty passes. Captain McDaniel made certain of that. "Do you think those Nazi bastards and those yellow-bellied Japs give a rat's ass about Christmas?" he bellowed at an assembly of students to explain the school's leave, or rather, no-leave policy. "That's the very time those miserable cutthroats would pick to torpedo a hospital ship, or dive-bomb a school, or commit mass murder of POWs."

Eleanor was in my thoughts a lot, mostly at night, just before going to sleep. I patiently listened to Cliff's bragging about wonderful Helen, and how he was going to get married after completing the course at SCTC, get assigned to a Destroyer Escort, stay in the Navy and have a bunch of kids after the war ended, become an admiral, and live happily ever after. And then I'd think about Eleanor, remembering the bus ride, and wonder if I would have worked up the courage to tell her my feelings if she hadn't first told me she loved me. Then I wondered if I really loved her. How did one know the answer to that question? I hadn't seen her that much. Not nearly as much as Dee. Or Betty. Why did my heart start thumping when I thought of Betty? She's too old for me. Then, I laughed out loud. And outranks me.

Eleanor's letters, not as frequent as I would have liked, did help ease my loneliness. After listening to Cliff's usual nightly discourse about his and Helen's future, I again read the latest news from Brookline, where she was spending the Christmas holidays. Eleanor and her mother had gone to one of the local movie houses to see "Holiday Inn," with Bing Crosby and Fred Astaire in the principal roles. She thought the story was kind of sappy, but she loved Bing's singing, especially "White Christmas," and Fred's dancing. No doubt about a white Christmas in Boston, with nearly two-feet of snow falling over the weekend. The new year brought even more intensive study of celestial navigation, piloting, and ship handling. Each student was given the opportunity to command an SC for miles along the Inland Waterway under the close scrutiny of our instructor, which called for nerve-wracking decisions and maneuvering to avoid colliding with ships, buoys, and other hazards to navigation.

Cliff and I were at or near the top of every class except a course on purchasing and maintaining ships' supplies. It was just as well. The last assignment either of us wanted was to be the supply officer on a destroyer escort, or on any other ship, for that matter. By the third week in January 1943, with graduation only a week or so away, fifteen of my fifty original classmates had fallen by the wayside for various reasons, mostly either from poor grades or chronic seasickness. The remainder of the group began wondering and worrying about their future assignments. "Anywhere but the Pacific," was the fervent and often spoken prayer. "Too damn hot."

The war seemed to be going well in North Africa. The Americans had pushed General Rommel's troops eastward. President Roosevelt and Churchill met in Casablanca to plan future strategy. American forces in the Pacific had been slowly built up. The feeling of panic had disappeared. But German troops still occupied vast areas of Europe, and the possibility of an across-channel invasion of Great Britain still loomed in the background, although the RAF had swept hundreds of German aircraft out of the sky, and the Russian armies had been giving Hitler more than he bargained for.

"Couple of letters for you, Bill."

I looked up from the desk where I'd spread a chart of the North Atlantic and was trying to work out a navigational problem with parallel rulers and compass. Cliff held out two envelopes. Mighty nice handwriting."

Both envelopes bore APO postmarks. Cliff was right. The handwriting on one was distinctly feminine and "nice" but unfamiliar. The other, a masculine scrawl, looked vaguely familiar. I ripped open the first envelope. From Lieutenant (j.g.) Elizabeth Marshall. Betty! A warm feeling shot through my entire body. I missed her. A whole lot. I eagerly started reading. She was home on leave and had saved up enough gas coupons to drive to Bethlehem. "I had a wonderful visit with your mom and dad and your Uncle Dan. Your mom gave me your address. She made me promise not to snitch on her. Loose lips sink ships, she reminded me. I hope training is going okay. I know you'll knock them dead." She was stationed in London, an aide to an admiral. Just like jerk Dobson had said, I thought. I read on. She and Dee had become good friends, lived within a block of each other; got together frequently for lunch, and "sometimes in our favorite bomb shelter," she added. "That is, unless Dee, who's got a civilian job, decides to stay in bed or keep on working or imbibing at her favorite pub. She can get away with it. I can't. The powers that be would frown on it." She loved her job. Loved her admiral. "He's over sixty and happily married. So don't worry about me." She wrote about her family. "Mom's doing war work, so she says. And good old Dad is making a ton of money on the war. It's a crime and a sin, as far as I'm concerned." Her closing lines sent a thrill through me. I read them maybe ten times. "I'll never forget you, Bill. You made a huge difference in my life. Stay safe. Much love, Betty."

I closed my eyes, and recalled that first meeting with Betty on the train, when Harry had made such an ass of himself. Then the picnics near Taughannock Falls, the concerts at Bailey Hall, the book reading sessions. Cliff must have heard me sigh.

"Well, old buddy, must be someone important. That sounded like air escaping from a tire."

"Yeah," was all I could think to say.

I looked again at the second envelope. Who else would be writing me? This letter was from Lieutenant (j.g.) George Dugan. He'd been promoted.

> January 25, 1943

Dear Bill:

Well, my friend, you're going to have to salute me when next we meet. An All Nav came through, and I made j.g. by three days! Close call. I guess you didn't qualify, because there was a requirement of training and duty at sea. But that means I've taken command of my ship, the SC 604, where I've been the exec for the past six months. And that, in turn, means I need an executive officer, and I can't imagine any one I'd rather have than you.

I checked with BuPers and learned that your next assignment will be as executive officer on an as yet undesignated subchaser. Sorry to be so damn nosey, but it's for a good cause. And so, if you agree, I can put in for you and when you finish up at SCTC in the next couple of weeks, you'll be ordered here. I can't tell you where "here" is, except that it's in the same hemisphere as your present location.

Please send me a letter by return mail and let me know whether you'd like the assignment. I hope you will.

All the best,

George

Would I like the assignment! During the past ten days, we had our skulls filled with stories, mostly from enlisted personnel serving as SCTC instructors, about tyrannical skippers, usually reserve officers, jerks who took advantage of the awesome power a ship's captain held over his officers and crew to make shipboard life miserable.

"You are a fortunate coot," was Cliff's laconic response to my good news. "I only hope lady luck treats me as well."

My enthusiastic acceptance letter to George was safely in the U.S. Post Office by 0745 the next day. Along with a long letter to Betty.

CHAPTER 27

"This tub'll never make it. Why should we risk our necks for them frogs?" Bosun's Mate First Class Schultz stalked from the forecastle of the U.S.S. SC 604, the object of his deprecating remark. We just received orders that our tiny subchaser would join a slow Atlantic convoy bound for Mediterranean ports, and upon arrival it would be turned over to the Free French authorities under the Lend Lease Program.

"That's where the damn war's going on," George had exulted after reading our orders aloud. "No more escorting the damn Sea Train." Prior to my joining the ship in mid-January, the SC 604's primary mission had been to escort a gigantic merchant vessel loaded with railroad cars, known as the Sea Train, from Key West to Havana and return, Key West being the "here" referred to in George's letter. I'd made one trip and had marveled at the swift Gulf Stream current that pushed relentlessly at the ship's hull, necessitating the helmsman to steer at least 15 degrees to the right of our course in order not to be carried far to the north of our destination, and 15 degrees to the left on our return journey. I had enjoyed the tour of Havana in an ancient open Buick, chauffeured by a West Indian gentleman sporting a straw hat, who pointed out the sights in a marvelous English accent, followed by a sumptuous meal at the Hotel Nacional. George and I had puffed on Cuban cigars while sipping after-dinner cordials.

Schultz's outburst served to deepen my own anxiety, and it took a great effort to restrain myself from rushing to the skipper for words of comfort. "He's got enough troubles," I thought. The bulk of the ship's complement had recently been replaced. George's two officers and most of the crew members had never been to sea. Bob Brown, the third officer, hadn't as yet attended SCTC. He would leave the ship in Miami, where a recent graduate of the school would come aboard as third officer.

Many questions spoken and unspoken crowded my

worried mind as we prepared for departure. Is the ship large enough to make it? How high do the waves get in the Atlantic? Would a German submarine even waste a torpedo on a subchaser?

George fought tooth and nail with the Key West Navy Yard personnel to procure equipment we were entitled to, and more. Bob and I did the best we could to help ready the ship for its new adventure. But our captain's shoulders would have to carry most of the load until we learned.

Preparations for a sea journey had finally been completed after several days of intensive activity. Bob and I celebrated our leisure by relaxing in our bunks in the tiny stateroom that served as the living space for the three officers. We busily planned a visit to one our favorite Key West bars. As we discussed the various options, George's feet appeared at the top of the ladder. I watched until his entire body filled the stateroom. "We've been ordered to get under way immediately for Norfolk," he announced, beaming with excitement. "We're going to war." He swung toward me. "Mr. Creelman, take the ship down to pier nine, and refuel her." He turned and headed back up the ladder. Jumping from my bunk, I followed him partway up. I opened my mouth to speak, but he looked down, clapped me on the shoulder, continued up to the deck, and disappeared from view.

I stood motionless for a few moments, stunned. I'd studied ship handling out of a book at SCTC. I'd brought an SC alongside an ocean buoy many times. I'd watched George handle the ship, but I never dreamed I'd be given the responsibility for docking the little vessel for months, and then only under his experienced eye. Trying desperately, but unsuccessfully, I'm sure, to hide my misgivings from the crew, I managed to get the lines off the dock without mishap. "Rudder amidships. All engines back slow. I leaned on the rail of the flying bridge, gazing anxiously astern. The ship began backing into the harbor. "One long blast," I ordered, and I confidently expected all traffic to keep the hell out of the way, as the comforting drone of the ship's horn followed that command.

I had not reckoned with the tugboats and other craft that jammed the harbor, moving in all directions. From the starboard quarter, a squat, filthy, ugly tug came tearing towards us with a bone in her teeth. "One long blast." I shouted, my voice somewhat shriller. Our horn bellowed in response. The tug bore down on us. "Sound five short blasts." I screamed down the voice tube. The tug maintained course and speed. "All engines ahead full." I shouted. What seemed to be a near miss, but probably wasn't even close, shattered my nerves. Desperately trying to regain my outward composure, I managed to maneuver the ship slowly up the harbor, avoiding the eyes of the crew members, who must have seriously doubted their executive officer's seamanship. As we approached the fuel dock on our port side, I didn't allow for the flow of the current that impeded the ship's forward progress. The heaving line fell yards short of the dock in spite of Schultz's strong right arm. And so, into the teeming traffic we backed to make another try. I allowed a bit for the tide this time. The line barely reached its target, and I sighed with relief as the line handlers hauled the little ship to the fuel dock with brute strength.

That night while underway for Miami, I had the first of a series of nightmares. George stood watch on the flying bridge. In my dreams, I relived the tugboat episode. This time, however, the situation got completely out of hand, with a collision imminent. I began to cry out for help. George, startled by my shouts and thinking a man had fallen overboard, ordered all engines stopped. He raced from bow to stern, trying to locate their source before he realized that the shouts came from the depths of our stateroom. He shook me awake. Heartfelt curses came from the bunk above me, where Bob had been peacefully sleeping. Anyone not accustomed to the top bunk of an SC can forget that one foot above his head a bank of pipes carried important fluids about the ship. Suddenly awakened, Bob had sat up abruptly.

Our radar failed that night. Since our course carried us through the congested shipping lanes of the East Coast, a serious problem had been thrust upon us. George drummed into the heads of his officers and deck crew the necessity of keeping a constant and careful lookout. He didn't have to warn me. I remained sufficiently nervous to be alert at all times, as we plowed relentlessly through the night at a steady 10 knots. All ships operated without running lights. Huge black objects seemed constantly to loom ahead. Another ship? My imagination? I didn't dare lower my binoculars for more than a second at a time.

But we made it. Safe and sound. To my relief and joy.

And to George's as well, I'm sure. After arriving in Miami, two new officers joined the ship. Bernie Thompson replaced Bob, who had been ordered to attend SCTC. The prospective French commanding officer of the SC 604, Jean Charles Devin DeFontenay, also came aboard.

Just over twenty-seven years of age, slim and about 5 feet, 8 inches tall, his black hair cut to military length, Jean's self assurance and obvious intelligence impressed George and me right away as he joined the ship's company. His dark, piercing eyes moved constantly, absorbing every detail of the little ship. After rather nosey questioning, we learned that Jean had graduated from the French Naval Academy several years before the war in Europe commenced in September of 1939. His wealth of training and experience qualified him, I thought, for a far more important command. After assisting in the scuttling of his destroyer at Toulon, Jean had endured imprisonment in Paris, where his jailers selected inmates at random to be shot in reprisal for hostile acts committed against the German occupiers. Jean escaped after relatives bribed the guards, and he made his way to Spain with the help of the underground. From there he traveled to North Africa and joined the Free French Forces. After several frustrating months, he finally received orders to the United States to report for duty as prospective commanding officer of the SC 604. He, along with many other French naval officers, had a burning desire to join a ship and fight the murderous Boche.

Jean spoke English with a pronounced British accent when he came aboard. Two months later he sounded more like a Yankee after his close association with George and me, and his loving perusal of Damon Runyon's stories. Women became "dolls," and men became "guys." Jean held the belief, a matter of amazement to him, that the American male had been completely subjugated by the so-called "fair sex." "Your country should not be called the United States of America," he observed on numerous occasions. "It should be called the 'Queendom of America.' In France, a woman's duty is to keep her husband and lover happy and contented. In America, it's just the opposite." George and I learned this momentous bit of information while plunging through the blue waters north of Miami during a two-day training cruise. We felt that discussion along those lines to be academic.

Jean also believed in living life to the hilt. "I want to

experience every possible sensation," he once confided. He imparted this news to me on a calm, moonlit night during the mid-watch, that depressing period between midnight and 4 o'clock when time always seemed to move at a snail's pace. But not with Jean as a companion. I didn't respond to this announcement, knowing that a fascinating example would be forthcoming from the little Frenchman. "I want to eat every kind of meat," he went on, then proceeded to recite his culinary adventures with great animation, involving consumption of a long list of strange animals and birds, including, so he claimed, the soft under part of the amputated arm of a shipmate, who was the victim of an exploding shell, a hangfire. The ship's cook had fried the morsel in a saucepan. In answer to my inquiry, Jean murmured, "it tasted like chicken."

One evening, while Jean performed the navigational duties, George and I finally learned the principal reason for his efforts to live the full life. "I'm going to die on February 27, 1947," he announced while squinting through the lens of the sextant. George and I glanced at each other but did not respond. The quartermaster jotted down the time from the comparing watch as Jean called out, "mark."

"It's too bad," Jean went on, "I can never get married. It wouldn't be fair to my wife." He completed his sightings and restored the sextant in its case.

"How do you know that's going to happen?" George asked.

"I just know it. It came over me one day that I will die then."

We gazed at the darkened horizon, our three navigational stars now joined by millions of others. "But suppose you're at sea? Will everyone else on board have to die with you?" I asked.

Jean smiled with his Gallic shrug. "Oh no, I've got that planned. All hands will be at battle stations, wearing life jackets on the night of the twenty sixth and all the next day. I don't want anyone else to die just because I have to."

George and I repeatedly tried to dissuade Jean from believing in his fate, but to no avail.

We cleared the swept channel at Miami at about 0930, signaled a farewell to the station ship, and settled on a course of 060, which would be maintained for a couple of hundred miles. We'd then turn north, well beyond the congested traffic that clogged the shore channels. Although already late February, the soft sky seemed spring-like, the shades of blue and pink contrasting with wispy white clouds. A gentle breeze ruffled the calm sea.

Jean accompanied me on a routine inspection of the ship to assure that all the starboard watch had taken their stations. I found his enthusiasm contagious. "No more training. No more school. We are now a part of your great fleet," he exulted, eyes gleaming with excitement. The inspection completed, I climbed into my bunk to relax until 1200, proud that the SC 604 had reached combat readiness at last.

About two hours after I took over as officer of the deck, the wind commenced whipping the canvas and swirling around the flying bridge. An incessant flapping drew my attention upward to the United States ensign streaming out horizontally from the force of the breeze. Instead of gently rolling, the ship began to pitch relentlessly, her bow rising from the sea then plunging into the waves, throwing spray across the deck, even though the noon sun high up in the cloudless blue sky reflected brightly from the emerald green ocean.

A feeling of foreboding crept over me, as I braced myself against the lurching of the ship. I never experienced seas this rough during our training at the Local Defense School and Subchaser Training Center. I deeply wished to be closer to land, instead of two hundred miles to the east of any safe haven. I repressed a desire to share my concerns with the lookout.

George appeared at my side, a broad grin on his face, his eyes beaming. "Damn. I enjoy being at sea when it's rough like this," he shouted over the rush of wind.

"I was beginning to think it's a little too rough," I shouted back. He laughed, patted my back, and went below. His short visit buoyed my spirits.

By mid-afternoon, the blue of the sky had changed to gray, and the sea, instead of sparkling, appeared oily and dirty, and, although not as choppy, higher than before. The wind blew with increased force, and now our little ship commenced pitching more violently. I joined George on the flying bridge soon after his watch started. "What do you think now, Captain?" I shouted over the din of the howling gale.

George set his jaw. No smiles now. "This is as rough as I've ever seen it," he replied. "What's the barometer doing?" he called down the voice tube.

"Falling, Captain," the helmsman's response floated up.

George ordered the officers and crew to don life jackets. They provided warmth, if nothing else. We slowed our engines that night until they little more than idled. I watched with increasing alarm as the helmsman strained to hold the ship's course against the powerful waves crashing against the ship and hurling green water across the bow. By morning the wind had risen to gale force and beyond. Low clouds raced across the sky. The waves increased in height, their windblown crests curling ominously, each a threat to swamp the ship. We struggled on against the gale and sea during the daylight hours, uncertain whether the ship had made any headway, and uneasy over our prospects. Toward evening, a Navy plane, probably checking on a possibly surfaced submarine, flew over low enough for me to make out the faces of the two flyers. The occupant of the rear seat saluted me as the aircraft roared by. I returned the salute with the depressing realization that within less than two hour they'd be on dry land.

The full force of the storm struck that night. Horizontal sheets of rain pounded my face with suffocating force, taking my breath away. The screaming wind churned the sea into a phosphorescent fury, surrounding the ship with howling demons. This must be what hell is like, I thought. I huddled with George on the flying bridge and apprehensively stared upward at the massive Atlantic rollers marching relentlessly toward our tiny vessel. The wind howled through the rigging, making conversation impossible. The flying bridge suddenly commenced shaking violently. "Get the hell out of here," George shouted. "The whole works are going." He shoved me toward the ladder. I slipped momentarily, but recovered and climbed down to the deck below. George had reached the halfway point on the ladder, when a large strip of canvas ripped loose and enveloped him for a terrifying moment. He flung it aside with one hand, holding on with the other, as it vanished into the sea. George leaped the rest of the way, as the remaining canvas flew by, landing next to me with a crash. He staggered, and I grabbed his arm to prevent him from falling.

The officers on duty gathered in the pilot house behind the helmsman, who strained every muscle, working desperately to prevent the wheel from spinning out of control. George ordered a course that took the sea two points off the starboard bow, following SCTC training instructions on how to cope with a hurricane or vicious gale, never dreaming we'd be forced to apply that learning so soon. Several times a huge wave tossed the ship wildly to port, and the helmsman frantically spun the wheel to starboard, unable to bring her back on course before the next gigantic roller descended. In those awful moments, we held our breath as the inevitable lift came, then the heart-stopping pause as the ship stood balanced on the crest, followed by the roller-coaster drop and the earsplitting crash as the wave broke over us. Each time, the sturdy little subchaser shook herself like a drenched mongrel and recovered with only moments to spare before confronting the next onslaught.

The storm continued unabated throughout the night. Once in awhile a lull in the roar of the wind caused my hopes to jump.   But soon the howling started again, sometimes even louder, perhaps a reminder by the storm of its omnipotent presence. On the third morning, my stomach reminded me that the only food I'd consumed for more than two days had been several oranges shared with me by our helmsman. I crawled across the deck to the galley and the aft crew's quarters, just barely making headway against the driving, stinging tempest, clinging to the life lines we rigged. I opened the hatch, climbed down the ladder, and entered the crew's quarters. The nightmarish sight, barely illuminated by a red night-light, momentarily stunned me. Was this the Black Hole of Calcutta? The place reeked of vomit and sweat. Groaning men sprawled on the deck of the crews quarters; a mixture of salt water, ketchup, broken eggs, and mayonnaise lapped around them. Hanging on to stanchions to keep my balance, I plunged into the galley, where I spotted a pan of fried potatoes secured to the range. Grabbing a fork, I raised a mouthful to my lips. At that moment, the ship's cook staggered in, stared at me with glassy eyes, turned green, and spewed vomit into the bilge. My hunger vanished, and I barely managed to avoid losing the meager contents of my stomach by rushing up the ladder to the fresh air above.

My spirits dropped to their lowest point after my aborted

effort to find food. I worked my way amidships through the buffeting gale, opened a hatch, and descended the ladder to the engine room, dimly lit by a night-light. I found myself at the ship's center of gravity, where the motion, far less violent, resembled a comfortable rocking chair. Our chief engineering petty officer, one of the few crew members still able to stand upright, extended a friendly invitation to rest for awhile in his clean and warm domain. I lay down in the middle of the floor between the two enormous diesel engines, using my life jacket as a pillow. The steady throb of the engines and the rocking motion soon sent me off to dreamland, where I remained for the next two hours, when once again I had to return to the maelstrom.

George radioed a message to Norfolk that morning in a highly classified code, describing our plight. We waited hopefully for a response. Nothing. Two hours later he sent another message in a code of lower classification. Another wait. Still no response. The next transmission went across the ether in plain language. "In middle of severe storm. Unable to make headway. Position not known. Ship in danger of foundering. Can you assist?"

Shortly after we dispatched our final plea, salt water flooded the radio transmitter, preventing the sending of further messages. Despite that setback, we were elated not long after to receive a reply—until we decoded it.

"Storm abating," it read. "Head for swept channel at Norfolk."

"Those fools," screamed Jean. "We don't even know where we are. What's the matter with your Navy?"

"If we don't know where we are, how the hell do they know?" George shouted back. "Forget about the damn radio. Let's keep the damn ship afloat."

George stared ahead in silence for several minutes after this outburst. His brow knitted. God, now what? I wondered.

"Have you checked the forward bilge recently?" George asked.

"No, sir," I replied.

"The ship feels sluggish in the bow. You better check it."

I went quickly on deck and crawled across to the hatch leading to the forward crew's quarters. I descended the ladder and removed the bilge covers. Salt water sloshed an inch below the floorboards. A wave of horror swept over me. No wonder the ship felt sluggish. I dashed up the ladder, and worked my way aft, buffeted by the howling gale. I burst into the pilot house. "The bilge is full." I yelled.

"Take it easy," George said calmly.

"Captain, you better take a look," I shouted, "the damn bilge is full."

"Take the deck, Jean," George ordered, and accompanied me forward. He reached down and lifted the bilge cover. He froze for a moment. Convinced.

"The strainer's stopped up with a bunch of junk, Captain." This report came from Henderson, our leading gunner's mate. Wearing only his skivvies, he stood waste deep in dirty, oily bilge water, after ducking down in the muck to check the bilge pump strainer. His blond hair lay plastered to his head, his face covered with grime. The strained eyes looked inquiringly up, as George, with a battle lantern beaming into the bilge, leaned forward for a closer look.

George stared at the brown swirling liquid for a chilling moment, his face turning red with anger. "My God," he shouted. "Who the hell stowed provisions in the damn bilge?" Bags of coffee and cartons of toilet paper had been carefully stowed in the bilge by Bernie, our inexperienced supply officer. The containers had burst open and their contents clogged the pump strainer.

Not waiting for a reply, George shouted, "Grab some buckets, we've got to bail this thing out." Only four of the crew not needed at the helm and in the engine room could be called upon in this emergency. The remainder lay hopelessly sick in their bunks or sprawled on the deck of the crew's quarters. Jean, George, and I formed a bucket brigade with the four crewmen. Henderson continued diving into the bilge, scraping coffee and toilet paper from the strainer. Bernie stood watch in the pilot house. He checked up on us a couple of times, enshrouded in oil skins, shouting encouraging words, beaming with excitement, giving us the thumbs up signal. The fool seemed to be enjoying himself.

The bucket brigade toiled on for several hours, while the ship reared and bucked, her bow plunging deeply into the angry sea. We rotated positions every fifteen minutes, the most dangerous being the one that required dumping the mixture of salt water, toilet paper and coffee grounds over the side. I'll always remember foaming green water tumbling and crashing towards me during that ordeal. And, as ever, the screaming wind drowned out conversation, and even thought at times.

Gradually the water in the bilge receded, and I could detect with relief that the ship's bow had lightened perceptibly. Henderson continued to scrape the pump strainer, and the bucket brigade continued its chore, finally emptying the bilge. George thanked Henderson profusely. What a courageous guy.

During the storm, Jean had no fear for his own safety because of the sure knowledge that he would not die until February 27, 1947. But he constantly and irritatingly voiced his anxiety about the welfare of the rest of us, expressing concern that George's and my Navy careers would be cut short and we'd never know who won the war, worrying and fretting that Bernie wouldn't be able to complete his graduate work at the University of Pennsylvania, and on and on.

One night as I tried to relax in my bunk, Jean came bursting down the ladder, shouting wildly, "We're going to sink. We're going to sink."

"For God's sake, what's happened now?" I yelled.

"Nothing has happened," he answered. "I just don't see how we can keep our little ship afloat in this terrible storm."

I lost my cool for a moment. "Haven't we got enough troubles without talk like that?" I shouted. "Get the hell out of here."

Jean drew back in surprise at my outburst. "I'm only worried about you and George and Bernie," he said mildly, then crept up the ladder and disappeared.

Now time seemed to stand still. My world consisted of a heaving platform, buffeted by smashing waves, screaming gales, and stinging pellets of rain. Travelling between the stateroom and the pilot house could be accomplished only with the utmost difficulty, each forward step taken only after firmly grasping a solid upright to keep from being hurled to the deck or over the side. None of the officers and crewmen had removed their uniforms or bathed since the beginning of our ordeal. Our sleeping quarters stank of sweat and filthy clothes. We kept our life jackets loosely around us at all times, in the hopeless belief that we'd possibly have a better chance of survival if the ship foundered.

Late one night as I lay rigidly in my bunk, my thoughts

turned to Jean's alarming prediction as to the fate of the SC 604. Bernie lay stretched out in the upper bunk, probably sound asleep. No apparent worries at all. I wondered whether the world would ever learn what had happened if the ship capsized. No one could survive such a calamity. After three minutes in that raging sea, we would all drown. What would Eleanor do? Find another guy? Probably. What would Dee think when she heard the news? And Betty? Wonderful Betty. And Mom and Dad and Uncle Dan. Footsteps rapidly descending the ladder interrupted my dreary thoughts. Jean dropped to the deck and started dancing a jig, hopping around, first on one foot, then the other, a broad grin on his face. He's finally cracked, I thought. "You are saved," he shouted exultantly. "We've sighted land."

Bernie and I jumped to the pilot house and peered into the darkness. Suddenly, through the black night and swirling clouds, a beacon flashed dead ahead. And again, and then again. George clutched a timing watch, and called out the duration of each flash and the interval in between—a two-second flash with a two-second interval; a one-second flash with a one-second interval; a three-second flash, with a two-second interval; and then a repetition of the sequence. Quartermaster Second Class Littleton jotted down the information and handed George the light list for the East Coast. We huddled in the pilot house while he turned the pages, the volume illuminated by the dim rays of a battle lantern held by Jean. George slowly ran his finger down the list, searching for a lighthouse or beacon with the same characteristics as the one shining through the darkness. His finger froze in the middle of the fifth page. After a few moments, he looked up, his eyes wide with surprise. "That's the Cedar Island lighthouse," he said incredulously. "We're forty miles north of Norfolk."

"Congratulations, Captain," Bernie said, his voice a bit shaky. We all congratulated George, and at that moment I realized the sea had calmed perceptibly, moderated by the point of land guarded by that heavenly beacon.

CHAPTER 28

One hundred and fifty merchant ships plodded in ten columns, extending over miles of ocean, their bows rising and falling in unison, sending white spray across decks loaded with cargo. Twelve sleek gray destroyers, armed with the latest antisubmarine weapons, fanned out on every side of the convoy, their underwater sonar pinging, searching for submerged U-boats, listening for the telltale echo that would indicate the presence of a target. The SC 604's assigned position day and night was two thousand yards on the port beam of the destroyer occupied by the escort commander which, in turn, was stationed a thousand yards directly ahead of the center of the convoy. The destroyers had impressive code names, like Neptune, Hercules, Samson, Atlas, Ajax, and Poseidon.

Ours was Kitten.

The weather continued rotten. The tiny ship plunged forward into the teeth of a rain-filled 30-knot gale that cascaded green water over her bow. While on duty, I clung to the flying bridge rail, braced to maintain my balance as the ship rose high on each foamy crest, then slid into the trough as the wave passed beneath. No big deal to the officers and crew of the SC 604, who road out the storm of the century, or so we decided. We learned later that many merchant ships in the convoy lost their deck cargoes. Destroyer officers had pointed to our plunging, rocking, minuscule vessel to complaining crew members as an example of the horror that could happen to a man in the Navy. A "tin can" looked good compared with a tiny subchaser.

Much to George's disgust, no sooner had we cleared Norfolk harbor when Kitten received a blinker message from the escort commander ordering us to "maintain your station and convoy course and speed at all times until further orders. Do not, repeat not, activate sonar equipment." So much for our chance to blast a submarine to hell, at least on this trip. I wondered how Captain McDaniel would have reacted to that humiliating directive.

"Just thank the good Lord for stormy weather," George said more than once. "Makes it tougher for Doenitz's wolf packs to hone in on the convoy." Highly classified messages warned nightly of the probability of encountering a dreaded wolf-pack, one of the groups of U-boats able to locate the position of a convoy by radio-direction finding equipment, then, travelling on the surface, swiftly converge on the lumbering merchant ships to carry out a devastating and deadly attack. So far we were unmolested.

George's reassuring words coursed through my mind as I gripped the flying bridge rail to maintain my balance as the SC 604 lurched and plunged into the heavy seas. My oilskin coat and sou'wester fended off the cold and rain-filled gale sweeping from the northeast. I wasn't cold, but I wasn't warm either. I glanced at my watch: 0015. I'd just relieved Bernie. The mid-watch. How I hated that seemingly endless duty. The officer being relieved always hung around, knowing he'd soon be in his warm and dry bunk. Bernie had been no exception this night. "Course zero eight five," he said. "Speed 10 knots. No change in course or speed expected. The captain says to call him if anything unusual happens, no matter how trivial." His admonition irritated me. I always read the Captain's night order book before going on watch.

Bernie had yawned and stretched, a big smile on his face. "Jean's in my bunk, so I'll take yours." With four officers and three bunks, Jean, Bernie and I shared the two bunks across from the Captain's bunk in the cramped stateroom. No one shared the captain's bunk.

"Yeah, I know," I muttered, wishing he'd leave me to my misery.

"What a night." He yawned again. No response from me.

"Oh, well, I'm off to the galley for a cup of java, and then it's beddy-bye for Ensign Thompson." He descended the ladder, leaving the bridge to me and the lookouts, Stubbs and Friedman. Too rough this stormy night to order one of them to the crow's nest. We learned the hard way, after vomit on several occasions had streamed down onto the flying bridge from a seasick lookout, spattering its occupants.

I raised my binoculars and squinted into the eyepieces. Ahead only the black night with swirling clouds and foaming wind-tossed Atlantic rollers marching toward us; to starboard,

I could barely discern Neptune, the escort commander's destroyer, making heavy weather despite her size. Astern, black shapes rose and fell rhythmically in the heavy seas.

"Bridge from engine operator."

Carson's voice from the voice tube interrupted my inspection.

"Bridge aye," I replied.

"Sparks reports condition red message from Neptune. Submarine contact."

My mind froze for a split second. Submarine contact. This was it.

I swung around to Stubbs. "Call the captain!"

George appeared on the bridge in less than a minute, wearing his helmet and lifejacket.

"Sound general quarters!"

The startling rasp of the horn brought running and thumping footsteps from the forward and aft crew's quarters. I scrambled below to retrieve my helmet and life jacket from the wardroom and returned to the bridge. If anything happened to George, God forbid, I would take command. Shadowy figures hastened aft along the deck headed for the K-guns, the depth charge racks and the two 20-millimeter guns; others rushed forward to man the 40-millimeter cannon. Jean joined George and me on the flying bridge. Stubbs and Friedman uncovered the two 20-millimeters, retrieved loaded magazines from the gun box and attached them.

"Captain, sparks reports immediate change of course ordered by convoy commander. New course three four five.

"Left full rudder," George shouted down the voice tube. "Come to three four five."

"Aye, aye, sir, three four five," came the response.

As we swung violently to port, the beam sea crashed into the ship, heeling her over to such a degree I felt sure she would capsize. The occupants of the bridge grabbed the rails, struggling to hang on until the rugged little vessel settled on the new course. My face must have turned blue from holding my breath.

"Steady on three four five," came the announcement.

I turned my glass toward where I last saw Neptune. The sleek destroyer cutting across our bow at about 2,000 yards distance, her churning wake indicating flank speed. "Looks like Neptune is on to something," I shouted in George's ear.

He swung around and raised his binoculars. George sighed deeply. "Damn, I wish we could get involved."

A hollow rumble shook the SC 604 from stem to stern. "She's dropped depth charges," Jean yelled. Six huge geysers rose high into the air astern of the charging destroyer. I trained my glasses on the churning water, eager to witness the remains of a submarine that had been blown to hell, but only the angry sea was visible. Either Neptune had been deceived by false echoes or she missed her target.

"Jesus Christ! The bastard must have slipped through the screen!" The exclamation came from George, who had directed his binoculars astern. I swung around. As though in slow motion, a reddish-white ball ascended from near the center of the convoy. It hung for several seconds, then, like a gigantic Fourth of July display, disintegrated into a million sparks and descended just as slowly. No celebration this time. We watched the frightful display, knowing that sailors on board the stricken vessel were dying.

"Captain, convoy commander has ordered new course zero nine zero," Carson called up through the voice tube.

"That'll throw the bastards off if there's more of them out there," George muttered. His command followed. "Right full rudder, come to zero nine zero." The ship lurched to starboard and once again nearly broached as the heavy seas struck her beam.

"Bridge!" Carson again.

"Bridge, aye."

"Sparks has message from Neptune: SS Pilgrim abandoning ship. Kitten follow me to pick up survivors." At that moment, Neptune loomed up on our port beam plunging in the opposite direction. As she went by, her stern light shown dimly through the murk. "Thank God!" George exclaimed, "at least we can see her." He leaned over the voice tube. "Left full rudder. Come to one eight zero." Friedman's rush to the rail and familiar retching sounds told us that he hadn't escaped this last violent turn unscathed.

"Why us, Captain?" Jean stood alongside of George.

"Well, I assume because our deck's closer to the water than the tin cans, and we can more easily pull survivors aboard." He paused. "And I guess all the destroyers are needed to protect the convoy."

"Do you think its a wolf pack attack, Captain?" I tried to keep my voice steady.

"Maybe just the lone wolf," he muttered. His effort at a joke reassured me.

George peered through his glasses for several seconds at Neptune's bobbing and swaying stern light, then turned toward me. "Mr. Creelman, proceed amidships, and ask Mr. Thompson to report to the bridge. Tell Schultz what's going on, then assemble all topside hands, including gun crews, and three of the engine room gang. Prepare life rafts for instant release. Have Schultz collect all the life preservers, secure lines around them, assign one man to each preserver, and get ready to haul these poor bastards aboard." A crooked grin crossed his face for an instant. "You're in charge. So get going."

"Aye, aye, sir."

I hurtled down the ladder and onto the deck in an instant, marveling at how George had thought of so many things so quickly, and wondering how Bernie would respond to George's ordering him to the bridge. Bernie had braced himself against an air vent adjacent to the galley entrance, water streaming from his helmet and oilskins. Instead of raising any question, a smile broke out. "Great. That's where the action's going to be."

Within minutes, my orders to Schultz had been carried out. A dozen crewmen assembled amidships, half on the starboard side, the other half on the port side, each grasping a life preserver. One man stood by each of the four life rafts, ready to release them overboard on command. Pale faces told me that most of them suffered from seasickness. Schultz's forceful language must have induced instant recoveries.

Was our ship slowing down? Yes, she lost headway and commenced rolling and pitching simultaneously. Stubbs appeared at my side, his eyes wide with excitement. "The captain's spotted survivors dead ahead, Mr. Creelman. He says get ready to take them aboard."

Now the engines had reduced speed so as to barely hold the ship's course. The violence of the rocking motion nearly catapulted me over the side. "Hang on," I shouted, "and be prepared to take on survivors!"

"There they are!" The shout came from Schultz from the starboard side. I peered into the rain-filled darkness, the salt water stinging my eyes, but could see nothing but foam-streaked waves. Then, suddenly, like a dream, there popped into my vision to starboard a dozen swirling objects in the sea. Were they boxes? No. Human beings. Tiny bobbing emergency lamps attached to the life jackets added an eerie dimension to the wild scene. The ship edged closer to the group. "Wait until they're near enough to reach," I shouted. "Wait for my order!" Seconds went slowly by.

We edged closer and closer.

"Now!"

A dozen life preservers sailed to starboard. The two starboard life rafts dropped into the sea. Now the scene became nightmarish. I lost track of time. The violent rocking motion of the ship endangered the lives and limbs of the men struggling in the water as they neared the side. I became dimly conscious of forms being dragged aboard, cursing, sobbing. As the ship lurched, a survivor fell heavily against me, knocking us both to the deck. I grabbed his arm, hauled him inboard, and propped him against the ventilator. His eyes stared out, not really seeing. "Jesus, she just broke in two," he moaned. "Broke in two. Broke in two. The engine room gang was trapped. Didn't have a chance. Oh, my God."

"Okay, sailor. You'll be okay. You'll be okay." Small comfort, I knew, but what else could I say?

"Mr. Creelman, the line to Number 2 raft has parted!"

I jumped up and leaned out over the starboard side. The life raft floated free, a single figure clinging to its side, trying to climb aboard. Before I could react to Schultz's shouted warning, he grabbed a life preserver from the deck, checked to see that a line was securely attached, handed the end to me, adjusted his life jacket, shouted "Pull us in," and to my amazement, just as a wave passed under the ship, dove into the swirling sea.

"Bates, Stone, give me a hand," I yelled to the two seamen who leaned against the pilot house, gasping from the strenuous ordeal of hauling in the eleven survivors, now stretched out on deck. They hurried toward me and grabbed the line. I could make out through the blinding rain that Schultz had reached the life raft and had dropped the preserver over the head of the survivor. He waved his arm, his mouth working, shouting an unheard command to start pulling. We strained to haul the two struggling figures aboard, fighting against the wind and sea, making no headway for a few frightening seconds. Then nature stepped in, for just as Schultz and the survivor seemed to be carried away from the ship, an outsized wave rolled in, raised the storm-tossed figures high in the air, and dumped them on deck with a resounding crash.

(WELL DONE KITTEN)

Neptune's blinker, hooded so as to direct its beam straight ahead, flashed through the darkness. A thrill shot through me. I instantly understood, but I refrained from calling out the information aloud, not wanting to embarrass Signalman Stubbs, who struggled to decipher the message.

After a request to "repeat your message," Stubbs finally shouted out, "Well done, Kitten." The four officers huddled on the flying bridge let out a rousing cheer.

"Congratulations, Captain," I said.

"Congratulate Schultz, he's the hero." George paused. "I'm going to recommend an award of some kind, maybe the Bronze Star. Poor guy. But I guess he's lucky to get off with a broken arm. How that damn sailor from the Pilgrim lucked out, I'll never know." In fact, all of the survivors from the torpedoed ship were in amazingly good condition considering they were blown up and tossed into the sea. A half-dozen sprained ankles and twisted knees and several broken arms. No worse than that.

"Neptune is trying to raise us, Captain."

"Tell them to go ahead."

The dimmed flashing light commenced blinking again, with Stubbs calling out the message. "Proceed at first light to rear of convoy and transfer survivors to Orion by breeches buoy. Weather clearing. Sea moderating. Ten-knot winds and 2-to-4 foot waves expected by dawn." The USS Orion, a huge Navy tanker, had been stationed at the rear of the convoy. Her mission was to refuel the escort vessels during the ocean voyage.

Breeches buoy? I vaguely remembered reading something about those contraptions in some long-forgotten sea adventure novel, and recalled viewing a couple of news reels showing wounded men being transferred from ships at sea to a hospital ship. But nothing at Local Defense School or SCTC had prepared us for this emergency.

"We don't have a breeches buoy, Captain." Supply Officer Thompson gazed anxiously at George.

"The Orion will have one, I'm sure," George reassured Bernie.

"But..."

"But who knows how to pull off this damn caper? Is that what you're worried about?"

"Well, yes sir, I guess I am," Bernie admitted.

George turned to the SC 604's prospective commanding officer. "What about it, Jean, have you ever been aboard a ship that transferred personnel or supplies by breeches buoy to another ship?"

Jean shrugged, a sly grin on his face, no doubt pleased to be able to teach something to the Americans. "Captain, I would say maybe ten times, at least."

George clapped Jean on the back. "Okay, my French ami, it's your baby."

Another shrug from Jean, who immediately took charge. "You'll want to bring her along the lee side, Captain, which will be the tanker's port side." His eyes roved around the ship. "The Orion'll throw us a hawser, which has to be strong enough to bear the weight of the passenger." He gazed back at the stern for half a minute, apparently deep in thought. "But where can we attach it? We need a stanchion that can withstand a lot of strain."

"What about the mast?" I suggested.

"Excellent, Bill!" Jean beamed at me. "We'll drag the hawser aboard along with the blocks and tackle for hauling the breeches buoy back and forth and secure them to the mast. When we're hooked up, the Orion will let the breeches buoy slide down the hawser. Her deck is higher than ours, and gravity will do the trick. Then we'll load those poor guys in one at a time, and they'll be winched aboard the Orion."

"Okay. Sounds damn good. Mr. Creelman will select a couple of seamen to give you whatever muscle you need. He glanced at his watch. "It's nearly 0400. Jean, you and Mr. Creelman get a couple of hours of shut-eye. I'll stand watch with Mr. Thompson and rouse you up in time to carry out this damn mission."

Only four hours had elapsed since I relieved Bernie. It seemed like four days.

One by one the frightened and exhausted members

of the Pilgrim's crew were lifted into the breeches buoy, slapped on the back with shouts of encouragement, and then winched across fifty feet of seething foam to the gigantic Orion, looming high above our tiny subchaser. Although the weather had moderated as promised by Neptune, still the surging wash between the two vessels continued to be so strong that Jordan, our most experienced helmsman, had to strain every muscle to hold the ship's course. Twice our stern began swinging like a pendulum. Jean held up the transfer of human cargo each time, seconds before we smacked into the tanker's side with a resounding crash. As the two vessels fell apart, cascading green water completely submerged the SC 604's stern, sending a thrill of anxiety up my spine until the gray deck once again appeared. After nearly two hours, our struggles ended, and our job was done, with the last of our guests safely aboard the tanker.

The four officers crowded onto the flying bridge, after waving our thanks to the tanker crew. A wave of exultation swept over me. We did it. Rescued a dozen American sailors and transferred them to safety. Smiles all around.

"Jean, you were damn terrific." George's face beamed as he hugged the embarrassed Frenchman.

"Thank our sturdy helmsman for holding the ship's course," Jean said.

George leaned over the voice tube. "Our sturdy helmsman will get a promotion. That's how I'll thank him," he shouted down the tube.

"Thank you, Captain." Jordan's voice reflected the pleasure he must have felt.

George breathed a heavy sigh and turned to Stubbs. "Let's get the hell out of here. Signal Orion and ask permission to cast off." Stubbs complied quickly, then waited for a response. But none came. Our ship continued swinging back and forth, sometimes grazing the side of our unwanted companion.

"What in the name of hell is going on?" George growled.

Orion's blinker flashed for our attention.

"Go ahead," Stubbs responded.

I groaned inwardly as I read the message, but I waited for Stubbs to pass on the bad news to George. "Captain, we've been ordered to stay alongside Orion and take on fuel."

"Jesus H. Christ!" George exploded. "I can't believe this. We don't need fuel." He turned to me. "Do we, Mr.

Creelman?" Serving as engineering officer happened to be one of my assignments. I left all the details to our efficient engine crew, in particular Polansky, our reliable chief. But I did check the level of our fuel twice a day. Thank God. "We've emptied number one tank, Captain," I replied. "But we can easily make it to the Med on number two. We switched over yesterday."

"Oh well," George growled, "there's nothing we can do. Signal Orion to pass over the damn hose, Stubbs. Mr. Creelman, get your engine room gang ready to refuel."

After ninety minutes of swaying and plunging, and several near collisions with the tanker's stern, we finally got the good news from Orion. "Fueling completed. Cast off." Every man aboard sighed with relief as the gap between the two vessels slowly widened, allowing us to proceed independently. "All engines stopped," George ordered. He swung around to me. "Tell Polansky to switch over to the tank we've just filled."

"Aye, aye, sir."

I went below to the engine room, gave Polansky the order, and returned to the deck. Instantly a muffled explosion rocked the ship, followed by a burst of black smoke billowing out from the engine room hatch. On the heels of the smoke came members of the engine crew rushing up the ladder, each paler than the one ahead of him.

Have we been torpedoed? My first frightened thought.

We quickly learned from the disgusted Polansky that our new fuel had been contaminated with dirt and water. The explosion represented no more than a gigantic backfire of protest from our ill-treated engines. Why hadn't we examined a sample of the fuel before we put it in our tanks? I didn't like to think about that question, since I was the engineering officer. But it had never crossed my mind that the Navy would present us with anything but the cleanest, purest diesel oil.

By now many of the ships in the convoy had disappeared into the mist and rain. Fortunately, one of our two tanks remained nearly full of uncontaminated diesel fuel. But our engines could not be started until the fuel lines were cleaned. Even then, we weren't sure they would start.

"Inform the tanker our engines have failed," George ordered the signalman.

Minutes passed as our blinker flashed out its efforts to attract Orion's attention. Only a few of the rear ships in the columns were visible now, the rest blocked from view by the rain and swirling clouds. "Shall I keep on sending, Captain?" I feared for our signalman's life at that point. But George replied in a pleasant voice, "Yes, Stubbs, keep on."

Jean stared moodily at the faint outline of the tanker. No doubt he had a few choice thoughts about the Navy of the Queendom of the United States, but he sensibly withheld expressing them. A wave of apprehension swept over me. What would a German submarine do if it spotted us? It wouldn't waste a torpedo. It would surface out of range of our pitiful weapons and blast us with deadly 5-inch shells. I glanced at Jean and George. Were they afraid? I wondered. Their faces showed no emotion. Jean probably was counting on his premonition of a February 1947 death.

"Orion's responding, Captain." Those welcome words interrupted by morose thoughts. A faint flicker of light from the tanker appeared through the misty clouds, signaling us to send our message. The tanker must have relayed our plaintive plea to the escort commander, for soon we learned by blinker that Atlas would take us in tow. I could imagine the purple curses blistering Neptune's bridge.

Our engine crew's labors proved to be successful sooner than we could have hoped, and our engines commenced their regular beat before Atlas's arrival. By then we'd dropped twelve miles astern of the nearest ship. Her top safe continuous speed was only two knots greater than the base speed of the convoy. The SC 604 would be lucky to regain her position in less than seven or eight hours, during which she'd be at the mercy of any submarine that caught sight of the tiny vessel.

But the SC 604 chugged ahead without incident in the teeth of a stiff breeze, plunging through the oncoming waves now higher than before, and finally reached her station abeam of the escort commander at 2035. We congratulated ourselves on our uneventful return to our position, and those not on watch rested comfortably for the rest of the night. We little realized the commotion that had been stirred up on Samson, the destroyer patrolling the port beam of the convoy. We later learned from Samson's officers in a bar in Oran that the crew of the ship had been aroused by the rasping signal of GENERAL QUARTERS! Man all battle stations! A surfaced submarine had been spotted on radar. Samson trained her 5-inch guns on the target. In the nick of time, just as the order to commence firing was about to be given, a lookout shouted, "Hold your fire! It's Kitten."

CHAPTER 29

There it was. Rising majestically through the misty rain and low flying clouds.

The Rock!

The convoy had completed the remainder of the Atlantic voyage after Pilgrim's loss without further enemy attack. We repeatedly blessed the weather, which had again turned nasty. George's surmise that we'd been attacked by a "lone wolf" proved to be correct.

The convoy, barely making headway, spread out for miles below the gigantic fortress. The United States escort group had been joined by a British battleship, six British corvettes, and a French destroyer that had escaped being bottled up in Toulon during the month following the North Africa invasion, when all of France had been occupied by Hitler's forces. Jean had been beside himself with excitement when he caught sight of the sleek vessel, his eyes glued to the binoculars, as she raced by, the French tri-color streaming in the wind. "The Victor Hugo," he shouted. "I served on her for nearly a year. My first duty after the Academy."

"Next stop, Oran," George announced breathlessly. "Or more precisely, Mers-El-Kebir. We're starting to move now. Should reach convoy speed by 1800." He'd just returned in Neptune's gig from a convoy conference which, to his great excitement, he was invited to attend. "You won't believe this," he went on, his eyes shining, "I was actually piped aboard Neptune. I thought the damn ship was having a damn fire drill. But, there they were, a guard of honor at present arms, and the bosun's pipe piping away like crazy. Like I was Admiral Hornblower. The same damn thing when I left the ship. Made me feel damn good."

He sat in silence, his eyes shut, a huge grin on his face. The officers of the SC 604 crowded into the stateroom, George seated on his bunk, Jean across from him, reclining in the lower bunk. I stretched out in the upper bunk. Bernie had the deck. Jean and I waited for George to continue. "Ah well, back to reality," he finally muttered. He glanced over at

Jean. "Neptune's skipper got the word that we're turning the 604 over to your countrymen in Mers-El-Kebir. She'll be all yours. A crew will be there waiting for their skipper. Frogs, of course."

Jean smiled, not at all offended.

"What's going to happen to Bernie and me, Captain?" I asked.

"It looks like we'll be reassigned to a ship operating in the Med. Either a PC or another SC. I'm hoping the three of us will be together. At least I've made the request." Another grin. "I've grown kinda fond of you damn guys."

I felt like I was just awarded the Medal of Honor.

The smile disappeared, replaced by a frown.

"Why so serious, Captain?" Jean asked.

George let out his breath. "Well, we're going to be running a gauntlet between here and Oran. Nearly every convoy during the last couple of months has been hit by dive bombers based in Southern France, mostly night attacks. Hence the beefed-up escort. This damn escort group is loaded with fire power. I mean loaded. Should scare the pants off the damn Germans."

The weather remained unchanged as the massive flotilla lumbered on in an easterly direction, hugging the north coast of Africa. In my imagination, I pictured the Mediterranean as being sparkling and blue, ruffled by balmy breezes. After all, Spring had come. Supposedly. Instead, a 30-knot gale and a beam sea buffeted us, prostrating half the crew.

"It's the mistral. A little token of welcome sent down from my native land," Jean informed us. "But be happy," he added. "No Stuka bombers will be flying."

Jean proved to be correct. The 400-mile journey to Oran, except for the rotten weather, came to an end without incident. Not even a "condition yellow" warning. A portion of the convoy broke off from the main body, and, along with the SC 604 and several destroyers, including the Victor Hugo, proceeded into the harbor at Mers-El-Kebir, arriving on March 26. We stood in silence as the SC 604 passed by the remains of a segment of the French Mediterranean fleet blown to smithereens by the British after the fall of France. "No decent Frenchman will ever forgive the British for what they did here," Jean announced grimly, as we maneuvered to avoid the superstructures of the once proud ships resting on the harbor bottom, battered and rusting.

The SC 604 tied up at a crumbling dock astern of a weather-beaten freighter. No sooner had the order "secure the special sea detail," been issued by George than a horde of ragged barefooted Arab kids tried to scramble up the vessel's side and had to be driven off. Cries in broken English reached us from the dock. "You wanna buy dirty pichers? Wanna sleep with my sister? Got any cigarettes?"

"Animals!" Jean growled. "Filthy animals."

My high esteem of Jean dropped several notches when I realized his contempt for Arabs. It seemed that he and most of the French population regarded Arabs as little better than animals. Worse, probably.

Preparations began immediately to ready the ship for transfer to the French. Much to our distress, Bernie received orders to proceed to Algiers for assignment to the PC 923. George and I stayed aboard with Jean to help train the new crew. We learned just enough "French" to give basic commands for steering the ship.

On April 2, 1943, we finished our work. A little ceremony followed, presided over by a high-ranking Free French officer and his staff. Someone made a speech. In French. I didn't understand a word. Jean seemed pleased. The United States ensign slowly descended, and after being carefully folded, was presented to George. I felt a lump in my throat. The French ensign briskly ascended skyward and snapped outward into the African breeze. The thrilling strains of the Marseillaise, rendered by a tiny military band, filled the air.

Jean glanced at George and me, and smiled almost imperceptibly.

"Good-bye, Kitten," I whispered. "Good luck!"

CHAPTER 30

"The two of you can hang out at BOQ until your orders are cut."

Lieutenant (j.g.) Steve Chapman had introduced himself as the Assistant Personnel Officer, Naval Headquarters, Oran. BOQ. Bachelor officers quarters. Visions of bunk beds, four to a room raced through my mind, with showers and toilets shared by thirty officers. Like Cascadilla Hall. Only worse. "I just got to this Godforsaken dump myself only last week," he informed us. "Hitched a ride from Gibraltar on the Victor Hugo, a French tin can. Same convoy you guys were in."

He handed George a mimeographed sheet of paper. "Here's the authorization. Hand it in to the desk clerk at the St. George Hotel, a couple of blocks down the street, this side. Turn to the left when you leave here."

Hotel. What a laugh. Chapman had a sense of humor, anyway.

"How long will we be at this so-called hotel that's named after me?" George asked.

"Oh Jesus, I don't know, maybe a couple of weeks. We're waiting for three PCs from the States. Their convoy's been delayed. Just arrived in Gibraltar. Tangled with a wolf pack, courtesy of Admiral Doenitz, and lost seven merchant ships. You'll probably be assigned to one of them."

Assigned to a PC.

Not the largest ship in the fleet, but considerably larger than an SC. I'd been aboard only one, the PC 1173, on a weekend cruise from Miami to Key West during SCTC training. A PC's mission was to patrol coastlines or escort coastal convoys. Just over 178 feet in length, steel construction, flank speed 21 knots; a 3" 50 caliber gun forward of the pilot house and flying bridge; a 40 millimeter Bofors gun aft; a half-dozen 20 millimeter machine guns; cannons; rockets and depth charges for attacking submarines; a complement of five officers and sixty crewmen. That sounded terrific.

The St. George was tucked back from the street, surrounded by gigantic palm trees, looking for all the world like a French villa, which it probably was before the war. The "desk clerk" turned out to be an aristocratic Arab, sporting a turban and attired in a flowing white robe. He stepped from behind the desk, bowed and smiled. "Welcome to the St. George. I am Abdul, at your service. I trust that your visit will be pleasant." At the snap of his fingers, two Arab boys dashed into the lobby, grabbed our luggage, and waited breathlessly for orders.

"Take these bags to the Suite Royale."

George and I exchanged astonished looks. "Are you sure we're in the right place?" George asked.

Our "clerk" glanced at the mimeographed sheet. "Oh yes, gentlemen, without any doubt." He smiled, and pointed. "Please, follow me. The lift awaits you. Your suite is on the third floor."

The three of us just managed to squeeze into the tiny, but elegant elevator. A bright overhead light recessed in the domed ceiling reflected from the brass interior walls and intricately tiled floor. Abdul closed the gate-like door, and we ascended ever so slowly. Our two bell boys waited down the hall, beckoning, as we thanked Abdul and stepped from the lift.

Well, I hadn't been around all that much. Neither had George for that matter. But we had to agree that our bachelor officers quarters must have been designed for visiting royalty. After all, it was the Suite Royale. A tour of our home away from home disclosed two gigantic bedrooms, each with a private bathroom and an enormous bed with a silk canopy flowing from the ceiling. "To defend against the mosquito," one of the boys explained. Persian prints adorned the walls of the living room, some depicting strange turbaned figures on horseback hunting wild animals with spears; others showing weird women, playing instruments resembling lutes. How could I be sure? I'd never seen a lute.

The living and dining quarters, definitely fit for a king and a queen, contained luxurious sofas and chairs, three low mahogany coffee and side tables, wall-to-wall Oriental rugs, and a carved wooden dining table surrounded by a dozen matching chairs under an enormous glittering glass chandelier. George sailed his hat across the room, where it made a soft landing on the thick Oriental rug, then sprawled on one of the sofas and stared around at our luxurious surroundings. "Just what the hell is going on here?" he exclaimed. A shrill bell interrupted any explanation I might have attempted. I noticed a telephone on a side table near the door. I hurried across the room and lifted the receiver. "Ensign Creelman," I said.

"Creelman, this is Chapman."

Here it comes, I thought. A reality check.

"I guess you're going to kick us out of this palace." I tried to hide my disappointment.

"Well, actually I'm not. The fact is you're in the VIP quarters. I just took this job a couple of days ago, and screwed things up. Put you in the wrong place. But my boss said to hell with it, let 'em stay there. We're not expecting any bigwigs."

"Well, gee, thanks," was all I could think to say.

"No problem."

"How much is this going to cost us?" I asked.

"No charge for the suite. You'll have to pay for any food or drinks you order. Feel free to splurge. It's dirt cheap. So don't worry. Have a ball. It'll be your last chance for a long time." The phone on the other end clicked.

"What do you suppose he knows that we don't know?" George asked, after I repeated Chapman's last remark.

"Probably going to be another invasion soon," I replied. "Now that the Germans are about to be kicked out of North Africa."

"Jesus, where do you suppose the damn thing will be? I can't wait."

"Let's have a look." I pointed to an enormous globe mounted on a metal stand next to one of the sofas.

We dragged the globe toward us and sat down. George traced his finger along the southern shore of the Mediterranean. "We're here and want to get there." He pointed to Berlin. "I say forget Italy. Invade Sardinia. Then hit the bastards in Southern France." He looked at me.

"Maybe attack Greece." I said. "At least the natives are friendly." I studied the globe. "Or Sicily. What about Sicily? Looks like a steppingstone to the Italian mainland."

"That would really be stupid," George snorted. "Sicily's full of mountains. If you want to get to Italy, bypass Sicily and then let the damn eyeties and Krauts try to fight their way out." He examined the globe closely. "Well, maybe you're right. That does look like the shortest way to Rome. Yeah. Sicily. Maybe we can blow the damn Mafia to hell."

A shrill ring interrupted our speculations. The telephone again. "We're out of here for sure," George grumbled. "I'll handle it." He heaved himself up and shuffled over to the phone. "Admiral Dugan here," he announced pompously. I watched him anxiously as he listened. The grim look on his face broke into a smile. "Terrific." More listening by George. "Yeah, yeah, I'll tell him." Tell him. What in the hell was I going to be told? Another seemingly endless message from Chapman followed. "Well, Lieutenant Creelman will be glad to see him, I'm sure." George dropped the phone into its cradle, the smile replaced with a huge grin.

Meanwhile, my jaw had dropped to my shoes.

"What the hell's going on, Captain?"

"You, my friend, have been promoted to Lieutenant (j.g), as of exactly one month ago. All Nav 435 did the trick. Chapman thought you'd like to know. Trade one gold bar for one silver bar, and add a half-stripe. Sounds like the title of a song."

I rose slowly to my feet, barely able to shake the hand that was offered. Promoted. No longer an Ensign. My head spun with excitement.

"I guess you won't have to salute me anymore, Mr. Creelman," George said.

"I'll always salute you, Captain," I replied.

For the first time, at least to my knowledge, George actually looked embarrassed. "That ain't all the news," he went on. "Do you know a Paul Michel?"

I sat down abruptly. Memories of Marie swept over me. Memories of...God. What the hell was he doing here? "Paul Michel?" I tried to steady my voice.

"Yes. Paul Michel." George stared. "Is he some kind of enemy? You look like you've been poleaxed."

"No. No. No enemy. It's just..."

"Just what, for Christ's sake?"

"Well, it's just that..." I stopped. I couldn't tell George about Marie. I couldn't tell anyone. "Well, it's just that I'm surprised," I said. "I rented a room in his home in Washington until I was transferred to Local Defense School. He's French. Now that I think of it, he was stationed in Algiers before the war. Some kind of diplomatic post." I felt my face getting warm as I recalled the exotic dinner prepared by Marie and the drunken session that followed, with her jabbering endlessly about herself and Paul.

"Well, I'm glad he's not an enemy, because he's on his way over here." George stared again. "You look like you've seen a ghost. Are you sure this damn guy doesn't want to kill you, or something?"

"No. No. I'm surprised, that's all. Surprised."

"I'll say you are. You are damn surprised. More like shocked, if you ask me." He walked to the phone, spun the dial, and waited. "Abdul, please send up drinks for three. Maybe your finest bottle of brandy and plenty of beer for Lieutenant Creelman." George winked and gave me a thumbs up. "And some tricky French hors d'oeuvres. You know what I mean. We're expecting an important guest. Monsieur Paul Michel." He hung up the phone and turned slowly. "I don't know what your problem is with this guy," he said, "and it's none of my damn business."

George joined me on the sofa. "It seems that Michel was a passenger on the Victor Hugo," he said, "and he and Chapman became pals. When Michel dropped by to chat, Chapman told him how he screwed up by assigning two lowly naval officers to this palatial establishment. When he mentioned your name, your friend or enemy Paul Michel nearly fell over. I guess he was surprised, too."

"Well, Bill, what a surprise."

I thought George would choke, trying to keep from laughing.

After our greetings and introduction, George had solemnly poured out brandy for himself and Paul, and a glass of Arab beer for me. Paul looked ten years older, his face lined. And deep shadows under his eyes. He'd lost weight. Lots. It had only been mid-September since I last saw him. Not even a year ago, when he mysteriously disappeared.

"Yeah, a surprise," I mumbled.

I longed to ask him about Marie, but didn't dare at first. But then I thought. maybe he'd be suspicious if I didn't. "What do you hear from Marie?" I asked, hoping my voice held steady.

"She's still in Washington. I've been moving around so much, it's hard to keep track of her. But she's fine. Working for the Free French group in D.C."

I cleared my throat. "She was really upset when you sort of vanished into thin air."

"I don't blame her." He placed his glass on the table

and took a deep breath. "It was tough to take off that way, without telling her where I was going, but I had no choice. Strict orders to keep my mouth shut. Fermer la bouche."

George chimed in, to my relief. "What was going on? Can you tell us now?"

"Pour me another drink, and I'll give you the story. Except for some of the details, there's no secret about the broad outlines of the mission I was involved with. It's had quite a lot of publicity."

George complied. Paul held the snifter to the light, contemplated the amber fluid, took a sip, leaned back, closed his eyes and started talking. "When I left Washington, I thought I was headed for Gibraltar but had no idea why. Instead, I flew by U.S. Navy Transport on an R5-D to London, stopping at St. John's and Horta for refueling. I hung around London for a couple of weeks, reporting every day to Free French headquarters, biting my nails and silently cursing my superiors. Finally, I received orders to report to General Giraud's headquarters in Gibraltar. He just escaped from a German prison and was quite the hero. The Rock was jumping with rumors about a possible invasion. Everyone knew about the allied troop buildups in England, Scotland, and Gibraltar. The French newspapers were wild with speculation, most of them targeting North Africa, but not knowing when or exactly where. The Vichy government was scared silly that an invasion would trigger the complete occupation of France by the Germans, which happened, of course."

He held out his glass for another refill. I quickly complied.

"I never saw General Giraud," he went on, "but met I with General Charles Mast and his deputy. An invasion of North Africa mostly by American troops was planned, but the general didn't know when or where, and for reasons I've never understood, wasn't told until just a few days before troops started landing in French Morocco. The Americans were anxious to persuade the French Army and Naval leaders in North Africa not to resist an Allied invasion. Someone familiar with the area was needed to go to Algiers and contact Robert Murphy, the top official at the American Embassy in Algiers, and act as a liaison between General Mast and him. I was their man. Everything had to be done in the utmost secrecy because the French officials were divided on whether to try to bring France back into the war or to roll over and play dead, figuring on a total German victory. Some of the key players were loyal to Marshall Petain, who was desperately trying to keep the Vichy government afloat."

Paul's voice rose, and his face flushed with excitement. "Well, as the whole world now knows, arrangements were made for General Mark Clark, Eisenhower's deputy, to meet secretly with General Mast and Mr. Murphy at a beach house near Cherchell, about seventy-five miles west of Algiers. Where I used to spend vacations." He smiled. "Where I met Marie." A long silence followed. I hoped my face did not reveal my guilty thoughts.

He shrugged. "I shuttled between Mr. Murphy and General Mast and attended secret meetings between the two of them in Algiers, laying plans for the rendezvous with General Clark. Unfortunately, I wasn't in on the Cherchell meeting. Only military personnel attended. A British submarine carried General Clark and his aides to about a mile from the beach, where they went ashore at night in rubber boats. What an adventure. What heroes." Paul sighed in obvious admiration. "I never heard any details about the meeting. The plan couldn't have been a total success, because the French fought back hard near Casablanca and also managed to slow things down at Algiers."

Paul stopped. A long silence ensued, while he relived his adventure. Finally, he turned toward us, his glass raised. "I salute both of you and wish you luck in your next great adventure." He downed his drink, then stood. "I must be going. I'm off to Algiers this afternoon. And then..." The typical Gallic shrug followed.

"And then what, for Christ's sake?" George demanded. "Where's the next big push? And when?" His voice rose with excitement.

Paul drew himself up to his full height. "I would be hung by my most manly parts were I to divulge that information."

"Oh, come on, Paul," George coaxed. "Bill and I aren't exactly spies. We've been through hell getting to this damn dump. We know enough to keep our damn bouches shut."

Paul glanced at me, maybe looking for some advice. I decided to let George handle the situation.

"Anyway, Bill and I've figured it's Sicily," George said. "So what the hell. It's no big military secret."

Paul flushed like he'd been slapped across the face.

George's shot undoubtedly hit the bull's-eye. "We're right, aren't we?" George exulted. "So you might as well fill us in on what's going on."

"Well." Paul held out his glass. "One more for the road, as you Yanks say." His glass refilled, Paul leaned back on the sofa.

"It's Sicily all right, gentlemen," he said quietly. "The decision was made in January, when Roosevelt and Churchill met in Casablanca. Even the exact date and hour's been decided. An early morning assault on July 10, when the moon will be mostly on the dark side, and the weather has at least a chance of being fairly decent. American and English troops. General Patton's 7th Army and General Montgomery's 8th Army. Admiral Cunningham will be in overall charge of the naval operations. Admiral Hewitt will command your 8th Fleet. Admiral Ramsey will command the British Fleet. The French Fleet will be represented," he added proudly. "This glorious invasion will be the most massive and powerful sea and land operation in the history of the world!"

A feeling of warmth rushed through my body. My armpits dampened. I inwardly prayed that my emotions didn't show. Was I going be a part of all of this? This what? This carnage? So far, I was lucky. Only the elements to cope with. Not the Germans. Except for the sinking of the Pilgrim. But I wasn't directly involved. My ship hadn't been blown apart. I hadn't been hurled into the sea. I hadn't seen my shipmates slaughtered or drowned.

George's excited voice interrupted my dire thoughts. "Haul that damn globe over here, Bill."

I quickly complied.

George turned to Paul, his eyes shining. "Where will the landings be?" he urged. "Do you know? Damn, I can't wait."

Can't wait! My captain actually looked forward to maybe getting himself killed.

Paul grimaced. He couldn't have been happy, spilling all these secrets. But I guess he figured, in for a penny, in for a pound, because, after a big sigh, he drew the globe toward him. "Here's where the Yanks will land, between Licata and Scoglitti." His finger traced a path eastward along the coast. "And here's the British sector, between Portopalo and Syracuse."

Licata! Scoglitti! Portopalo! Syracuse! Places where

I might die. Places I never even heard of before. Except Syracuse, New York. Why wasn't I there?

George leaped to his feet. "This is fantastic," he shouted. "Fantastic. We're bound to be in on it. Why else would we be waiting around here for reassignment? Chapman said we'd probably get assigned to one of the PCs headed this way from Gibraltar."

"Well, Lieutenant Dugan," Paul paused and smiled at me, "and Lieutenant Creelman, I wish you Godspeed and good hunting. Maybe I'll be aboard the Victor Hugo, and we'll meet in Palermo after we've run the Boche's derrieres out of Sicily."

"I'd like to drink a damn toast," cried George. "Come on Bill, fill up that damn stein. One more, Paul."

We lifted our glasses.

"Okay, let's get corny," George said. "What the hell. We'll all yell 'victory in Sicily,' then down the hatch."

We raised our glasses.

"Altogether, one, two, three," George called out.

"VICTORY IN SICILY!" we shouted in unison.

CHAPTER 31

"The target area of the Western Naval Task Force is the Gulf of Gela. The code name of this operation is Husky. Your ship's assigned to the Joss Force landings in the Licata area, specifically the segment of the Molla Attack Group that will land on Green Beach 1. You're a part of Task Force 86.3 under command of Admiral Dubose."

A large chart of the northeast coast of Africa and the south coast of Sicily hung from the wall of the dingy room, held in place by a string of thumbtacks along the top. As he spoke, Commander Campbell's pointer traced a path from seaward to a position halfway between Torre di Gaffe and Licata. "Those landings will take place more or less contemporaneously with landings by three other attack groups in the Gulf of Gela, the first designated as Gaffi, landing on Beach Red to your west, the second, Salso, landing on Beach Yellow to the east; the third, Falconara, landing on Beach Blue further to the east." The pointer tapped each location on the chart as he spoke.

The stubby, prematurely gray-haired officer, a 1933 graduate of the Naval Acadamy, held the position of assistant operations officer on Admiral Hewitt's staff. His responsibility, just one week before D-day, was to make certain that the commanding officers of small craft assigned to the Beach Identification Groups for the several invasion beaches or for reconnaissance and patrol duty understood their tasks perfectly. Our turn had come to receive instructions.

"The Green Beach landings are set for at or near 0300 on 10 July. The PC 823 will sail from Bizerte Roads with the Joss Force medium convoy at daybreak on 8 July, taking the station assigned by your escort commander. After orders from him, you will break off from the main forces and proceed ahead toward the invasion site in time to rendezvous with the British submarine HMS Safari at 0030 on 10 July. She's due to arrive seaward of Licata near midnight on 5 July, and send scouts ashore by rubber boats to reconnoiter. She'll be submerged during daylight hours. In the early morning of 10 July, Safari will be patrolling five miles off the beach in the Licata area. The challenge recognition signal will be HUS. Your reply will be KY. Use hooded lamps for signaling. She'll order you to take up Station Fox 4,000 yards to seaward from her. Precisely at 0130, 10 July, you will commence blinking the letter fox to seaward to guide the YMS group assigned to sweep Green Beaches 1 and 2. They will commence sweeping after passing you. A group of LCIs carrying a segment of the 3rd Infantry Division to Green Beaches 1 and 2 will shortly follow. You will proceed to lead the columns of landing craft to within 3,000 yards of the beach. Don't run away from them, and do not, and I repeat not, operate your sonar. When you break off, reverse your course and commence patrolling on a 5,000-yard line about 10,000 yards from the beach seaward of the cruiser and destroyer fire support. Take whatever action is needed to deal with hostile aircraft. Remain on that patrol until further orders."

"Where will the orders come from, Commander?"

George's face flamed with excitement. Seated at a battered wood table with the commanding and executive officers of nine other PCs and SCs in a stuffy, windowless conference room on the first floor of U.S. Naval Headquarters, Bizerte, he had furiously written every word on a white tablet.

"From the Biscayne, the Task Force 86.3 flagship. She'll be stationed about 6,000 yards southeast of Licata breakwater in case you need..." Commander Campbell stared at the chart, a faraway look in his blue eyes. Probably wishing he had a ship to command in the coming drama. It seemed strange, I thought, just nineteen months ago when war was declared, all of the ten ship captains in the room were civilians, most of them just out of college. Now each commanded a U.S. Navy vessel operating in a war zone on the eve of a historical invasion. This officer, trained for war at Annapolis, had no command.

"If you don't hear from Biscayne, just use your own judgment," Commander Campbell said. "Maybe take up station close to one of the cruisers to guard her against air attacks or underwater saboteurs. I'm sure you'll figure out what to do."

Commander Campbell turned to the few remaining officers not yet briefed. I barely heard what he said. My mind raced with a mixture of excitement and apprehension. The PC 823 would be going into the beach ahead of the invasion forces. Could we get away with that? Wouldn't the shore batteries blow us to pieces? Or bombs from the Luftwaffe? Or even the Italians? I yearned to be in Boston. With Eleanor. Should I write her and hint at what was going to happen? Officers' letters were not censored. Enlisted men's were. I never figured out the reason for the difference in treatment.

"Let's get a damn beer. Man, we have to celebrate." George tugged at my elbow. Officers in khaki uniforms headed for the door in silence. All subdued. Except George. His eyes looked like he'd just won a million dollars at roulette. He dragged me from the building and along the waterfront, lined with palm trees and jammed with naval vessels of all sizes and descriptions. We stopped at the U.S. Navy Officers Club, a crowded, noisy, sweaty, hot room—the local house of prostitution before the Americans took over. So we learned within an hour after docking the PC 823—a one-bell landing by George despite the 6-knot current. Beer sold for five cents a bottle, fifty cents a pitcher. Hundreds of gallons were consumed by thirsty naval officers every week.

When we entered, the cacophony of shouts, laughter, and music from a jukebox, turned up to its maximum level, physically jarred my ears. Cigarette and cigar smoke hung like a low-lying fog, inflicting God knows what damage on our poor lungs. Added to the confusion, a raucous group of LCI officers belted out a popular ditty:

> "Roll me over in the clover, roll me over lay me down and do it again. This is number one and the fun has just begun, roll me over lay me down and do it again."

After lining up for ten minutes, we caught the bartender's attention, ordered two pitchers of beer, grabbed two glasses, and elbowed our way to a table, just deserted by members of the glee club who quit their yowling after reaching number ten and staggered toward the exit. George tossed his hat on the table and took a deep breath when we got seated. "This is too damn good to be true. We've got to get loaded." He poured the beer into two glasses and raised his toward me. "Good old Captain McDaniel would be proud of us. I'm going to drink to him. Then to Chapman for getting you and me assigned to the same damn ship and getting you assigned as my exec." With that, George chugalugged his drink and quickly poured a refill.

I watched him as he sat there reveling in the orders we just received. I thought back to the day, just six weeks ago, when Chapman had telephoned us early one Monday morning at the St. George. We'd been drinking most of the night, royally entertaining officers billeted at the BOQ. I answered the ring, barely able to keep my eyes open, my head pounding with pain.

"It's wake-up time in more ways than one," Chapman had announced. "Hustle your butts down here. Better pack first. Be prepared to board the PC 823 by 1800."

"What's going on?" My headache seemed to have vanished.

"Your former commanding officer is still your commanding officer. He's taking over the 823. The skipper and exec have been relieved of their duties. You've been assigned as executive officer. I'll have the orders cut before you get here."

And take over the PC 823, George did. No doubt about it. The morale of the crew hovered below zero when we boarded her. We learned from Bixler, the ship's quartermaster first class, a solid man in his late thirties hailing from Baltimore, that the former captain and executive officer had repeatedly abused the crew: captain's mast nearly every day, restrictions handed out by the dozen on a regular basis, liberty cancelled for the slightest offenses. Meanwhile, a few favorites received promotions and liberty whenever possible. The captain and his executive officer frequently spirited liquor and women aboard, winking at the gangway watch, who was promised special treatment for turning his head away as the unauthorized guests boarded and left the ship.

Ensign Donnelly, the engineering officer, bit the bullet and reported their conduct to the captain in charge of Naval Operations at Oran. After a week's investigation, the two misfits were relieved of their duties. Ensign Donnelly remained aboard, as did Ensign Stocke and Ensign Pierce.

Within a few weeks after George took command, the crew's morale ascended to the highest possible point. At least it seemed so to me. Bixler agreed. He and I became close friends through our mutual Maryland connection. My duties as executive officer were mostly administrative. Because of my knowledge of celestial navigation and piloting and because I could send and read blinker and semaphore, George appointed me navigation officer and communications officer. He selected Pierce as gunnery officer and aircraft recognition officer, and he also assigned him to conduct training courses and examinations for crewmen seeking promotions. Stocke served as the supply officer and first lieutenant in charge of the deck crew.

The three officers varied in origin and background. A husky red-head with no college education, Jim Donnelly grew up in South Boston, where he acquired a half-Boston, half-Irish accent. He served as an engineer aboard a cargo ship for eight years before Pearl Harbor. Carl Pierce hailed from Salt Lake City. The devout and scholarly Mormon graduated from Utah State University in 1938 and spent the next year as a missionary in Kenya, spreading the word of the Latter-day Saints. To my amazement, he donated ten percent of his Navy pay to the church. He called it tithing. I'd never heard the term before. Jack Stocke, a tall, rangy guy with huge hands, a crew-cut and a "show me" attitude, was born and raised in St. Louis. He played varsity outfield at the University of Missouri, was a steadfast Cardinals fan, and openly and unashamedly worshiped Number 7, Stan Musial. We bemoaned the low caliber of the wartime major league teams and argued endlessly with me over the relative abilities of legendary baseball heroes, especially Musial and Joe DiMaggio.

I glanced at George, as his third beer disappeared down the hatch, a happy smile lighting up his eyes. Probably dreaming of the coming battle. It suddenly occurred to me that I knew hardly anything about him. He never talked about his personal life. That figured, since, as the captain, he treated his officers, even me, with formality at all times. I wouldn't dream of calling him anything but "Captain." He addressed all of his officers as "Mister." He had become less formal when we shared the suite at the St. George Hotel. Once in awhile, he called me "Bill," but I always addressed him as "Captain."

I did know he wasn't married. As executive officer, I kept on file the personnel records of all the officers and crew. Did he have a girlfriend? I wondered. Maybe this was as good a time as any to find out. I cleared my throat. "Captain, do you mind if I ask you a personal question?"

He snapped out of his reverie, and shot a glance at me.

"Well, I don't know. Depends on how personal." He held out his empty glass. "Fill 'er up and give it a try."

"Well." I hesitated. Maybe I was going too far. I complied with his request. But said nothing.

"Send your message, Mr. Creelman. That's an order!"

"Well, you heard me go on and on about Eleanor and Dee and Betty when we were at the St. George, and it occurred to me that you just listened and never talked about any girlfriend you may have."

The smile slowly faded. I immediately regretted asking as a grim look appeared on his face.

"I'm sorry, Captain," I mumbled. "I shouldn't have been so damn nosey.

"No. It's okay." George examined his hands carefully for at least a minute. "I was married before the war. Beautiful girl. Terrific figure. We were kids. Got boozed up one Saturday night and eloped to Elkton, Maryland, not far from your hometown, where we got hitched for twenty five bucks. Stayed together for a year. I worked during the day, attended college classes at night. Not much time for her. She got a job. Her damn boss drove a Cadillac, handed out expensive gifts, took her to nightclubs, treated her like a damn queen. She dumped me." He snapped his finger. "Just like that. Sued for divorce. Charged neglect. End of story." He raised his glass. "Here's to good old Rosemarie. She taught me a damn good lesson. I'll never get mixed up with a damn woman again. Not as long as I live." He swallowed his beer in two gulps and slammed the glass on the table. "Screw them all. The young and the short and the tall."

The silence lasted forever. Or so it seemed. He must have noticed my embarrassment. "Come on, Mr. Creelman, don't think I'm upset. I'm not. I'm glad she's out of my damn life. I'm happy the damn war came along. Helped me forget that damn bitch. Now I can't wait until we run those damn eyeties and krauts out of Sicily." He stood abruptly. "Let's get back to the damn ship, and fill in Pierce, Stocke, and Donnelly on what's going on." He reached for his hat and squared it on his head.

"Look out, Benito. Here we come."

CHAPTER 32

"Can't you read the damn thing, Casey?"

George lowered his binoculars and turned angrily toward the signalman, who, for the third time, flashed the Swanson, asking her to repeat her message. Moments later the gray camouflaged destroyer, 3,000 yards off our port beam and barely visible, disappeared completely into a trough, then as a wave carried her upward seemed to jump clear out of the water. Columns of LSTs and LCIs beyond the Swanson rose, fell and rolled in the stormy seas whipped up by a force 6 gale that chilled me through my oilskins. The dim light continued flashing, at times hidden by the angry white caps rolling toward us.

"Captain, can you move in closer? I'm only getting part of it." Casey's strained eyes pleaded with George.

I struggled with my conscience. I read the message from the escort commander twice, interrupted by Casey's blinkered requests that words be repeated. Should I embarrass him by translating the signal for the captain? Maybe I should give him one more chance. And yet...

George brought my hesitation to an end in a hurry. "Damn it to hell. The Swanson must think we're a bunch of ignorant turkeys." He swung around toward me. "What does it say, Mr. Creelman? I know damn well you've read it."

George meant business. I had no choice. I mouthed a silent "sorry" to Casey. "We're to break off at 2000, and proceed to rendezvous with the Safari, and carry out previous orders."

"Send a roger to the Swanson."

The single letter, dit dah dit, flashed out from Casey's blinker.

George glanced at his watch. "Okay. This is it. In forty-five minutes, we'll be on our way." His eyes lit up. "Damn."

"Oh, by the way, Captain," I said, "the Swanson wished us good luck."

George grinned. "Mr. Creelman, we are about to embark

on the most momentous enterprise of the war. Striking for the first time the enemy on his own land."

I recognized the opening lines of Admiral Cunningham's stirring message relayed this morning to every Allied ship.

We clutched the flying bridge rail and held on for dear life as the PC 823 lurched to starboard then slid down the side of a beam wave. George finally spoke when we recovered our breath. "I'll need the course from our position at 2000 to a point 10,000 yards seaward of Licata. Plot it out and have Bixler bring it to me. Then grab some chow and get some shut-eye. Ask Mr. Pierce to come to the bridge. I'll stand watch with him. I'll expect you back here at 2300. We're due to rendezvous with the limey sub at 0030."

"Shall we come to general quarters, Captain?" I asked.

George thought for a couple of seconds. "No. Let's give the crew as much rest as possible. We'll have plenty of time at general quarters before this thing is over."

I made my way down the ladder to the deck and entered the chartroom just aft of the pilot house. Bixler stood alongside Rodriguez, an inexperienced helmsman who joined the ship in Bizerte, counseling him in the task of holding the ship's head in a beam sea. In the next couple of minutes, I plotted and jotted down the course on a sheet of notepaper and handed it to Bixler.

"Wish we were in the fair state of Maryland, Mr. Creelman." The quartermaster smiled wryly.

"We'll be there just as soon as we win the war," I said. Please take this to the captain." The salt air stung my eyes as I stepped from the charthouse. I struggled down the deck to the wardroom, staggering as a particularly vicious wave crashed into the ship. Carl Pierce looked up as I entered. A small, black leather-bound Bible lay open on the green cloth that covered the table occupying most of the room. "The captain would like you to report to the flying bridge," I said. He closed the Bible and shoved it in the pocket of his jacket. I shrugged out of my oilskins and draped them over a chair. "Do you think reading that religious stuff will bring us good luck?" I asked.

"This religious stuff, as you call it, isn't supposed to bring anyone luck," he said. "Reading the word of God gives me faith, and that's all I can expect."

"Well," I said, "I'd feel better if a little good luck was thrown in."

"Okay. I'll buy that." He smiled, squared his hat on his head, and was gone, slamming the door behind him.

Pierce had pretty much given up his efforts to convert me to his religious ways. We had many discussions about the Mormon beliefs. They sounded crazy to me. I once asked if he planned to have more than one wife. He just laughed. Didn't get mad at all. But I admired him. A really decent guy in every respect. He actually did practice what he preached. At Pierce's request, the captain had two-blocked the church pennant the Sunday before we sailed from Bizerte. Pierce conducted a short, impressive service in the crew's mess hall, attended by the entire ship's company except for the men on watch.

"Well, Mr. Creelman, looks like we're going to have a little fun before long. This'll help get you ready. Hang on to it, though. Don't want it all over the deck." Steward's Mate First Class Page entered from the pantry adjacent to the wardroom as he spoke. He placed a plate on the green cloth and handed me a knife and fork wrapped in a cloth napkin. Steam rose from the corned beef and cabbage in front of me. Judging from the smell, it would be perfect. I thought of the poor G.I.'s and their miserable K rations, and the dozens of times we handed out onions and oranges and lemons to LCIs coming alongside, their occupants begging for something, anything to add flavor to the tasteless crap that passed for food. My early resolve to stay out of the Army at all costs had paid off in more ways than I expected.

Page never failed to dish up the tastiest chow no matter how rotten the weather. One of three steward's mates attending the needs of five officers, his cooking had become legendary among officers of the escort-sweeper group assigned to Task Force 86.3. Superb crayon drawings of ships, including the PC 823, and ports he visited during his Navy career also reflected his artistic talents. He completed three terms at a fine arts college in Philadelphia, and, in a burst of patriotism, signed up at the Philadelphia Navy Yard for a four-year hitch the day after Pearl Harbor. Only to end up being a nursemaid to a bunch of officers.

"Thanks, Page," I said, "you never let us down."

"Wish I could see some action. Wish I was assigned to the 3-inch fifty crew, passing ammunition at least." His usual smiling face turned sad.

I never figured out why members of the Negro race had

been relegated to subservient positions on naval vessels—none in the engine room, none among the deck crew, no negro quartermasters, no negro signalmen. Page's station at general quarters was the crew's mess hall, which would serve as a hospital, and where, if needed, he'd assist Cathcart, the ship's pharmacist's mate, in tending to the wounded.

"You'd be heading up the gun crew if I ran this Navy," I said.

"I'll give you an extra scoop of ice cream for those nice words, Mr. Creelman."

After my three scoops, I went out on deck and worked my way amidships to go below, hanging on to the rail as the ship rolled and plunged. The force of the gale seemed to have diminished in the short time I was in the wardroom. Maybe we'd get a break and have reasonably decent weather for the invasion. I couldn't help laughing. Like wishing for good weather at a wedding or a picnic.

George and I shared a stateroom, he in the lower bunk, me in the upper. A small desk with a lamp occupied a space along the bulkhead at the foot of the bunks; our uniforms and coats and oilskins had to be crammed into a tiny closet, the rest of our gear stuffed in drawers below the lower bunk. Our life jackets served as pillows or footrests. I slipped out of my jacket, pulled off my shoes, climbed into the upper bunk and lay back. When had I last worn pajamas? I couldn't even remember. Maybe at the St. George. Our sojourn in that palace seemed like a wonderful dream. I shut my eyes, but sleep would not come. In less than twenty-four hours some German or Italian, or both, might be shooting at me. Would I panic? In front of the crew. In front of George. He couldn't wait for the action to begin. But, then, the Germans and the Italian guys probably would be just as jittery as me. Eleanor's face swam into my mind's eye. Two letters had finally caught up with the ship a week before we sailed from Bizerte. One dated May 15 told me that the commencement exercises at Vassar had been scheduled for June 6. More than a month ago. She accepted a job with the Red Cross in Boston. "Doing her part," she said. The other letter really surprised me. She received a telephone call from my SCTC roommate, Cliff Mills, who was ordered to Boston to report for duty on a destroyer escort. The great planned wedding with Helen never occurred. "She chickened out, didn't want to sit at home waiting and worrying," Eleanor wrote. "We went to a movie. I tried to console him. He's sweet. Thinks you're the greatest. I agreed. Tomorrow he's off for places unknown, but he guesses convoy duty in the North Atlantic."

Would I ever see her again? That thought had crossed my mind once before. When our little subchaser, the rugged SC 604, had been caught in that terrifying storm. I was almost certain that we would go down. There was no time to think about it then. But now. Too much time. I shouted at the overhead: "Forget it. Get some sleep, Lieutenant Junior Grade Creelman. Or you won't be worth a damn."

A sudden increase in the beat of the diesel engines, followed by a sharp turn to starboard, shook me out of my morbid thoughts, and nearly shook me out of the bunk. I raised my arm and stared at my watch. 2000! We were headed for our rendezvous with HMS Safari. My apprehension turned to elation. "I wouldn't miss this frigging frolic for all the beer in Milwaukee," I cried out. "Oh death where is thy sting." Where had I heard that? Probably something Mom had read aloud from the Bible. But what the hell did it mean? Maybe Pierce would know.

Feeling foolish, I shut my eyes again and fell asleep. I dreamed I was in Boston, rowing a small boat across the harbor to Charlestown, wearing a tricorn hat. As I glanced upward, a glimmer of light appeared in the belfry arch of the Old North Church. Then another light!

They were coming by sea!

But that was supposed to be us. Not them.

"Mr. Creelman. Mr. Creelman."

Someone shook my shoulder, interfering with my rowing. I snapped awake to look into Casey's anxious eyes, level with mine. "Nearly 2300. The captain wants you on the bridge."

CHAPTER 33

I joined George in a matter of minutes. The two lookouts, Slowinski and Adams, occupied their stations on the flying bridge, one on the starboard side, the other on the port side. A first quarter moon hung in the western sky, about 15 degrees above the horizon, dimming the starlight and throwing a narrow shimmering path along our frothy wake. The sea had definitely diminished in violence as had the force of the wind. An eerie feeling crept over me, as I scanned the horizon through my binoculars. Not another ship to be seen. For days we sailed in the company of dozens of vessels. Alone now. And lonely.

"Course is 085," George said. "I've followed your plot. It's right-on. Damn good. Should bring us to our rendezvous point within the next ninety minutes. Briggs has had radar contact with the beach for the last half-hour. Screen looks like a damn chart. Licata's a couple of miles east of Monte Sole. Sticks out like a sore thumb."

"Has radar spotted the Safari?" I asked.

"Not yet. She's low in the water, and the damn waves are still pretty high."

The throb of the diesels indicated our speed to be about 10 knots. Despite the reduced speed and moderated seas, white foam cascaded over the bow and hissed along the deck as the ship knifed through the waves.

"What's that?" George seemed to freeze in place, his head cocked to one side.

"What's what, Captain?"

"That noise." His eyes lit up. "The damn flyboys saying good morning. Listen."

Then I heard it. A chill shot through me. The thump, thump, thump, thump, like the beat of distant drums, originating somewhere in the interior of the island, too far away for the aircrafts' engines to be heard.

"That'll soften up the bastards," George exulted.

"Do you suppose they're bombing the beaches, Captain?" I asked.

"No. I doubt it. Not part of the plan, anyway."

Twice more in the next hour we heard rapid booms like thunder from a distant storm, cheered on by George each time. How many innocent women and children had died or been mangled by the air strikes? Not a question to ask George.

"Brought you and Mr. Creelman some java, Captain."

Casey's head appeared above the deck of the flying bridge, holding out two mugs, probably still embarrassed and smarting from his inability to read the Swanson's message.

"Thanks, Casey," George responded. "That's damn nice of you."

I gratefully took the mug of steaming black coffee.

As Casey started down the ladder, George leaned over and patted the sailor's shoulder. "Sorry I was a little testy awhile back. You're a damn good signalman. I'm just too damn impatient."

Casey looked up at him, obviously embarrassed.

"Gee, Captain," he choked, "thanks. But it was my fault. I should read faster. I'll work on it. I promise."

A silence, except for the constant rhythm of the diesels and the rush of wind and water, hung over the flying bridge after Casey's departure. Slowinski and Adams glanced at each other, clearly approving of what they witnessed. I thought again of the huge difference George had made in the morale of the crew, after their awful experience with the two misfits, and reflected for the fiftieth time on how lucky I was to have him as my skipper. I swallowed deeply from the coffee mug, feeling the warmth take the chill from my bones, then cleared my throat. "That was a nice thing to do, Captain, if you don't mind my saying so."

He gave me a quick glance and turned away. Now it was his turn to be embarrassed. "Well, thanks. It's true, though. I am too damn impatient with some of these guys. All of them are trying to do the best they can."

"You've treated them like men, Captain. You always compliment them when they do a good job. If they foul up, you let them know straight away. They're getting better and better just because of that."

George braced himself against the port rail of the bridge, raised his binoculars with one hand, holding his coffee mug in the other, and began scanning the horizon, obviously not wanting to continue this particular conversation. He lowered the glasses and stared ahead for several seconds, then turned toward the ladder. "This damn stuff is going right through me. Better hit the damn head before we get busy. Suggest you do the same at some point. Meanwhile maintain course and speed."

"Aye, aye, sir."

He half-smiled and disappeared down the ladder.

I slowly drank the heavenly brew, then turned to Slowinski and held out the empty mug. "Would you take this to the galley? Bring up a couple of cups for you and Adams. I'll keep tabs on your area."

Slowinski grinned broadly. Ski, as his shipmates called him, seemed always to bubble over with good cheer. Never complained. An outstanding deckhand. And only nineteen years old. One of millions of kids in the armed forces, their lives disrupted, torn from friends and families, with a good chance of never seeing them again.

"Thanks, Mr. Creelman." He paused. "Do you mind if I get hot chocolate, instead? That's what John Quincy and I like best."

"John Quincy?"

I stared at the lookout.

"Is your name John Quincy Adams?"

Adams giggled and rubbed his nose.

"Uh, no sir. Not really. That's just a name Mr. Stocke gave me. I never did know why, and he never explained. Some of the guys picked it up and it stuck."

I couldn't help laughing. "Well, it's a damn good name, as our captain would say."

I turned to Ski. "Hot chocolate for you and John Quincy, by all means."

"Captain. Radar here. I've got a small target bearing 45 degrees on the starboard bow, range 8,000 yards, moving slowly to port. Looks like a vessel of some kind."

George emitted a huge sigh and stepped back from the voice tube. "Damn!" His voice shook with excitement. "That's got to be the Safari. We're right on time." George looked around the bridge. "Slowinski, get Casey up here on the double. I want him to be ready to send the recognition signal, or respond if the Safari challenges us first. Tell him to bring the hooded hand lamp."

"Aye, aye, sir."

The eager sailor practically jumped down the ladder.

Within a few moments, Casey appeared at George's side, the lamp held tightly in his hand. Another five minutes elapsed. The ship plowed forward with a pitching and rocking motion. The lower tip of the enlarged crescent touched the horizon, just about to disappear, the stars brightening as the lunar light faded. The sea and wind had moderated even more than before. Too beautiful a night to kill people, I thought. Or for people to try to kill us. What was the point of war, anyway? I wondered about George's thoughts, and whether his heart pounded anywhere near as hard as mine. If so, probably with excitement.

"What's the range now, radar?"

"Four thousand yards, sir. The target's 10 degrees off our port bow. Moving at the same rate of speed."

George glanced at his watch. "Okay, radar. Let me know when the range is 3,000 yards, and give me another bearing."

"Aye, aye, sir."

Another minute crawled by.

"Captain, we're being challenged." Casey's voice cut through the silence.

"Read it to me."

A light flickered dimly across the tossing waves from about 20 degrees off our port bow. I easily read "dit dit dit dit, dit dit dah, dit dit dit." H U S! The challenge.

"It's H U S, Captain," Casey called out.

"Respond with K Y."

I could hear the clicking from Casey's hand-carried blinker. "Dah dit dah, dah dit dah dah."

The letter R, dit dah dit, flickered from the other ship's lamp.

"Damn, it's Safari!" George shouted.

"Left standard rudder. Come to 055," George called down the voice tube.

"Aye, aye, sir. 055."

The PC 823 swung to port for several seconds.

"Steady on 055, Captain."

"Very well."

"She's trying to raise us, Captain," Casey called out.

"Tell her to send her message."

Once again, closer and clearer now, the light commenced flashing. Casey called out each word. "Welcome to Sicily.

Please take station as ordered. Continue blinking fox until YMS group and landing craft arrive. Then assume patrol as previously ordered. Good luck."

"Tell her wilco and thanks." George pumped his fist in the air, as Casey complied with the order. "Right full rudder. Come to 180. All engines ahead standard." The PC 823 swung to starboard, and within less than a minute reached her new course. George shouted down the voice tube. "Radar, let me know when we're 12,000 yards from that bulge in the coast east of Monte Sole."

"Aye, aye, sir."

George stepped back and swung around to me. The wild gleam in his eyes startled me. "Okay. Okay. Okay. We should be on station in thirty minutes. At about 0100. We'll slow the engines to idle and cruise back and forth until 0130, then start signaling."

George stood rigidly, as though frozen, staring upward. "This is it! Damn!" He shook his fist at the stars. "Come on, you bastards. I can't wait."

I hoped he did not notice my shocked look when he turned toward me. "Mr. Creelman, please tell Mr. Stocke to report to the bridge. I'll stand watch with him. You turn in for awhile."

"But Captain," I pleaded, "you've got to get some rest. Let me stand watch with Mr. Stocke. I'll call you in plenty of time before we start signaling."

"No. Damn it."

I could only obey. I went below and roused Jack. "The captain wants to stand watch with you until we start the signaling from Station Fox."

Jack rolled over, sat on the edge of his bunk, and slowly started buttoning his shirt. No pajamas for him either. "For Christ's sake, doesn't the old man trust me?" He sounded and looked crestfallen.

I tried to reassure him. "Yeah, he does. It's not that. He can't miss anything. He's wound up like a top. I've never seen the guy so excited. He wants to take on the entire German army, as well as the Luftwaffe. It's like he's waited all his life for this moment."

"Well, I could live without it," he mumbled. "I'm just worried that our lives will be a hell of a lot shorter than we figured." Jack reached for his trousers hanging over the desk chair. We learned the hard way how to dress while the ship rolled and pitched in a stormy sea. Trousers had to be the toughest. You grasped the side of the bunk with one hand and carefully worked your foot through the first trouser leg, then repeated the procedure with the other. A slip of the hand, and you ended up hopping across the room on one foot to avoid crashing to the deck. Jack accomplished his objective without injury and grinned triumphantly. "If this war ever ends and I survive, I'm going to join a road company and demonstrate how a small-craft officer gets dressed in rough weather."

"You'll be the star of the show," I said. "Maybe I could be your agent."

"Maybe. But first things first." He waved and disappeared through the hatch.

Yeah, I thought as I lay in my bunk, staring up at the overhead pipes. First have to win this stupid war. I turned on my side, shut my eyes, and fell asleep. No dreams this time. I never did finish rowing to Charlestown. Our side won that war, anyway.

"Bill. Time to go."

Jack stood over me, shaking my shoulder.

My eyes snapped open in an instant.

"Okay. Thanks. What's going on?"

"It's 0145. We've started signaling. Wind's abated. Sea's still choppy. But not too bad. No moon, but plenty of starlight for our German and Italian friends to see us by. We heard a couple of bombing attacks by our boys before midnight. Saw some fires and flashes inland, nowhere near the beaches. Don't know what they're up to. Wish they'd take out the shore batteries." He snorted. "That's the good news."

"Well," I said, "let's have it."

"Our radar's conked out. Kaput. Gone."

That was bad, real bad. Our eyes gone. "You've got to be kidding. What's wrong? What happened?"

Jack shrugged. "Who knows. Problem with the wiring. So they say. Kelsey's working on it."

I rolled over and eased myself down to the deck and retrieved my helmet and life jacket from the foot of the bunk. "How's the skipper doing?"

"Doing the caged animal routine, pacing back and forth on the bridge until a few minutes ago."

George had calmed down by the time I joined him. "Gotta

keep a sharp lookout," he muttered. "Damn radar's let us down."

I looked around. Casey stood behind the starboard blinker. Ski and John Quincy had been replaced by Henderson and Reynolds. They and the Captain wore helmets and life jackets. Three pairs of eyes stared through binoculars. I followed suit, but only wind-tossed white caps filled the lenses. The squeaking blinker hinges operated by Signalman Casey confirmed the repeated flashing of the letter F, dit dit dah dit, in the direction of the oncoming armada. Or was it oncoming? Maybe the columns had been driven off course by the choppy seas and wind.

My arms and shoulders ached from gripping the binoculars, but I dared not lower them, except to wipe salt water from the lenses. Twice a black object jumped into my vision, and I nearly shouted, but as the objects ascended slowly skyward and disappeared, I realized I was hallucinating. Time seemed to stand still as George, the two lookouts, and I stood rigidly, training our glasses seaward, the silence broken only by the wind swirling around the bridge and the flapping of the U.S. ensign just below the dome of the defunct radar. Thirty minutes dragged by. And then out in the darkness, another black object jumped into my vision. But this one did not float upward. A second black object appeared. Two columns of YMSs slowly bearing down on the PC 823, their stubby bows bucking and rearing in the waves.

"Captain, I've spotted them. On the starboard beam. About 3,000 yards."

"Yeah, I see them." George's voice shook with excitement.

Six of the 136-foot wooden ships passed by in two columns, and then fanned out to the right and left to commence their indispensable assignment—to rid the pathways to Green Beaches 1 and 2 from deadly mines. I had met several YMS officers at the officers club in Bizerte, and had admired the casual manner in which they discussed their work, an enormously important and dangerous task. The unofficial motto of the Minesweepers was "Wherever you go, we have been."

I kept my glasses on the sturdy little vessels until all of them had disappeared in the darkness.

"Okay," George muttered. "The LCIs should be along

soon. "Keep signaling, Casey."

"Aye, aye, sir."

Again, four pairs of eyes gazed seaward through binoculars. The silence among us again broken only by the whistling wind and flapping U.S. ensign.

"Captain, there they are." The shout came from Reynolds. "Two points on the port bow."

"Yeah. Thanks. I can see them now."

At that moment, I caught sight of the stubby bows of the landing craft, bucking and rearing in the heavy seas. Within minutes, I could make out masses of humanity huddled together on the decks of the lead landing craft. Two hundred soldiers packed in each tiny vessel. Most of them probably prostrated from seasickness.

George turned to me. "You made sure the depth charges are disarmed?"

"Yes, sir. I checked them myself."

"Okay." George leaned over the voice tube. "Sound general quarters."

The blast of the horn startled me, even though I knew it was coming. Henderson jumped to the bridge 20-millimeter cannon and removed the cover. Reynolds opened the ammunition box, removed a clip of shells and fastened it to the gun.

"Signal the LCIS to follow us, Casey. Keep signaling until we get an acknowledgement."

The message flashed out. Then again. And again.

A "roger" finally flickered from the lead LCI.

George leaped to the voice tube. "All engines ahead slow. Left standard rudder. Come to 045." The ship methodically swung to port and reached her new position, now with a following sea, giving us a smoother ride than before, the ship settling in the stern, then lunging forward as each wave passed underneath, pushing us along. Thumping footsteps and clanging hatches evidenced the responses to the call to general quarters. Reports flashed up through the voice tube. "Three-inch fifty manned and ready." "Forty millimeter manned and ready." "Mid-ship twenty millimeters manned and ready." "Engine room manned and ready." "Ship's hospital manned and ready."

"Keep a sharp eye out, Mr. Creelman, and make sure they're keeping up with us."

"Aye, aye, sir."

"We'll have to clock real carefully so we come as close as possible to where we're supposed to let them go," George said. He studied his watch. "We're 12,000 yards from the beach," he mumbled to himself. "It's 0215." He glanced at me. "We should reach our release point in about fifty minutes. We might be a bit closer than 3,000 yards, but, what the hell. They'll have a better chance of hitting the right spot."

A haze hung over the wind-tossed waves. Too dark to see any part of the coast, not even Monte Sole, which, according to our chart, reached a height of 540 feet above sea level. Not much of a mountain. I trained my glasses astern. Our charges tagged along behind, in good formation, each vessel within eye contact of the one ahead. What thoughts ran through the minds of those GI's, I wondered. God knows, maybe the poor guys longed to be ashore. Preferring bullets from the enemy to the hell of seasickness.

No bullets. Not yet.

"Searchlights two points off starboard bow, Captain," Reynolds called out. "Looks like from the beach." Five streams of light, converging on one spot about 6,000 yards distance. "From Beach Yellow," George said. "That's about where the Biscayne should be." I could practically hear his teeth grind. "Damn, I wish we had our radar."

I held my breath, waiting for the inevitable gunfire from shore. But none came. We plunged along, our glasses trained to starboard, too dark to see the Biscayne if she were the object of interest. After about twenty minutes, the lights began shifting aimlessly, then vanished abruptly. George glanced at me, shaking his head. "Can't figure out why the damn eyeties don't open up."

I'd scanned the overall invasion plan, a gigantic volume of material. Out there on either side and behind us, scores of ships loaded down with troops and tanks and trucks and artillery moved slowly and silently toward the beaches. Like a gigantic tidal wave. Thousands of hearts must be beating wildly, just as wildly as mine. I marveled at the ingenuity of the planners of such a massive operation. George broke into my thoughts with sharp commands. "All engines stop. Casey, signal the lead ship. Tell her to steer 045, and goodbye and good luck."

The hooded signal lamp clicked out its message. A "roger wilco" responded. Then "thanks." The PC 823 rolled and wallowed as the rearing and bucking LCIs passed by on either side, so close that I could make out the netted steel helmets of the human cargo. I resisted an impulse to wave. It was not as though the troops were off on a vacation trip.

"Okay, let's get out of here." The churning wakes from the last LCIs had vanished in the darkness. The PC 823 turned in a 180-degree arc at George's command and settled on her new course at standard speed, plowing into the oncoming sea, forcing spray and foam over the bow. George gazed at his watch. "It's 0315. We should be approximately on station in fifteen minutes."

"Captain, radar reporting."

George leaned over the voice tube.

"Captain here."

"Radar now working, Captain."

"Damn. That's great. That'll be extra liberty for you when we hit port, Kelsey. What's on the screen?"

"Targets all around us, Captain. Too many to count."

"What a blast. What a damn blast." George's eyes gleamed. "We should be close to the fire support ships. They'll be opening up soon after first light."

The invasion plan called for support in the Licata area from the cruiser Brooklyn and several destroyers. Cruisers Birmingham, Boise, and Savannah, as well as minesweepers and other destroyers operating in the Gulf of Gela, would provide massive assistance to the invaders, should they be pinned down on or close to the beaches by enemy troops. The PC 823 plunged through the dark waves, the haze rising from the churning sea blotting the starlight and limiting visibility even with binoculars to less than 1,000 yards.

"Radar, what's the range to Monte Sole?"

"Ten thousand yards, Captain."

"Okay, Monte Sole's at an angle from us. We've got about another thousand yards to go. We'll start the patrol in two minutes." He called down the voice tube. "Pass the word to secure from general quarters. Starboard watch has the duty."

"Aye, aye, sir." I recognized Bixler's voice.

Members of the port watch silently left their battle stations and disappeared below. Hopefully to sleep.

George leaned over the voice tube. "When's first light, Bixler?"

"About 0500, Captain," came the prompt reply.

"What about sunrise?" George called down.

"0550, sir."

Bixler didn't miss a trick. An expert quartermaster eased the life of the navigation officer. Me, in this case. George glanced at his watch. "Okay, let's start the patrol. We'll steer 285 at 10 knots for thirty minutes, then reverse our course for another thirty minutes. "We'll come to general quarters at first light." He grinned. "Unless some damn thing happens before."

It crossed my mind that George had been on the bridge for more than six hours without a break, except for his one visit to the head. "Captain," I said, "why don't I take the deck so you can get some rest? I'll call you ten minutes before first light. That's less than two hours from now."

To my surprise, he agreed. "Okay, thanks, Mr. Creelman. I could use a little shuteye."

A feeling of loneliness crept over me after George's departure. And so, Bixler's appearance on the flying bridge came as a pleasant surprise. "Rodriguez's got the hang of it, Mr. Creelman. I thought I'd come topside to see what's going on. I'll take over when we come to general quarters. If that's okay," he added.

"Great. Fine. You can help us keep an eye out for the damn enemy, as our captain would say."

Bixler laughed. "I get a kick out of him. What a great guy. He's by far the best of the three commanding officers I've served under. The crew loves him."

"Yeah," I said, "I agree. He's the only skipper I've had. I'm really lucky. Some commanding officers I've run into act like they think they're God Almighty. Treat their officers and crew like dirt." I thought of Fraley, and wondered if he'd ever put in for sea duty. What a disaster for anyone stuck onboard a ship with that tyrant as C.O. Probably remained a shore-based bastard at the Receiving Station.

"Well, I hope the captain gets some satisfaction from the invasion," Bixler said. "I shouldn't say this, I guess, but he strikes me as being an unhappy man who's trying to find himself. Or maybe looking for something to live for." Bixler shrugged, then grinned. "How's that for a bit of psychology, Mr. Creelman."

"You may be right," I said. "He sure doesn't open up very much. You have to drag information about his personal life from him." I thought of George's marriage and the unhappiness that it must have brought. Maybe after the war, things would shape up for him. I hoped so. He deserved the best.

We silently scanned our sectors, along with the two lookouts. My thoughts went out to the G.I.'s we'd led into the beach area. From the frying pan into the fire. Any gunfire from shore would have been drowned out by the swirling sea breeze and the rush of sea water alongside and over the bow. How many had drowned before wading ashore? How many had been shot?

The PC 823 had completed three laps of her patrol and had begun the fourth, when Bixler interrupted my concentration. "It's 0445, sir. Should I call the captain? I glanced at the horizon. Still dark. The haze continued to prevail. Visibility even with binoculars remained only about 1,500 yards. "Yes. Please."

In less than five minutes, George ascended the ladder beside me. He looked rested. Alert. A broad grin on his face. "Man, I really was knocked out. I'd have slept forever if good old Bixler hadn't shaken me awake." He laughed out loud. "I feel like a damn million bucks." He patted my shoulder. "Bring on those damn Nazi bastards!"

"It's starting to get light, Captain."

The warning came from Henderson.

"Sound general quarters."

Once again, the startling rasping horn reverberated throughout the ship, followed by the now familiar thumps of running footsteps.

Reports from stations all manned and ready came pouring in.

Now we could make out the dark shapes of ships along a seven-mile line about 8,000 yards from the beach. Silent. Waiting. A chill went through me. This really was it.

The ship completed the fourth lap of her patrol and turned once more on a course of 285. I wanted to talk to George. Say something. Hear something reassuring in return. Did anyone notice my trembling hands holding the binoculars to my eyes? I hoped not. Why should they? No one paid any attention to me.

One of the larger dark shapes suddenly erupted with flame and smoke. Loud booms rolled across the wind-tossed sea. "Captain," Reynolds screamed out, "that ship just suffered a direct hit."

"No, damn it, she's fired a broadside, probably at some inland target. I'd bet it is the Birmingham. For God's sake, I'll send you below if you don't take it easy."

Reynold's face fell to his shoes. "Sorry, sir."

At that moment, flames spurted from a dozen other ships, probably destroyers and cruisers, adding their support to the invading allies.

"Two aircraft on the port beam, Captain, altitude about 5000 feet." This time Reynolds' tone sounded controlled. Even relaxed.

Our glasses swung to port. There they were. Just like I'd seen in the newsreels. My first glimpse of the enemy—headed for the Birmingham.

"Dive bombers." George shouted. "Hold your fire 'til they pass over the Birmingham."

The roar of engines could easily be heard now. Two huge geysers shot up on either side of the cruiser. Two near misses. "Open fire." George shouted. Ear-splitting cracks of the three-inch fifty, and the rapid clatter from the 40-millimeter and 20-millimeters shocked me to my bones. We'd never before fired all of our guns simultaneously.

For nothing.

The two dive bombers thundered by unscathed, headed toward the now brilliantly lit horizon. Streaks of red, blue and green radiated skyward near dead ahead. "Damn." George shook his fist at the rapidly disappearing enemy, mere dots by now, headed toward the red arc of the rising sun.

Guns thundered all along the line of ships, belching smoke and flame, fascinating to hear and behold. How could anyone on the receiving end of such powerful explosives survive? A dozen geysers of sea water appeared mysteriously and silently, some disconcertingly close to the fire support vessels. "Shore batteries have opened up," George shouted. "Now the damn fun begins." We watched spellbound. Like we had a ringside seat at the war.

"Sun's up, Captain." A report from Reynolds.

I swung my binoculars to a point a few degrees off the port bow, blinded for a few seconds by the enormous red ball of fire.

"Captain. Captain." Reynold's voice rose. "Aircraft just off the port bow, coming in low. Headed right at us."

My heart stopped beating for an instant. Out of the blinding sun, skimming the waves, came the messenger of death, angry red flashes spurting from its nose. Henderson swung the bridge 20-millimeter around and opened rapid fire, joined instantly by blasts from the three-inch fifty. I crouched down, head between my legs, hanging on to my helmet, stunned and deafened, completely confused, wondering if this would be the way I'd finally end up. A thundering roar overhead, quickly fading, told me that the aircraft had passed over the ship, untouched by our gunfire.

The comparative silence overwhelmed me. No sound but the rush of water and the throbbing of the ship's diesels. I expected angry words from George. But none came. I pushed up to my knees. "God, Captain, that was too close for comfort." I was barely able to speak, my voice strangled, my nerves shot. I looked up when no response came. George lay back against the canvas, staring toward me, as if in a trance. Reynolds leaned over him. "Are you okay, Captain?" he asked anxiously.

George turned his vacant stare to Reynolds and reached under his life jacket. A shock wave passed through me when he withdrew his hand. Blood streamed down his wrist, and dripped from his fingertips onto his trousers.

I leaped to the voice tube. "Get Cathcart to the bridge," I shouted. "On the double." I knelt beside George, who continued to stare curiously at his bloody hand like it was some strange and unnatural object.

"Captain, you've been hit. Cathcart's on the way up here. He'll fix you up in no time."

George's gaze slowly shifted to me. His lips moved. But no words came. I leaned down, my ear a few inches from his face, our helmets making contact.

"Captain," I choked out, "what is it? What are you trying to say?"

Then I heard him. Low. But distinct. And firm.

"Damn!"

CHAPTER 34

"Mail call, Captain."

I looked up from the letter I was struggling to write. A letter to George's mother. There'd been no time until now to sit down and try to figure out what to say to her about the disaster of five weeks ago. The terrible moment when George died on the flying bridge of the PC 823 that awful morning. Just as the sun rose on his last day on earth. July 10, 1943. I'd always remember that date.

Carl Pierce stood in the doorway of the wardroom, holding out the familiar blue envelope with the familiar handwriting. A letter from Eleanor.

"Thanks, Mr. Pierce."

Carl removed his hat, sat across the table from me and laid the blue envelope on the green cloth. I didn't have the heart to open it now.

"Were you able to finish the letter, Captain?"

I stared at my handwritten scrawl. "Well, no. Not yet." I choked out the words. "What the hell can I say that'll help Mrs. Dugan? Nothing. Nothing could help. Jesus Christ! Why wasn't it me? Why did it have to be the captain?"

Carl cleared his throat. "I've seen how you've really suffered, Captain. It's a terrible thing. Seems like it's impossible to understand." He glanced at me quickly, then spread out his hands on the green cloth. Carl Pierce had been appointed Executive Officer, upon my learning that I no longer was acting commanding officer of the PC 823. The orders reached us an hour after we tied up at the battered dock in Palermo one month ago. The harbor had been first opened for shipping by the U.S. Navy in late July, after General Patton's Army drove the Germans from the devastated area. The PC 823 had been on antisubmarine patrol constantly since our arrival, clearing the harbor at sunset and returning to port at sunrise. The Luftwaffe finally gave the weary civilians a respite, after weeks of pre-invasion and post-invasion bombing attacks, first by the Allies then by the Germans. But not before two U.S. subchasers nested at pier 6 only fifty yards from the PC 823 had been blown apart in a pre-dawn bombing raid by JU-88s, setting fire to a freighter and a naval tug. The disastrous hits had been made possible by the flashes from the SC's 40-millimeters, which served only to attract the bomber's attention at the cost of dozens of casualties. More young men slaughtered in a strange country, thousands of miles from home. An awful lesson learned the hard way.

Pierce coughed discreetly, drawing me back from my morbid thoughts. "I know you don't go in much for anything religious, but there are verses that would help you come to grips with this. I'll mark them and leave my Bible on your desk."

"Thanks, Mr. Pierce. That's very thoughtful of you."

"The Captain would have been pleased at your getting command of the 823," he said. "You should take a lot of comfort from realizing that. He had tremendous respect for you." Pierce paused. "As do the officers and crew."

"If I get to be one-half as good a skipper as George Dugan, I'll be satisfied."

"Well, you'll be more than satisfied. I'd bet the farm on that."

Pierce stood. "I should tell you that SOPA has sent orders that the officers and crew of the ship have been given one week's R and R commencing tomorrow at 0800. And that includes you. Especially you. I don't know what's still standing in this poor bombed out city, but I've read that there are some interesting old palaces and churches, and nice scenery in the surrounding countryside." He chuckled. "And believe it or not, the Palermo Opera Company has scheduled a performance at the Opera House next Saturday evening. I really admire the Italians' spirit. Nothing interferes with their music. Not even the hell of war."

He left me alone with my thoughts. The enormity of my unexpected responsibilities, first as acting commanding officer and then as commanding officer of the PC 823, had nearly overwhelmed me. I constantly wanted to run to George for advice. But there was no George to run to. The next best thing, I decided, would be to pattern my conduct after his. Keep the officers at arm's length. No fraternizing. Not even ashore. Except maybe with Carl Pierce. The officers would always address me as "Captain." I would never use their first names in addressing them. Only in that way could I be sure that discipline would be maintained, that my orders would be obeyed without question. A good relationship with the crew should not be difficult to preserve. George treated the men fairly and firmly. I would follow his example. I hoped that Carl Pierce had accurately reported the crew's feelings toward me.

The two letters, side by side on the wardroom table, attracted my attention. The one from Eleanor unopened and unread. The other to George's mother unfinished. I studied the first few lines again—those awful words I struggled with, cursing and hurling crumpled sheets of paper all over the wardroom. How could one soften the blow? Everything I wrote sounded so formal.

"Dear Mrs. Dugan. I regret to inform you that your son George was killed during the invasion of Sicily."

Terrible!

"Dear Mrs. Dugan. I am terribly sorry to have to tell you that George was killed during an air attack on our ship."

Worse!

"Dear Mrs. Dugan. George was killed during an attack on our ship by enemy aircraft. He died quickly and quietly without pain. Nothing that I can say will ease your suffering and unhappiness. But I do want you to know that the entire crew admired and respected George. He was a great skipper. He was both my Captain and my close friend." That would have to do. I held up the silver dog tag I removed from around George's neck. I stared at it. "George Francis Doyle. 117899." I gripped it tightly. "So long, Captain," I whispered. Carefully wrapping the dog tag in a blank sheet of paper, I tucked it into the envelope. I went on to tell Mrs. Dugan that George's possessions would be packed up and mailed soon but would take weeks to reach her. I closed by asking her to write me. I'd try to answer any questions that could be answered without violating security restrictions. I sealed the envelope before I had second thoughts about revisions and placed it alongside Eleanor's letter.

Raising the blue envelope to the light, I could make out the delicately slanted handwriting that used to make my heart beat faster. Why not now? And why had I delayed opening this one? Just a few weeks ago in my excitement I nearly ripped apart the contents of the two envelopes that caught up with the ship in Palermo. As I tried to make out individual words through the envelope, the opening bars of the first movement of Beethoven's Fifth Symphony filled the wardroom. V for Victory! Pouring out from the shortwave radio speaker attached to the bulkhead. Probably BBC. A source of both news and pleasure. Memories of the first concert I attended in Bailey Hall with Betty floated through my mind. A feeling of guilt swept over me, and I quickly tore open the blue envelope. A one pager. But at least on both sides.

Dear Bill:

I finally have a few minutes to spare to write you. The Red Cross is becoming a bit of a pain. They actually have me working from four o'clock in the afternoon until midnight! Except on Sunday, when I go into the office from eight until noon. Lucky me. I'll give it a try for awhile. See what happens.

Last Saturday I was surprised to get a telephone call from Cliff. His ship was docked at Commonwealth Pier. He told me he was just back from convoy duty in the North Atlantic, although I don't think he should have. Or maybe it's ok. I don't know. We went to the Copley on Sunday afternoon. Remember? He's a terrific waltzer. I asked if he'd heard from Helen, and for a couple of seconds I thought he was going to cry. She's married! Already! To a doctor in Dallas, who was classified 4-F by his local draft board. He's probably making a fortune with most everyone else his age in the service. So I guess Helen got what she wanted. What a silly fool.

Cliff came to dinner last night with mom and me. He looked fabulous in his white uniform. He told us a little about his adventures after mom pumped him for information. Poor guy. He really has had a rough time. In more ways than one. Tomorrow the three of us are going to a concert. Koosey again. Ugh! But Cliff loves the classics. Hope he wears whites again. Write me when you have a chance.

Lots of Love,
Eleanor

P.S. I told Cliff you were on the PC 823.

I hope that's okay.

I read the letter again, then once more, and wondered about the change in tone from earlier letters. No "darlings," no "sweethearts," no "Os" and Xs" for hugs and kisses—childish but welcome. Not even an "I love you." A sister might have written the letter to her brother. My one letter from Betty had been warmer and more loving. I tucked it away in my official file and had fished it out to read at least six times. But I wondered even more why Eleanor's omissions didn't particularly trouble me. And why her seeing Cliff did not worry me. Or her waltzing with him. Or her going to a concert with him.

I leaned back, closed my eyes, and massaged my forehead, trying to find relief from the nagging headache that had plagued me ever since that fatal moment off the coast of Sicily. We transferred George's body to the Biscayne. "We'll give him a proper Navy burial." So the signal from the Biscayne had read. Then we were ordered to resume patrolling to help cope with the sporadic bombing attacks that had continued throughout that dreadful day. By then thousands of troops and vast quantities of equipment had reached the beaches and had advanced miles into the interior.

The next two days, July 11 and 12, had brought vicious but unsuccessful counterattacks by the Germans and Italians. The PC 823 patrolled seaward of the cruiser Savannah while she pounded enemy shore batteries and troop concentrations. Our mission again was to repel attacking aircraft. Whether the "curtain of fire" sent up on several occasions by the PC 823's three-inch fifty, 40-millimeter, and 20-millimeters played any role in frustrating the dive bombers, I'd never know. For whatever reason, the Savannah continued her troop support bombardments unscathed. When Allied air support belatedly showed up at mid-day on July 12, our efforts were no longer needed.

The morning of July 13 brought a welcome blinker message from the Biscayne as she passed our stern headed for the open sea. Maybe to bury George. I didn't want to know. Casey relayed the message to me without once calling for a repeat. "Proceed immediately to Bizerte for ship's maintenance and to pick up relief officer and await further orders," Casey shouted, his voice rising with excitement after each word.

I managed to cope with the 6-knot current sweeping down the man-made canal into Bizerte harbor. Like sliding on ice! Docking the ship never failed to be a tense operation, even under perfect weather and current conditions. Officers and crews of other ships walking by would invariably pause to watch the performance, hoping to witness a collision with the dock. Previously, I had George at my side, ready to ward off any potential misstep. But in Bizerte there were only the watchful eyes of the special sea detail and the fascinated spectators. Not quite a one-bell landing, but almost. The disappointed audience had moved on.

The harbor had been occupied by a variety of warships, mostly U.S.—a couple of hulking aircraft tenders, more than a dozen destroyers and destroyer escorts, preparing to get underway to rendezvous with the next westbound convoy forming up, the sleek gray shapes tied up three-deep at the dock, the barrels of their 5-inch caliber guns pointed skyward, radar antennas slowly rotating. Further along the seemingly endless pier, a half-dozen YMSs and groups of PCs and SCs lay nested together. There was constant movement aboard the ships and on the dock—supplies and ammunition being loaded, decks swabbed, and rust, acquired from hundreds of hours of exposure to wind and sea, scraped. To add to the confusion, the ugly, ear-splitting racket of handy billies, those ubiquitous light-weight gasoline motors used to supply power for numerous tasks aboard ship, filled the air.

I couldn't wait to leave the ship after the special sea detail had been secured. I needed to go off by myself and think. To get my head on straight. There'd been too many reminders of George. One sleepless night, shortly before we reached Bizerte, lines from the Walt Whitman poem that Betty had read aloud kept running through my head. We'd just finished one of our picnic lunches near Taughannock Falls. Her voice was soft and intense, a sad expression on her face, brushing her dark hair back as she spoke. "Exult O shores, and ring O bells, but I with mournful tread walk the deck my Captain lies, fallen cold and dead." If only I could talk to Betty. She'd understand. She suffered horribly from the death of her fiancé but had managed to go on living. That had to be tougher than losing your commanding officer.

At Pierce's suggestion, I requisitioned a jeep after reporting to Operations. "Get out of town," he urged. "Take a drive. Visit Tunis. Life's slowly getting back to normal there since the Germans evacuated the city, even though hundreds of poor Arabs are sleeping on the sidewalk and trying to stay alive by begging. The French treat them like animals."

What else is new, I thought. The French could be as brutal as the Germans.

"And talk about exciting history," Pierce went on. "Tunis is near the site of ancient Carthage. There's a bunch of Roman ruins and interesting Islamic buildings. You'll have a ball. Here, take this with you." He held out a brochure prepared and distributed by the American Red Cross loaded with information about Tunisia. "It tells you all about the area, going way, way back, before the birth of Christ."

My progress in the battered olive drab vehicle on the road to Tunis had been retarded by dozens of swarthy men, veiled women, and children, plodding wearily along the pitted macadam highway. No one had asked for a ride, to my surprise. Maybe time meant nothing to those poor subjugated people. I wondered where they were going. And why. I wheeled by ugly burned-out tanks on either side of the road, a harsh reminder of the disastrous battle that had raged in the Kasserine Pass only a few months ago, where the U.S. divisions suffered a humiliating defeat. As my jeep edged slowly through the throng of humanity, I spotted a turbaned figure astride a magnificent mahogany-colored steed heading toward me at a brisk trot. As the figure drew nearer, I sucked in my breath. This proud Arab looked totally amazing—the youthful head held erect, one hand holding the reins loosely, the other grasping a rifle held across his knees, like an Arabian prince. As this noble character out of the tales of Aladdin came abreast, his piercing black eyes looked straight through me and beyond. Here's a man to be reckoned with, I decided. Strangely, the imperious figure and the weary passersby ignored each other completely.

I had slowly wound through the maze of narrow, pot-holed streets, tooting gently on the horn at a throng, now consisting mostly of dogs, goats, and children, impeding my progress. Curious stares of black-robed Arab men and women, seated in open doorways of crumbling shacks, rhythmically fanning themselves with filthy towels, greeted my efforts to clear a pathway.

What had passed for a street mercifully smoothed out and widened. The crowds diminished, and I finally reached what appeared to be a major intersection. A wooden sign dangling slightly askew from a two-story yellow stucco structure proclaimed the establishment to be L'Oasis. I pulled over to the curb directly in front of the darkened entrance and stared into the open door. The interior looked cool and inviting. I could make out several tables in the dim light, two of them occupied by respectable looking young men, wearing brilliantly white turbans and robes. An oasis from the oppressive heat and humidity that wore me down. If I dared leave the jeep, I could cool off, have a cup of tea. Relax. Think.

A tall, slim Arab, maybe in his mid-twenties, clothed in the inevitable robe and turban, had hurried through the open door, all smiles, his even-white teeth contrasting with his dark complexion. He bowed slightly. "Good afternoon, sir. Would you care to enter?"

I marveled at how quickly well-educated Arabs picked up the English language. This one even had an English accent. No way could I learn to speak any Arabic, except perhaps "Yes" and "No" and "How do I find the dock?"

"Can I leave the jeep here?" I asked.

"Absolutely, sir. It's safety will receive my personal guarantee." He glanced into the interior of L'Oasis. "To further ease your mind, I will arrange a seat at a table so that your vehicle will be under close observation by yourself."

I thanked him, removed the key from the ignition, and jumped quickly to the sidewalk and stretched to overcome the stiffness that had set in from my uncomfortable journey.

"My name is Ali," he volunteered. "My honorable father is the proprietor of L'Oasis. We welcome all soldiers and sailors who fight against the murderous Germans." He smiled wryly. "Even the French."

"Where did you learn to speak English so well?" I asked.

His smile broadened. "I thank you for the compliment. I learned a great deal from a tutor in Tunis. Then I studied for two years in Cambridge. Before the war, of course. Unfortunately, I was back here between terms, already having purchased passage to Southampton, when the cowardly Germans perpetrated the attack on Poland. And so I was stymied, as you might say. I had to keep a low profile until the English and Americans cleared out the filthy Hun."

I pulled out my wallet, fished out a 100-franc note, and held it out to him. The smile vanished. He held up his hand. "Please! We are honored to have such as you as our guest." Ali swung around and strode through the door. I stuffed the note in the side pocket of my trousers, and sheepishly followed him into L'Oasis. As promised, I was seated at a bare wooden table, positioned so that the front half of my jeep was in view.

"I deeply regret that we cannot serve you an alcoholic beverage," he said rather somberly. "My honorable father is devoted to Islam and the teachings of the Koran." He brightened. "But we do offer a variety of delicious Arabic teas, and the most delectable cakes."

"No problem," I said. "I shouldn't drink and drive, anyway. Tea and cakes would be perfect. Very English, wouldn't you say, old chap?"

Ali raised his eyebrows at my feeble attempt at humor and remained silent.

"You select the tea," I hurried on. "And bring me a couple of those tricky looking pastries that young lady is working on." I nodded toward a woman seated two tables away, leafing through a magazine. She held one of the interesting-looking cakes in her hand, popping it into her mouth as I spoke. Probably French. She had that Gallic look about her. The dark hair and eyes and smooth white skin reminded me of Marie.

"Michelle's favorite," Ali whispered confidentially. "She's a regular customer of ours. Impeccable taste."

"That's good enough for me," I whispered back.

Ali disappeared through a door adjacent to the front entrance. I caught a quick view of what appeared to be a kitchen and an elderly dark-skinned, bareheaded man leaning over a long wooden table.

The tea tasted overly sweet, but good. A wonderful thirst quencher. Far better than the flat, warm, tasteless Arab beer we were afflicted with at the off-limit bars in Bizerte we surreptitiously visited. Michelle's favorites—light, crisp, and delicious—lived up to Ali's endorsement.

My host appeared at my side. All smiles. "Did you enjoy your refreshments?" he wanted to know.

"Fantastic. My compliments to the chef." I glanced

at Michelle, who seemed absorbed by the contents of her magazine. "And to Michelle." I meant to keep my voice low, but obviously had been overheard, for Michelle glanced up at me. Her smile warmed the room. I held my breath for a few seconds, then returned the smile.

"The commander was pleased with the tea and cakes?" she called over. Just the right amount of French accent. Enough to send a quiver through me.

"Excellent," I replied. "Like Ali said, your taste is impeccable."

She raised her eyebrows and returned to her magazine. I wondered what article could be so fascinating. My mind did a few acrobatic tricks. Should I continue the conversation? Or should I leave well enough alone? Ali poured out more tea, and I examined her covertly as I raised the wine glass to my lips. I guessed her age to be in the late twenties. She wore a silky black dress that exposed white shoulders over which the soft dark curls clung. Her breasts, unrestrained by a bra, were beautifully shaped and partially exposed. Enough to arouse my interest. Her reddened lips were full. Not too much lipstick, I noticed with approval. She licked her finger as she turned a page, her head bent slightly to one side. The sight of the darting pink tongue brought a certain memorable twinge. Shades of Marie! What could it be about French women that aroused a guy's passion?

I cleared my throat loud enough for her to hear, and also the two Arabs who were quietly conversing at the table adjacent to Michelle's. They shot a glance at me, then at Michelle, shrugged and continued their conversation. I looked more closely at them. Both lean, dark, and athletic appearing, they reminded me of the noble horseman I saw along the road to Tunis.

"By the w way," I called over to her. My voice cracked a little. Was my stammer back? I tried again. "By the way, I'm not a commander. Just a junior grade lieutenant."

"You look very important in your khaki uniform, Monsieur Junior Grade Lieutenant." She raised her wine glass as if to toast me. "And very handsome."

This brought the two Arabs to attention. Obviously they understood English.

Now I really did feel warm. I tried to muster up some courage. Should I ask to join her? Would she be insulted? Why was I so damn shy with women? Another long clearing of the throat.   She probably thought I had some horrible lung problem. I took a deep breath and plowed ahead. "Uh, could I join you and buy you another pot of tea? And maybe another order of Michelle's specials?"

There came the smile, lighting up the room. She closed her magazine, pushed back her chair, squeezed by the table occupied by the two Arabs, now interested spectators, and glided toward me. For the first time I took note of her classic legs, encased in black netted stockings. Also silk. The shoes seemed to be made of black velvet. I vaguely wondered where she obtained the elegant clothes, and how she could afford them.

"Let me join you, Monsieur Junior Grade Lieutenant," she said. "I would love tea. And one or two of Michelle's specials, peutêtre."

Ali must have been watching and listening, because he rushed up and placed a chair close to mine. "Merci, Ali," she murmured, then sat down slowly, placing the now closed magazine on the table. I noted the title. "Amour."

Ali quickly left, then returned with a fresh pot of tea and a pewter plate overflowing with Michelle's specials. I fished out the 100-franc note and laid it and a twin note on the table. Ali thanked me and again disappeared into the kitchen.

"Everyone speaks such good English," I ventured to say after a long awkward silence, during which she raised the wine glass to her lips, her dark eyes fixed on me.

"My late husband was assigned to the French embassy in London before the war," she told me. "We had many British friends. And some Americans," she added.

I thought for a few seconds. Her late husband. I hesitated, wondering if I should ask questions, or would that be too intrusive. She brought the subject up. Maybe she wanted to talk about him. "What happened to him?" I finally asked.

A shrug followed that question. "He entered the French underground. I had to join my parents in Marseille, and then, after the Germans occupied all of France, escaped in a small bateau to Oran. As the fighting went back and forth in North Africa, I managed to dodge the bullets, so to say, and when the blessed English and Americans finally chased the Boche off, I found a haven in Tunis, where I waited for word from Yves-Alain, my husband." She spelled his name for me. "When word did come just one month ago, it was that he was captured and executed by the bloody Nazis. Shot." She wiped a hand across her forehead. "At least not hung." She reached for a cake. As her hand went out, I placed mine on it. That smile again. My heart seemed to stop.

"I'm so sorry, Michelle," I said.

"Merci, Monsieur Lieutenant Junior Grade," she whispered.

"Please! Can't you call me Bill," I urged.

Now she grasped my hand. I felt a slight squeeze. "Okay, Beely." Marie's face shot through my mind's eye.

"What will you do now?" I asked. "Do you have a job? How do you live?"

She sighed. Deeply. "I have very little money." She glanced down at her dress. "These clothes I managed to carry with me from Marseille. Soon they will be rags." She managed a woeful smile. "But Ali has been very kind. He arranges jobs for me from time to time and lets me live here. Yves-Alain and he became acquainted because of their interest in politics. They had the same ideas about what Hitler was up to and tried to warn the British and French of his obvious plan to subjugate all of Europe. That's why I came here. I knew Ali would be a friend. She smiled up at Ali, who appeared once more to replenish our glasses.

"Mon cher ami," she murmured, "what would I have done without you?"

Now it was Ali's turn to shrug. He said nothing.

Michelle still clung to my hand, and now I felt a faint pressure. Or could it be my imagination? She gave me a quick sideways glance, then as quickly turned her head away. I vaguely wondered what kind of jobs Ali got for her. I couldn't see her waiting tables or tending bar. A sales clerk? Well. Maybe.

Another squeeze of my hand. "I miss him so," she whispered. Those eyes again. Boring through me, it seemed. Like a beam of light. "He was nearly as tall as you and just as handsome. Just as..." She stopped, then reached over and stroked my cheek.

"Just as what?" I felt a bit dizzy at this point. All kinds of stirrings going on.

"Just as... How do you say it? I don't know." She made a little face, and the smile returned, her lower lip caught in her teeth. "Oh, you know what I mean. I feel so bold. I don't know you at all. But I think of Yves-Alain when I look at you." There was a long pause, during which my mind exploded. As I stared at her, a huge wave of desire swept over me. God! Marie all over again. She seduced me. Would it be Michelle's turn?

"And it's been so very long, my Beely," she whispered.

My entire life seemed to flash through my mind. Betty. Eleanor. Dee. Uncle Dan. Mom. Dad. Is this how a drowning man felt? I wondered. I guess the turning point had come when Michelle's hand left mine, crept across the table, then to my knee, then worked its way up and a bit to the center. I narrowly averted an explosion. Sheer willpower, I guess. "Just look at a spot on the wall," Erwin used to say.

"Please, Beely, will you come to my rescue?"

I couldn't believe my next words. "Where can I meet you?" I gasped. "And when?"

Michelle drew my head down to her breast. I could feel the soft flesh against my cheek. "My room's upstairs," she murmured. "The first on the right of the landing." She glanced at a tiny silver wristwatch. "Meet me in trente minutes, one-half of an hour from now. Let me get ready for you."

With that, she slipped from her chair, glanced toward the two Arabs as she brushed by their table, and disappeared through a red velvet curtain at the rear of the darkened room. Before the curtain swung shut, I could make out stairs leading up to the next floor. An uneasy sensation crept over me. Something didn't seem right. Everything had happened too fast. I'd lost control of the situation. After she was gone five minutes, during which my spinning head slowed down a bit, I suddenly thought about the jeep. I couldn't leave it unattended and unwatched. I glanced quickly around the room. A single Arab now occupied the table. I wondered vaguely how I could have missed seeing his companion leave the building. The door to the kitchen opened. Ali came through and began removing the dishes and utensils from the empty place at the table now occupied by the remaining Arab, the two of them conversing inaudibly.

What would he think, I wondered, about my having a liaison with Michelle? The wife of his dead friend. No way he wouldn't know. Or find out. Maybe I could tell him some kind of a story. Like maybe that Michelle wanted to show me photographs of Yves-Alain. I couldn't help smiling ruefully.

He wasn't that stupid. But I'd have to have some excuse.

"Oh, Ali," I called over.

He crossed the room in an instant. "Yes, sir. What is your pleasure?"

I let out my breath. I kept my voice low. "Michelle has some old letters from her husband she wants me to look at. And some photographs. She has to search through her apartment to find them." This lie probably went over like a lead balloon. But what the hell.

Ali didn't seem at all surprised or disturbed. "That will be very helpful to her, sir, to talk about Yves. It would be doing her a great kindness. Poor young widow," he went on sympathetically, "no husband, no chance of getting one, and…" he paused, sighing, "in dire financial straits. I've tried to help her find work. But times are hard. He shrugged.

"But I can help her," I said excitedly, without thinking. "I have a fair amount of cash with me. I'll let her have some now, and I'll bring more in a couple of days." I felt exhilarated. Helping a young widow in distress. How noble could you get. Then my high-minded thoughts crashed. Would it be so damn noble to go jump in the sack with a young, vulnerable, impoverished widow? But I wouldn't have to go all the way, or even part way. I could actually look at photographs, give her some money, and leave. Still…A wave of excitement swept over me. I shut my eyes, thinking of Marie. It would be terrific. How could it not be?

Ali must have seen my hesitation. He spoke rapidly. "Oh, sir, you are a friend indeed. Americans are so very generous and kind. We've learned that many times." He shot a glance into the street. "If you're concerned about your jeep, I can take care of that. This is a slow time of day. I'll have Mohammed sit in your vehicle." Before I had a chance to argue or think, he reentered the kitchen. I could hear his voice in Arabic. Immediately the elderly dark-skinned man appeared, now wearing a turban, bowed, smiled, shuffled through the open door, and climbed into the front seat of the jeep, folded his arms on his chest, and leaned back.

I glanced at my watch. Michelle had been gone for only ten minutes. But why wait any longer. Why impose on Ali any more than necessary. I took a quick look at the young Arab. He placed his head on the table, his eyes closed, the white turban contrasting sharply with the dark stained wooden table. I rose, grabbed my hat, and hurried to the velvet curtain. I swung it to one side and slowly climbed the scarred steps to the unlighted upper landing. I stopped to get accustomed to the darkness, then noticed a door just to the right, as described by Michelle. I stood in front of it and listened. Silence. And then a rhythmic, creaking noise. Maybe some kind of an overhead fan. I tapped at the door. The creaking noise ceased instantly. I leaned my head against the door. Listening. After what seemed to be forever, it suddenly swung open.

The next few seconds were a bad dream. Michelle stood framed in the doorway, her dark curls a tangled mess, her eyes bulging from her head like marbles, clothed in a filmy silk wrapper. "Beely! Not now. I told you trente minutes."

Looking over her shoulder, I saw the young Arab, sitting up in a low bed, without headboard, naked, so far as I could tell, his eyes as startled as Michelle's. My mind froze. My body froze. The sudden disillusioning realization that I'd been taken in by a prostitute overwhelmed me. "Jesus Christ!" That was the best I could do. I wheeled around, rushed down the stairs, past the sleeping Arab, out of the building, to the side of my jeep. I opened the door, reached over, grabbed Mohammed, and jerked him to the street. "Get the hell out of here!" I shouted. He staggered toward the open door of L'Oasis, his eyes wide with alarm. I leaped into the driver's seat, pulled out my key, inserted it in the ignition, started the engine with a roar, and screeched down the street, ignoring pedestrians who dodged out of my way to avoid being executed on the spot. I made a squealing U-turn and roared passed the L'Oasis, where Mohammed had been joined by Ali. "You miserable pimp!" I yelled out, then slammed the jeep into second gear and tore along until I spotted a Navy shore patrol vehicle, which, thankfully, served to jolt some sense into my inflamed skull.

I was probably more angry with myself, than Ali or Michelle, I had been so stupid. They were trying to earn a difficult living under difficult circumstances. I was just trying to, well...

Betty's face appeared in my mind's eye. What would she have thought of me if I'd... I shut down my thoughts. Or Eleanor. My fling with Marie had been bad enough. Guilt feelings had swept over me many nights, fending off sleep. I cooled down as I drove along. I thanked Michelle for her greed in fitting in the young Arab ahead of me. "Merci beaucoup, Madame Hooker," I shouted to the darkening sky. I felt like such a fool, how could I have failed to realize what the setup was? And then I laughed out loud, thinking of Michelle's words. "Cher Ali, he arranges jobs for me from time to time."

Our replacement officer, Ensign Henry Schneider, had reported for duty within twenty-four hours after my disastrous liberty in Tunis. I guess "brash" would be an appropriate word to describe him. He was short and stocky, with curly black hair and flashing dark eyes that did have a twinkle. I had to admit that. I learned quickly that he hailed from Brooklyn, born and raised two blocks from Flatbush Avenue. His accent would have given him away. "Call me Hank," he said after I read and endorsed his orders. Carl Pierce's jaw nearly dropped to the deck at that suggestion. "Mr. Schneider," I informed him in the sternest voice I could muster, "I will call you Mr. Schneider, and you will address me as 'Captain' at all times." Was I a son of a bitch? I wondered. I worried that we got off on the wrong foot, but I needn't have. There was only one more confrontation when I insisted he wear a tie when he went ashore.

"Why do I have to wear a tie, Captain?"

"Because I say so!"

Not the best reason I guess but it worked.

His brashness fell a few notches when he lost his dinner during his first night on watch while we were underway. Schneider and Jack Stocke quickly became great pals, and they constantly bickered about the merits of the St. Louis Cardinals versus the Brooklyn Dodgers. Stocke wounded the new officer repeatedly by reminding him of the infamous ninth-inning third strike in the 1941 World Series when, with Brooklyn leading 4-3, Mickey Owen let the ball get by him, allowing Tommy Henrich to reach first base, resulting ultimately in a 7-4 Yankees victory. "Those lucky damn Yankees," Schneider would moan, "We got the lousiest breaks during the entire series."

Our stay in Bizerte had been prolonged by three weeks when the port generator conked out. Spare parts and equipment were at a premium, and we were forced to wait impatiently for a replacement. "It's aboard a supply ship somewhere between here and Gibraltar," Mr. Donnelly had been informed on each occasion he made an inquiry.

A thrill of excitement had pervaded the entire base when the news came over the BBC on July 26 that Mussolini had been deposed. King Emmanuel turned the Italian government over to an aging Marshall Badoglio, who, we all hoped, would quickly surrender to the Allies. Maybe the war would end soon. We could go home. But the euphoria was short lived. "No way the lousy Germans will let Italy go by the board. You watch. The Huns will slaughter any eyeties that oppose them." Ensign Schneider's humble opinion. No one had disagreed. He proved to be correct.

The lives of the officers and crew had been made miserable by the commanding officer of the escort/sweeper group attached to Bizerte, and under whose supervision the PC 823 temporarily fell. Lieutenant Commander Opie had long since been retired to civilian life when war broke out. Like hundreds of other passed-over regular officers, he was recalled into the service. Now he reigned in his glory. Unfit to command a U.S. Navy vessel, he vented his frustrations on the reserve officers who commanded the YMSs, SCs, and PCs assigned to his group, demeaning them at every opportunity. Jackets had to be worn at all times despite the intense African heat and humidity; ties must be two-blocked; hats worn squarely on the head; anyone who failed to salute a superior would be put on report. All ships must be ready for a surprise inspection, day or night, decks scrubbed down, brass polished, deck lines appropriately flaked down, guns covered, and many other "chicken shit rules," so called by Lieutenant Commander Opie's entire command.

"What an asshole," I overheard Schneider mutter, as our nemesis had saluted the colors and marched stiffly down the gangplank and on to the dock after one of his surprise inspections. This time he chewed out the gangway watch for what he called a "sloppy salute," obviously frustrated at not being able to find anything important to criticize.

"Amen," Carl Pierce had intoned.

"Hey, Carl," Jack Stocke had called out jokingly, "are you, a devout Mormon, condoning such nasty language?"

Carl shrugged. "When the shoe fits. You know." He laughed sheepishly.

We rejoiced when Ensign Donnelly finally had reported the arrival of the spare generator. Within twenty-four hours we made the repairs and were underway. A feeling of relief had swept over the entire ship's company, as the PC 823 passed Cap Blanc to starboard and set a course for Palermo.

Back to the war.

CHAPTER 35

During our journey from Bizerte to Palermo, the stormy Med had been a huge lake, with only ripples from a soft breeze from the north ruffling the green waters. The PC 823 had rolled gently as she chugged along at a steady 15 knots, as though bent on a pleasure cruise rather than sailing in hostile waters during wartime. The crewmen shed their shirts when off watch, basking in the warm sun, regaling one another with a wide variety of tall tales, each laced with dozens of Anglo-Saxon expletives, the one resorted to most often by a wide margin being the ubiquitous F word used indiscriminately as a noun, verb, or adjective.

Now, seated in the wardroom alone after Pierce's departure, I began mulling over past events—George's death, what we might have done to avoid that awful tragedy, my inadequate letter to Mrs. Dugan, my Tunis adventure with Michelle, Eleanor's letter, her news about Cliff—when Pierce reentered the wardroom. He slumped into the seat across from me and placed his hat on the table. "Just got word, Captain, Operations has made final arrangements for the week's R&R for the entire crew. A skeleton crew will take over tomorrow at 0700. We can shove off anytime after that."

"I'm staying aboard," I said. My response even surprised me. I hadn't given any thought to the news that Carl had brought earlier about R&R. But my letter to Mrs. Dugan followed by reading Eleanor's letter had left a cloud of depression hanging over me.

"Gosh, Captain," Carl pleaded, "you need a break. If the palaces or the opera don't suit your fancy, I've learned there's a terrific beach in Mondello, just up the coast. You can really relax there. Lie in the sand. Read a book. Read two books. Or you can walk around the city. Meet some of the people. They love Americans. They're so happy that the Krauts have been kicked out of Palermo, you'll be treated like a king."

"I don't want to be treated like a king," I said. "I'll feel guilty, having a good time when the captain is...when the captain..." I stared out through the door at a warehouse on the dock. A swarm of sailors and soldiers moved past, headed toward town. The port had been more than 75 percent restored. The CBs had done a marvelous job. "Look," I said, "I'll be okay. Please don't worry. Have a good time. I'll see you and the other officers at chow this evening, and maybe by then I'll have changed my mind. But I doubt it."

"Well, Captain, I'm going to figure out some way to get you off this bucket." He stood. "Maybe I'll search for some kind of prayer that'll work."

I managed a smile. "You never give up. But maybe it's not a bad idea. Pray for something good to happen for a change." I sat alone, staring at Eleanor's letter. I read it once more. Yes, there was a difference. I missed the earlier eager warmth.

"Pardon me, Captain."

Page peered from the pantry.

"Yes, Page. What's up?"

Page stepped into the wardroom, holding a large piece of drawing paper. "I thought you'd like to have this, Captain." He placed the sheet on the table.

I gasped in amazement at a crayon sketch of George on the flying bridge of the PC 823, looking seaward, his binoculars half-raised, his jaw squared, a smile on his face. I could hear him saying, "Damn! Bring on the Stukas!"

"Page. This is marvelous."

"Well, the captain was a marvelous man. I did this from memory."

"You did a wonderful likeness."

I held the picture up and stared at it. My mind raced. Mrs. Dugan should have this. "Page," I said, "would you mind if I sent this to the Captain's mother? I know she'd love to have it."

"Gosh, Captain. No, of course not. What a great idea." He stared at the picture for a few seconds. "I'll borrow this one, if you don't mind, and do another one for you."

I leaned back after Page reentered the pantry and closed my eyes. I pictured once more George's staring up at me, that puzzled look on his face. A wave of depression hit me again. Would I ever get back to normal? Would I ever not have a lump in my throat? Not have an empty feeling in the pit of my stomach? Another knock at the open wardroom door jarred my senses. What the hell was going on? Why couldn't I be left alone? I opened my eyes. The gangway watch, Bosun's Mate Second Class Cassidy, stood in the open door.

"Yes, Cassidy. What is it?"

Cassidy stepped into the wardroom and removed his hat. "Lieutenant Mills requests permission to come aboard, sir."

Cliff! My heart leaped. Then sank fast when I recalled Eleanor's letter. What an amazing coincidence. "Thanks, Cassidy." My first instinct was to rush out of the wardroom to greet Cliff. Then, I thought, I needed to compose myself. Can't make him think I'm not glad to see him. "Send him in." Cassidy restored his hat, saluted and headed for the gangway.

"Page," I called out. I felt like a coward, but in truth I wanted the steward's mate nearby when I first saw Cliff.

"Yes, sir?" Page emerged from the pantry.

"Rustle up some coffee, would you? We've got a visitor."

"Yes, sir."

I squeezed by the table and stood in the doorway. And there he was. All smiles. His hand extended. My Texas friend. What a great guy. I relaxed immediately. He looked fifteen pounds lighter. His uniform hung on him like a flour sack. His eyes looked awful. Like two piss holes in the snow, Erwin would have said.

"Bill!" he exclaimed. "I'm mighty glad I caught up with you."

I grasped his hand. "Where in the hell did you come from?" I asked. "I didn't see any DEs tying up."

"We're over at the fuel dock. Refueling and taking on ammunition and supplies. We're shoving off at 1800. Have to pick up a homebound GUS convoy at first light tomorrow forming off Bizerte Harbor. I was coming back from Operations, after picking up our orders, and nearly dropped my front teeth when I spotted the PC 823." His face flushed suddenly. "Uh, your friend Eleanor told me the number of your ship."

"Oh, yeah," I said, hoping my smile was not strained. "I know. She wrote that she saw you when your ship tied up in Boston."

Cliff shifted back and forth uneasily. Now his smile seemed a bit weak.

No way for two old friends to behave. "Come on in. Take the load off your feet. Page will bring us some coffee. I hope you have time for that, anyway."

Cliff glanced at his watch. "Okay, I'd like that. I don't have to report back to the ship for several hours."

When Page had served us, I raised my coffee mug. "Cheers. When we leave here, we'll have a few beers at the officers club."

We sipped our coffee in silence, except for the drone of the ship's generators and strains of a Mozart violin concerto from the radio speaker. The BBC kept the armed forces well supplied with classical music. "Eleanor said you've had a rough time," I finally ventured. "In more ways than one."

Cliff made a face. "One of the ways I was more or less prepared for. I knew convoy duty would be hell." He grinned wryly. "Didn't old fire-eater McDaniel warn us?" He bit his lower lip. "The other hit me like a ton of bricks."

"Helen?"

"Yeah. Helen." Cliff drained off his coffee. The ever-alert Page promptly refilled the mug.

"I'm sorry." Not much help. I tried again. "Maybe it was for the best." How trite can you get!

He glanced up quickly, then stared into his mug. "Yeah. Maybe so."

The silence thickened like a storm cloud to the point of embarrassment. Cliff finally cleared his throat. "The gangway watch said you're in command." He held out his hand once more. The smile returned. Genuine this time. "Congratulations, Bill. That's really terrific."

My face must have given away my feelings. He immediately asked what was wrong, and I spent the next fifteen minutes talking about George and what a wonderful skipper and great friend he was, and I described the awful morning of July 10. "I'll never get over it," I said.

"Oh, but you will, in time," Cliff said. "You'll never forget him, but the pain will ease. You'll remember the good things. I've been going through the same sort of thing for the past two months. Not my captain, but my closest friend. Killed in an air attack near Bône. A squadron of JU-88s hit us at dusk. Ironically, he was the aircraft recognition officer. He no sooner made the identification when a bomb grazed our fantail. Shrapnel got him, along with a signalman and three of the 40-millimeter gun crewmen. The ship suffered only minor damage. I couldn't sleep for a month, but I'm doing a hell of a lot better now."

Page poured our third cups of coffee during the ensuing silence. He's right, I thought. My terrible grief after losing Spike had finally eased. And I now only thought of the great times we had, and the joy of our reunion after Dee and I found him. But that had taken much longer than a month.

"Bill."

I glanced at Cliff. His face was drawn up, as though in pain. I waited for him to continue.

"Bill, I've lost a lot of sleep for another reason," he said. I knew what to expect. I asked anyway. "How come?"

He looked to one side and stared at the bulkhead for what seemed like forever, then finally spoke. "I've got to tell you that I visited Eleanor more than once."

"I know. She wrote me about it. Just got the letter today."

Cliff cleared his throat. "Look Bill, I feel like a shit. In fact, I am a shit." Another pause.

Strangely, I didn't feel upset. Betty's face flashed into my mind's eye. My heart beat a little faster. The kindest thing would be to put Cliff at ease.

"Have you and Eleanor got something special going?"

He startled with surprise. He began to speak but stopped when I held up my hand.

"It's okay," I said. "Please don't worry about it. Eleanor's a lovely person, but..." But what, I wondered. "But I don't think I love her," I finally went on. "Probably never did, although I admit I told her I love her." I leaned back and couldn't help smiling, a bit ruefully. "Maybe I'm the shit, not you, if you're looking for someone to blame."

The look on Cliff's face, like he'd suddenly lost a huge weight, made me want to laugh. "Jesus, Bill, you're some kind of a terrific guy. I really didn't expect it to happen. Certainly not so soon after Helen. And I'd hate to do anything to hurt you." He went on hurriedly. "I thought I might be on the rebound. It worried the hell out of me. And she was worried sick about how you'd react. We talked it over for hours, it seemed like. I really don't think I'm on the rebound. She's so...so..." He glanced at me uneasily.

"Oh, go on," I laughed, "say it. She's beautiful and wonderful. I agree. I don't mind. Honestly."

"Thanks, Bill. You don't know what this means to me, your taking it all so well. She felt miserable, thinking what she'd done, with you overseas in a war zone and all. She said she'd write. He downed his third cup. "I guess you haven't heard from her?"

"Only the one letter," I replied. "Maybe it'll get here before we leave Palermo."

"I hope so," Cliff said, "but I'll write her tonight and let her know I've talked to you."

"Okay. In the meantime, what do you say we go ashore and have a few beers at the officers club. I'd like to hear what else you've been up to on that Destroyer Escort of yours."

The officers club occupied the rear of the Excelsior Hotel, a dingy, elegant old structure only a short distance from the harbor, the number one Palermo hotel before the war, now taken over by the U.S. Navy, and used mostly to accommodate visiting brass. We entered the nearly empty cocktail lounge. Two officers from the PC 596 sat at a table in the corner with two young dark-haired female representatives of the friendly citizens of Palermo, who, as Pierce had said, loved their American liberators. I gave the two officers the traditional thumbs up signal. They waved back, big grins spread over their faces.

A young Italian waiter, probably no more than sixteen years old, wearing a thread-bare, dingy white jacket, rushed up to our table, eager to please. He announced that his name was Antonio Marino and stood ready to fulfill our every need. I'd been continuously surprised at the courteousness and cheerfulness of the Palermo civilians. Most of them spoke at least broken English. Many claimed to have a cousin or uncle in America, usually living in Brooklyn. This one must have been lucky enough to avoid military service because of his youth.

Antonio quickly brought us our beers along with a basket of pretzels. I raised my glass. "All the best to you and Eleanor. And I really mean it." Or did I? How could my feelings change so quickly? Then, I thought, how come her feelings had changed so quickly? It sure couldn't have been true love.

Cliff watched me intently. "Thanks, Bill," he finally said. "That's mighty decent of you." His Texas drawl had never been more pronounced.

I leaned back, placed my right leg on an empty chair, and waved my hand at Cliff. "Okay, my friend, I want to hear more about some of the adventures you've been having that Eleanor hinted at in her letter."

"First of all," he replied, "I want to tell you something you'd never believe in a million years."

"What in the world could that be?"

"Do you remember a guy named Steve Dobson at your alma mater?" A half-smile broke out on Cliff's face.

"Steve Dobson!" This was a surprise. To hear his name after all this time. I grimaced. "Yeah, I remember the little jerk. Where in the world did you run into that misfit?"

"That particular misfit was assigned to my ship as a signalman third class. He was on my watch during our last east-to-west crossing. I nearly fell over when I learned his brother was none other than Harry Dobson, the creep that stole your ordnance manual at Local Defense School."

"Yeah, that's right. Not one, but at least two born losers in the Dobson family. But what about the little twerp. Did he mention me at all?"

Cliff chuckled. "The first time he and I stood watch together, I learned that he attended Cornell University. Naturally, I asked if he knew you and I was amazed when he said yes and then proceeded to regale me with the way you screwed up an important baseball game. I didn't believe the little jerk for a minute and managed to avoid any future conversations with him."

My mind shifted back to that miserable day when Steve had practically thrown the ball game, followed by the measles, then Dee and Erwin going to the Spring Day dance with me languishing in the infirmary in a jealous snit. It seemed like another world. Would there ever be that kind of world again?

"Well, you were right," I said, "he was not only a jerk, but a liar of the highest order, and full of b.s. to go along with it." I signaled Antonio, who scampered over. "A pitcher of suds this time, per favore."

"Okay, sir."

"Did he say what happened to Harry?" I asked.

"Yeah, he sure did. Our old amigo Harry was given a chance to apply all he learned about ordnance in LDS. He's in command of an armed guard crew on a Navy troop transport in the Pacific."

"I hope he falls overboard and drowns." And I really meant it. I wondered dozens of times what would have happened to my Navy career if I hadn't been blessed with ESP. We watched in silence as Antonio placed the pitcher of foamy beer on the table with fresh mugs.

"Grazie," I said.

"You're welcome, sir."

Cliff burst out laughing. "It tickles the hell out of me the way you speak Italian and Antonio responds in English."

"Yeah, we do learn from each other. Isn't that what we're fighting for? One world. Or something."

Cliff snorted. "For my money, we're fighting to kill those German and Japanese sons of bitches that started this frigging war."

"Speaking of the frigging war, tell me what you've been up to these past months?"

Cliff held me spellbound with tales of high adventure escorting UGS convoys across the Atlantic, through the Strait of Gibraltar, past Torpedo Junction, on to Bizerte. "It was tough enough in the Atlantic, but there was no way to keep our presence secret from the Krauts, once we hit the Med. We had to pass through the Strait in broad daylight. Everybody and his brother, including the lousy German spies along the north coast of Africa, knew where we were and where we were bound. Convoy speed was only eight knots, and sometimes we felt like sitting ducks. Our problems came mostly from the air, with an occasional U-boat attack. We lost one DE in our last convoy. An acoustic torpedo slammed into the ship's forward magazine. Blew her in half. It was a hell of a mess. Guys blown apart, guys struggling in the water, drowning in front of our eyes." Cliff's face turned rigid as he spoke. "We didn't stop to pick up any survivors. We made sonar contact and messed up the situation even more by dropping a pattern of depth charges. Our captain wanted to be a hero. I could have shot him. God knows how many guys in the water he managed to kill. And we lost contact almost immediately. Searched for more than three hours without any luck. She may have been waiting us out on the bottom the entire time. We'll never know."

"Was your captain reprimanded?"

"Hell, no. None of us had the guts to file a report." Cliff barked out a nasty laugh. "That was par for the course. God knows how many times we've fired at either British or U.S. aircraft. Friendly fire. Sheeit!"

It must be terrible, I thought, to have no respect for your commanding officer. I changed the subject. "How active was the Luftwaffe?"

"I told you about the time my pal was killed. My first convoy. The next one was even worse. Some of the time it was like a peacetime cruise. Other times all hell broke loose. We could predict the rough days when we caught sight of a shadow plane. You could safely bet the farm that we'd soon have unfriendly visitors, usually just after sundown, and usually torpedo planes and glide bombers coming at us from different directions. You've never heard such a racket or seen such fireworks when every escort vessel, including a British battleship, let go with everything they had. Really effective firepower. Only three of four merchant ships were hit, and they managed to stay afloat."

During Cliff's saga, we drained the last drop of beer. Where was the usually attentive Antonio? I raised halfway up in my chair, when I noticed Pierce, standing under the curved arch of the entry to the lounge, hat in hand, gazing anxiously around, obviously searching for someone. I didn't have to guess who.

I waved my hand. "Mr. Pierce," I called out, "looking for me?"

A wave of relief swept over his face as he hurried across the room. He was breathing heavily when he reached the table. "Captain, I'm glad I found you. I figured you might be here. We've been ordered to get underway at 2000. Something big's in the wind. Don't know what. The specific orders are for your eyes only. I stuck them in the ship's safe."

"So much for a week's R&R," I said. I pointed to Cliff. "Carl Pierce, meet Cliff Mills. He and I were in Local Defense School and SCTC together. Cliff's been making sure that the slow convoys from the States get here safely."

Pierce and Cliff shook hands.

I glanced at my watch. "I assume we've got sufficient supplies and ammunition on board."

"Yes, sir." He hesitated. "I hope you don't mind, Captain, but after the message was delivered, I took her down to the fuel dock and topped off. She's back in the same berth."

I patted his shoulder. "Hell no, Mr. Pierce, that's terrific. Well done. Your action's what our Navy calls 'forehanded.'"

Pierce laughed. "I don't know about my being forehanded, but it was forehanded of you to order me to take the ship down to the fuel dock a few weeks ago, then walk off the ship, leaving me in shock. I nearly died on the spot. But it was a good way to learn."

Pierce was recalling the time when I thought, what the hell, he's got to dock the ship sooner or later, and the best way to make him swim is push him in the water. So, I did just that. Ordered the refueling and walked off the ship before he had a chance to know what had hit him. Then I hid behind a palm tree, nerves on edge, and watched while Pierce backed the PC 823 out of the slip and slowly maneuvered her to the fuel dock. I waited until refueling ended, then, less nervous, watched as he brought the ship back to her original berth. I never told Pierce about my spying on him. George had pulled the same stunt on me, and I always appreciated his confidence. Come to think of it, maybe he spied on me. Now, I'd never know. I caught sight of Antonio. "I'm happy to say that your forehandedness has given us the time needed for a farewell beer." Antonio quickly rushed off to comply with my request. Three beers and another glass rapidly appeared. We raised our mugs.

"Farewell to you, Cliff," I said. "Temporarily, I hope. Goodbye to Palermo." We downed the contents of our mugs.

"And hello mysterious orders."

CHAPTER 36

The ship's officers crowded into the wardroom. Pierce stretched his neck to follow the words as I read aloud the instructions contained in the secret envelope I retrieved from the ship's safe. Stocke, Donnelly, and Schneider listened eagerly.

"The main landings will be in the Gulf of Salerno. D-day is 9 September. The operation has been designated AVALANCHE." A chill swept through me. Another invasion. George's figure flashed in my mind's eye. Lying on the deck. Dying. I cleared my throat, then went on reading, my voice so low that the officers strained to listen. "The PC 823 will be a part of the group assigned to escort a convoy of LCIs from Bizerte to the beach area. You will get underway at 2000 this date, proceed directly to Naval Headquarters, Bizerte, and report to the Commanding Officer of the Escort/Sweeper Group, Lieutenant Commander John Opie, for further orders."

A chorus of groans like the moaning of cows who'd just lost their calves filled the wardroom. "Opie." Pierce's voice reached C above high C, wherever that is. "Are we going to have to deal with that maniac again?"

"Oh, hell," I said, "Opie's the least of our worries. We're going to have to contend with the damn Krauts." I tossed the orders on the wardroom table. "Okay, let's grab some chow, then get the ship squared away so we can leave this lovely city as close to 2000 as possible."

At 2003 exactly, the PC 823 backed from the slip, threaded its way through dozens of anchored ships in the harbor, and rolled and plunged up the coast in a quartering swell from seaward, operating at standard speed. Our route would take us past the hulking shape of Mount Pelligrino, past Mondello Beach, where Pierce said I should relax and read, then a turn to port, and on the new course until abeam of Cape San Vito. We would then steer 270, due west. After holding that course for two hours, we swung to course 235, past Isola Marttimo, and on into Bizerte Harbor.

The officers gathered on the flying bridge debated the chances of successful landings on the Salerno beaches. Hopes for easy pickings had been fanned by recent persistent rumors that the Italians were on the verge of surrendering. Bagdolio had proclaimed allegiance to Hitler, but many politicians and military experts did not believe him, predicting that he'd seize the first opportunity to dump his former ally. Other so-called experts expressed concern that the unconditional surrender demand announced by the U.S. and Great Britain would be too much for the proud descendants of Julius Caesar to swallow.

"Okay, let's break up this bull session," I finally announced. "I'll stand watch with Mr. Schneider until we change course off Cape San Vito." The flying bridge emptied quickly except for Schneider, the two lookouts, and me. By now the sun had set, an enormous red fireball that had sunk majestically beyond the horizon, leaving streaks of red, yellow, purple and green blazing across the deep blue evening sky. "Red sun at night, sailors delight," the old adage went. That was okay by me. A flat, calm sea like the proverbial millpond added to our enjoyment, my mental picture of the Mediterranean until I learned how miserably rough and unpleasant it could be. What better sailing could one ask for? If only the black cloud of invasion would disappear.

"Radar," I called down.

"Radar, aye, sir," Kelsey responded immediately.

"Let me know when Cape San Vito is directly on our beam. It'll stick out like a sore thumb. You can't miss it."

"Aye, aye sir."

I wondered whether Schneider resented my remaining on the bridge. He probably thought I didn't trust him. Actually, he'd done quite well for the most part since coming aboard, but I'd been a bit shaken when, upon reaching the flying bridge on his watch several weeks ago, I'd spotted a floating mine only about twenty yards dead ahead, bobbing and rolling in an angry sea. I had immediately ordered right full rudder, and we watched in silence as the ugly black horned ball passed by our port side. The expression on his face made it clear that he'd learned a lesson. The lookouts, especially the crow's nest lookout, also had been remiss, but I refrained from imposing any discipline after a brief lecture on the vital importance on being alert at all times.

"I hope you don't mind my standing watch with you, Mr.

Schneider," I said. "You're catching on fine, but I'm a little edgy, and know I couldn't sleep if I did hit the sack."

"Gosh no, Skipper, I enjoy the company." Pierce had gently suggested to Schneider several times that he be a little more formal in his manner of addressing his superior officers, but to no avail. We finally gave up. His good nature more than made up for the rough spots.

Within the hour, we viewed astern the slow ascent of a brilliantly yellow gibbous moon, which dimmed the brilliance of the Milky Way's path across the dark sky. "What a night for romance, Skipper," Schneider exulted. "Can't wait to hook up with my petite French cheri when we hit Bizerte." With that cogent remark, Schneider commenced scanning a wide arc of the horizon with his binoculars, softly whistling the Marseillaise.

"Well, you better work fast," I commented, "because we're going to be plenty busy getting ready for Salerno."

The PC 823 proceeded for the next hour at a steady 15 knots, each of us with his own thoughts as we scanned the horizon, the ship softly pitching in the gentle swells moving in from directly ahead, the swishing and gurgling sounds mingling with the throb of the engines and the incessant pinging of our sonar gear.

"Bridge, from Radar."

"Bridge, aye."

"Just passing Cape San Vito on..."

Kelsey's complete message never reached me. At that moment, a loud metallic clanging filled the air for a few seconds, then ceased as abruptly as it had begun. The port engine immediately shut down. The ship veered to port.

"Maintain your course," I shouted down the voice tube. "What's going on?"

The ship swung back to its previous heading.

"Engine room shut down the port engine, sir," the engine telegraph operator called back. "Don't know for sure, sir, but sounded like we threw a connecting rod."

I quickly called down the voice tube. "Starboard engine ahead one-third."

"Aye, aye, sir."

"Ask Mr. Donnelly to report to the bridge," I called down.

"He's on his way, Captain."

"Bridge, from radar."

"Go ahead radar."

"We've passed by Cape San Vito, sir."

"Very well." The time had come to change course.

"Left standard rudder, come to course 270."

"Aye, aye, sir."

I was conscious that Donnelly stood at my side. "Captain, we've thrown a connecting rod in the port engine. I'm afraid it can't be repaired without going back to port."

"How long are the repairs likely to take?"

"Well, we won't have to go into dry dock, sir. That's good news, anyway. But it will take a couple of weeks at best, and that assumes spare parts will be available and there are no other ships with higher priorities."

"Very well, there's no use moaning and groaning about it." I raised my glasses and scanned the entire horizon. Nothing in sight. "Please tell sparks to radio headquarters, Palermo, using the secret cipher, and tell them we have a serious mechanical problem, and are returning to port."

"Aye, aye, sir."

"I'm sorry, Captain." Donnelly looked crestfallen.

"It wasn't your fault. The old bucket has taken a beating for months. It's a wonder we haven't had worse problems than this. Then I couldn't help smiling. Cheer up, Mr. Donnelly, at least we won't be terrorized by Lieutenant Commander Opie."

U.S. and British warships of every size and description crowded Palermo harbor— cruisers, destroyers, troop transports, LSTs, LCIs, LCVPs, supply vessels, minesweepers, PCs, SCs, and more. A German spy, gazing down from the rugged surrounding hillsides would quickly have reached the conclusion that something BIG was brewing. And soon. The question would only be where. After much maneuvering and waiting, and many blinker signals, at mid-morning the PC 823 finally received permission to tie up next to the dock at Pier 21. I sweated through the one-engine docking, accomplished with no damage to the dock or the ship, and was gratified to hear Pierce's murmured commendation, "Great seamanship, Captain."

Donnelly soon brought the news. It would be days, maybe weeks, before repairs could be made to the port engine. Facilities had been strained beyond the limit. Hours later, I sat alone in the wardroom, having ordered all the officers to go ashore and relax. Pierce had urged me to take a break from the ship, but I refused. Nursing the mug of coffee that Page had poured, I pondered the situation. The chances of the PC 823's participating in the planned invasion were close to nil. But was that bad? As I conned the PC 823 through the awesome armada crowding the harbor, I was left with thoughts I wouldn't wish to share with the other officers. I hated to admit it even to myself, but the prospect of another invasion brought feelings of anxiety and depression. Did that make me a coward? I hoped not. Anyone anxious to get shot at must be some kind of nut. Then I thought about George. He'd have relished the prospect. And George wasn't a nut. Or maybe he was. In a nice sort of way.

A wave of sadness crushed down on me. Maybe I should have gone ashore. A couple of stiff shots of bourbon or Scotch or gin or all three, or maybe more than a couple, might help. I'd never been on a drunken spree in my life. Nor had I ever wanted to. Anyway, I never could afford to spend money on booze. The closest, I guess, was that memorable evening when I got pleasantly crocked with Marie. Memories of the elegant dinner and my sparkling French landlady's continuous chatter flitted through my mind. I couldn't help smiling. She virtually put me to bed that night. To sleep. But there was no use thinking about getting drunk. Not today, anyway. I couldn't leave the ship without an officer on board.

"Captain, there's someone at the gangway requesting to see you."

I looked up in surprise. Pierce stood in the open doorway, hat in hand, an odd, crooked smile on his face. Completely unlike Pierce. Maybe the devout Mormon had tied one on.

"I thought you went ashore," I said. "What happened?"

"Oh, I had a few cokes and pretzels at the officers club and chatted with the guys from the PC 596. They had a couple of women with them, and it was pretty clear I was a fifth wheel. So I said to heck with it." He glanced to his right down the deck. "Maybe you better check on your visitor."

"Who the hell is it? I really don't want any damn company."

"Well, it's a lieutenant." His smirk remained. What was going on with my executive officer?

"A Navy lieutenant?"

"Yes, sir."

"A U.S. Navy lieutenant?"

"Yes, sir."

"One-and-a-half striper or two-striper?"

"Two-striper, sir."

"Well, who the hell is it?"

Pierce shrugged. "Didn't give a name, sir."

Now I was really irritated. "What's his business? What does he want with me, for God's sake?"

Another shrug. "Didn't say, sir."

"This is just what I don't need," I muttered. "Probably some shore-based bastard wanting to know how come the captain was killed. I've already answered a ton of questions, and my action report spelled out the whole miserable business in detail."

"What should I do, Captain?" Pierce waited, his eyebrows raised.

"Oh well, send him in. He'll just come back another time if I don't see him now. Let's get it over with."

Pierce backed out of the doorway, placed his hat squarely on his head, and headed toward the gangway.

I leaned back and shut my eyes. Would I ever rid my thoughts of George? Would I ever forget the horror at sunrise on July 10? Would I ever be allowed to forget it?

"Request permission to enter the wardroom, Captain."

I turned cold. Then hot. Then faint. I opened my eyes.

Lieutenant Elizabeth Marshall stood framed in the doorway, standing at attention in her blue uniform with the two gold stripes on each sleeve, her white summer hat under her right arm, a black bag slung over her shoulder, her dark curls a bit longer than I remembered, a huge grin on her face.

"Betty!"

I squeezed around the table and, without thinking, took her into my arms. She dropped her hat and returned my embrace. I'd forgotten how tall she was. Her soft hair pressed into my lips.

"Bill," she gasped. Then laughed. A shaky laugh. "Is this any way for a ship's captain to carry on? And with a superior officer."

"Oh, Betty. Jesus. God. I don't know what to say. I've never been so glad to see anyone in all my life." It was my turn to laugh. A shrill, hyper laugh. "Except maybe when I found Spike."

"I'm really in good company," she smiled.

We sat down, staring at each other. I clung to her hand. "No wonder Pierce acted so damn silly," I said. "He really acted strange. Now I know why."

"Well, I asked him to let me surprise you." Her low familiar laugh filled the wardroom. "He did a good job of carrying out orders."

My voice rose excitedly. "But what are you doing in Palermo? How long have you been here? How long are you staying? Where are you quartered? How did you know I was in Palermo? Can we go somewhere and talk?"

"Whoa, Captain, slow down." She extricated her hand, reached over and squeezed my arm. "Yes, to answer your last question. We can go to the Excelsior. I'm staying there. My admiral's here for a conference. We flew in from Gibraltar this morning." She shuddered. "What a rotten ride. The weather suddenly turned awful. Pouring rain, lightning, thunder. Nearly scared me to death. We bounced all over the sky, even dodged some enemy aircraft, so our pilot claimed. I don't know. He was a bit of a windbag. Typical flyboy. We'll be in meetings for a couple of days, maybe more, at least Admiral Wilson will. We're occupying VIP quarters. Separate, of course. Suites are rundown, but all kinds of service. I checked on the location of your ship at Operations, and, lo and behold, discovered you were right here in Palermo. I couldn't wait to see you." She leaned over and stroked my cheek. "My dear friend. I'm so happy to find you." To my amazement, her eyes filled with tears.

"Gg gosh, Betty..." I choked up. I could feel my eyes filling up.

"We're a soupy pair," she said. She withdrew her hand, cocked her head and eyed me intently. "You don't look all that great, Bill. What's been going on?"

"Too damn much," I replied. "The worst thing is I lost my captain. Killed during the Sicilian invasion." Betty's pained expression surprised me. She'd never met George. I hurried on, relating the events of that awful morning. She only listened, staring at the tablecloth, her slim fingers slowly kneading her bag.

"He was the best commanding officer anyone could have," I said. "And a great friend." A lengthy silence followed. I sensed that she wanted to tell me something, but couldn't find the words. The look in her eyes, a quiet sadness, was troublesome and disconcerting.

"Oh hell," I finally said, "let's get out of here. The officers club's in your hotel. We can find a quiet table and catch up with each other."

Antonio greeted me like a long lost uncle, his eyes rolling with excitement when I introduced him to Betty as my favorite waiter.

"Welcome back, Capitano. Please to follow me. I have nice quiet table for you and the bella signora." With that, he hustled off toward the far corner of the room, a huge grin on his face, looking back twice as he went, and waving us on. With a grand flourish, he pulled back a chair and bowed. Be seated, if you please."

Betty smiled graciously. "Grazie, Antonio."

Antonio soon hustled up to the table with a pitcher of beer and two glasses. I filled our glasses, then raised mine. "To a wonderful reunion with a wonderful girl."

Her quick smile brightened the room for an instant. Then was gone. "And with a wonderful guy," she said. The sadness in her eyes remained.

An awkward silence settled on us after we downed our drinks. Betty kept glancing at me, then frowning into her empty glass. She cleared her throat a couple of times, as though she wished to speak, but no words came. She had something on her mind. What could it be? It couldn't be her reaction to George's death. Was she about to tell me she was in love with some guy? Or worse still, engaged? With all my heart, I hoped not. If I hadn't realized it before, I suddenly knew. I couldn't say how or why, but I knew that I loved this beautiful person. Really loved her. Had loved her for years. Ever since Cornell. Not like it had been with Eleanor. Or Dee. And, God knows, not like it had been with Marie.

"Gosh, Betty," I finally said, in a whisper, "you're acting real strange all of a sudden. Is there something wrong? If so, is there anything I can do to help?"

She reached across the table and grasped my hand. The strained look in her eyes startled me. She finally spoke, her voice barely audible. "I'm afraid I have some terrible news for you, Bill. I hate to add to your troubles."

My mind performed a dozen somersaults then raced ahead like an express train. Had something bad happened to Mom or Dad? Or to Uncle Dan? But how would Betty know that, and not me? Now my mind went blank. "What are you trying to tell me? What's the bad news?" I finally asked.

"It's Dee. She was killed during a bombing raid. In London."

For a few seconds, I couldn't breathe. It wasn't true. Not Dee. Not my happy-go- lucky friend, who cheered me up when I was down, who helped me find Spike.

Betty's words rushed on in a monotone, like she was reciting a hated school lesson. The full impact of her message slowly set in as she spoke. "It happened just a week before I left England to come here. Dee refused to go into the bomb shelter. She made up her mind to stop running for cover every time there was an alert, especially after she received word that her relatives had died in a concentration camp. Instead, she'd head for the nearest pub and toss down the booze until the all-clear sounded. I tried as hard as I could to get her to go into the shelter that awful night when all of London seemed to be on fire. We were having dinner together when the alarm sounded. I jumped up to head for a shelter, but she said to hell with it. She was sick of hiding like an animal in a cave. I didn't want to leave her, but I was under strict orders to take cover during a raid. She died instantly. No pain. No suffering." Betty squeezed my hand, and looked anxiously at me. "I'm so sorry, Bill. After all you've been through. I was going to write you. I never dreamed I'd be able to give you this terrible news in person."

First George. Then Dee. And her aunt and uncle. It was too damn much. This goddam war, I thought. This lousy war. Those lousy Huns. Those lousy murderers. "This goddam war." I moaned. My voice rose. "Those miserable bastards." Every head in the room snapped around toward me. Antonio scooted over, his eyes popping out of his head, unable to speak from surprise.

Betty looked around, then reached into her shoulder bag, took out her wallet, fished out a U.S. five dollar bill, and tossed it on the table. "We're leaving, Antonio," she said. "Come on, Bill, let's get out of here." She grabbed my arm, pulled me out of the chair and dragged me from the room. More heads turned. To hell with them. What did they know. What did they care.

"We're going to my suite," Betty announced. "It was stupid of me to break that awful news in a public place. I'm sorry, Bill."

"What the hell difference does it make?" I choked out. "Dee is dead. George is dead. Jesus Christ is dead. Everybody in the whole damn world is dead. I wish the hell I was dead." As I raved on, Betty pulled me through the lobby and into the elevator. "Third floor," she called out to the ancient operator, who seemed oblivious to the scene I was making. Just another drunken Yankee.

The next thing I knew, a door opened in front of me, and Betty shoved me into a cavernous living room, crowded with furniture. In the dim light, I could make out bookcases, side tables, floor lamps, a roll-top desk, several stuffed armchairs, and a wooden floor covered only by a small Persian rug in the center of the room. Incongruously, it crossed my mind that these shabby accommodations couldn't hold a candle to the luxurious suite occupied by George and me in Oran for those few blissful days.

I stumbled, as Betty pushed me into the center of the room. "Sit down over there," she ordered, pointing to an enormous blue velvet sofa in front of the damask-covered wall. I meekly obeyed her, leaned my head on a matching velvet pillow, and closed my eyes. A huge dark cloud of despair swept over me. Dee was dead. That wonderful, courageous girl. How could that be? What kind of God would let that happen? For that matter, what kind of God would let this murderous war happen? I wanted to laugh. There was no God. How could anyone believe otherwise? To my great embarrassment, tears streamed across my cheeks, down my chin, and onto my jacket, like someone had turned on a faucet. I hadn't cried like this since learning of Spike's death. I was alone with my grief then. No one had been there to watch me make a fool of myself. I buried my head in my hands, hoping that Betty wouldn't notice. But she came to my side in an instant. She pulled me toward her, pressed her lips against my head, and gently rubbed the back of my neck, all the while murmuring words I couldn't understand. That did it. I really broke down, sobbing like a child who'd lost his mother.

"I'm sorry, Betty," I finally managed to blurt out. "It's just..." Just what? I couldn't think of a damn thing to say. But I did feel better.

"Oh, Bill, don't apologize," she whispered. "I'd have given anything, my right arm, both arms, not to have had to tell you about Dee. I know how close you two were, and how much you cared for her."

I pulled away from her, and pushed her back at arm's length. I looked directly into her eyes, dark eyes brimming with tears. She'd never looked more beautiful. I don't know how I had the nerve to say what came next. I'm glad I did, though.

"I cared for Dee a hell of a lot. She was a wonderful friend." I took a deep breath. "But, I love you, Betty. It's you I love, not Dee, or anyone else. And I've loved you for a long time."

Now it was Betty who burst into tears. Now it was my turn to draw her close to me and bury my face in her lovely dark hair. Now it was my turn to murmur consoling words, mostly repeating that I loved her and always would. The next words from her were soft and barely audible. But I heard them.

"I love you, too, Bill." She buried her head into my chest.

A huge weight slipped away from my mind. Like a newly-constructed ship sliding down the runway into the cool waters of the harbor.

Peace at last!

The End